HE HELD HER TO HIS HEART

Laurel fought to control her feelings. For Penn Allandale, she knew, love was a game. But she was feeling so many different emotions for the first time: jealousy, admiration for a man, longing to impress him and finally, deep, burning desire. She closed her eyes as Penn's hands moved from the formal dancing position to her waist. Then he kissed her again and she cried out. Something within her answered the desire in him and she felt she would do anything to please him, if only he would ask. He kissed her ears and her neck, her throat and the rise of her breasts. Laurel pulled back, trembling.

"Is this how you act with all the women you meet?"

"Only the ones I want," he murmured huskily. . . .

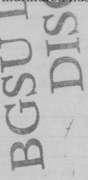

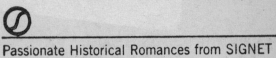

Passionate Historical Romances from SIGNET

JOURNEY TO DESIRE

HELENE THORNTON

A SIGNET BOOK

NEW AMERICAN LIBRARY

Publisher's Note

This novel is a work of fiction. Names, characters, places, and incidents either are the product of the author's imagination or are used fictitiously, and any resemblance to actual persons, living or dead, events, or locales is entirely coincidental.

Copyright © 1984 by Helene Thornton

SIGNET, SIGNET CLASSIC, MENTOR, PLUME, MERIDIAN and NAL BOOKS are published by New American Library, 1633 Broadway, New York, New York 10019

First Printing, July, 1984

1 2 3 4 5 6 7 8 9

PRINTED IN THE UNITED STATES OF AMERICA

1

Blenheim Palace, Oxford, England,
Late Summer 1898

Laurel drove the gig at high speed through the gates of the palace. She smiled roguishly at the porter in livery, who, in return, raised a tasseled ebony staff to acknowledge her. These ancient English customs amused her, despite her awe at the Duke of Marlborough's impressive palace and estate. Here, everything was a world apart from the green backwoods of Vermont and the white clapboard house that was home.

Wheeling around a circle of chestnut trees, Laurel paused to enjoy the view over the lake, with its Vanbrugh Bridge and waddling ducks. How beautiful everything was, how majestic and grand, like something out of a fairy tale. The house with its roofline of finials and coronets, statues of warriors and goddesses stretched over seven acres of floor space. For a moment Laurel wondered what it must be like to be transplanted from America, as Consuelo Vanderbilt had been, and become a duchess in such a stately home, where the social rules took weeks to learn and the servants were as autocratic as their masters.

Laurel was unaware that as she sat in the gig daydreaming about life, a man was watching her from a vantage point nearby. He was tall, fair-haired, handsome, and very curious about the honey-haired nineteen-year-old whose powerful personality and unconventional turn of phrase had made her the talk of Woodstock. So this was Laurel Holman. First he weighed Laurel's hair, as it shone amber gold in the sun, then the flawless peaches-and-cream complexion and slanting amber eyes. Her neck was long, her cheekbones high, and as she sat looking intently at the magnificent house, he thought that, in her blue-and-white batiste dress, she resembled a Tatar princess masquerading as an English lady. Taking care not to startle her, he rode forward until he was at her side. He bade her good morning.

"It's a beautiful day, Miss Holman."

Laurel turned and gazed into his face, her amber eyes catlike in their watchfulness. "Who are you?"

"Pennington Allandale at your service. I live at Wentworth Saye in Woodstock, a stone's throw from the gates of Blenheim."

When he said his name, she looked startled and he wondered why, unaware that Laurel had been told by Consuelo that Penn Allandale was not only the handsomest man in Oxfordshire but the biggest womanizer as well. Penn was pleased that the young lady's voice was husky, as unusual as her appearance.

"I'm Laurel Holman. I came over here four weeks ago from America with my father. Poppa's doing a portrait of the Duchess of Marlborough for the State Apartments."

Penn thought how much he would love to hold the young lady close and waltz with her under the stars. On the spur of the moment, he decided to make certain he could see her again.

"I was about to call with an invitation for you and your father."

"What kind of invitation?"

"Today's my sister's birthday. Clarissa's twenty-one and we're having a party for her at the house. I thought the Marlboroughs might bring you and your father to dinner."

Laurel gazed into Penn's cornflower-blue eyes, at the way his ash-blond hair fell in soft waves to his neck. His skin was brown from the summer sun, his shoulders broad, and there was a hardness in him that was both forbidding and fascinating. Suddenly nervous at being alone with the biggest womanizer in Oxfordshire, she took the reins and made ready to leave.

"I have to get back to the house, Lord Allandale."

"You didn't accept my invitation, Miss Holman."

"I'll have to ask Poppa if he's free."

"Nonsense! Your father will do whatever you tell him, like every other man in your life."

Laurel hesitated, then smiled despite herself.

"You're a very insolent man."

"Renowned for it, I'm afraid."

"There are no other men in my life, anyway."

"There should be. A beautiful woman like you should be pursued until she can't run anymore."

"You make love sound like a stag hunt, sir."

"Not at all, it's only the chase that's similar. The stag hunt ends in death, while the chasing of a beautiful woman sometimes ends in paradise."

Two pink spots appeared in Laurel's cheeks and with a nod she drove on past the Englishman toward the forecourt of the palace. To her alarm, Allandale galloped at her side.

"Have I offended you, Miss Holman?"

"No, not really. I'm just not used to talk like yours. Since I arrived in England I've realized that the local sense of humor's very different from ours in America and I never quite know when I'm being teased."

"Let me waltz with you tonight and show you the beautiful and rare orchids in my conservatory, though they will be nothing compared to your exquisite looks."

Laurel felt herself blushing again, apprehension entering her heart.

"Poppa's busy right now trying to finish the portrait, and he's as stubborn as a mule when he's working, so I'm not sure I can come to your party. You won't be missing much, though. I'm not famous for my dancing, except for treading on folks' toes, and when it comes to small talk, I'm absolutely deficient. It's best if we forget the idea."

"Capital! I shall call for you at seven-thirty. Tell your father Lord Allandale will be waiting for him in the Long Library, and do see that you wear something special. It's Midsummer's Eve and it could be a night for us all to remember."

Before Laurel could reply, Penn had gone, an impressive figure in his English tweeds, elegantly seated on his splendid chestnut horse. Pulling the gig to a halt in front of the palace, Laurel rushed up the stone entrance steps two at a time, colliding with Consuelo, who immediately led her into the salon, where she ordered hot coffee and ice water to calm her down.

"What's the rush, Laurel?"

"I met Lord Allandale in the park and he's invited us to a party at his house. He's a most dreadful flirt!"

"Most of the women I know think he's something of an expert at the art."

"Will you be going to the party at Wentworth Saye?"

"Penn does give wonderful parties. And now that he's taken a fancy to you, he'd be desolated if you didn't charm the birds clean out of the trees tonight. You must borrow one of my dresses, perhaps the lemon-yellow faille or the white satin with stars."

"But I'm not sure I want to go to the ball. Men like Lord Allandale think all women will do their bidding."

"And they're right—most will. Penn's handsome, charming, a true English gentleman; plus he's comfortably well-off. What more could any woman want? He's also far more elusive than most women think; after a while they usually give up trying to tie him down."

"How old is he?"

"He's thirty-four. I don't think he'll ever settle down. His standards are just too high. He wants the kind of marriage his grandfather had and I don't think *those* perfect matches exist anymore."

"Is he *very* rich?"

"No, not very, but his family owns that lovely house and he and his brother Hugo have a comfortable income."

Laurel became pensive, then suddenly rose and excused herself.

"I must go and help Poppa set up his paints. You're sitting at eleven-thirty, aren't you?"

"That's right. We'll be joined today by the Prince of Wales and his cousin, the Grand Duke Andrei Vladimirovich from St. Petersburg. They're passing through Oxford en route to Stratford and I invited them to lunch. Your father might get another commission from the grand duke, so see that you're charming to him. The Romanovs all *love* having their portraits painted."

"I never met a Russian before."

"Andrei's twenty-seven, unmarried, very Russian, full of moods and temperament. He's also one of the richest men in the world. If you're not tempted by Penn Allandale, *he* would be a *real* catch!"

"You're forever matchmaking, Consuelo!"

"And you're forever dreaming of romance. I can't wait to meet him, anyway. Charles tells me he likes bear hunting, building palaces, and dancing the mazurka. Whoever *heard* of such a man!"

The duchess was posing in a dress of frothy white organdy with pink satin ribbons trailing from waist to hem. Her dark hair was dressed in the Gibson-girl style, her long neck accentuated by a thick band of black velvet held in place by a solitaire diamond. The portrait accentuated her height and exotic but elegant beauty. The background was the park of Blenheim and the classical statues of the parterre.

James Holman was working on the right hand that was holding a solitary pink rose. His brows were furrowed, his face intent, and he appeared to have no interest at all in the important guests who were watching his every move.

The grand duke's attention wandered from the small spry painter with the impressive leonine head to the daughter, who had taken his fancy on first sight. He looked from Laurel to Consuelo, thinking that though both were American they were as different as a lion from a lamb. The duchess was fragile and mysterious, strangely virginal in the white organdy, and impossibly remote. The younger woman, with her amber hair and tiger's eyes, was astonishing. He looked from Laurel's face to her small hands with

11

their long oval nails and from her hands to her body with its full breasts, tiny waist, and long legs. Her dress was an emerald-green silk with a tiny white collar and jet buttons from neck to hem. Catching her glance, Andrei smiled, hoping fervently that she would not know he was longing to undo every one of the black buttons, to reveal the exquisite body beneath. To take his mind off the desire that was pounding in him, he addressed her.

"Are you enjoying England, Miss Holman?"

"I am, sir, though it's very different from Vermont, where my father and I live. We're only just getting used to the strange customs of the country."

"My country is even more different. Like its people, Russia is a land of extremes."

Laurel smiled, obviously interested in what he had to say. Suddenly the grand duke had an idea that took his breath away. He made an effort to appear as casual as possible, but it was obvious that he was growing increasingly excited.

"Your father is a very talented man, Miss Holman."

"Indeed he is, sir. Last year he exhibited in New York, Paris, and Milan. He's done four royal portraits since October, and now this beautiful painting of the duchess. I think it's going to be my very favorite of all he's done in the past five years."

Andrei walked over to where the painter was working.

"I invite you to St. Petersburg, Mr. Holman, to paint some of the Romanov family."

Holman turned, stared intently at his new patron, then nodded.

"Why, I'd be honored to visit your country, sir."

"You must come as soon as the duchess's portrait is complete, so you can arrive before the winter freezes the railway lines. That will give you time to get accustomed to our Russian weather."

Laurel stared at the grand duke's dark, shining eyes, at the clipped black mustache, the tall, thin body and pale high-cheekboned face. Did he mean what he was saying? And if so, for how long would they be expected to stay in Russia? Her father was habitually unbusinesslike; he would simply set off for the unknown without confirming arrangements, so Laurel took the role to which she had become well-accustomed.

"Where will we live if we come to Russia, and how long will be our stay?"

"You will live at the Vladimir Palace on the Nevski Prospekt, which belongs to me. I imagine you will need to stay for one year—there are many Romanovs and all of them will want to be painted by your father, once they see some of his work."

Andrei watched Laurel's tawny eyes widen, the nostrils dilate with excitement. He again felt his yearning for her. If only she would accept the invitation, if only she would leave everything and everybody behind and come to Russia, he would have a chance to woo and win her in the legendary Romanov style.

The grand duke's scheming was interrupted by the arrival of tea. Silver pots of China and Darjeeling were placed next to piles of cucumber sandwiches, pâté de foie gras, and the Prince of Wales's customary lobster salad. While the staff bustled and poured and set out napkins and plates and cups, the duchess took a rest and regaled everyone with a mischievous account of a ball she had just attended in London, in which a leading society lady had disgraced herself by falling asleep on the dinner table after imbibing too much champagne.

The Prince of Wales laughed delightedly at the tale, while Laurel and her father sat in the corner discussing the grand duke's offer.

Andrei watched his prey. Would they come to Russia? Would they agree that living in St. Petersburg for a year was an opportunity not to be missed? Thinking of Laurel's golden hair spread across his pillow, he decided to do everything he could to tempt her father. He walked over to Holman, sat in an armchair, and addressed the painter.

"I must tell you more about my offer, Mr. Holman. You and your daughter would travel from London to Paris at the start of your journey, staying for two nights at the Ritz Hotel, and then taking the early-morning train from the Gare du Nord to the Russian-German border. From there the Imperial Train would meet you and bring you to me in St. Petersburg. All the costs would be covered by me, of course, as would the cost of your accommodation and all other requirements during your stay in the city."

"You are aware, sir, that I charge a minimum of five hundred guineas for a portrait?"

"When you paint the Romanovs, you will charge a minimum of a thousand. Otherwise they will not appreciate it."

Holman stared dumbfounded at this. If there were as many Romanovs as the grand duke implied, and each of them willing to pay one thousand guineas for a portrait, he would return home to America as rich as a Rockefeller. Turning to his daughter, he looked questioningly at her.

"Could you stand to be away from home for a whole year, baby?"

Laurel was gazing at Andrei, a curious look in her eyes. It had all been such a shock she had not noticed that he was as tense as she and her father. Now she saw the way he was gripping the arms of his chair, the rigidity of his back, and the sudden softness in the wild black eyes. She thought how untamed he was, almost a savage creature full of desire, despite his cultured background. He was the complete opposite of Penn Allandale, whose English good manners and reserve were new to her. A frisson of forbidden excitement filled her at the thought of being pursued by such a man and perhaps making the remote Penn jealous. She turned to her father and replied. "I'd love to visit Russia, Poppa. It'll be an experience to remember. I thank you for your kindness, sir, in inviting me and my father."

The Prince of Wales and Consuelo exchanged glances and smiled knowingly. Then the prince sauntered over to his cousin.

"Come, Andrei, we must unfortunately leave this

delightful company. If we are to be in Stratford by six-thirty we shall have to make haste."

The grand duke rose and kissed Laurel's hand. Then, having bowed to the duchess, he turned to Laurel's father.

"You will hear from me, Mr. Holman. My staff will forward tickets for you and your daughter in due course, with full instructions for the journey."

When they had gone, Laurel ran to the window and watched as the prince and the grand duke stepped into their carriage. They were almost ready to leave when Penn Allandale appeared on his horse at the forecourt of the palace. Seeing the Prince of Wales, obviously a friend, he dismounted and made the customary bow. The prince greeted him warmly with an outstretched hand. Laurel saw the grand duke eyeing Lord Allandale and the Englishman's polite but distant nod to the Russian. For a moment the two men assessed each other. Then the prince signaled for the coachman to drive on and Penn mounted the steps to the entrance of Blenheim. Laurel rushed to the top of the stairs to see if she could hear what he had to say.

"I see you had a call from the grand duke. What did he make of your American visitors?"

"Fell for the girl, so Wilson tells me. He invited the Holmans to visit Russia, and they accepted."

There was a pause while Penn digested the news. Then came his autocratic reply: "Strange-looking fellow, looks as if he has formalin in his veins instead of blood, regular vampire I'd say. Best tell the

Holmans to hang garlic in their bedrooms and to keep their necks covered at all times!"

Laurel heard the duke's loud, irreverent laughter and almost burst into laughter herself before the door of the library closed on the two men. Smiling delightedly at Lord Allandale's caustic wit, she hurried downstairs, intent on going for a walk in the grounds to clear her head after all the excitement of the afternoon. She was about to leave for Russia, because the Grand Duke Andrei had taken a fancy to her! Why, she might become as famous as Madame de Pompadour before the year was out. The thought made her laugh. She rushed out into the meadows of Blenheim and lay daydreaming of passion and forbidden pursuits. She was puzzled when Penn Allandale's face kept intruding into her mind. She had met him for only a brief moment those few hours ago, yet she could not keep from thinking about him. She liked his way of admitting his faults, of challenging her when she tried to criticize him. She adored the color of his eyes and the scent of his skin and the golden hair that glowed in the morning sun like that of a young Greek god. Blushing at the wantonness of her own thoughts, Laurel told herself she must stop daydreaming of passion. Penn Allandale was a womanizer and a very dangerous man.

Later, Laurel was picking red poppies and white dog daisies when a shadow fell over her path. Looking up, she saw Penn on his chestnut stallion gazing down at her.

"I hear you enslaved a grand duke this afternoon."

"I did nothing of the kind."

"But you leave for Russia in three weeks' time—at his invitation?"

"Poppa's going to earn a thousand guineas a portrait in Russia. It's more than he ever had in his whole life. He didn't even get to be known until he was over fifty."

"Why are Americans so interested in money?"

"Because it buys the things we want. And why not?"

"Don't get angry, Miss Holman. When you're angry your face turns quite red."

Laurel stood her ground, unable to think of a reply. Then she realized that Penn had been teasing her, and tried to pretend she felt an inner calmness.

"What are you doing here again, Lord Allandale? You said you'd call for us at seven-thirty."

"I shall, but I heard that the duke can't come tonight and I had something urgent to discuss with him. Have you decided what to wear yet?"

"The duchess is lending me a lemon-yellow dress."

"I detest lemon-yellow!"

"You're supposed to have a lot of charm, Lord Allandale. Why don't you just try for a few minutes to be charming with me?"

Penn guided his horse at her side as she moved toward the house.

"Too much charm isn't good for women, Miss Holman. They should be beaten soundly at least three times a week. Well, I must leave you. I'll be back at seven-thirty promptly, lemon-yellow dress or not."

Laurel ran all the way back to the house and upstairs in her usual tomboyish fashion. In the salon she begged a word with the duchess, who was en route to her room to change for the evening.

"I need a favor, Consuelo."

"Of course, but what's wrong? Since this morning you've been as nervous as a kitten."

"Can I change my mind and wear the white satin dress instead of the lemon-yellow one?"

Consuelo noted the pink cheeks, the excited look in Laurel's eyes. Penn Allandale had called, and it had not escaped her notice that he had been seen walking through the fields of Blenheim with her young guest. Was it possible his brief appearance had provoked this change of mind? She smiled indulgently at Laurel, amused that the girl seemed to spend most of her days dreaming of falling in love with some legendary knight in shining armor. Had her girlish romantic ideal been realized in the handsome, if enigmatic form of Penn Allandale? She led Laurel to her dressing room and pointed to a rack of exquisite dresses in rainbow colors, all in the finest lace, satin, tulle, and silk.

"Take your pick. You can wear whichever you want for the party tonight. However, I happen to know that Penn's favorite color is lavender blue."

With that, Consuelo returned to her room, leaving Laurel alone and wide-eyed among the dresses, hats, shoes, and furs of the mistress of Blenheim. The room was heavy with the scent of Consuelo's perfume, a mysterious blend of Eastern spices, violet, coriander, and ylang-ylang. Laurel wished she were just like the duchess, tall, delicate, elusive as a moonbeam, and mysterious, instead of a strapping lass from Vermont without an ounce of sophistication. Taking off her dress, she surveyed her reflection in the mirror. Her shoulders were too broad, her breasts too heavy, though her waist was small and her legs long. She must do her best to accentuate the good points and also find herself a beautiful perfume that would be immediately recognizable as hers alone. She went patiently through each dress on the rack, trying to imagine herself in it and envisaging what she would look like through Lord Allandale's eyes.

At last Laurel made her decision, took the chosen outfit and the stole that went with it, and hurried to her room. There she sent for the maid and asked for the duchess's perfumer from the village to be brought to her at once. This was Midsummer's Night. Penn Allandale had said it could be a night to remember, and as far as Laurel was concerned, it surely would.

At seven-thirty Lord Allandale called for his guests. James Holman and Consuelo were already in the Long Library, standing together before a blazing log fire enjoying a glass of champagne. Laurel had not yet appeared and one of the maids was sent to find her. While waiting for her, the duchess ordered more champagne and the three stood together chatting about people who would be present at the party that evening.

As the clock struck the quarter-hour, Lord Allandale turned and saw Laurel at the far end of the room. The library was one hundred and eighty feet long, and as she walked toward him, he had time to take in every detail of her appearance. She was dressed in a ravishing outfit of shimmering white satin, with a tiny waist and a wide, undulating skirt that fell in a train behind her. The neckline was décolleté and encircled by diamante stars that cascaded in a shimmering mass from neck to hem. At her throat Laurel wore a choker of black velvet ribbon with a single white camellia. In her hair there were more camellias arranged with diamond star pins loaned her by Consuelo. The effect was stunning and for a moment Penn was entranced by the vision. When he had first seen Laurel in the grounds that morning, he had thought her a beautiful and fascinating tomboy who might someday become a ravishing young lady. Now she seemed the most beautiful and unusual creature he had ever met, a temptress and an angel, a mischievous, titillating conundrum who smelled of camellias and lilac and the green fields of Oxfordshire. He walked forward and took her by the hand.

"You are beautiful, Miss Holman. I wish I were a famous poet so I could do you justice with my praise, but Shakespeare's words will have to suffice. You are surely 'a lass unparalleled' anywhere in England on this night."

Consuelo surveyed Laurel's burning cheeks and the touching look of joy in her eyes. Penn Allandale was enchanted, that was certain. Holman was pour-

ing himself more champagne instead of asking the
servants to do it. Consuelo sighed. The painter was
forever preoccupied with his sitters and seemed to
take little notice of his daughter's reaction to people
and places. She knew in her heart that Holman had
no idea how much Laurel had grown up in the last
few months. She watched him closely as he turned
and saw the girl. At that moment a look of surprise
and delight lit his face and he walked forward and
kissed his daughter.

"You look wonderful. I should do your portrait
next, because you're the most beautiful young woman
in the world for me."

"I commission you to do just that, Mr. Holman."

Penn smiled briskly at the painter, taking the matter as settled.

"I would like Laurel's portrait to be painted with
the conservatory of Wentworth Saye as the background.
I shall show it to you tonight, Miss Holman, when
we arrive at the house, and I have no doubt you'll
find it a most worthy place to show off your beauty."

In the carriage, Laurel sat between her father and
Consuelo, facing Penn, who now seemed unusually
withdrawn. On reaching the entrance to the grounds
of Wentworth Saye, she looked about her, enjoying
the pastoral English scene—the white swans preen-
ing on the lake, the famous avenue of beech trees,
and the paddocks full of chestnut horses. She realized how much the Englishman loved his home when
he began to speak of it.

"Wentworth Saye was built in the reign of Elizabeth I and rebuilt in part in the early nineteenth century. The grounds were laid out by Capability Brown, and those yew trees are famous as the largest and oldest ones in England."

Laurel looked ahead to the Elizabethan house, a square, solid white structure heavily timbered in black. Around the door there were yellow and pink roses and looming over the courtyard was a massive magnolia tree. The windows were leaded in diamond shapes, and amber light shone through from the interior, which was candlelit. Smoke rose from tall, oddly shaped chimneys, and all around the walls of the property were vast stone urns full of headily scented verbena and night-scented stock, lavender, and heliotrope. To the right of the facade, Laurel could see an orchestra playing under the trees in the hazy light of the summer evening. Couples were waltzing dreamily on a floor specially laid over the lawn. The women were elegant, the men in white tie and tails. Laurel gazed through the arched stone door that led into the flagged hall of the house and saw liveried servants and maids in black and white putting the finishing touches to a buffet.

Following her gaze, Penn explained the significance of the style of the buffet.

"My sister is mad about history, so we designed the meal in the form of a seventeenth-century banquet, with ptarmigan in aspic, roasted quail, dove, and peacock, jellied veal and lobsters, chickens stuffed with pigeons, thrushes, and herbs. The cooks have been exhausting themselves for a week, I can tell you, and some of the staff think it more trouble than it's worth. But as you can see, it is a fine and very English show."

Laurel continued to stare at the sensational view through the front door into the house. After a while, she realized that her father and Consuelo had already descended and were walking toward the trees where the orchestra was playing. She was alone in the carriage with Lord Allandale and he was smiling at her, his blue eyes soft on hers. Excitement fluttered within her and she felt the onset of something she did not understand. His voice was gentle and affectionate.

"Now I know why Consuelo calls you Dreamer."

"She teases me about my daydreaming, but I didn't know she'd given me a nickname."

"Everyone in the Marlborough Set has a nickname. The Prince of Wales is called Tum-tum for obvious reasons."

"What do they call you?"

"I'm not sufficiently sociable to be one of the set, but they call me Penn and sometimes Lucky."

"Your house is wonderful, Penn, so warm and old and different from the other places I've seen."

"You've only really seen Blenheim, and that's a great palace, but not a home. Come, I'll show you around Wentworth Saye, so you'll have something of me to remember when you go to Russia. The grand duke is offering a fortune for that pleasure."

Laurel paused and turned to face Penn, disturbed by his choice of words.

"It isn't like that at all! You make it sound as if the

24

grand duke's buying me, and not Poppa's talent as a painter!"

Looking down at her, Penn wondered if she could be as innocent as she seemed. Was it possible she did not know that Russians were accustomed to buying everything they wanted with emeralds, diamonds, and sheer blinding wealth? Determined to understand Laurel better in the brief time at his disposal, Penn rose and held out his hand.

"To hell with grand dukes. Tonight you are *my* guest and I want to show you my home. I might even risk dancing with you. Perhaps I should put on a suit of armor so you can tread on my toes to your heart's content."

Laurel laughed, delighted at the joke.

"That's about the only way you'll escape getting hurt when I'm in the dancing mood."

Penn showed her the drawing room with its magnificent stone fireplace, so tall she could stand inside it. The sofas were covered in English chintz; the curtains were of soft silk velvet. Everywhere there were dressers and cupboards displaying the Allandale collection of blue-and-white Spode pottery. On stairs and hallways there were armored figures holding torches—trophies, Penn told her, brought back by an ancestor who had fought with Marlborough at the Battle of Blenheim. The master bedroom had a carved oak four-poster with a stunning white lace spread and roses in crystal bowls on the tables. The view from the windows stretched over the undulating hills of the Oxfordshire countryside. In a field beyond the limit of the Allandale land there were black-and-white cows drinking from a brook, and on the wall of the kitchen garden a cockerel was calling, as if mistaking the lantern-lit party arena for dawn.

Laurel passed from the bedroom to the portrait gallery, where her companion showed her the family paintings. One caught her eye and held her attention.

"Who's this handsome gentleman? He looks like you."

"That's my grandfather, Ridley Allandale. He was an explorer and went overland to the Pamirs from a base in India. They tell me he was the finest shot in England and the biggest womanizer, too."

"They say the same of you."

"Do they? They're probably right. A pretty woman is one of life's great pleasures."

Penn was pleased by the frown that darkened Laurel's face for a moment, and amused when she reached the portrait of his grandmother, the famous American beauty Alice Franklin. He watched as she assessed the lady's fiery red hair and challenging green eyes.

"Who's this lady? She doesn't look at all like an English aristocrat."

"That's my grandmother, Alice Franklin. She was one of the most beautiful women of her day."

"And she ended up marrying the biggest womanizer of his day. Poor Alice!"

"Poor nothing! Grandpapa was forty when he wed. He'd chased women and caught most of them all over England, America, Asia, and Europe. When

Alice came into his life she was twenty-two and had already had two millionaire suitors. She fell in love with Grandpapa, but never told him just how much she adored him, and he spent his entire life in utter devotion to her, wouldn't leave her for a day in case some tall-dark-and-handsome stranger carried her off. They were absurdly happy, never had a row, though Alice once cracked a favorite Spode bowl over Olivia de Lisle's head when she thought the lady was flirting."

"I wonder how she learned to cope with her husband's philandering?"

"He didn't have any affairs after they were married. We Allandales chase women *until* we meet the perfect wife, then we only chase happiness. We're very English, you see, Miss Holman. We can only dedicate ourselves to one pursuit at a time, and one woman, too."

Laurel gazed into his eyes, and for a moment, time was suspended. Then, fearful of her own feelings, she tore her glance away. She had a contrary urge to cry and to be held in Penn's arms and hugged to his broad chest. Impatient with herself, she hurried out of the gallery and downstairs, her white satin dress shimmering in the candlelit hall. As they approached the crowded salon, she turned to her host with a wistful smile.

"Thank you for the tour, Lord Allandale. I must let you join your guests now."

"Call me Penn, as you did before, and let me call you Laurel."

"Very well."

"Do you like Wentworth Saye?"

"I love it and I am touched by the story of your grandfather and his wife. I hope someday to find a man who'll love me like that, though I know love's not too fashionable right now in these modern times."

"Fashion is for the empty-headed and folk who live their lives caring what others think of their thoughts, words, and actions. Never try to be fashionable, Laurel. Pursue love if you must, and let it rule your life if you wish, but *never* try to follow the rules of society. Society can be something of a bore. Now, let me introduce you to my brother, Hugo. He's six-feet-four and the shyest man in Oxfordshire. I do hope he doesn't fall in love with you. I swear he'll follow you all the way to Russia if he does. Hugo has always had the instincts of a bloodhound. It's one of the family traits, I'm afraid."

Laurel waltzed with Hugo, then gave her next dances to a host of handsome young men, all eager to pay court to the pretty lady with stars on her dress that matched the stars in her eyes. While she danced, she watched as Penn first led his sister to the floor, then a procession of attractive women, many of whom seemed to know him well. Laurel sighed, telling herself she could never love a man who had made love to half the women in Oxfordshire. For a moment she wondered if his reputation for womanizing was well-founded. Then she saw one of the ladies dragging Penn outside to the terrace to dance in intimate closeness under the tangled vines of scented jasmine. Laurel thought of Penn's grandmother, who had broken a Spode bowl over a rival's head. She could never do that. She could never marry a man of whom she was jealous. Her ideal man was one she loved just a little, not with the violent passion and desire that a man needed to feel. Otherwise life would become nerve-racking and no longer enjoyable. That was Laurel's theory. She was too young yet to know that theory and practice are often irreconcilable in real life.

As the night wore on and the guests grew more noisy, Laurel allowed Hugo to show her the grounds of Wentworth Saye. At the end of the west wing there was the conservatory about which Penn had spoken. It was constructed of white-painted iron in an onion-dome shape, modeled, Hugo informed her, on an Austrian schloss gazebo designed by Ludwig II. The orchids on the shelves were rare, the scent intoxicating, the atmosphere humid, warm, and full of hanging green tendrils that made the place seem like a jungle rather than a glasshouse in the English countryside. While Hugo went away to bring glasses and champagne, Laurel thought wryly that Penn had forgotten his promise to show her around his conservatory. Was he always so unreliable? Was he one of those men whose apparent good character is in reality only a facade?

At that moment one of the men with whom Laurel had danced entered the conservatory and locked the door behind him. Laurel laughed delightedly at the expression on his face.

"Are you locking the door to keep folk out or to keep me in?"

"I am intent on being alone with you, Miss Holman."

"Why?"

"Because I intend to kiss you."

"I don't kiss strangers, Mr. Endicott, not even handsome ones like yourself."

"But when we danced you let me hold you tight."

"Where I come from that's the custom, and anyway, how was I to stop you? You're far too big to throw to the floor!"

He was tall and stockily built, with a small brown mustache in a thin line across the top of his lip. Laurel moved back as he came nearer, but despite her reserve, he continued to pursue.

"You look like a dream in that tempting dress. Surely you expected someone to kiss you on Midsummer's Night?"

"I had thought of it."

"Really, Miss Holman, I believe you're making fun of me!"

Laurel saw, out of the corner of her eye, Hugo hurrying across the courtyard with two glasses, an ice bucket, and a bottle of champagne. When he observed Endicott leering at her, he tried to open the door. Then, realizing that it was locked, he hammered on it furiously.

"Open up at once. I don't wish to have to ask twice."

Endicott turned and unlocked the door.

"Can't a fellow have any privacy in your house, Hugo?"

"Not with Miss Holman. She's spoken for."

"Not by you, surely. You wouldn't know one end of a lady from another!"

"I'm asking you to leave now, Samuel. Will you go or do I have to persuade you?"

Laurel watched as Hugo put the glasses on the table and the champagne in its bucket of ice. He smiled down at her from his great height, his fair hair tousled, his blue eyes merry behind the thick spectacles.

"I'll just go and fetch something tasty for you to eat, Miss Holman. Excuse me, will you."

Laurel watched the tall, powerful figure disappearing toward the house. Then she stood, gazing up at the moon through the open glass windows in the roof. Pink, rose-scented candles had been placed on tables and shelves in the warm, damp air, their scent mixing with that of the orchids from the jungles of South America and the islands of the South China Sea. Laurel was wondering what had happened to Hugo, when she saw the light of someone's cigar at the dark end of the conservatory. She backed toward the door, fearful that Endicott had returned. Then, as the figure came nearer, she realized that it was Penn. Her heart missed a beat and she thought of his reputation and wondered if it was wise to be alone with him on a magic night like this.

He paused to look down at her as Laurel waited breathlessly at his side.

"I see Hugo brought the champagne. Flannegan's on his way with some of Cook's veal pasties and saffron cake. I wasn't sure if you liked sweet or savory with your champagne."

"Where's Hugo gone?"

"He came to tell me he'd delivered you to the conservatory as I asked. I promised to show you around this place, if you recall, and I never forget a promise. Take my arm in case you slip—it's rather dark and these marble floors can be tricky when they're damp."

Laurel took his arm, and together they walked in the flickering light along avenues full of sensational flowers. Some of the orchids were yellow spotted with green. Some were pink and fleshy, some dark and forbidding. One was carnivorous. Laurel watched as Penn put a moth on the plant's lower lip, recoiling when the tiny, fluttering shape disappeared into the cavernous aperture.

"That's a horrible flower!"

Penn smiled at her distress on the dead moth's behalf.

"Obviously it's a Russian plant. It swallows up everything it desires in a second, and is powerful enough to do what it wants."

"I think you should throw it out."

"I hope you think the same of the grand duke on better acquaintance."

Laurel smiled at this. Then the orchestra under the chestnut trees struck up with the mysterious, lilting waltz from *Bal Rosé*. She was thrilled when Penn turned and took her in his arms.

"Let's dance. This is one of my very favorite melodies."

His arms were gentle but firm and Laurel forgot she was not the best of dancers and relaxed against his body, content to let him whirl her around on the white marble floor under the scented foliage and in the light of the harvest moon. When the music came to an end, he continued to hold her and she felt herself trembling at his touch. His voice was low and she closed her eyes when he bent his head to hers.

"Kiss me, Laurel. Kiss me because you want to or because it's three A.M. on Midsummer's Day. I have longed to do this ever since the moment I first saw you sitting in your gig gazing at Blenheim with those big amber eyes."

She smelled the faint scent of cigar smoke on his skin and the healthy fragrance of grass and meadows and flowers. Then his lips touched hers lightly, barely brushing them. Impatient to be kissed like a real woman, Laurel stood on tiptoe. For a moment she opened her eyes and saw that Penn was raising his hands to cup her face. Then his mouth was on hers and the fire of his passion ignited her. She swayed, breathless from excitement. Then she let him kiss her as only lovers kiss—deep, inquiring, titillating kisses that lull the mind and make the body float in paradise. Suddenly her whole being was on fire, her back bending so she was pressed hard against his body. As Penn lifted his face from hers, she rested her head on his chest and let her fingers wander over his neck and shoulders.

"No one ever kissed me like that before."

He was silent, but she knew now that his seemingly casual attitude concealed a passionate man, a man of towering desire and infinite subtlety. She looked with longing into Penn's eyes.

"Say something or I'll think you're angry I was so forward," Laurel whispered.

"I need a glass of champagne. I'm feeling like Grandpapa did the first time he kissed the beautiful Miss Franklin. I remember he wrote in his diary on that occasion: 'Met a young lady today who made my hair stand on end and my heart give a fearsome lurch.' He wrote something else too, but I'll not tell you that until we know each other very well."

Penn poured the champagne and they ate the tiny veal-and-bacon pies Cook had prepared. Then, as the orchestra began to play some of the soft, early-morning tunes that come at the end of a party, he led Laurel by the hand from the conservatory to the bank of the river and together they watched first pink and gold streaks of dawn touching the night sky. When she shivered, he took off his jacket and placed it lightly over her shoulders, his fingers touching her skin for a moment and making her heart turn over. The look in his eyes was gentle and she wanted to throw her arms around him and never let him go.

"Are you glad you came to the party, Laurel?"

"Very glad. I love your house and the garden and

all the old English furniture you've collected over the generations."

"I'm pleased the country doesn't bore you."

"It's where I come from, remember. Vermont's all green and quiet and peaceful. I miss it, and so does Poppa."

They were returning to the house, when Laurel heard the last waltz being played.

"Dance this with me, Penn. Let's go right back to the conservatory and dance it all alone."

As he held her to his heart, Laurel fought to control her feelings. For Penn Allandale, she knew, love was a game. For her the evening had been a revelation. She had felt so many different emotions for the first time—jealousy, admiration for a man, longing to impress him, and finally, deep, burning desire. She closed her eyes as Penn's hands moved from the formal dancing position to her waist. Then, as she had hoped, he kissed her again, and she cried out, because something within her answered the desire in him and she felt all at once so weak and pliable she knew she would do anything in the world to please him, if only he would ask. He kissed her ears and her neck, her throat and the rise of her breasts above the décolletage. Laurel pulled back, her body trembling like an aspen.

"Is this how you act with all the women you meet?"

"Only the ones I want." He looked down at her, realizing that she believed he was merely going through the usual routine of seduction. "I would like to pay you a compliment, Laurel. I may have the reputation for being a womanizer, and perhaps it's one I've earned, but even my worst enemy wouldn't call me a liar. I like you. Indeed, I fear I more than like you. I certainly desire you, and there has never been a woman in this house who affected me on as many levels of emotion as you have. I'm only sorry you have to go out of my life as soon as you entered it."

"I don't leave for Russia for three whole weeks."

"Then I propose to monopolize you until you do. Say I have permission to call on you each day. We'll go to Woodstock Fair together tomorrow and I'll win you a prize in the horse race. We'll go to London, too, and we'll have lunch at Claridges, chaperoned by my Great Aunt Elvira."

Penn was about to complete his plans for her amusement, when Laurel wound her arms around his neck and kissed him full on the mouth.

"Invite me to Wentworth Saye to be with you. That's the most important thing of all."

"Of course I invite you."

Penn's quicksilver tongue darted here and there and he could feel Laurel's body moving instinctively against his own. Provoked as he had rarely been before, he grasped Laurel and pulled her against him, his masterful hands touching her bare back and the long slim neck. Desire filled him and he kissed her again, bending his head to caress her shoulders and the full breasts that had edged out of the satin dress when he reached for her. He heard a sharp intake of breath and a sigh of ecstasy. Then, as he took her and kissed her more insistently, Laurel fell into his arms in a fainting swoon. Penn had forgotten how young and innocent Laurel was.

With a sigh, Penn walked the silent Laurel back to the house, motioning for his brother to follow.

"I'm afraid Miss Holman isn't well, Hugo. Do go and bring Consuelo and tell her what's happened. I shall put Laurel in the Blue Bedroom."

"Don't worry, Penn, it's probably a bit too much champagne combined with this humid weather. We need a storm to clear the air. I've been sweating like a damned racehorse all evening."

Hugo hurried ahead, opened the bedroom door, and turned on the lights. Then he ran downstairs and went in search of Consuelo. He was in a state of considerable excitement. From childhood he had worshiped his brother, always siding with Penn in arguments with their sister and doing all he could to support him. Today, for the first time that he could remember, he had seen his brother anxious about a woman. Now that he had met Laurel, Hugo understood why. A fellow had to steel himself not to fall madly in love with the lady when she fixed him with her tawny eyes. Now she was off to Russia and out of reach of any courtship. What would Penn do? He was not a man to pine his life away for a woman. On the other hand, he was as stubborn as a mule and it was not in his nature to give up easily on anything that was important to his future. Hugo hurried toward the gazebo, where Consuelo was listening to a young girl singing.

"I think Miss Holman fainted, and Penn asked me to bring you to her in the Blue Bedroom."

"Well, that's unexpected! What did Penn do to provoke it?"

"He gave her two glasses of champagne. That's *not* excessive."

"She turns scarlet every time his name's mentioned. I do believe Laurel's a little infatuated with your brother."

"She's beautiful and charming and I won't hear a word against her. Usually women never get past making rude comments about my ears. Laurel told me I was a fine dancer. She is kindness itself, and a true lady."

In the early morning, when all the guests had gone, Penn walked alone among the tables and left-over food, making his way to the riverbank. The sun was rising and it was going to be a beautiful day. He was thinking of Laurel and how she had struggled to control her feelings when they had led her from the Blue Bedroom to the carriage that would take her back to Blenheim. She had said a polite good night to him and had insisted on seeing Hugo and Clarissa to thank them for inviting her. Then she had stepped into the carriage and disappeared from view, but not before a tear had fallen from her cheek onto his hand as he helped her to her seat. Penn gazed over the river at an elderly shepherd leaving his cottage en route to the day's work. Would this green and idyllic English countryside be enough to compete with the undoubted splendors of St. Petersburg? Could he hope to triumph against a charmer of ruthless dimension like Andrei Vladimirovich Romanov? With a sigh, he turned back toward the house. He had not a thousandth of the Russian's wealth, nor his legendary flair and impulsive nature. He was just a home-loving English gentleman who enjoyed his horses, his family, and his land.

While servants bustled about on the ground floor of the house, clearing up the debris of the party, Penn looked wistfully into the Blue Bedroom on his way to his room. There, in the early-morning sunlight, a solitary diamond star shimmered on the pillow. With it was a note in Laurel's hand: *I'm leaving this star with you to remind you of the ones we danced under last night. It's to make sure you come to Blenheim to give it back to the duchess, who loaned me all my finery. I loved your house and your party and the daisy meadows by the river. Wentworth Saye made me realize all over again that I'm just a country girl at heart and that's all I'll ever be. Laurel.*

Penn folded the note and put it in his pocket. Then he went to his room and lay fully clothed on the bed. *She was a country girl at heart and that was all she would ever be.* Pray God the stifling salons of Russia would bore her to death and the frenetic pursuit of pleasure prove too shallow for her nature. Looking at his watch, he saw it was eight-fifteen. He rang for breakfast and went to have a bath. At ten he would call for Laurel and take her to the fair. And from that moment on he would show

her his countryside, his England, his world. He began to sing in the bath, and by the time Flannegan,
the butler, appeared, he was feeling almost cheerful.

"It's a fine day, sir."

"Indeed it is, Flannegan."

"You won't forget that Lady Harmon asked you to
visit her today."

"I cannot go. Send one of the grooms with a bouquet of flowers and my apologies."

"Yes, sir. Miss Clarissa said you would doubtless
be taking Miss Holman to the fair."

Penn looked startled at this, and the butler concealed a smile.

"Did she indeed. How did Clarissa know what I'd
be doing?"

"She took a liking to the young lady, sir, and said if
you hadn't already invited Miss Holman she would
do so. I'll order William to deck the gig with roses,
shall I, sir?"

"Yes, please do."

"And a special picnic would be in order. Shall we
say jellied beef, potato salad, chocolate cake, and a
raspberry-and-strawberry flan?"

"That sounds perfect."

"And I'll prepare the Blue Bedroom in case the
young lady needs it again, sir. Perhaps next time she
should be invited to stay the night, as she obviously
needs plenty of rest."

"You're incorrigible, Flannegan."

"Indeed I am, sir."

Penn ate his bacon and eggs, all the while thinking

of his sister. She actually liked Laurel Holman. The only people he had ever known Clarissa take to were long-dead relatives and characters from novels. Puzzling this strange change in his sister, he dressed and went to the stables for his morning ride. It was going to be a perfect day and he would have to wait only one more hour before seeing Laurel. He walked his horse for a while, picking a vast bouquet of wildflowers as he moved through the meadows. Then, half an hour early, he galloped furiously from the grounds in the direction of Blenheim.

Laurel was sitting in her room dreaming of the moment when Penn had kissed her in the conservatory. How beautiful it had been, how perfect. She had almost finished breakfast when her father arrived with a message from the grand duke.

"That Russian wants us to leave for London a week from today. Did you ever hear such a thing? He must think paintings get finished by looking at them!"

"But why the hurry, Poppa?"

"I'm darned if I know. He just wants us there right now. He's obviously a man used to having his way. I'm not sure I like him for that."

Laurel sighed wearily. She had thought there would be at least three weeks with Penn, weeks in which she would learn more of him and his life and of herself and her own true feelings. Now everything was ruined. She would be leaving England in just seven days. She was about to write Penn a note, when she saw him riding through the park toward the house. Forgetting about her father, she rushed down the corridor and out of the building, hesitating when Penn stepped off his horse and smiled at her.

"Good morning, Laurel. Thank you for your note. I brought back the star for Consuelo, though I should much rather have kept it as a souvenir of a perfect evening."

Penn ran up the stairs to her side and together they walked toward the main hall.

"Poppa just heard from the grand duke. We've leave for Russia in seven days. Isn't it *awful!*"

A frown touched his face and sadness filled his eyes, but his voice was strong and firm and there was an obstinacy about him that Laurel had not suspected.

"Then we'll do all we planned to do in one week instead of three. Give me *all* your time, Laurel. I'm greedy for it, as you well know. And don't worry about leaving for Russia. I believe young women should travel and experience the world before they marry and settle down."

"That's unusual. Most men prefer women who are innocent of the world."

"Women who are innocent of the world have a tendency to go off after a few years of marriage with the first dashing foreigner who crosses their path."

"And I suppose you know all about bored wives?"

"Indeed I do. Now, let me tell you my plans. In this one week that remains of your stay in England, I want to show you my world. It's the only world I have, and very different from the one you'll experience in Russia. We'll adventure in it together and I'll do my very best to make each moment unforgettable."

They walked hand in hand into the house, each thinking his own thoughts. Penn was saddened by the news, but determined not to show it. Laurel was torn between honoring her father's arrangement with the grand duke and being with the man who had touched her heart. From this time on, she knew, the two men could compete for her affection. Who would be the winner of the contest? Would it be the passionate grand duke with his palaces and his pavilions and hunting lodges and chests full of jewels? Or would it be Penn Allandale, the English gentleman and biggest womanizer in Oxfordshire? Suddenly, as she looked up at the masterful profile, Laurel smiled. She was at the beginning of a great adventure—and she was looking forward to every moment of it with all her heart.

2

Blenheim–Paris, September 1898

They had been to the fair together and Penn had won her a silver cup in the horse race. During the subsequent days they had visited the oldest public house in London and lunched on steak-and-kidney pie with English treacle tart to follow. They had had tea at Claridges Hotel and had followed it with an evening at the Theater Royal, Drury Lane, where they had enjoyed the play. Laurel had laughed till the tears rolled down her cheeks when Penn took her to the music hall. She had cried, too, at the sight of some poor orphaned children in a village workhouse near Oxford. She had met an English peddler, two peers, and a formidable relative of Penn's named Great Aunt Fifi. They had watched a cricket match together and had played croquet on the lawn at

Wentworth Saye. All the pursuits of an English summer had been theirs and they had loved every minute of their time together.

For the last two days of her stay in England, Laurel would be Penn's guest at the house, chaperoned by his sister, Clarissa, who hated to travel farther than the nearby village, but loved hearing of America and the scandalous doings of the rich and famous. The invitation had not included Laurel' father, because he was too busy finishing his port of the duchess to socialize. Holman had visited Wen worth Saye, however, on a number of occasions a Penn's invitation, and the two men had enjoyed each other's company. The sketches of the conservatory that would provide the background to Laurel's portrait had been completed and the commission promised for the earliest possible occasion. Penn had even arranged that the finished work be sent by diplomatic courier from St. Petersburg to London. Holman had noted the Englishman's anxiety about this and his desire that everything be done to make the portrait a truly memorable one. When he pondered the reason for the fuss, Holman smiled. Lord Allandale, he told himself, was surely just a little in love.

It was a golden early September afternoon and Penn and Laurel had been blackberrying by the river. The air was still, the sun warm, and Flannegan and three manservants were walking toward them from the house with a picnic. Looking disapprovingly at their purple-stained fingers, the butler turned to his master with an arched eyebrow.

"Will you and Miss Holman wish to wash before you eat, sir?"

"Of course not. This juice will be hell to get off and we're hungry. Don't be so antiseptic, Flannegan."

"No sir, of course I shan't."

"What have we to eat?"

"I brought some cold grouse, sliced venison in aspic, mixed salads, pippin tart for the lady, and a selection of cheeses, including sage, Derby, and Stilton. We also have strawberries and cream."

"I'm half-dead from thirst. What is there to drink?"

"We have two quarts of water, sir, and some iced tea. Also I took the liberty of bringing champagne and some of your special cider. With respect, sir, do remember that after two glasses of it most normal human beings have a tendency to snore."

"Thank you, Flannegan."

"Will that be all, sir? Oh, I almost forgot, Lady Arran called. I told her you had the mumps and were fearfully infectious. She left in a hurry and won't be back for some weeks. Miss Holman, Cook made you some of those sultana pasties you liked. They're under the napkin."

A light breeze rose over the river, bringing a welcome coolness to the air as they ate. Laurel listened to the sounds of the English countryside, bees buzzing in the clover flowers, a field hand singing a country song, a cuckoo calling, and the lapping of river water on pebbles. When she had eaten some of the venison, she took a slice of pippin tart and held out her glass for more champagne.

"I love this English food. If I stayed on here I might end up as fat as a hog."

"You'd be a beautiful hog, at least. I can't stand women who don't enjoy eating. One of my sister's friends eats only hard-boiled eggs, lean meat, and lemon sorbet. She's so thin her husband bruises himself on her extremities."

They smiled at each other, their eyes bright in the sun. Then, when they had eaten their fill, they closed the hamper, leaving out only the champagne in its fast-thawing bucket of ice.

In the nearby field, farm workers were bringing in the hay and children were sliding down the ricks, squealing delightedly. Penn turned to Laurel with a pensive look.

"Do you like children?"

"I shall love my own, because they'll be raised with lots of love and discipline."

"You'll be a regular martinet, will you?"

"A very affectionate one, but I'll never let my children be ill-mannered like some of the modern ones are."

He was silent while he digested this information. Then he turned to Laurel. "Are you all packed for your trip to Russia?" he asked.

"I have my new maps, my fly swats, my bug-killing powder, and everything else folks have told me to buy."

"How do you feel about leaving us?"

"Poppa's looking forward to it, and in a way, so am I. Until I came to England I'd never even been out of Vermont. Now I've seen New York and London and Oxford and I'll soon be traveling right across Europe to Russia. I have to admit, though, that St. Petersburg sounds a pretty odd place. Someone told me yesterday that even the czar's palace is full of vermin."

"There are advantages and disadvantages in all foreign cities. In Russia you'll be given a fine welcome. You'll see sights you could see nowhere else in the world, strange and wonderful buildings and families who are so rich their women have dresses and jewels to match them for every day of the year. The drawbacks are the fleas and the foreign ways of the people."

"You talk as if you know it well."

"I'm second cousin to the Prince of Wales and he's a first cousin of the Czar of Russia. That makes me distantly related to the Romanov family."

Seeing Laurel's sudden change of mood and the apprehension that came on her whenever he talked of Russia, Penn hurried to change the subject.

"Let me tell you about the dinner party we're having tonight. This is my sister's small tribute to you. The Marlboroughs are coming, and your father, of course. Lord Marchmont's accepted with his wife, and Sir Basil Stevens, our nearest neighbor. He's a wondrous talker. I shall pall into insignificance by the side of him."

"I doubt that you pale into insignificance by the side of anyone! By the way, I meant to ask you, Penn, what's that object on the lower field? I couldn't make it out."

"It's my balloon. Hugo and I are both mad about the new sport of aviation."

"But it's very dangerous! You're not to try any such thing!"

"I've always been interested in it. You're not to worry."

Laurel fell silent, troubled by this piece of information. Then she held out her glass again.

"Can I try out some of that deadly cider Flannega was warning you about?"

"Certainly not. I want you as sober as a judge for tonight. I intend to show you off and brag about you to everyone in sight."

The dining room of Wentworth Saye, with its oak-paneled walls, faded tapestries, and turquoise Savonnerie carpet had been hung with hundreds of pink Malmaison roses that fell in magnificent fern-framed profusion from the crystal chandeliers. The doors to the garden were open and the smell of lavender and scented stocks drifted in. There was a log fire in the grate in case the night turned chilly, and a five-gallon solid-silver punch bowl on the sideboard.

Penn inspected the arrangements with his sister before the guests arrived.

"You've done us proud, Clarissa, and I thank you."

"This is an important evening for you, Penn."

"I know it is."

"Be kind to her and don't be flippant when you

mean to be serious. Laurel's young and impression-able and unused to our English ways."

Penn looked at the blazing fire and then at his sister, who knew only too well how much it was costing him to keep up the pretense of cheerfulness.

"You're in love with her, aren't you, Penn?"

"You ask the darnedest questions, Clarissa."

He gazed into his sister's pale, placid face with its faded blue eyes and prematurely graying ash-blond hair. She was trying to help him and he was grateful to her for her consideration. Impulsively he bent and kissed her cheek, shaking his head resignedly when she spoke.

"This will be the first woman you ever met that you couldn't have for the asking, and the first one you had to compete for. Your rival will be Russia and the entire Romanov family. That's certainly a challenge, even for you!"

"I've no intention of competing with the grand duke."

"Of course you'll compete. Laurel's the only woman who ever gave you a second glance who's worthy of you and worthy of Wentworth Saye and our heritage. She's special and we both know it."

"What can I do, Clarissa? He'll give her a palace, a yacht, half the world if she asks for it. I have ten thousand a year, this house, the home farm, and two hundred acres of land that I have to work like the dickens to make profitable. I'm hardly in Andrei Vladimirovich's class."

"Nonsense! You're an Englishman, and that counts.

Half of those Russians are crazy, and the other half are arrogant enough to believe they can buy everything and everybody. If Laurel is a mercenary young woman, you're best without her. But she isn't, and you're not, and I think you'd best start planning how you can chase her to the ends of the earth."

Penn stared into his sister's deceptively still face. He had never suspected that Clarissa could feel passion about anything. Yet here she was recommending that he pursue a young woman to the ends of the earth. He put his arms around her and hugged her to his heart.

"I love you, little sister, even if you are a bit of a dragon."

"I'm a dragon who cares for you, remember that. I long for you to be settled and happy, Penn. Your life will really begin when you're married to a wonderful woman."

Penn walked upstairs to the gallery and stood for a long time looking at his grandfather's portrait. He was wondering how the gentleman had made Alice love him and how he had been able to keep her when every man in England had coveted her. He thought that Laurel was a woman who could inspire jealousy in any man, and he hoped he would not fall prey to such a violent emotion.

A few minutes went by. Then Penn heard the faint rustle of taffeta and smelled the now familiar scent of camellias. Turning, he saw Laurel in a dress of lavender-blue satin, the fichu and hem edged with lilac flowers picked out in amethysts and pearls.

Around her throat was a necklace of tiny solitaire diamonds, at her wrist a bracelet of amethysts that matched the shimmering stones on the skirt. In her hair, nestling among the red-blond curls, were dozens of satin violets held in place by the now familiar diamond stars. As she stepped into the light, Penn moved forward, holding out his arms and twirling her around, so the billowing, shimmering skirt filled half the width of the gallery.

"You're even more beautiful than before. I fear you're doing all this to enslave me just before you go."

"I'd love to enslave you, but so would half the women in England. The duchess told me that a long time ago."

"Did she, begad. I shall tax Consuelo with it in the morning. Come, we must go and meet our guests. Hugo's going to lose his appetite and suffer severe infatuation when he sees you in that dress."

"And you, Penn, what are you going to do?"

"I'm going to kiss you in the moonlight and try to cast a spell on you, so one day you'll come back to me at Wentworth Saye."

Laurel stood quite still, wondering if he was aware of the commitment inherent in his statement. The words had touched her heart, and suddenly she felt less enthusiastic about leaving England for the wilds of Russia. Penn Allandale had said he wanted her to come back to him. She felt almost exultant with joy.

They ate a very English meal that night, with celery soup and trout from the river, baron of beef with horseradish sauce, and a creamy syllabub scented with Madeira. Afterward, instead of the women adjourning while the men passed around the port, Clarissa made them all go to the terrace, where champagne was being served.

As night fell and the sky turned a misty dark blue, fireworks exploded over the gardens, exquisite orange, gold, and scarlet displays in the form of moonbeams, flowers, and sunbursts. The sky darkened imperceptibly and the colors glowed all the brighter, till the feast of sound and color took the breath away.

The Duke of Marlborough kept exclaiming in his upper-class English voice: "Gad, sir, what a sight!"

Consuelo was too busy watching Penn to say anything at all. Laurel's father was doing the same, and both were exchanging knowing glances.

The other guests were simply thrilled by the display, a sight never seen before in that rural corner of England. Shrewdly Sir Basil Stevens looked at his host and then at the beautiful young woman at his side. His voice was mocking when he spoke: "You've gone to a lot of trouble for us, Penn."

"Clarissa did it all."

"How did you arrange such a show, my dear? I should have thought the locals rather lacking in knowledge of such pyrotechnic spectacles."

Clarissa's haughty reply made the entire company laugh. "I sent Hugo to arrange for the Royal Artillery Regiment from Stratford to come and give us a display. They gave one last year for the queen and I saw no reason why they shouldn't come to Wentworth Saye.

You know how they love showing off what can be done with gunpowder."

Laurel applauded one of the most beautiful set pieces, a golden extravaganza that seemed like the fountains of Rome. Then, to her surprise, the night was lit by a thousand silver stars and her name appeared under a simple message: "BON VOYAGE TO OUR FRIENDS THE HOLMANS." Tears filled her eyes as she stood staring at the glittering message that faded gradually, leaving only the darkness of night. At that moment she understood for the first time the irrevocability of her decision to visit Russia with her father. Once she left England, Penn would not find it hard to forget her, because every woman in the area wanted to spoil him. But how would *she* forget the memorable days at Wentworth Saye, the moments of magic there had been between them?

While the Duchess of Marlborough chatted to Lord Marchmont and his wife asked James Holman to paint a portrait of her with her five children on his return to England, Penn led Laurel through the laburnum walk that had been planted in his grand-mother's day from the east wing of the house to the river. In this scented tunnel of undulating golden fronds, he bent and kissed her hand.

"Thank you for making my night so wonderful."

"What did I do to make it? Tell me so I can do it again."

"Your tears made me realize that you'll be just a little sorry to leave us all."

"I never realized until tonight that you could grow attached to a place in a few short days."

"I've grown accustomed to a person in a few short days."

They paused at the spot where the laburnum walk ended at the waterfall. There they kissed, their lips hot and eager, their bodies pressed hard against each other. Laurel held Penn tightly, her arms around his neck.

"When you kiss me, strange things happen to my body and I feel as if I'm floating or about to faint."

"That's how it is for a passionate woman."

She smiled, pleased by the compliment.

"Am I really a passionate woman, Penn?"

"I fear so."

"Why do you fear it?"

"Because you may be passionate for someone else, too."

"I'm nineteen, and until you kissed me, no one else had ever touched me. I was beginning to think I wasn't very attractive to men."

Amused by her innocence, he kissed each of her fingers.

"I could have awakened feelings in you that need to be satisfied, Laurel. In Russia the grand duke will pursue you, and he's a man used to having his way, a very passionate man who has never been in love, so they say. Take care and don't make the error of trifling with him, or he might pursue you with a ruthlessness you'll find unacceptable."

"Are you trying to scare me, Penn?"

"No, I'm telling you the truth. Now, let's go to the conservatory and I'll pick you an orchid to press in your journal."

"Will we meet again when I come back from Russia?"

"That's for you to decide."

"What do *you* want, Penn?"

"I want everything, but I'm not in a position to demand it of you."

"Sometimes you talk in riddles."

"You're leaving for Russia shortly. If, once you're there, you want to forget England and all the things you did here, that's your prerogative. If you want to see me again, we'll find a way to be together. But first you have to be free to choose your man and your life. I wouldn't want a woman who was hurried into choosing me as her potential suitor."

Laurel pirouetted merrily around him, secretly pleased by this subtle hint of his intentions. Then, as Penn stepped aside, she entered the warm interior of the conservatory. Tonight there were no pink candles, only the silvery light of the moon on the exotic flowers that filled every surface. There was champagne on the table and a plate of her favorite pigeon savories covered with a linen serviette. Laurel watched as Penn filled their glasses, smiling delightedly when she heard a solitary violinist playing the waltz from *Bal Rosé*, as the orchestra had played it that first magic evening at Wentworth Saye. She could not tell where the sound was coming from, but when it began, she waited breathlessly for Penn to take her in his arms and waltz with her.

He watched her reaction as the violinist was joined by a pianist, other violins, and finally by the entire orchestra, who were hidden under the chestnut trees in the lower meadow. He was touched to see the joy and surprise, the passion Laurel could no longer control. Taking her glass, he held out his arms.

"This is our waltz, I believe."

"Where are the musicians?"

"Under the trees, like last time, only tonight they're playing just for us."

He led her out of the conservatory and onto the deserted terrace, where they waltzed together under the moon. Above them, pink and yellow roses grew over a trellis, their petals falling on Laurel's hair. Now and then Penn kissed her cheek, and once he brushed some of the petals from her shoulder, making her shiver with pleasure. Then, as the clocks struck midnight, he bent and let his lips find hers. He heard the sharp intake of her breath and felt the pounding of her heart against his own, and he longed as he had never longed before to love her. Instead, he picked her up in his arms and carried her to her bedroom.

"If I waltz with you one moment longer I shall forget I am a gentleman and want more from you than any man has the right to ask."

"Don't go, Penn! I don't want you to leave."

Laurel stood looking down at her hands, shocked

by what she had said. Then she gazed eagerly into Penn's face.

"You really don't have to go away."

He hesitated, closing his eyes in an effort to shut out the sight of her desirability and willingness to allow him to stay. Then he moved to the door.

"Indeed I must go, Laurel. You see, for us there will be a time and a place, and it isn't now. Good night, sleep well. I shall breakfast with you on your terrace at eight in the morning."

Laurel closed the door and walked to the window to breathe in the scented air. The music drifted up to her and she realized they were playing all her favorite songs. For a moment she paused to look at her reflection in the mirror, smiling wistfully at the beautiful ball gown Consuelo had given her. It was a wonderful dress and the gift had been a generous one, made, Laurel knew, to help her tempt Penn into some kind of statement of his feelings. Suddenly conscious that she had only twenty-four hours left in England, she lay down and stared at the ceiling. He liked her, that was certain. But did Penn more than like her? And what of her own feelings? She had experienced such intense desire whenever he was near; the whole week had been one long crescendo of fevered anticipation. Was this love or infatuation or the feelings of an inexperienced girl when confronted by the aggressive lovemaking of a passionate man?

Laurel rose and took off her dress, putting it carefully on its satin hanger and covering it with gauze.

She was thinking of the dinner they had eaten, the fireworks display, the orchestra playing under the trees, and the looks Penn had cast her way whenever he thought no one was watching. At Wentworth Saye all the nights had been enchanted and all the days magic moments to be remembered and savored to the end of her life.

On Monday at ten in the morning, Laurel and her father were driven to the station by the Duke of Marlborough's coachman. Consuelo rode with them to see them off, her beautiful face watchful as Laurel sat stiff-backed and silent beside her father, watching the scarlet poppy fields of Oxfordshire as they passed by. The girl's eyes were swollen and there was no doubt she had been crying. There was something else, too, an aura of uncertainty and disappointment. Consuelo knew well that the reason for this was the absence of Penn Allandale.

Holman was consulting the itinerary sent him by the grand duke and making notes in violet ink of things he must buy for himself and Laurel before leaving Paris. He looked across at the duchess as she addressed him.

"How are you feeling, Mr. Holman—all ready for your great journey?"

"I'm just fine, ma'am. I plan to enjoy this trip to Russia and to make so much money I'll be able to retire on my return and leave Laurel comfortably off when I die. After Russia I'm only going to paint women I want to paint, and none of those awful ones with big teeth and red noses."

Consuelo laughed at his irreverent attitude. "You may find plenty of big teeth and red noses in Russia."

"I'll overlook them for a thousand guineas a throw."

Holman took his leave with affection, kissing Consuelo's hand and beaming with genuine pleasure into her beautiful, wistful eyes. "Thank you most kindly for all you've done for me and my daughter. Our stay at Blenheim's been unforgettable and I'm so glad you like the portrait I did."

"I love it, Mr. Holman, and I thank *you*. Laurel, are you feeling well?"

"I'm fine, thank you."

Consuelo knew she was not. From the moment they had left the palace, Laurel had been looking for Penn, who was nowhere to be seen. The duchess watched as Holman and Laurel stepped on the train and took their places in the coach reserved for their exclusive use. Then, as the guard blew his whistle and waved the green flag, Consuelo stood blowing kisses until the train disappeared from view into the mist of a fine September morning. As she walked back to the waiting carriage, she was pensive. Where *was* Penn Allandale? Why had he not come to see Laurel off? For the first time that she could ever remember, Consuelo felt cross with the gallant Englishman.

The Holmans traveled from Dover to Calais on the night boat. The crossing was rough, and for hours Holman was seasick. At seven A.M. they found themselves pale and tired on the quayside of Calais, their luggage stacked neatly by their side. As Laurel sent a porter to buy some coffee from a stall, servants appeared as if by magic and soon they were sitting in deep velvet seats on the express to Paris.

While her father sketched her, Laurel looked out at the flat fields of northern France, the cornfields of Picardy, and the idyllic green banks of the River Oise. France was not unlike England, except that the people were smaller and more given to expressing themselves in a voluble manner. The farms and estates seemed larger, the fields stretching endlessly to the horizon. A vision of Penn Allandale on his chestnut mare came into Laurel's mind and she asked herself for the hundredth time why he had not come to say goodbye at the station. He had told her on many occasions that he hated goodbyes, but even so she had expected at least a brief appearance.

Laurel's eyes were sad as she continued to watch the changing scene, the appearance of small towns of grey granite and then the stately suburbs of Paris. For a moment, in her excitement at being in the legendary French capital, she forgot Penn and stared at the houses, the startling skylines with the white cathedral of Sacre Coeur and a thousand intriguing rooftops, chimneys and tiny, ancient alleyways that appeared as they neared the center. In Paris, she saw, the people walked quickly about their business. Children in school smocks of blue and white check ran home with long loaves under their arms after an early morning visit to the baker. Midinettes in grey hurried to deliver expensive hats from exclusive shops in the city and everywhere there were flower sellers, news vendors, chestnut roasters and beautiful women in ornate equipages riding through the streets under the admiring eyes of mounted Chasseurs à Cheval in blue and silver.

At the Ritz Hotel, Laurel found herself with a bedroom almost as large as the ground floor of her home in Vermont. She wandered restlessly back and forth, looking at the paintings on the wall, delving into the drawers of the dresser and hanging her overnight clothes on hangers. Next to her room were a sitting room and then her father's bedroom. He had retired there on arrival, exhausted by the rigors of the voyage. Laurel looked in on him and ordered him some hot milk with brandy and a bowl of chicken soup.

"You've got to eat, Poppa. You've had nothing since you left Blenheim."

"I'll be all right, you'll see. It's just that my stomach still feels as if it's in my throat and my legs as if horses galloped over them. I'm sorry, dear, I'm going to have to rest today. When I've slept the clock around, I'll be just fine."

Left to her own devices, Laurel wondered what to do. Should she go out and look at the fashion shops of Paris? Was it safe to do that, or were women alone viewed as loose and followed around the streets by men? She could eat in the hotel restaurant or order food in her room. She rebelled against remaining all day in her room. If she did that, she knew she would spend the entire time thinking of Penn and wondering why he had ignored their departure. If he could not even come to the station to say good-bye, he could not think so very much of her. Laurel tried to tell herself she must forget Penn Allandale for the moment.

Putting on her new hat and the moleskin coat Consuelo had given her, Laurel went out, locking the bedroom door behind her. She had decided to walk around the rue de Rivoli and the Place Vendôme because she was dying to see the windows of the legendary jeweler's, Cartier, and the fashion houses of Rouff, Worth, and Doucet. She was planning to sketch some of the new season's dresses in order to have them copied by the dressmakers in St. Petersburg. She was aware, from Consuelo's warnings, that her wardrobe would be sadly insufficient for Russia and was desperate to know how to augment it from the meager cash available.

Laurel had reached the corner of the rue de Rivoli when she heard footsteps behind her that stopped when she stopped and continued again when she did. Convinced that she was being taken for a member of the demimonde, she hurried on. The footsteps behind her quickened their pace. Panic-stricken, Laurel picked up her skirts and ran like the wind, never stopping for a second until she reached the corner of the Champs Elysées. There were more people on the streets in that area and she felt safe from harm. Not hearing the pursuing footsteps anymore, she continued up the wide, tree-lined boulevard, pausing at a café to order coffee. She was so relieved she could barely keep from singing out loud that she had eluded her pursuer.

Laurel was savoring the dark rich espresso when she became aware that someone was standing over her table. Her cheeks turned pale and she knew in her heart that it was the man who had followed her from the Ritz. Looking up with all the defiance she could muster, she was shattered to see Penn Allandale smiling down at her. He had followed her from England to Paris! Overjoyed to see him, she leapt to her feet and threw her arms around his neck.

"Oh, my dearest Penn, whatever are you doing here in Paris?"

"I followed you. Never did like saying good-bye, and thought I'd put off the dreadful moment for as long as possible. Nearly lost you just now, when you decided to do a passable imitation of a racehorse. Did no one ever teach you that ladies *never* run?"

"I thought I was being followed by, . . . by . . . an undesirable person."

"Some people have called me that."

"They haven't and you know it. When did you arrive here, anyway?"

Laurel wondered suddenly if he was planning to follow her all the way to Russia. She smiled, however, delighted by Penn's presence and touched by the sentiment that had brought him to her side. She almost laughed out loud when he described his journey.

"The channel was so rough when I came over, I

swear my stomach was very near scrambled. Couldn't sleep a wink last night, either, for worrying in case I missed you. I say, Laurel, let's go to lunch. You don't have to hurry back to the Ritz, do you?"

"Of course not, I'm a free bird. Do you know Paris well enough to suggest some place for us to eat?"

"I was here at school for two years when Father was at the British embassy. We could go to the Orangerie in the Bois de Boulogne, you'd like that, and tonight to Maxim's for dinner. Where's Mr. Holman?"

"Poppa was sick on the crossing. He's gone to bed and won't be getting up again till we leave."

"I'm so sorry he's ill, but it means that Paris is ours for the taking. Let's make the very best of our last few hours together."

They took a carriage to the Bois, where they walked together through the green lanes. They passed the pavilion and skirted the racecourse to the Orangerie, a white iron structure that reminded Laurel of the conservatory at Wentworth Saye.

Fashionable Parisiennes were lunching with their friends, lovers, and husbands all around them. They were dressed in the latest fashions, their scent filling the air with tempting odors of chypre and musk.

Laurel watched waiters rushing back and forth with coffee and kümmel on ice for the clients whose meals were over and who were sitting under the trees watching children in small sailing boats on the lake. She looked across the table at Penn.

"I was upset when you weren't at the station to see

us off. I couldn't think why you hadn't come, and debated the reason for it all the way to Paris."

"And what did you decide in the end?"

"I decided you couldn't care much for me or you'd have wanted to say good-bye."

"I'll never want to say good-bye to you, Laurel. In future please give me the benefit of the doubt. Why, I could have been ill, for instance."

"If you'd been ill you'd have sent Hugo to give me a message."

"You've come to know me quite well in our crowded week together."

Laurel looked down at his strong hands and the gold hairs on his wrists that shone in the sun. She was longing for him to touch and hold her, to give her a kiss that would melt all her emotions and make her weak with longing.

Feigning ignorance of her scrutiny, Penn asked her what she wanted to eat.

"I'm so hungry I could devour the entire menu!"

"Dearest Laurel, I am *so* happy to be with you again."

After lunch they walked together under the weeping willows by the lake, arm in arm like a young married couple. As previously, Laurel found herself entirely at home with Penn and at ease in his presence. She was not ashamed to talk with him of her apprehension about her scanty wardrobe for the visit to Russia.

"I've the blue evening dress the duchess gave me and a black taffeta that was made for me in America

67

before I left. I've two emerald silks and three voiles in pink, white, and green. But I don't know what I'll *need* in Russia. Do the women there change clothes four times a day like they do in England, and will I be expected to do the same?"

"I doubt it. You'll be invited to parties and balls and social functions, and for those you'll have to dress, but at home you'll do as you please. There are many good dressmakers in Russia, who'll run up clothes for you, and in any case, the grand duke will understand the situation. He'll probably make you a gift of some special things."

"Do I accept them?"

"Of course. He'll expect you to accept all the gifts as if they were your due. He's a Russian, and Russians function along very predictable lines."

"What will he expect in return?"

"If he's a gentleman, only your company. He'll be quite content to wear you on his arm like a beautiful jewel and to have half of St. Petersburg imagine you're his mistress. If he's not a gentleman, he'll want you to become his lover."

Laurel blushed to the roots of her hair, suddenly out of her depth in this world of men and love affairs.

"I never heard of such a thing. I don't want to talk about Russia anymore."

"You brought it up, my dear."

"I know. I'm so worried all of a sudden about going there. I wish I'd never met the man."

"Come, we'll have some cassis on ice and a strong cup of coffee. Then I'll take you for a carriage ride around Paris. We'll see the beautiful shops of the Madeleine and the Cathedral of Nôtre Dame. I'll buy you some flowers at the market and then we'll say a prayer in the chapel. You can pray that you'll be looked after on your long and arduous journey. I shall pray that someone keeps the grand duke under control when he sees you again!"

"Where are you staying in Paris?"

"At the Ritz, of course. My bedroom's just across the hall from your own."

Penn was amused by the look of surprise on Laurel's face and pleased by the relief and mischievous glee when she spoke.

"Do you ever sleepwalk, Penn?"

"Only when invited to do so by a beautiful woman."

In the early evening, as she changed her clothes in the hotel bedroom, Laurel heard an accordionist in the street below playing a lilting French love song. She ran to the window and looked down at the hectic scene of Paris in the rush hour. Every inch of roadway was a jumble of fiacres, broughams, horse-drawn imperials, barrel organs, barouches, flower-sellers' carts, and bicycles all trying to make their way through the crowded square to the place they called home.

She was about to move away from the window when she noticed Penn walking between the buses and carriages, a bouquet of camellias in his hand. He was dressed in evening clothes and so handsome many of the passing women paused unashamedly to stare at him. One woman in a wondrous hat of bois-de-rose feathers leaned out of her carriage and addressed him. Penn shook his head and bowed politely, continuing to move steadily toward the Ritz, despite the lady's annoyance. Laurel sighed. Women found him irresistible, and what man would refuse the endless invitations to dinner, tea, and intimate four-to-fives?

Returning to the dressing table, Laurel stood in her camisole and drawers, trying to decide what to wear to Maxim's that night. All her best clothes were packed and she had left out only a white batiste dress. She had been so certain she would have to dine alone at the hotel. Penn's arrival seemed like a wonderful bonus, but she was conscious she was ill-prepared for it. Her deliberations were interrupted by a knock at the door. Throwing a pink silk kimono over her underwear, Laurel hurried to open it, surprised to find Penn standing there, his arms outstretched offering the flowers.

"You said you'd come at seven-thirty and it's only six-fifteen. I'm in my drawers and not fit to receive a man!"

"I was feeling miserable without you and decided to come early. I know you like camellias and I hope you'll wear some of these in your hair tonight."

"Of course I will, Penn."

Stepping into the room, he watched appreciatively as Laurel put the flowers in a crystal vase on the table. He looked from the open silk kimono to the perfect long slim legs and the voluptuous breasts at odds with the fineness of the rest of her body. Desire came to him and he asked himself despairingly how he could ever let her go and if he could do anything to stop her leaving for Russia.

When Laurel turned to face him, Penn was still gazing at her.

"What are you thinking? You've a strange look in your eyes, Penn Allandale!"

"I was wondering if we should cancel Maxim's and eat here in your suite, so I can admire you in your kimono and then go to bed full of fearful lust."

She kissed his cheeks, caught off balance when Penn pulled her onto his knee and kissed her full on the mouth. The kimono fell open and Laurel struggled to rise, her heart beating wildly, her cheeks flushed.

Penn's voice trembled with emotion. "Don't pull away like that. I can't bear it when you try to run away."

She ceased all resistance and closed her eyes as his lips met hers and the familiar thrusting, searching, titillating began, rousing all the fires in her soul. His hands gently caressed her shoulders, her neck, one straying to the opening of the kimono and the camisole underneath with its three pink satin ribbons. Laurel felt one of the bows being undone, slowly, gently, with infinite finesse. Then the erotic hardening of her breasts began as Penn ran his hands lightly over them. Sounds of pleasure and longing came from her and again she knew the overwhelming feelings of desire he had first awakened in her. His fingers found her nipple and gently rolled it back and forth, causing something within her to contract and then to give her the most exquisite and electrifying reaction. Laurel cried out, writhing so violently and pulling back so they fell together onto the ground. The kimono slipped from her shoulders, exposing her legs. She was bewildered when Penn rose suddenly and walked to the window. She wanted more than anything in the world to be loved.

"You're not angry, are you, Penn?"

"Only with myself and my unpardonable behavior. I want you too much, you see, and when you're near I cannot control the force of my emotions. The sight of those curls of yours and the scent of your body drive me wild and I have to kiss and caress you. When I do, I want more than kisses and caresses, and that cannot be."

She walked to the sofa as if in a daze and lay back in her white camisole and drawers, not caring that she was uncovered. His words had inflamed her and she could do nothing but rock gently back and forth, trying to still the agitation and the elation within. After a while, she spoke softly. "I want more than kisses and caresses too."

"I know you do, and that's the agonizing part of it. You're a most sensuous woman, a woman for whom love will be one of life's joys and necessities. But I cannot just make love to you and then see you off blithely to Russia. In any case, I'm unwilling to treat you as I might treat a lesser woman. I shall love you only when we've made a commitment about our future, if there is ever to be a future, and that can only be decided when you've been exposed to the temptations of life. If you can resist the grand duke's diamonds and his winning ways, if you still want me when you've experienced life in the atmosphere of wealth and power that surrounds the Romanovs, then I shall be waiting for you."

"Penn, do you love me?"

He stiffened, as though unwilling or afraid to answer.

"I've told many women I adore them, that I think them fascinating, beautiful, exquisite, titillating. I've made a point of *never* telling one that I love her. We Allandales reserve that for the women we want to marry, so I'll not answer your question at this time."

Laurel rose, put on the kimono, and walked barefoot to the window where he was standing. Rising on tiptoe, she kissed his cheeks and looked into the deep blue eyes.

"I don't know anything about passion and I've never been in love. I don't even know the difference between love and infatuation, but in my family we're very open about our feelings, so I'll tell you mine, Penn. I think of you all the time. I know I'm going to miss you dreadfully when I leave for Russia, and I know that every time you touch me I feel as if my body and yours were parts of the same jigsaw and meant to fit together. I wanted you to love me just now. I didn't give a damn what happened afterward. I just wanted you to be with me, in me, opening my body to your own."

"Dear God, Laurel, say no more! I can scarce control myself as it is."

"I'll be leaving in the morning and I've heeded

your advice. I'm going to enjoy everything the grand duke has to offer, and who knows, I might feel the same way about him. I might turn out to be one of those women who need *men*, not one man. I think I'm too young yet to know what I am or what I'll be. But if I still want you and think about you all the while, I'll come to Wentworth Saye and tell you so."

"I shall be waiting for you, I promise."

"Now I'd best dress for dinner. Will the white batiste be all right for Maxim's? It's all I've got out, so if it's not   'l have to eat elsewhere."

Penn   at the dress and then at the pink marks on her breasts, where his hands had touched her. The kimono had fallen open again, revealing the strong-boned, full-breasted body and the long, slim legs. With an effort he looked into Laurel's eyes.

"In the white dress you'll look like an angel among all the painted harpies of the demimonde. I must tell you that no respectable woman would be seen dead within a mile of Maxim's, though no doubt you'll find it fascinating, as you're an American and not subject to the normal rules of society. Some mothers even cover their daughter's faces when passing the place so they won't be contaminated."

Laurel's irreverent laughter rang out and Penn joined her, his face glowing with happiness.

"I'll go to my room while you change, and will return in fifteen minutes. Is that enough time?"

"Yes, that will be fine."

The manager of Maxim's looked up at the handsome Englishman and the beautiful girl at his side.

She was demurely dressed in white with pink camellias in her hair. The Frenchman thought wryly that she looked like a virgin, though surely not even an Englishman would bring an innocent to a private dining room at Maxim's. Then, out of the corner of his eye, the manager noticed that one of his Russian diners was beckoning him. Handing Penn and Laurel over to the maître, who led them upstairs to a pink-shaded salle privée, he hurried over to the Russian and bent solicitously forward to hear his request.

"Can I be of assistance, Excellency?"

"What is the name of the couple who came in just now?"

"He is Lord Allandale from England. The lady was not named. As you know, sir, at Maxim's ladies *never* have names."

"I should like to know who she is, if you please."

The manager sighed as the Russian began to pile gold pieces on the table without even looking up. The gold pieces were duly pocketed and the Frenchman made his way to the desk, where the maître was conveying Penn's order to the waiter. Words were exchanged and the maître returned to the salle privée carrying a bottle of champagne with the manager's compliments. As he poured the foaming gold liquid, he looked closely down at Laurel's wide-eyed face.

"Will you be in Paris long, Lord Allandale?"

"Only until tomorrow morning. Miss Holman leaves for Russia at six A.M. and I shall be returning to England when I have seen her off."

"And how is your brother, sir?"

"Hugo's well, thank you. He'll be over here in the Christmas Holiday for the Embassy Ball, so you can expect him."

"We shall be honored, as always, sir."

The manager went at once and conveyed the lady's name to the Russian, pleased to receive another mound of gold coins for his trouble. Russians, he reflected, were his favorite clients, so generous and willing to spend their money to enjoy themselves, even if they had an unfortunate tendency to dance on the tables when drunk and to stick forks into courtesans' breasts when overinflamed by passion. Moving through the raspberry-pink velvet banquettes full of the wealthy, the famous, and the infamous, the manager was well pleased with his little transaction.

Behind him, the Russian was thoughtful. What would Andrei Vladimirovich say if he knew that his latest passion had dined with a man in a private room at Maxim's on the eve of her departure for St. Petersburg? He had sworn the girl was a virgin, and indeed she looked like one, though one could never tell with foreigners. He had also sworn to have the American within six months of her arrival and had taken a number of bets on the outcome of his desire. The Russian smiled, his face flushed with pleasure. On his return home to Russia, he would bet against the grand duke being successful with the girl. He would say nothing of what he had seen this evening and put a large part of his fortune on Andrei's failure. A gambler, the Russian ordered more champagne and told the woman at his side that within the hour he was going to make her the highest-paid courtesan in Paris.

Laurel and Penn drank champagne and he ordered the meal, because she was too entranced by the forbidden atmosphere of the room to be able to concentrate on the menu. He chose a terrine of wild boar, followed by a ragoût of chicken and oysters with Argenteuil asparagus and pommes dauphines. For dessert they ate an extravagant concoction of meringues, cherries, and fresh peaches soaked in absinthe, honey, and lime. The waiters moved around them like phantoms, disappearing at the right moment to hurry to the kitchen and gossip furiously about the couple.

As he watched Laurel eating, Penn kissed her cheeks and held her hands.

"All of Paris will think you a sinful woman now that you've dined in a private room at Maxim's."

"Good, I'm sick of being thought of as a paragon of virtue."

"You'd best not tell your father where I brought you."

"I shall too. I tell Poppa everything, though I don't know if he always listens."

"Would you excuse me for a moment, Laurel?" Penn went outside and called the manager of the establishment. "When Miss Holman and I arrived, I noticed that one of your Russian guests was particularly interested in the lady. May I ask that gentleman's name, sir?"

The manager stared. The English were a surprising race, often seeming half-asleep, but with eyes in their backsides when the need arose. He answered without hesitation. "That was Count Cherchenko, sir, a good friend of the Romanov family. He is leaving for St. Petersburg on the early-morning train, though no doubt he will soon be back in Paris, as he is a regular visitor to Maxim's."

Penn returned to the room where Laurel was finishing her champagne. He poured her another glass, only stopping when he realized she was becoming a little tipsy.

"Now what shall we do, young lady?"

"Let's walk by the River Seine in the moonlight. Then you can kiss me and tear off all my clothes."

"Your word is my command."

Penn held her firmly as they came downstairs into the main public section of the room. As they passed the Russian's table, Penn kissed Laurel playfully on the cheek, gratified to see the count's manservant following them at a distance and jubilant to know he found a way of letting Andrei Vladimirovich know that he had a rival—and a serious rival—for Laurel.

On the stone sidewalk of the Seine, the only sound was the lapping of the water and the occasional plop of an oar cleaving the dark surface. Silver moonlight lit the scene, so the river resembled a sheet of shimmering satin dotted here and there with golden pools that were the reflections of the ornate iron lamps on the bridges. An old man was asleep on one of the benches and a young couple were kissing in the shadows of the Pont Neuf.

Laurel held Penn's arm, looking up at his profile outlined against the starry night sky. His forehead was high, his hair soft, his nose straight and long, his chin determined. He had the head, she decided, of a king or an emperor. She rested her cheek on his shoulder as they walked along, feeling happier than she could ever remember.

After a while Penn's deep voice invaded her most secret thoughts. "What are you dreaming about?"

"I was thinking how happy I am."

"What else?"

"I can't tell you the other thoughts. To tell the truth, they were a bit wanton. Am I drunk, Penn?"

"Only delightfully uninhibited."

"What time is it?"

He looked down at his watch and into her eyes.

"It's nine-forty-five. At five in the morning you have to leave the hotel for the station. I'll take you and your father there, of course. Would you rather return to the Ritz immediately?"

"No, I don't want tonight ever to be over."

"What then? Shall we go for a carriage ride to Montmartre or to the Folies Bergères to have a drink in the bar with the people of the night?"

"I'd like to go to the Folies. Poppa's always wanted to go there. He'll be green with envy when he knows we went."

The foyer of the Folies had always been a love market for hordes of pretty women. As Laurel and her escort entered, the intermission had recently begun and already the air was full of cigar smoke and the sound of a dozen different languages. The scene was colorful and bizarre. Elderly gentlemen in full evening dress were busy pursuing beautiful young women in feathers and satin, their faces alight with anticipation. Foreign millionaires mixed with Turkish diplomats, local characters, tourists, and members of the demimonde, all parading back and forth waiting for something sensational to happen. Behind the bar, a dreamy-faced young girl with blond plaits was serving absinthe and a potent wine from the vineyard of ̇   ̇ ̇tmartre farther up the hill. An American tourist smo᷍   ̣ ̣ Havana was in the process of purchasing a painting from a young artist. An English lord was buying an hour of love from a lady in yellow satin, and everywhere folk were chattering, ushers were calling, musicians playing, the con men picking their prey for the evening.

Penn watched Laurel closely as she sat at a table near a young couple as wide-eyed as herself. He ordered champagne, frowning, because the smoky atmosphere displeased him. He was delighted when Laurel spoke with her usual candor: "This smoke will cling to my clothes for a month!"

"It's a place to see once for the sake of seeing it, but rarely again."

Laurel gazed at the scene, comparing the noise and the smells and the hard-eyed look of the people of Pigalle with the peaceful scenes she had witnessed at Woodstock Fair, the shepherds leading their sheep to auction, the gun-dog trials, the handsome young Englishmen competing in a horse race and the countrywomen selling golden homemade butter wrapped in cabbage leaves. This was not the kind of world she wanted for herself, though it was fun to experience for a few minutes. When she had finished her champagne, she turned to Penn and held out her hand.

"Let's go for a walk to Montmartre, as you suggested before."

"Capital! I could do with some fresh air. If you'd rather wait for me at the entrance, Laurel, I'll pay the bill as quickly as I can."

She was standing at the street entrance to the theater when a young man walked by, paused, and raised his hat to her.

"Are you free?"

"I'm waiting for a friend."

"Will I do? I'm an awfully good friend."

"My friend's upstairs paying the check, sir."

"Are you sure he is?"

Laurel was amused to find herself being accosted for the first time in her life. Then Penn appeared and the young man hurried away into the night with a startled backward glance. Laurel linked her arm in Penn's.

"That young fellow was about to pick me up."

"I must be more careful and not leave you alone in future, though I have to admit he has good taste."

They climbed the ancient stone stairways to the cobbled streets of Montmartre and stood together in the darkness, looking down at the twinkling lights of the city. The night was fine, the breeze warm, and there was a smell of roasted chestnuts in the air that was typical of Paris.

Penn stood slightly behind Laurel, kissing her ears and her neck and her shoulders.

"It's almost midnight. I must take you home very soon or you'll be very tired in the morning. Tell me first, though, that this is one of the loveliest sights you ever saw."

"The loveliest sight I ever saw was the moon shining through the roof of your conservatory at Wentworth Saye and the orchids glowing in the candlelight."

He turned her around so she was facing him and hugged her to his heart.

"Thank you for saying that, Laurel."

"It's the truth. I keep thinking about that night and how we danced together under the moon. I'll never, ever forget it."

"Let's dance together again and to hell with what people think."

In the moonlight, they waltzed around and around the square, humming the tune from *Bal Rosé*. At the end of the song, Penn bowed and Laurel curtsied and a wave of applause came from people watching from open windows in the apartments above. With a wave to the romantic men and women of Montmartre, they ran down the steps, pausing under a lamp to look into each other's eyes.

Penn could barely keep from showing his distress at the nearness of her departure, but he put on a brave face and whispered tenderly, "Promise me you'll write often."

"Of course I will, and see that you reply. I'll be waiting for your letters like a starving woman."

"This is the damnedest thing. Can you not cancel the visit to Russia? Do you *really* have to go there?"

Laurel thought of Andrei, whose intense desire had communicated itself to her like a forbidden kiss. She realized that her previous desire to be wooed by him and to go to Russia was now outweighed by her eagerness to be with Penn Allandale. To withdraw at this point, however, would be to ruin all her father's plans. She spoke firmly, though her face showed clearly the dejection and apprehension she was feeling.

"It's Poppa's big chance to earn enough money to retire on, and I can't deprive him of that. He can't go alone, either, because he's sixty-two and not in the best of health."

Penn was delighted to see Count Cherchenko's servant following them back to the hotel, but relieved the man remained downstairs when they went to their rooms. Outside Laurel's suite, he kissed her good night and then went his separate way. He was trying not to tell himself that the idyllic days of their friendship were over. From this moment on, Laurel would be subjected to the greatest temptation any woman could endure and exposure to a way of life that would both intrigue and intoxicate her. Russia was another world. What effect, he wondered, would it really have on her? Penn shook his head perplexedly, experienced enough in the ways of women to know that the only thing that was certain was that they were unpredictable.

Laurel looked in on her father and found him sound asleep, a note pinned to the curtain around his bed: *Dearest Laurel, I set the alarm for 4:45. Am feeling much better for having rested. See you in the morning. Hugs, Poppa.*

She closed the door gently and went to her room, her mind still full of the events of the evening. When she had undressed and gotten into bed, she turned off the light and tried hard to sleep, but she was restless, and at one she rose and walked to the window. Below, the Place Vendôme was deserted but for a solitary gendarme making his rounds. The night was chilly, the sky mottled storm-gray and silver-white. Laurel tried to cool her burning cheeks by pressing them on the glass of the window, all the while struggling to settle her mind to the inevitability of saying good-bye to Penn. She could find no way of accepting that separation, but knowing she must try to sleep, she went back to bed. There she tossed and turned until she suddenly heard the door open. Penn walked into the room. Her heart thundered with excitement as he stood for a moment looking down at her.

"I can't sleep. My head's full of nightmares about your trip to Russia, and I keep trying to find ways of stopping you and your father from leaving. Forgive me for intruding, Laurel."

She held out her arms to him and pulled him down so he was sitting on the edge of the bed. Then she pulled him again, so he was lying on the top of the bedclothes at her side.

"You shouldn't be here, but I'm glad you came anyway. I haven't slept either."

"If your father wakes and finds me here, there'll be a fearful row. He might even challenge me to a duel, and he's such a charming fellow, I should hate to have to harm him!"

"Poppa won't wake. He takes a pill every night and has to have a loud alarm clock to wake him in the mornings. Kiss me, Penn."

His lips met hers and he whispered that he adored her. As their passion mounted, Laurel let him explore her body as he had not done before, and he knew then the extent of her desire and the beating, relentless longing she was experiencing was the same as his own. His hands moved over her thin silk nightdress. He was stunned when she lifted it over her head and threw it to the ground, and she lay naked before him. Penn moaned softly as his hands reached the curves of her hips, the gentle rise of her stomach, the muscles of her thighs. Laurel, he realized, was beyond reach of good sense, transported into a world of sensual delight. He whispered his adoration to her and kissed every inch of her body until she cried out.

"Oh, Laurel, you are the most beautiful creature I ever saw or touched or adored, but you know we cannot make love."

"I want you so much. Don't tell me it's not possible."

Unable to remain at her side without hastening further toward the ultimate act of passion, he kissed her once again on the lips and then rose and left the room with one brief backward glance of regret. Laurel was the most exciting woman he had ever known, a saint and a goddess, a beautiful, innocent, lusty young woman made for love. Penn left the hotel at once, lest he be tempted to return to her, and spent the night pacing back and forth in the deserted streets of the capital, his mind preoccupied by the struggle to regain control of his emotions.

At six o'clock the following morning Penn put James Holman and his daughter on the train at the Gare du Nord. Laurel was so pale he wondered if she were ill. She assured him that she was simply very distressed to be leaving him. He looked appealingly into her father's eyes.

"I've asked Laurel to write to me, sir. Do remind her if she forgets."

"I doubt she'll do anything of the kind, Penn, but I'll make sure anyway."

"You're most kind, sir."

"And I'll start painting your commission as soon as I get to Russia. It'll be my best recommendation, and I plan to make it a masterpiece."

Holman saw something in Penn's face when he heard this that touched him to the heart. Unless he was mistaken, the Englishman had fallen in love with Laurel and was suffering terribly at the moment of parting. Holman put his hand through the window and grinned a cheerful final good-bye.

"Don't you worry about a thing, Penn. I'll look after my little girl till we come back to England."

"Godspeed, Laurel. My compliments to you, Mr. Holman."

Penn stood to attention when the guard blew his whistle and the train began to move. His eyes were fixed on Laurel, his body longing for her as it had longed ever since that moment when he had first seen her in the park at Blenheim. As the train pulled out of the station, he stood tall, waving a blue silk scarf until Laurel was gone. Then he sat on the bench in the station concourse, clenching his fists to keep from breaking down. Tiredness, elation, distress, and confusion filled his mind. Laurel was gone and he was alone again. He had never regretted the departure of any woman, so why was he feeling so empty, so upset, so lonely, before she was even a mile from the station? He knew the answer to the question, but could not bear to admit it to himself, even now. He was trying to rally his spirits, when he heard a sound nearby and saw Flannegan holding out his hand.

"Time to get back to the hotel, sir. We have to leave almost immediately for Calais. I thought it best to come for you in the carriage in case you were feeling a trifle . . . indisposed."

"I'm perfectly well—don't treat me like a child!"

"Of course, sir, face up to the upset with a stiff upper lip like a true English gentleman."

"Do shut up, Flannegan."

"You're in love, sir, so I shall forgive your bad temper."

*　　*　　*

87

Laurel stared out of the window until Penn was a tiny dot in the distance. Then she walked to the compartment that had been reserved for her use while her father went to check on the schedules. It was over. Now he would go back to England and return to his bachelor ways. She thought of the happenings of the night and shivered from passionate excitement. How lovely it had been and how perfectly natural. As she remembered Penn's kisses, tears began to fall down her cheeks, and she found it impossible not to sob. Was it possible, she asked herself, that she was in love? She cried even harder at the thought, though she had always dreamed of being swept off her feet by passion. Dear God, in her case love was going to be worse than measles, hives, and consumption combined! Love would make an idiot out of her and she would lose the independence she had always valued and spend her life in tears, thinking of Penn.

When Holman returned to his compartment, he found Laurel sobbing her heart out. He fell to his knees before her.

"What's wrong, baby? I don't recall you crying like this since you were a child."

"Don't call me baby, Poppa. I'm not a baby any longer, I'm a woman."

"Of course you are, and a beautiful one, too."

Holman shook his head, puzzled by the ways of women. Here was Laurel, about to start out on a great adventure, and all she could do was cry like a six-year-old. He handed her his handkerchief and hugged her in his arms, just as he had when she was little. In his heart he knew her tears were for Penn and told himself he should be glad, because the Englishman was a fine young fellow, full of fun and charm and kindness. Holman had liked him from the start. As Laurel's tears increased, he patted her shoulders and kissed her gently.

"Don't cry, dear. Everything'll work out fine, you'll see. We're going to have a great time in Russia. I'll paint some portraits and make us enough money to buy you a whole new wardrobe of clothes ready for your return to England."

At this Laurel cried harder than ever and had to retire to her sleeping berth before lunch. There she fell into a restless sleep and dreamed that Penn was riding by the side of the train on his chestnut mare. When she woke, however, there was nothing but darkness all around. Penn was far, far away and she knew she might never see him again. Alone in her small room, she began to cry again and she was still crying when they crossed the border into Switzerland.

3

The Journey, September 1898

The railroad station of Grodno was painted corn-flower blue, with filigree white wooden shutters. The stationmaster, wearing his best uniform and shiny boots that creaked as he led the Holmans from the Paris Express to the Imperial Train, had been told that the couple were the Grand Duke Andrei's personal guests. He was anxious to impress with his efficiency, his polite manners, and his dignity.

Rounding the corner of the platform, Laurel and her father paused to stare at the strange sight before them. The Imperial Train was royal blue and gold, every inch of its brass fitments polished to a mirror-like sheen. Lined up along the platform were the drivers, porters, waiters, and muzhiks, whose sole job it was to attend the imperial family and their guests whenever they wished to travel. There were one hundred and fifty of them, their faces solemn, their uniforms impeccable, their eyes curious about this small gentleman in the cream tussah suit and wide panama straw and lady in dove gray, whose tawny eyes and glowing hair drew the attention and admiration of everyone. The grand duke had had many women from the ranks of the aristocracy of St. Petersburg, and his affairs were common knowledge. But this was the first time that he had ever sent the Imperial Train to collect one from foreign parts.

Laurel turned to her father with a twinkling smile.

"Well, this is certainly a change from the train we just left. Surely, we're not the only passengers?"

"I gather we are."

"They seem to be waiting for someone."

"Probably for orders. The Duchess of Marlborough told me Russian servants don't move till someone gives them instructions to do so. Initiative's not highly prized in these parts."

At that moment a tall Russian with dark, graying hair and a goatee approached, followed by a manservant and twelve porters carrying luggage. When he reached the spot where the Holmans were standing, he paused, debated what to do, and finally introduced himself.

"I am Count Cherchenko. I shall be traveling with you to St. Petersburg. I understand you are coming to Russia at the invitation of the Grand Duke Andrei Vladimirovich?"

"That's correct, sir. I'm James Holman and this is my daughter, Laurel."

"At your service, sir, Miss Holman. Now, let us get on board. Boy! Trunks, if you please. Follow me, Mr. Holman. I think it is going to rain, so we shall be much more comfortable on the train."

The Holmans followed the count, unable to keep from staring in rapt astonishment at the interior of the imperial wagons. The lounge they entered was upholstered in blue silk velvet with Aubusson carpets and solid gold fittings. While the count was taken to his sleeping quarters, Laurel and her father followed another servant to their own, two rooms with an interconnecting salon decorated entirely in yellow and white. The brocade covers were interwoven with gold thread that matched the tops of the crystal bottles on the dressing table.

Overwhelmed by the luxurious atmosphere of the train, Laurel sat on her bed and looked up at her father.

"I'll be scared to hiccup in this place, in case I break something."

"So will I. It's not what I'd call homey."

"What did you think of Count Cherchenko?"

"Not much. He looked at us the way a cobra looks at a mouse."

Laurel laughed despite her fatigue.

"I love you, Poppa, and I love your funny old-fashioned sayings."

"I love *you*, dear, and I want you to be happy. While we're in Russia you've just got to have fun and see a bit of life. Don't spend your days pining for Penn, because he'll be there when you get back to England."

"Will he? Every woman in Oxfordshire's in love with him; I can't take him for granted."

"If he's worth his salt, he'll be waiting. Now, let's go right back to the dining car and ask for something to eat. I'm so hungry I could even manage one of those odd-sounding Russian dishes you told me about when we were at Blenheim."

"Even roast wolf?"

"No roast wolf! I draw the line at that."

The scenery they passed was typical of Russia, flat fields stretching as far as the eye could see, most of them now emerald green since the wheat was sown immediately after the harvest in August. There were woods of birch, oak, and aspen, the leaves turning scarlet, crimson, and ocher. The villages were built of flat logs with a single street of one-story straw-thatched houses. Some of the buildings were oddly shaped, and many leaned at a perilous angle. And everywhere there was mud, after the heavy rains of the previous few weeks. The only touches of real color in this immense panorama of green and brown were the country churches painted red or emerald. Sometimes these had been gilded and built with a cupola of bright ultramarine. The peasants, for the most part, looked hardy. They had flaxen blond hair and were dressed in dark gray or brown, though the children wore vivid vermilion cotton smocks and the women cornflower wreaths in their hair.

Holman was waiting for his food to be served and feeling a little nervous in these alien surroundings. He was not completely sure Laurel was teasing about the roast wolf. After all, she had spent hours in the Blenheim library, reading everything she could find on Russia. He thought with longing of the clambakes they had enjoyed at home on the beaches of New England, the thick steaks and pot roasts that were his favorite food. It would be good to be home again when he was through with his work in Russia. It would be even better to know, at last, that his financial position was secure for the first time in his life.

Waiters appeared with silver salvers and walked past the table in a procession, raising the lid of each dish to display it to the three diners. The meal began with Russian hors d'oeuvres that included smoked salmon, pickled cucumbers, caviar, salted herring, and ham. Then red-cabbage soup with sour cream followed by baked sturgeon and roast venison with yellow plums. The dessert was fruit, cream, and nuts, and tiny amber-colored cigarettes were offered between each course, with copious quantities of Georgian wine. The service was elaborate and the meal took two hours to complete.

Holman looked wryly at his daughter.

"I hope they don't do all this again for dinner, or I might arrive as broad as I'm long."

"You must ask for a boiled egg or some cold meat, Poppa. We're guests, remember, we don't have to eat a feast twice a day."

After dinner, Count Cherchenko spoke with them

again, taking his place at their table and doing his best not to appear too inquisitive, though he was longing to know the reason for their visit—at least the official reason.

"May I ask what you plan to do in St. Petersburg, Mr. Holman?"

"I'm to paint the portraits of some members of the imperial family, sir. The grand duke assured me they'd all want a portrait when they see my work."

"I'm sure they will. The Czarina is very beautiful, and if you can persuade her to sit for you, everyone will follow."

"I hope so."

Holman lapsed into silence, suddenly apprehensive as to the reaction of the Russian aristocracy to his work.

Cherchenko turned to Laurel.

"And you, Miss Holman, how will you occupy yourself while your father is busy?"

"I always work as Poppa's assistant, and sometimes he lets me help paint backgrounds or parts of them for him."

"You're arriving at a good time of year. Before the Christmas social season begins, you will have had time to settle to our Russian climate. St. Petersburg was built on marshy land near the sea, and many visitors find the air enervating."

Laurel looked concerned at the thought of living on a flat, humid plain.

"Is there any real countryside near the city?"

The Russian was amused by her ignorance of his land.

"We have many millions of acres of forest and countryside, Miss Holman, a great deal of it very beautiful. If you prefer the country life to city life, you must ask the grand duke to allow you to use one of his dachas or a summer pavilion. Andrei prefers city living himself."

"How many houses does he own in all?"

The count shrugged, as if it had never occurred to him to count them.

"Who knows, perhaps ten or twelve, but you will see only the ones nearest the city. I doubt that you will visit the ones in the south and in Yalta, though they are truly unique."

"But we are to stay a whole year."

"In Russia a year is nothing. The distances in our country are very great, and nothing can be hurried. You will soon learn how isolated we are from the rest of the world and the normal communications you take for granted in Europe and America. Paris fashions, for example, reach us one year late. News arrives months after it has happened in London or Paris, and sometimes not at all. Our postal system is very primitive. Nothing of this really improves because we *like* our isolation. We do not want the rest of the world to know us, nor do we ourselves feel a great desire to know what is going on in far-off places."

The Holmans arrived in St. Petersburg on a cold autumn evening. The trees around the concourse of the station had turned to orange, red, and gold, and fallen leaves were blowing in swirling clouds around the passengers on the platform.

Laurel paused to take in this alien city and the sight of the River Neva turning bloodred in the spectacular reflection of a crimson sunset. The buildings of St. Petersburg were very grand but very bizarre to her eyes. Some had been constructed in the European manner, with gray stone facades and elegantly pillared entrances. Many were painted according to Russian custom in vivid colors of peach, emerald, rose, and yellow. The Winter Palace was dark green and white, and adjacent ministries cherry red, sienna, and brown. Many of the houses and churches had cupolas of shimmering gold that were now turning from rose to bronze in the light of the sun. St. Petersburg was said to be Russia's Western face, but to the Holmans it had an aura of the East and the unknown.

Laurel was still gazing at this unfamiliar scene when tendrils of river mist began to obscure the cobbled roadways of the city. As the mist drifted in, thickening to a fog, St. Petersburg became blurred like a city in a dream or a fairy story, and she wanted to rub her eyes to make sure she was not imagining it all. Her observations were interrupted by a sudden commotion. It was the grand duke.

Andrei appeared on the platform in a sweeping cloak of black karakul lamb that billowed and flapped behind him in the wind. His jacket was of ebony and silk velvet herringboned in leather, his shirt of white lawn held at the neck by a solid gold pin fashioned in a death's-head motif. Servants ran at his side, bowing whenever he turned to them, and Andrei kept calling orders to one or another and snapping his fingers imperiously. When he saw Laurel and her father he threw out his arms and hugged them as if they were old friends.

"So! You are here at last. Was your journey comfortable?"

"Very comfortable, thank you."

"You are cold, Miss Holman? Stepan, bring the lady's cloak."

A tall, handsome manservant stepped forward, and Laurel saw that he was carrying a voluminous cloak, of imperial sable. This he placed gently over her shoulders, inhaling her perfume and looking in bewilderment at the golden eyes and spirited face. Another cloak, of luxurious gray fox, was placed over Holman. Then the grand duke motioned with a flourish for them to follow him.

"We shall go at once to the Vladimir Palace, so that you can rest and supervise the servants as they unpack your luggage. I shall come to dinner tonight, and tomorrow or the next day you will lunch at my own home, farther along the Nevski Prospekt."

The coachman was six-feet-five and dressed in dark blue serge. He sported a round black hat with a tuft of shiny cocks' feathers, his fierce blue eyes staring out from above a long, tangled beard. His voice was strident and startling as he urged the horses on with ever greater speed.

Laurel clung to her father as they swept down the road by the canal and onto an immensely wide boulevard lined with massive houses, fashionable establishments, and palaces with campaniles, gilded domes, towers, and turrets. Her sense of being in some sort of fairy tale increased when the grand duke began talking of his homes.

"The building painted blue and yellow is the Vladimir Palace."

Laurel looked curiously at a building that filled a whole block of the Nevski Prospekt and on whose roof stood the gilded statues of naked Greek goddesses. Two massive guards with beards like that of the coachman were at the door. She looked into Andrei's eyes.

"The palace is huge, not at all as I expected it to be."

"Not so large, really—it is less than half the size of my own house, which has eight hundred rooms and one thousand servants."

"I never heard of such a thing!"

"In Russia we know how to live, Miss Holman. We could never survive in those small English houses."

Laurel thought of the four-room saltbox that was her father's home on the edge of the pine forest in Vermont. Then she looked more closely at the grand duke and saw that he was watching her intently, his black eyes almost mesmerizing in their force. As the coachman pulled into the courtyard, Andrei leaned forward, eager for her approval.

"How does the city please you, Miss Holman?"

"It's amazing! I never saw anything like it in my life."

"And you, Mr. Holman?"

"It's big, sir, very big. I'm afraid I'll get lost every time I go out."

"You have only to ask and a servant will accompany you everywhere during your first weeks in the city. I shall see to it personally."

The fog came down and Laurel could see very little as they reached the entrance to the palace. While the grand duke strode inside and servants ran to take their baggage to their rooms, she paused, listening to the foghorns hooting in the bay. On the Nevski Prospekt, people with lanterns were making their way cautiously along the pavements, their faces stoic. Unlike the grand duke, the ordinary folk of St. Petersburg wore drab black and brown wool with scarves wound tightly around their heads. Russia was obviously a land of contrasts, of rich and poor, ancient and modern, servility and autocracy. With a brief, questioning glance at her father, Laurel moved inside the palace.

The palace had an air of baroque splendor and decadence, and it smelled of incense and musk. The main salon was white with a marble fireplace and heavy satin draperies that fell from a ceiling so high it could barely be seen. The dining hall was in red, with priceless Persian tapestries and erotic statues everywhere. The walls of the principal withdrawing room were of Byzantine tooled leather in shades of gold, bronze, and cinnamon. Sofas of tobacco velvet were drawn in a square formation before an open hearth, and gold-etched chests ten feet long and five feet high lined the walls. These were full of treasures for which there was no room in the rest of the palace. On the walls, here and on every corridor, there were portraits of Romanovs long past, dark men with saturnine features and ladies with languorous, arrogant eyes.

The grand duke ended his short tour and turned to the new arrivals.

"I have shown you only three principal rooms in the palace, because these are the ones you will need to find tonight when we dine together. I will send someone to guide you, of course, but if you should rise early in the morning, you may wish to find your own way down. Now Stepan will show you to your accommodations."

Down endless corridors—so long the palace laundresses were in the habit of traveling them by bicycle—lay the suites selected for the Holmans. Laurel entered hers with mixed wonder and dread. She found a bedroom in pink with white lace curtains, and bowls of formally arranged hothouse tulips. She was examining her room when a servant hurried past her with a solemn-faced individual in black pin stripes, who turned out to be the city's leading vermin eradicator. The servant was carrying a bucket of dead cockroaches and Laurel knew from the smell in the room that it must have been fumigated shortly before her arrival. She followed Stepan to the blue salon next to her bedroom, then to a writing room, the servants' pantry, a storeroom, and a woodstove for the fires in that part of the house, and finally her father's room. She was amused to see her father standing in his red-and-gold bedroom, scratching his head in puzzlement at the sight of yet another ceiling so high it was almost impossible to see.

She returned to her own room and gazed apprehensively at her dresses, which had been hung in a small corner of the vast wardrobe. The bed was also vast, and curtained in heavy pink satin with bows held by grinning satyrs. Disliking the furnishings intensely, she walked to the windows and found herself looking out at a courtyard that served only the rooms allocated to herself and her father. It was hemmed in on all sides by high walls covered in scarlet autumn creeper. A formal statue of Pan in white alabaster stood outside the window and two rows of standard roses had been planted—recently, Laurel imagined—near the other door. They had been put in the ground at intervals of precisely one and a half feet. She sighed, remembering her father's garden in America, with its masses of morning glory, its ornamental grasses, venerable apple trees, and yellow broom covered in butterflies. In America everything grew where it pleased, unpruned and unmolested. Laurel remembered the majestic eighty-foot-high magnolia in the courtyard of Wentworth Saye and the flowers that grew in profusion all over the meadows, the banks of the river, and the garden. Penn had told her he detested formal bedding and preferred flowers to spread as they felt inclined, and not according to the wishes of the gardeners. Waves of longing over-whelmed Laurel as she reminisced. She felt a fore-boding sense of profound depression at being in this alien place far away from everything and everyone that she loved.

James Holman walked dejectedly to his daughter's room and saw her standing alone and pensive in the courtyard. Joining her, he looked around with cau-tion to make sure they were unobserved before he spoke.

"I expected a pretty big place, but not Grand Central Depot! That bed of mine's so large I'll need a servant to guide me out of it in the morning."

"It's certainly unlike anyplace we ever visited before."

"It sure is. I'd give twenty dollars right now just to see a photograph of home, and two hundred dollars to be there."

"You told me you were never homesick."

"I never was before, but right now I'm homesick enough to make up for it."

Laurel put her arm around her father to comfort him.

"We'll settle in, Poppa. You came here to make money so that you could retire. We must both remem-ber we didn't come to Russia for a holiday."

Holman fell silent, impressed by his daughter's good sense. She was a woman now and no longer his little girl, and he was forced to admit it at last. He sighed at the thought of the lonely years ahead once Laurel married. Then, putting on a cheery smile so she would not know how low he was feeling, he walked with her back to his room.

"I'd best go change for dinner, and get along to the salon, if I can find it. If I stay around here, I'll get more miserable by the minute."

"What do you think of the grand duke?"

"He's very certain of himself and I'm not too sure I like that, but then, I don't need to. You're right about our reason for coming here. I came to paint portraits at a thousand dollars each. I don't have to enjoy the experience. I'm sure Andrei'll be just fine as long as things are going his way."

Laurel's maid was named Polinka, a tall, country girl with yellow hair, who, on arriving in the city, had aped the habits of the servants of the rich by painting her flawless skin with a white concoction containing mercury. Now, four years later, her teeth had turned black due to the mercury and her once flawless complexion was pockmarked with spots. She wore a black dress that had seen years of service and a spotless white frilly apron. On seeing the few gowns in Laurel's wardrobe, Polinka felt an instant sympathy for the poor young visitor. Tonight the new arrivals would dine alone with the grand duke, but most nights the young woman would be invited to a party, a formal dinner, or a ball. Polinka eyed the batiste dresses disapprovingly. The grand duke had better send his new friend to Madame Lototsky's to have some new clothes made or he would be the laughing-stock of St. Petersburg. Everyone knew he had been taking bets on the outcome of his passion for the

American, but who would understand his desire if the poor child went around dressed like a convent girl? The maid's irreverent soul was half amused and half outraged on her new mistress's behalf. If she got the chance, she must talk some good sense into the young lady. Obviously the American had no idea how to act in a manner befitting the future mistress of one of the richest men in Russia.

In the dining room Laurel and her father sat and watched as staff brought in salvers of food for their host's approval. Andrei took a spoonful here and a forkful there, passing the plates along the table with disdain and smiling apologetically in their direction.

"Eating has always bored me, though there are a hundred cooks in this house and two hundred in my own. We use them mainly for entertaining. My sister says I could get by with only one for my own needs."

"I love to eat and I think about food often."

"Do you really, Mr. Holman, how very odd. And you, Laurel, are you like your father?"

"Yes, I love sharing a meal with friends. At home in America we often have clambakes on the beach and sometimes twenty or thirty guests. It takes a whole day to cook the meal and sometimes half the night to eat it."

"I must tell the chef to make some of our special Russian dishes for your approval once winter comes."

"When does it start?"

"Very shortly. In Russia autumn and spring are our shortest seasons. Winter comes with rain and fogs and beautiful colors in the countryside. Then we have the first snowfall, which does not stay. After that, at the beginning of November, we have the second snowfall, and then winter is here. It is my favorite time of year because I love the feeling of being isolated by the ice on the frozen River Neva. Sometimes also the rail lines cannot be used and we are imprisoned here in St. Petersburg. That is a fine feeling. We can expect no unwelcome visitors from abroad during those months."

Laurel looked sharply at the grand duke. If he was anxious to have no unwelcome visitors from abroad, was it possible he knew about Penn? She had been half hoping the Englishman would miss her so much he would follow her to Russia, but what chance had he if the ships could not come to St. Petersburg because of the frozen sea and the trains were prevented from making the journey because of the frozen rails? She sighed as the grand duke explained his plans for her.

"In the morning at ten you have an appointment with Madame Lototsky, the leading dressmaker in the city. You will probably have to stay with her for most of the day. Later, perhaps on Wednesday in the afternoon, I shall take you and your father for the promenade on the Nevski Prospekt and you will see all the finest citizens of St. Petersburg in their carriages. On Saturday we dine with my friend Boris Vasilievich and his wife, Anna, at their house on the Zagorodny Prospekt. He is an aide to the Czar and a fine upstanding fellow with the finest collection of bearskins in the city, all of which he shot himself."

Holman sighed, uneasy because his host had mentioned nothing of the purportedly eager relatives who were going to sit for portraits. Andrei had also avoided mentioning the fact that there was no room in the palace set up as a studio. Holman decided to take the bull by the horns.

"May I ask if I can chose one of your rooms to be used as my studio, sir?"

"By all means do. There are three hundred to choose from and you may have whichever ones you like, Mr. Holman. Just tell the servants what you require."

"And when shall I need to be ready for my first commission?"

The grand duke's face remained bland.

"When you are rested from your journey, of course. In Russia we do not believe in haste."

"I'm eager to get started, sir."

"Of course you are, and it will all be arranged in time."

Andrei looked at Laurel's pensive face and the dimity dress, which he disliked intensely. Madame Lototsky had been given full instructions on how to clothe the American. Until then, he would expose the girl only to chosen members of his private circle of friends. He looked appreciatively at the curve of her breasts and wondered if Laurel was really as innocent as she appeared. Had no man ever touched her body? Had none seen her naked and helpless on a bed? The image tormented him, and to take his mind off the desire that had plagued him ever since their first meeting, he rose.

"I must retire now. I traveled from Yelagin this morning and rose at five to be sure I would have time to check all the arrangements that had been made for your stay. I am tired, I fear, and not the best of company. Do excuse my ill manners."

"We're tired too, sir, and eager to get some sleep. So with your permission, Poppa and I will say good-night."

"Good night, Mr. Holman, Miss Holman. I shall see you tomorrow at tea, after your visit to the atelier of Madame Lototsky. My man Stepan will be calling to collect you at nine-thirty."

When the Holmans had gone, the grand duke went to the forecourt of the palace, where his carriage was waiting. Within minutes he was at the gaming table of Ortolani's, throwing down gold pieces and shouting excitedly, "Horosha! Horosha!" each time he won. By one A.M. he had a pile of gold two feet high in front of him. By three he had lost it all. Determined not to leave empty-handed, he gambled on till dawn, leaving the club on the arm of a leading courtesan of the city, the faithful Stepan walking behind, stumbling under the weight of a bag of gold coins. They drove back to the grand duke's home, four hundred yards farther west along the Nevski Prospekt from the spot where Laurel and her father were sleeping. While Stepan put away the gold, his master chased the lady upstairs. An hour later she would leave well paid but dismissed like a servant, because Andrei Vladimirovich was known to have a horror of waking up to find himself lying next to a prostitute.

The next morning, Laurel and her father breakfasted on cheese, white rolls, orange marmalade, and the bitterest coffee she had ever tasted. No amount of sugar made it palatable, and seeing her dislike of the drink, the leading waiter in the morning room brought a samovar of fresh tea.

They could hear the sounds of the city outside the palace. Tradesmen were calling their wares: "Scissors sharpened, knives sharpened!" "Cranberries for sale!" Laurel remembered the cries of London: "Buy my pretty lavender, two bunches for a penny," and the day Penn had bought her twenty bunches to scent her linen and clothes for the journey. While her father poured himself more tea, she looked around the room. The fireplace was so large it would have filled half their living area in Vermont. She turned to Holman with a wry smile.

"Since we arrived here I've felt like Gulliver must have on his travels."

"Me too. It's an odd feeling living in a place with three hundred rooms and four hundred servants. What do they *do* all day?"

"I bet they spend half their time gossiping. What are your plans today, Poppa?"

"I'm going to search this house for a room to use as a studio. I think I'll be able to do one wing before lunch, and the upstairs section later. It'll take a week to search the whole house!"

"I have to go with Stepan to the dressmaker."

"Have fun and choose some pretty things. Andrei's a man with a lot of determination to have his own way, so see he doesn't try to get you to buy something that doesn't suit you. These Russians have a different style from what we're used to in America. You need to keep with familiar things or you'll look swamped."

"He won't be there, Poppa. He said only servants go out before noon."

Holman stared in surprise.

"Did he really say that? It strikes me that Russians are even more class-conscious than the English."

"Penn Allandale is not class-conscious!"

Holman gazed at his daughter, stunned by her vehemence. Then his face softened.

"I didn't say a thing about Penn, honey, but he's not typical of the English anyway. His grandmother was American, remember, and his great-grandmother too."

"Who told you that?"

"I asked Consuelo. She told me the entire history of the Allandale family. I found it most interesting."

"You're full of surprises, Poppa."

"The duchess accused me once of not taking enough interest in your life, but I do. Believe me, I do."

At nine-thirty Laurel left the Vladimir Palace in the grand duke's open carriage. The coachman drove at breakneck speed as he had before, and she had to cling to the side of the door to keep from falling to the floor.

Outside an exclusive pastry shop nearby, beggars were gathering in the hope that the owner would give them bread. As the carriage passed by, the door of the shop opened and a large black-bearded man hurled out a shower of stale bread, cakes, pastries, and rolls. The beggars leapt to catch them before they fell to the ground. Some were successful, but most were obliged to fight in the dirt over the scraps, pushing and jostling each other, oblivious of passersby.

Laurel turned away, alarmed by the sight of the squabbling beggars. As before, the contrasts of the city struck her. To her right there was the orange-and-white extravaganza of the Stroganov Palace with its eight hundred rooms and superbly gilded cupola. By the Moika Canal some boys in bright red smocks were singing on their way to school. Near the spot where a drainage tunnel was being dug under the street, a workman called out a bawdy comment to Laurel. He earned a crack of the coachman's whip for his indelicacy.

Stepan turned from his seat beside the driver and apologized to Laurel in his excellent English.

"Forgive that fellow, milady. Great personages of St. Petersburg do not usually go out at this hour of the day, and the rogue was stunned by your looks into forgetting himself."

"That's all right, Stepan. I didn't understand a word of it anyway."

"It is most fortunate."

"Who taught you to speak English?"

"The grand duke insists that all the bedroom and personal servants learn English and French. It makes us superior to other staff in the city, apart from the English and Scottish governesses, who are very popular. In that way we reflect favorably on the master's household."

Madame Lototsky's establishment was in a shopping arcade of luxurious dimension, skirted on one side by the shop of a Bukhara shawl dealer and on the other by a currently fashionable jeweler, whose creations in pearls and gold were causing much comment in court circles. On the ground floor of the dressmaker's shop there were lifelike models made of wax and dressed in outfits of Madame's own design. On the second floor were her reception rooms, fitting rooms, and workrooms. What was on the third floor was unclear, though close friends knew that this was where Madame lived during the week, when she was not at her dacha on the island of Kammeni Ostrov.

Laurel followed Stepan toward the dressmaker's shop, stopping several times to gaze at the astonishing displays in the nearby windows. In one shop, pearls had been piled in foot-high mounds in solid gold bowls, their lustrous exteriors ranging in color from cream to yellow, snow-pink to storm-gray. In a childrens'-wear shop adjacent to the jeweler's, long christening robes were on display, each one made of priceless antique lace studded with diamonds. Even the patisseur had made his exhibition of cakes into a work of art—a grandiose gâteau in the form of the Winter Palace with a garden of marzipan trees, lakes, and flowers.

Madame Lototsky was forty-five, a small, plump, bustling Hungarian with a riveting accent. She had settled in the city twenty years previously, after her Russian lover died in a duel. She was immensely rich, a fearful gossip, and as cunning as the arctic foxes that wandered the backwoods around the city. On finding her new client waiting patiently in the reception area, Madame invited Laurel upstairs to share some coffee, to give them both strength for the task ahead.

"I have cakes from Densov and a whole samovar of tea, if you prefer. There is also some *wonderful* smoked ham that you will find irresistible."

Madame said "smoked" as if it were two words, and Laurel smothered a laugh, gazing in awe at the lady's dark blond hair with its soft curls and the heavy-lidded eyes that missed nothing. Madame Lototsky had once been a rare beauty. Now she was aging and a shadow of her former self, but she was nonetheless a figure to be reckoned with, or so Stepan had said. In contrast to her world-weary face, her clothes were the essence of chic and beauty, and Laurel knew at once that she liked this new acquaintance.

Madame looked at Laurel with interest, making her assessment within seconds. The child was obviously a virgin, though the sensuous mouth and slumberous eyes augured well for some lucky man. She was tall, which was good, because it meant she would be able to wear almost any style. She was full-breasted and narrow-waisted, which would not only please the grand duke but was also unlike most of the solidly built women of St. Petersburg. Madame poured out a cup of delicious coffee and filled it with cream.

"You are going to be with us for a year, so we must be friends."

"Yes, ma'am."

"Do call me Lotty, all my friends do. Now, the grand duke has given me my orders for your clothes. I have to tell you that he is a man with very definite ideas on how women should be dressed, in particular any women who accompany him to balls and parties. Obviously I must keep within range of colors and styles of his choice."

"Does the grand duke dress all his women alike, so they're instantly recognizable in society, or does he have some other reason for this whim?"

Madame's deep blue eyes widened and she laughed delightedly.

"So, you have claws under those gentle white fingers. Andrei Vladimirovich likes his women in certain colors. He is a man of habit, though he would die rather than admit it, and any departure from his habit disturbs him *dreadfully*."

Madame eyed Laurel's tawny, tiger's eyes, freckles, and curly amber hair piled on top of her head. Dear me, this was going to be entertaining! What *was* the young lady going to say when told that the grand duke wanted her dressed only in scarlet, chartreuse, orange, and silver? He had insisted that the entire wardrobe be made in those shades, with nothing but black sable to go with them. She brought out swatches of fine-quality lace, satin, silk, and embossed velvet and handed them to Laurel.

"You can choose the materials, bearing in mind that winter is coming. Outside, the streets will be cold enough to take your breath away. Inside, the palaces will be as hot as glasshouses in the summer."

Madame was quick to note the faraway look that came into Laurel's face on mention of the word "glass-house." And what did that mean? Did the young lady love flowers? She pursued the question with her usual cunning.

"Do you have a glasshouse at home in America?"

"No, but a friend of mine has the most beautiful hothouse in the world at his house in England. Sometimes, at night, they light it with pink candles so the orchids can be seen to advantage by the dinner guests."

Madame's eyes twinkled and she was hard pressed to conceal her delight. If Andrei thought he would get this young woman into his bed within a few weeks, he was making a great error. Unless she was very much mistaken, the girl had enjoyed more than a look at the rare orchids in the gentleman's glasshouse. Perhaps he had kissed her there and set her heart aflame. But who *was* he? Lotty knew she must not ask, at least not yet. Her romantic speculations were cut short by Laurel's response to the samples of material.

"All these swatches are red, orange, chartreuse,

and silver. I don't wear any of those shades. They don't go well with my freckles, nor with the color of my eyes."

"The grand duke insists we make your new wardrobe in those shades, my dear. They are his favorites, you see."

Laurel rose and paced back and forth, suddenly very angry at Andrei's presumption.

"I've decided I don't want any new clothes, Lotty. I brought some things with me, and I'll manage with what I have."

"But have you ball gowns for every day of the week, Laurel?"

"No, I haven't, and if I can only have them in these colors, I don't want them. It's best if you send Stepan to ask for instructions from the grand duke. I don't want *you* to get into trouble on my account, but I won't be labeled as one of Andrei's women, nor will I make myself look like a lobster by wearing red and orange, whatever he says."

Leaving Laurel in her private room, Madame instructed Stepan to drive her to the grand duke's home. The order she had received was a large one and she was reluctant to lose it, but she was enjoying this unexpected turn of events immensely. She had met many of Andrei's women in the past ten years, and none had ever argued about what his friends called their "uniform." Not until now. Instinctively Madame knew that Laurel would never change her mind. She was less certain of what Andrei's reaction would be.

On her arrival, Lotty was summoned to the breakfast room, where the grand duke was drinking his morning coffee. He looked up in some surprise when she was announced.

"I expected you to be with Miss Holman. What happened, Lotty?"

"She won't wear red, orange, silver, or chartreuse. She says they don't go with her complexion. Further, she informed me that if the only clothes she can have are to be made in those shades, she won't have them. She prefers to manage with what she brought from England."

"Laurel has only a dozen dresses, most of them in white or governess shades. I dislike them all intensely, and I will not take her out in any of them!"

The grand duke rose and paced the room. How dare the girl disobey him. It had never happened before, and he found it impossible to believe. He looked angrily in Lotty's direction.

"You should have been more forceful with her, Lotty. After all, she's only a foreigner, and a very young and innocent one."

"She has character, sir, and she knows what suits her. Remember that she's an American, and they are not at all like Russians. You'll have to learn her ways if you're to understand her moods and her opinions."

"Very well, make whatever she wants, and to hell with it. But I am displeased with her, greatly displeased. You may tell her that."

Lotty took a deep breath and voiced her thoughts. "I don't think Miss Holman realizes she has to please you, sir. After all, she came here to be with her father, who's a famous painter. She's unaware that she's to be your possession. Perhaps *you* should inform her of her position."

The grand duke looked sharply at Lotty, uncertain whether she was mocking him. Then, with a wave of his hand, he dismissed her. "I leave it all to you. But please do make the girl understand that in my country we dislike women who argue and are disobedient to their lovers' desires."

"She's not a woman who'd care about such things."

"What is she, then, a witch who always walks alone?"

"Perhaps. She certainly has the power to bewitch, but then, you already know that, don't you, sir?"

Before he could reply, Lotty strode to the door.

"I shall return to my establishment and do all I can to please Miss Holman *and* you, but it will not be easy and I shall be very tired and very cross by the end of the day."

"I am obliged to you for your trouble, Lotty."

"I am obliged to you, sir, for the order."

Lotty and her new client spent two hours going through swatches of material and another hour agreeing on the designs for the evening wear. By lunchtime they adjourned to the upstairs apartment for a splendid meal of veal cutlets with shallots. They shared a bottle of rosé together and Lotty praised Laurel on the good taste she showed. She also asked many questions about James Holman, enjoying the anecdotes Laurel told her about her father's clients and his way of tackling commissions.

As she watched Lotty smacking her lips at a peach soufflé, Lotty understood why the dressmaker was well-rounded. As Lotty ate, she leafed through the order they had agreed on so far—one dozen ball gowns to be made to the Parisian designs Laurel had copied from the shop windows of the Place Vendôme. The colors and fabrics that would be used were heavy ivory satin, heavy deep rose satin, violet chiffon, amber chiffon over bronze tissue, two black velvets, two emerald-green silks, one shot with royal blue, a white lace crinoline in the early-Victorian style, and another white lace over magenta silk to be worn with rubies. To complete the order, Laurel had chosen two black dresses in a shimmering satin exclusive to Lotty's establishment. One would be made with sleeves reversing to violet and the other over a hundred frothy lace petticoats designed to show when she walked, turned, or danced.

The grand duke had asked Lotty to supervise the choosing of jewels to match each dress, and simple diamond necklaces and stars for the hair had been purchased to go with the black dresses, rubies to go with the white, ancient amber in Tatar designs to match the dress of that color, and emeralds to go with one of the whites. All the jewels chosen were unusual. Laurel disliked the conventional ornate settings of rubies or colored stones, square-cut and surrounded by tiny diamonds. Her jewels, she said, must be of only one color at a time. Square-cut emeralds or pavé diamonds must stand unadorned. The rubies, however, must be massed by the dozen like vivid cerise flowers in chokers around her neck. The jeweler had left, thrilled to the bone by the order and astounded by the young lady's ideas. He felt every society matron in St. Petersburg would soon be copying the foreigner and he would be kept busy for weeks with orders from women doing their best to outshine her.

By four in the afternoon, Laurel was exhausted. She and Lotty had agreed on the day clothes, the underwear, the afternoon dresses, winter cloaks, coats, and also the traveling suits the grand duke had insisted be bought. Almost the entire order had been designed to fit within the color ranges of black, white, amber, emerald, and ultramarine. Styles for dancing shoes in satin and brocade and boots in the finest kid had been chosen and lasts taken of Laurel's feet. Hats had been agreed on, after a fierce argument with the traditional milliner, Madame Vera, who returned to her shop trembling at the astounding ideas of this new woman about town.

One thing was clear to Lotty. The young lady was nobody's fool, nor a character who could be manipulated. The toughest business people had accepted this and there was bound to be much speculation as to what would happen when the grand duke realized that the American was totally different in every way from the women he had known before.

Lotty was lost in admiration. Laurel, she knew, had style—unorthodox, fascinating style. Andrei was about to be shaken up, jolted out of his confidence and complacency, and put back together again. Lotty beamed at the very thought, her rouged cheeks glowing. For as long as she could remember, the grand duke had been the spoiled darling of the Romanov family. Only the Czarina Alexandra loathed him, every other woman in sight spoiling him to death. No woman had ever said no to him, not because he was particularly fascinating, but because he was rich and could buy everything he wanted. He had never been in love and he treated all his women like servants, to be manipulated for his own satisfaction. His infatuations were brief, and once he was satisfied they grew boring to him. Now he would meet his match in this unassuming but spirited young lady from a far-off land. Lotty looked out of the corner of her eye at Laurel, who was gazing yet again at a book of wedding-dress designs.

"These are truly beautiful, Lotty. Did you design them yourself?"

"I did. They are dream dresses, just like the one I would have worn if any man had asked me to marry him. Unfortunately, no one ever did!"

"I can't imagine why not."

Madame shook her head sadly, shrugging her shoulders at past memories.

"There are some women in this world that men marry, and others they do not. I was one of the ones to have fun with, to be seen around the city with. I was not the kind to take home to the family. I tried to be, but I was not successful."

That night, after she had told her father everything that had happened during the day and had done her best to cheer him from his malaise at the continuing lack of both a studio and clients to paint, Laurel went downstairs to the dining room, where she found the grand duke standing by the fire with an attractive older woman.

On seeing her, Andrei rose and introduced her to the lady. "This is my eldest sister, Varvara Vladimirovna."

Like Andrei, Varvara was tall, slim, and dark, except that her hair was bisected on either side of her part with a thick streak of white. Unlike Andrei, she was direct and intimate in her manner.

Laurel felt at ease with her and was happy to sit at her side, telling the lady about her visit to Madame Lototsky's and all the wonderful clothes they had chosen.

Andrei poured himself a glass of wine and handed another to James Holman, who appeared shortly after his daughter.

"To America, to you, and to your daughter, sir."

"To Russia and the czar."

"I thank you, Mr. Holman. Now, tell me, have you found a suitable room for your studio yet?"

"No, sir. I have not. I'll be looking again tomorrow."

"Look on the third floor of the palace. There are many rooms with very large windows that open onto the garden. Get Oleg to show you. I feel certain the light will be best in that region of the palace."

"Have you told your relatives that I've arrived?"

123

"Indeed I have, and they look forward to meeting you very soon."

"And are they still interested in having their portraits painted?"

"I am sure all of them will be, but first we have to organize you, Mr. Holman. One cannot have an artist without a studio."

They were enjoying a dinner of wild turkey stuffed with lemon rice and talking of the Duchess of Marlborough's portrait, when a young woman burst into the room. She was ashen pale and had extremely light blue eyes. Her mouth was wide and painted red and her cheeks were rouged, contrasting like a Lautrec portrait with the chalky color of her skin. Her dress was crimson satin with a four-foot-wide fan of ostrich-feather plumes in the same startling shade. She was somewhat unsteady on her feet as she approached the table, and when she spoke, her voice was sharp, like a lash.

"Forgive me for being late, Andrei. I do so *hate* getting up before seven."

The grand duke was staring at the newcomer in horrified fascination. His face had turned even paler than usual and his dark eyes glinted like those of a trapped animal, betraying his feelings despite the calm tone with which he greeted this unexpected guest.

"What are you doing here, Yelena Ivanovna?"

"I came to see *her*, my dear Andrei. I knew she'd arrived because already people are talking about her. They say she's headstrong and fierce. I'm disappointed,

I must say. She looks like a schoolgirl to me. Whatever were you thinking of when you invited her to St. Petersburg? Everyone will laugh at you for your stupidity."

With one movement the grand duke rose and propelled the young woman out of the room. The diners heard her voice rising hysterically as he dragged her along the corridor, and then there was the slamming of a door and then silence.

Holman looked across the table at the grand duke's sister. "What's all this about, ma'am? I think you owe us an explanation."

"That young lady has been in love with my brother for two and a half years, ever since she left the Smolny Convent, and perhaps even before. She follows him everywhere and is frequently given to jealous scenes at the most inopportune moments. I beg your forgiveness, Laurel, and yours too, Mr. Holman."

When Andrei returned, he called for champagne and with a roguish smile made his own apologies.

"Do forgive Yelena. I have known her since she was thirteen, and even then she was damnably possessive. Her behavior tonight, however, was unpardonable and I beg most humbly for your forgiveness."

Holman glanced across the table at his daughter, whose face was unfathomable. He had no idea what Laurel was thinking and could only tell how angry she was from the whitened knuckles of the hand which gripped her wineglass. Within minutes he rose and motioned for her to follow him.

"You must excuse me, Madame Varvara. My daughter and I are still tired from our journey, and Laurel's had a busy day at the dressmaker's. We'll retire now, if you don't object."

"Of course not, Mr. Holman. I hope you both sleep well. I fear it will take some time for you to grow accustomed to our weather in St. Petersburg. It has a tendency to make visitors to the city very tired."

"Yes, indeed. No doubt we'll grow acclimatized in time."

Andrei rose and walked to the door with the Holmans.

"Tomorrow I shall take you to lunch in the country and in a few days the first of your new clothes will arrive. Then, perhaps, we shall go to the ball at the Winter Palace to celebrate the birthday of the Grand Duke Sandro. I am sure you are going to cause a sensation."

When he had made sure his daughter was sound asleep, Holman walked alone down the heavily carpeted corridor from his room and stood listening to the voices coming from the dining hall. He was relieved to hear that Andrei and his sister were speaking in English, although, like most of the aristocrats of the city, they often spoke in French. Moving down the staircase stealthily, he stood gazing up at a massive seascape on the wall outside the dining room. Andrei's voice came to him from inside the salon.

"I tell you, Varvara, there's nothing I can do about Yelena. She follows me everywhere and is less than sober half the time of late. She accused me the other day in front of Alexandra of having deprived her of her innocence."

"At least she speaks the truth."

"What was I to do when she appeared in the country in all her finery? I'm only human."

"You should never have invited her to the country in the first place. You should have sent her home to her mother. It's one thing to chase married women, Andrei, but to romance innocent girls is dangerous. You only wanted Yelena because she was a convent girl and a virgin. Coldness has always ignited your feelings."

"You know me too well."

"We must do something about Yelena or your reputation will be ruined. She should go and live in the country, where you can visit her. Her temperament is far too delicate to cope with the tensions of the city."

"I once sent her away, remember? She returned to Petersburg within forty-eight hours, having begged lifts on every farm cart in Christendom!"

"Well, you were mad about her until this new woman came into your life. You *were* talking of marrying her, and Mama agreed it was a splendid idea."

"I have other plans now. I will not be tied down by Yelena. She's beautiful and in love with me, but I need a special person as my wife."

"I know what you have in mind, and I tell you it won't work. The new girl cares nothing for you and she never will. Perhaps that's why you're crazy about her. Each new woman is the same for you, Andrei—

always cold and then enslaved within a week or two. This one is different, though. This one will make you lose your sanity if you are not careful."

Holman made his way back to his room and sat for a long time thinking perplexedly of all that had been said. What did it mean? Was the grand duke a philanderer and no gentleman, despite his exalted breeding? Getting into bed, the painter looked at the sketches he had prepared of his daughter during their journey to Russia. Laurel was beautiful, innocent, and interested only in Penn Allandale. Her father took off his spectacles and gazed into space, then blew out the candles, annoyed that the palace had not yet been electrified, because he hated the smell of tallow. In the morning he would think more about what he had overheard, and from this moment he would forbid Laurel to be alone with the grand duke, until they knew him a great deal better.

In her room, Laurel was tossing and turning restlessly. Images of the scarlet dress with its gaudy feathers kept entering her mind and she knew that Yelena was the grand duke's mistress and a potential enemy in the city. It seemed ridiculous to have an enemy when there was no reason at all for the girl's jealousy. Sitting up, Laurel rubbed her eyes at the very moment when a shadow passed by her window. Someone was in the courtyard between her room and her father's. She rose, put on a wrap, and hurried to see who it was, reaching the window in time to catch a glimpse of a red-feather fan disappearing through the door that led to the servant's pantry.

Laurel hurried to the entrance that led to the outer passage and locked it. Then she went back to bed, her heart pounding from uncertainty and fear. In the morning she would think about everything that had happened and write to Penn about it, asking his advice on how to treat Yelena if they should ever meet again. The thought of Penn warmed her heart and settled her nerves and in a few minutes she was sound asleep.

4

Despite all the grand duke's efforts, Laurel had adamantly refused to attend any major functions in his
company until after all her new clothes had been
delivered and she had had lessons from a dancing
master in the complicated quadrilles, mazurkas, and
cotillions that were still popular in Russian society.
She had also taken lessons in French, so she could
understand when the master of ceremonies called
instructions during the dancing, in particular during
the more intricate maneuvers of the mazurka.

November had passed and both Laurel and her
father were relieved. It had been a month of fog,
rain, and sleet, with high humidity and misty mornings.
At night the wind had howled around the corridors of
the palace, and once there had been snow, though

by the morning it had vanished. Now the snow had returned and the grand duke was exultant that winter had come at last.

At first Andrei had tried to cajole Laurel into appearing on his arm before his friends in society. Then, infuriated by her independence, he had called her to his office and for the first time had lost his temper in her presence. He had been surprised to be met with a return display of temper that left him shocked and contrite. He thought of her response and shook his head in perplexity. *"I'm not your woman, your possession, or your plaything. I'm here with my father whom you invited on your whim to come to St. Petersburg and who's been twiddling his thumbs in idleness ever since. There are no Romanovs to paint and you know it. You brought us here because you wanted to philander with me. Well, you can think again if you're hoping to philander me, because unless you get a new heart and a new brain and a new character, I wouldn't think of looking in your direction."* Andrei had rushed from the house on hearing this and had not been seen for a week.

During that time, Holman found a room in the palace and set it up as a studio. Laurel continued her lessons in dancing, French, and had a crash course from Lotty on the interests and characters of the leading citizens of St. Petersburg. She now felt confident enough to accept Andrei's invitation to attend the Christmas ball at his sister's house on the Fontanka. It would be Laurel's debut in Russian society and an important moment in her life. Laurel had written to Penn about it and had given her letter to the British consul to send back to London in the diplomatic bag, no longer trusting the Russian post. In the eleven weeks of her stay in St. Petersburg, she had received not one single letter from England and was growing gradually more disillusioned by what she imagined to be Penn's neglect.

Five hundred carriages were parked in the grounds of Varvara's magnificent home. Some of the coachmen were still in them, their heads covered with a light layer of snow. The exterior, glass-enclosed terrace around the ground floor had been turned into an exotic garden for the evening, with boxes of rare shrubs and flowering plants brought from hothouses in the country and kept warm by the wood-burning stoves. The entrance to the house was lined with mirrors from floor to ceiling, with a fountain in the center full of tiny black-and-white fishes. There were miniature palm trees in porcelain pots around the hall and on the wide, curving staircase. Most sensational of all, the house was lit by ten thousand colored candles, white for the salon, yellow for the dining room, and scarlet in the ballroom.

Laurel held her father's hand tightly, suddenly nervous at the thought of her debut. She had no interest in impressing the grand duke, but her pride decreed that she acquit herself well in this first meeting with Russian society. Seeing how nervous she was, Holman squeezed Laurel's hand, concealing her own edginess and the exasperation he was beginning to feel with Andrei as time passed.

"You look like a princess, honey. Just remember we're American and you're *you*. Don't ever try to be like these people. The way to success for you is to be Laurel Holman."

The grand duke returned from greeting his sister and watched as Laurel handed her sable cloak to a servant.

"Are you ready, Miss Holman?"

"You can call me Laurel from now on."

Andrei was pleased by this small concession to intimacy. Taking his place at her side, he walked with Laurel and her father up a grand staircase of thirty marble steps to the presentation area. There, high above a salon full of two hundred of St. Petersburg's most celebrated citizens, they were announced by a majordomo in powdered wig and eighteenth-century livery.

"His Excellency the Grand Duke Andrei Vladimirovich. Mr. James Holman from America and his daughter, Laurel Diane."

Suddenly the babble of chattering, gossiping, laughing people ceased and the men and women of St. Petersburg turned to look with avid curiosity at the young woman everyone had been longing to see for weeks. They were stunned by the simple line of her clothes, which made every woman in the room seem overdressed. Laurel's gown was of heavy white satin, with a generous décolleté and a deep V at the back that plunged to the tiny waist. The skirt undulated like a shimmering satin sea, forming a train behind. The interior of the train was lined with sparkling diamonds, a piece of understatement and disdain for direct ostentation that raised every eyebrow in the room and caused one matron to exclaim loudly, "She has hidden her diamonds under the train. Whoever heard of such a thing!"

In contrast to the deceptive simplicity of the dress, Laurel's jewels were opulent. She wore a choker of brilliant-cut single diamonds, the centerpiece of which was a large square stone more magnificent than had been seen in many a year. In her hair, disdaining further artifice, she was wearing simple camellias held in place by a dozen tiny diamond stars. The effect was alluring and yet perfect in its innocent beauty. Every woman present envied the lady her gown, and every man wanted to know more about the young woman who had the audacity to wear white when on the arm of Andrei Vladimirovich Romanov.

When Laurel reached the foot of the stairs, there was an instant babble of comment. The American had obviously refused to wear red or silver or any of the colors normally allocated to Andrei's women. Everyone had heard that she had refused Lotty's evening-dress designs and had brought her own direct from Paris, but they had not realized that she had put together an entirely new and original look, one not seen in St. Petersburg before. Her beauty was accepted without comment, though some of the women pronounced her far too thin. Her manners aroused the greatest curiosity of all, for on meeting the Grand Duke Serge, Laurel asked about the horses that were his pride and joy. She then proceeded to capture a leading countess's heart with a long and amusing chat about the Ritz Hotel in Paris, and to please a famous retired general with comments on Napoleon.

The czarina normally refused to attend frivolous functions of a social nature and had only come to this one because even she could not resist the opportunity of meeting the young American about whom there had been so much discussion. As Laurel passed around the room, Alexandra watched her, amused by her manners and touched by her obvious innocence, which was in direct contrast with the decadent faces of St. Petersburg society.

On meeting the czarina, Laurel excelled herself. First she curtsied prettily. Then, when the czarina motioned for her to sit at her side, she did so happily, chatting and at ease as if talking with a school friend.

"I had no idea that Russian society would be so elegant. Are all these different uniforms the men wear real or invented by their tailors?"

"I believe they are designed by the tailors of St. Petersburg. They are very colorful, are they not?"

"And how do the ladies find jewels in such outrageous colors to match their dresses? This is something I'll remember for always, ma'am. We don't have anything quite like it where I come from."

"Tell me about your home, Miss Holman."

Laurel looked pensive. Then she began to describe Sour Apple Farm.

"Poppa's house is an old farm with one big room,

two bedrooms, a kitchen, a bathroom, and a barn. That's all there is to it. It's made of wood painted white, and there are morning glories in the garden and hundreds of acres of pine woods all around. Sometimes we get bears, and once one came to the front door and tried to get in the house."

The czarina looked startled at the thought of such a happening.

"May I ask what you did?"

"I threw stones at it and shouted for it to go away. Bears hate noise."

Alexandra smiled at the young lady's natural manner. She was thinking of the little white house in the pine woods of Vermont and telling herself how lucky the Holmans were to reside far away from Russia with its bizarre and godless aristocracy. She continued to ask about Laurel's life in America.

"What do you do all day when you are at home?"

"My father's a painter of portraits and I help him. I'm a painter, too, though I don't have Poppa's talent. He just painted the Duchess of Marlborough's portrait for the state bedroom of Blenheim Palace in England. She's American and was Consuelo Vanderbilt before she married the duke. She's truly beautiful, with a long neck and lovely shiny dark hair. Her clothes fill three whole rooms of the palace."

"Whom else has Mr. Holman painted?"

"Oh, all the society women of New York and also the Princess of Wales in London. She was the one who recommended Poppa to the Duchess of Marlborough. And Blenheim was where we met the Grand Duke

Andrei. He invited us to Russia to paint all the members of his family, but no one wants a portrait and Poppa's spending his days wandering around like a lost soul and painting me, because he hasn't anything better to do. I don't think the grand duke was telling the truth when he said that the Romanovs loved having their portraits painted."

The czarina looked disapprovingly across the room to where Andrei was dancing a quadrille with yet another red-clad society lady. Then she turned to her husband the czar and presented Laurel to him, at the same time beckoning a servant and giving him instructions to bring Holman to her side.

Laurel's father appeared and Alexandra studied the small, thickset man with curly white hair, a neatly cut beard, and humorous eyes. She was pleased when he made an elegant bow to her.

"Your daughter has been telling me you are tired of waiting to find someone to paint, Mr. Holman."

"Indeed I am, ma'am."

Holman weighed the exquisite face with its strong cheekbones, perfect straight nose, and wonderful clear blue eyes. The czarina was even lovelier than the Duchess of Marlborough and almost every other woman he had met. He was so engrossed in studying the color of her hair and the line of her neck that he forgot to answer her next question. The czarina leaned forward and asked the question again.

"How long will you be staying in Russia, Mr. Holman?"

Holman smiled and asked her forgiveness. "Sorry,

ma'am, I was daydreaming. To be honest, I was trying to remember every line of your face so I could sketch it when I get home. How long shall Laurel and I stay here? The grand duke told us we'd need to be a year in St. Petersburg, because so many of his family would want portraits, but there's been no rush to commission me. I haven't had a single request for a portrait since I arrived, so I reckon my daughter and I'll leave as soon as spring comes and we can get out without being trapped by the snow."

The czar led Laurel to the floor and held out his arms somewhat stiffly as the orchestra began to play a Viennese waltz. They did three turns around the ballroom before the other couples joined them. Then Nicholas relaxed and smiled down at Laurel in his lazy, preoccupied way.

"I always think I shall tread on my partner's feet when we have to dance alone around the room. It is like being an animal in the zoo at such times."

"I'm well known for my awful dancing, sir, so you've nothing to be anxious about. I can ride a horse, swim, skate, and play tennis, but dancing's always been a mystery to me."

"My wife is very interested in your stories of America, Miss Holman. May I ask if you are free on Tuesday next? Alexandra is having a tea party for her sister, whose birthday it will be, and I am sure she would enjoy it if you could come. Shall we say at four?"

"I'd be delighted, sir, and thank you so much for giving me such a wonderful welcome to Russia."

Champagne was served by fifty black waiters in red livery and fifty blond Circassians in white and gold. A buffet that ran down the side of the room was constantly replenished with mounds of caviar, foie gras, chickens stuffed with truffles, and tiny white doves flambéed in butter, brown sugar, and brandy. There were peaches soaked in vodka, grapes from the Crimea on solid gold cornucopias, and a fountain that gushed violet-tinted punch made of white wine, rose petals, and peach liqueur.

The grand duke walked alone around the room, listening to his friends' comments about Laurel. They all agreed that she was beautiful and very different from the usual women in whom she showed interest. Many remarked on how well informed she was, conversing with most of the leading members of the aristocracy on matters close to their hearts. A retired general of the army called her a formidable young lady. His wife added in an overloud voice that the American should leave the grand duke's residence at once or compromise her spotless reputation.

When he had toured the ballroom, Andrei stood alone in the warmth of his sister's private living room, thinking of Laurel's beauty and the way she had ignored him from the moment they entered the house. Varvara said he was attracted by coldness, and she was right, but the American was not cold. She was just a young, headstrong girl who was not in the least interested in him. He decided there and then to make an effort to study everything that pleased Laurel, to forgo his mistresses, and to concentrate on courting her. With something of a shock, he realized that he cared nothing for the loss of the wagers he had made about making love to her within six months of her arrival. He made wagers on everything, especially on women, and had enough money to lose every one of them if luck deserted him. The truth was, he wanted Laurel, and one way or another knew he must have her. It would not be enough to take her by force. Andrei wanted her to want him, if only for a single night. For that he would risk everything.

Finishing his wine, Andrei put the glass on the table, returned to the ballroom, and stood before Laurel, his arms outstretched.

"I hope you saved just one dance for me."

She stepped forward, suddenly sorry for him.

"Of course I did."

"Then it must be this one."

He guided her to the floor and whirled her around under the crystal chandeliers. The music quickened and he held her a little closer, shivering when his hand came into contact for a brief moment with the naked skin of her back. The eyes of every man and woman in the room were on them, provoking Andrei, until he was mad with longing for this spirited and endlessly independent woman from another world. He smelled Laurel's perfume and savored the luxurious scent of camellias. Then, as the music ended, he held her for a moment, looking into the elusive golden eyes.

"Thank you for dancing with me. I hope we shall do it again very often."

"Of course we will. If all the parties are as nice as this one, it's going to be a very enjoyable winter."

"You are the most beautiful woman here tonight, but you will already know that."

"The czarina's the most beautiful lady here. In fact Poppa says she's the most beautiful he's seen in many years. He's hardly been able to take his eyes off her since they met."

"She *is* lovely, but her heart is hard. She treats me always as if I were a barbarian about to invade her territory. She recoils when I speak with her and openly chastises me at every opportunity."

"You must be gentle with her, Andrei. She's a delicate creature."

"She is hard and cruel. Sometimes I think she dislikes me so intensely she will send me someday to Siberia."

"You're imagining all this!"

"Perhaps she just detests the Russian aristocracy because to her it is decadent and interested only in gossip and scandal. She is a most moral woman, I can tell you. She would send us all away if she could, and live alone in her tiny suite with the czar, pretending to be a housewife. God, how I despise that woman and her bourgeois ways!"

After midnight, Laurel went from the ballroom to the rear of the house to take a breath of air. On the back stairs, outside the kitchens, she saw dozens of servants sitting on the ground, enveloped in their mistresses' fur cloaks. There were coats and wraps of wolf, bear, and fox, cloaks of sable and ermine, and this was the customary way of guarding them, not by watching them, but by actually wearing them. Laurel thought of the fleas for which Russian servants were known and shuddered. Was Raster, the coachman, sitting in some far-off place with her sable cloak around his shoulders? She thought wryly that she had best shake it well before putting it on.

Laurel was leaning against the rear door of the house that led to the garden, when she saw Yelena Ivanovna coming toward her across the lawn. The girl's eyes were as red as her dress and the ornate velvet cloak she was wearing. Laurel remained where she was, unwilling to retreat because of the other woman. She was surprised when Yelena hurried over to her and spoke apologetically.

"Miss Holman, I am so sorry I was rude to you when we last met. I was very unhappy, you see, but that is no excuse for behaving like a woman of low breeding."

"I've forgotten all about it and so must you."

Yelena's eyes filled with tears and she wiped them with a tiny silk handkerchief.

"I wish you were unpleasant and vain so I could detest you."

"I need a friend, not an enemy."

"You cannot expect friendship from me, Miss Holman."

"My name's Laurel and I don't see why not."

"I have been the grand duke's mistress since the

time I left the convent. My mother and I were invited to Andrei's house in the country at that period and I thought he was planning to ask me to marry him. He had pursued me for so very long, you see, but the chase was what interested him, nothing else. Afterward, for a while, he remained kind, but then he just drifted away from me. I was too young and innocent and in love to understand."

"How long ago was all this?"

"Two and a half years. Andrei still comes to visit me and I wait for him and am proud he chooses me most often. What else can I do? I love him and will never love another man. But now *you* are here and he will begin all over again his pursuit and his passion and his mania to have his own way."

Laurel spoke patiently. "I came to Russia to help my father paint portraits. I didn't come for the grand duke's pleasure."

"That is why you were invited, though, and Andrei always has his way."

"I'd like to offer you a word of advice, Yelena."

The girl turned her back and looked angrily out at the garden. How dare the American offer her advice! She was shocked when Laurel continued imperturbably.

"First, you must stop drinking vodka. No man respects a woman who drinks a little too much. Second, you have to stop crying. You've known for two and a half years that the grand duke wanted the chase and not your love. Accept it and start a whole new life right now. Third, and this is the most important of all, next time Andrei calls at your house, be out. Tell your servants to inform him that you won't be able to see him again."

Yelena's eyes flashed with sudden anger.

"You say all this so he will come to you instead."

"I don't want him, Yelena. I have my own life and my own home far away from here. There's no place in that life for a man like Andrei. Now, I must go back to my father. He said he'd save the last waltz for me. Think on what I've told you. It's the best and most honest advice you'll ever get. Right now you're a mess, and a lot of people in this city know it. Get your self-respect back by telling the grand duke to go to hell. Who knows, he might be one of those men who only wants what he can't have. Now you know where I'm staying. Come and see me and tell me when you've made a decision. I shall look forward to hearing from you."

"You wish me to call on you?"

"I do, Yelena, if you have time."

Yelena came closer and stood for a moment staring into Laurel's eyes as if trying to decide if what people said of the newcomer was true, that she was honest to the point of rudeness and nobody's fool. Then she ran away into the garden and sat alone in the moonlight, her mind struggling to take in Laurel's advice. One thing was certain: the American was right about her lost reputation and self-respect. Yelena walked away from the house without a backward glance and made her way to her carriage. The coachman was surprised when she asked him to drive her to the dacha in the country forty versts from St.

Petersburg. He had expected her to go home with the Grand Duke Andrei as she so often did after celebrations. Yelena looked anxiously out of the window, knowing that within the next few weeks she must make some decisions. Would she dare follow the American's advice? Or would she go on forever being the woman Andrei treated like a lapdog? She tried to think as Laurel thought, instinct telling her that the foreigner's independence had been one of the attractions to Andrei. With a sigh she closed her eyes, deciding to make the great decision another day.

At one A.M., when they had danced the last waltz together, Laurel and her father went to thank Varvara for inviting them. Then they moved to the imperial dais and bade good night to the czar. The czarina smiled down at them, her face soft and almost eager.

"I hear you will be attending my tea party on Tuesday, Miss Holman. I shall look forward to hearing more of your stories of America and the fashionable ladies of society."

"I look forward to it, too, ma'am."

"Mr. Holman, have you any examples of your work with you in St. Petersburg?"

"I have a portrait of my daughter, ma'am. It's the only thing I've had to do these past few weeks and I never enjoyed a portrait so much."

"I should like to see it, if I may. Please bring it to the Winter Palace on Tuesday when Laurel comes to tea."

In the carriage, on the way home to the Vladimir Palace, the grand duke looked curiously at the painter.

"I too would like to see your daughter's portrait, Mr. Holman."

"It's in the studio, sir. You can see it anytime."

"Then I shall look on my return." Andrei turned to Laurel, his face full of admiration. "Your debut was a great success. Now everyone will wish you to attend parties and balls. I accepted on your behalf only one invitation—that was to the czar's special soiree at the Imperial Ballet at the Maryinsky Theater. I recall your mentioning that you love the ballet, and in any case, one cannot refuse an imperial command."

"I'll look forward to that. Madame Lototsky told me lots about the ballet and the beauty of the theater."

"Lotty obviously told you many things also about the leading figures of the city. You talked to the Grand Duke Serge about horses, his wife about Paris, Marshal Oblimov about Napoleon, and the czarina about everything except Russia, which she hates. You were very well informed of everyone's interests. May I ask what Lotty told you of mine?"

"She left you out of our conversations, though if I had to hazard a guess I'd say yours were bear hunts and having your own way."

To Laurel's surprise, the grand duke threw back his head and laughed resoundingly.

"You ignore me, insult me, and treat me like a serf. I have never received such offhand treatment from a lady, and I fear its effect on me."

"You have nothing to fear. In a few weeks I'll be gone from here."

Andrei's face showed his alarm. He spoke sharply. "But you agreed to stay for one year."

"We agreed to stay for a year because we thought Poppa would have so many portraits to paint he'd need that time. But he hasn't, so we've decided to leave for London as soon as spring comes."

In the gilded room James Holman had chosen as a studio, the grand duke looked at a portrait of Laurel that took his breath away. He knew at once that he must own it. His eyes moved from the curved white iron roof of the conservatory at Wentworth Saye to the passionflowers and rare orchids climbing up the glass walls. The floor was white marble, the flowers pink, red, and violet. And there, in the center of the canvas, surrounded by foliage, ferns, and exotic blooms, was Laurel, her face full of anticipation, her statuesque body dressed in a gown of shimmering white satin with diamond stars falling from shoulder to hem. In her hair there were camellias held in place by more of the stars. Andrei saw on closer inspection that the painting depicted the scene in late afternoon or early evening, one side of the canvas touched by the glow of sunset that intensified the color of the flowers and made Laurel's hair look like a halo around her head. It was a masterpiece and he had no hesitation in offering to buy it.

"I want that painting, Mr. Holman. Please be so kind as to state your price."

"It's not for sale, sir. I've already been paid for it by the man who commissioned it."

"You can do him a copy. He won't know the difference. Then I can have this one and put it in—"

"I never do copies, sir. Also, on Tuesday I have to take this painting for the czarina to see. After that, I intend to use it as a sample of my work if anyone should inquire."

"I will give you a thousand guineas for it, two thousand, ten thousand, name your price."

Holman's eyes turned steely. He had come to Russia to earn enough money to retire, if he so chose, but he was not about to trade Penn's portrait to this spoiled and selfish man. He turned out the light in the studio and moved with Andrei to the door, locking it behind them.

"I'll do you another portrait of Laurel, sir."

"But that is the one I want."

"That belongs to someone else, and neither you nor I would resort to thieving, now, would we?"

"You are a hard man, Mr. Holman. I did not expect it."

"People never do, sir."

By morning fifty invitations had arrived at the Vladimir Palace for Laurel. Polinka rushed upstairs with them, her face shiny with excitement. Since the American's arrival, she had been astounded at the young lady's poise. In the early days, Polinka had thought the visitor in need of advice, but Laurel was doing very well without it. She had started out with one-tenth of a wardrobe full of plain, dowdy dresses and now had sixty evening, morning, and afternoon gowns that were among the most beautiful in the city. Her furs were sensational, her jewels the talk of St. Petersburg. As for the grand duke, Polinka knew he was lost, unable to work out how to proceed along the pathway to romance with a woman who rarely looked his way. The maid chortled merrily at the thought as she tripped into Laurel's room.

"You have fifty invitations, ma'am."

Laurel leafed through them, amused by the quaint form of the phrasing of some. There was one for a ball, another for a bear hunt, a Christmas party, a skating party, and a treasure hunt. Uncertain what the latter meant, Laurel looked to her maid.

"What's a treasure hunt, Polinka?"

"You're not to go to that, ma'am! It's immoral. They only call it a treasure hunt as a kind of code. It's a party when a woman gets chased by a whole load of fellows from society. Disgusting, I'd say."

Uncertain what this meant, Laurel decided to change the subject.

"Did you wash your hair like I showed you? I see you finally threw away your mercury powder."

"I did, ma'am."

"I'll show you how to put your hair in rags later, so you can have ringlets like you said."

"What will the grand duke say if he knows?"

"It's none of his business if I choose to help my maid improve her appearance."

"You'll drive him mad with your difficult ways,

ma'am. I reckon you're his retribution for all the bad things he's done to women in the past."

"The experience will do him good."

Polinka laughed raucously, delighted that Andrei was at last getting his comeuppance.

When the maid had gone, Laurel sat in her room and wrote a letter to Penn. She told him about her debut in Russian society and about her father's meeting with the czarina. She paused for a moment to wonder what the chances were of the royal lady sitting for a portrait. The czarina was known to be shy. Was it possible she would sit for a Holman portrait when she had been notoriously reluctant to pose for others? Laurel smiled at the thought of the czarina of Russia, locked away in the tiny rooms she had chosen in the palace, trying to pretend she was a real housewife and not empress of all she surveyed.

For the first time that day Laurel agreed to accompany the grand duke for a two-P.M. ride along the Nevski Prospekt. This was known to the wealthy of the city as gulanie, or the daily promenade. At noon, the street would be full of governesses of all nationalities with their charges in dark gray dresses with white voile collars. The young ladies were being taught how to deport themselves, how to shop, and how to make sure they were not subjected to the cheating that was a game with most of the city traders, as everyone knew. Then, at two precisely, the carriages of the rich would appear. Diplomats, leading civil servants, gentlemen in frock coats, and ladies in afternoon dresses and feathered hats would parade, gazing at each other through golden lorgnettes and gossiping furiously despite their air of respectability.

Laurel's reason for accompanying Andrei was that she wished him to do all in his power to help her father secure a commission to paint the czarina. If he was in a happy mood, she knew, he would be generous. If he was angry, who could tell what he might do to obstruct her father's ambitions? She watched him out of the corner of her eye as he waved regally to his friends.

"Who are the handsome soldiers, Andrei?"

"The Gardes à Cheval are the ones in red with black boots, and the Preobrazhensky Guard are in green. The ones behind are the Pavlovskies. They all have snub noses, because that regiment was formed by the Emperor Paul I, who himself had the very ugliest Kalmuck features."

"And who's the woman in the dark blue carriage, the one who keeps glowering at me as if she wants to make me disappear?"

"That, my dear Laurel, is my mother. She returned to the city yesterday from a protracted visit to Italy. You will meet her at the ballet or the theater at some point, and I must warn you she is a very jealous woman who hates every female friend I have. I am her only son, you see, and Mama believes I should marry only a princess."

"I hope she finds a suitable one for you someday."

Laurel turned her head from the intense gaze of the Princess Sophia, though in her mind she was going over every feature of the unusual face with its shock of white hair and black piercing eyes, so like Andrei's. Sophia was fifty-eight and a mother used to power. Her brother was one of the Czar's leading advisers. Her father had occupied the same position with a previous ruler. Laurel decided she was a lady to be avoided at all costs.

On Tuesday at four Laurel and her father arrived at the Winter Palace with the grand duke. They were shocked when he excused himself and left them at the gate.

"You will have more luck in what you plan without my presence. If I am there, the czarina will be in far too great a temper to be able to think clearly about sitting for a portrait."

"I had no idea she disliked you that much!"

"She does, believe me. She would do anything to make my life unhappy."

"You're making too much of her shyness, that's all."

"No, I'm not, but you will only believe me when you have seen proof of what she is like when I am near. I shall look forward to hearing your news on your return home."

The Winter Palace had fifteen hundred rooms and a hundred staircases. Looking north across the River Neva to the fortress of St. Peter and St. Paul, it was a towering symbol of immense wealth and power to most of those who entered it. On this day of the Holmans' first visit, the Chevaliers Gardes were on duty, their chestnut horses immobile as statues as the Americans walked from the courtyard to the inner entrance and the hall. There they saw a massive stairway of snow-white marble and walls of gilded boiserie so ornate the whole enormous room shimmered in the afternoon sunlight.

Count Orlov walked ahead of them to an anteroom, where they were handed over to a stern-faced servant.

"The czarina is awaiting your arrival with impatience, sir, milady. Boy! Take the painting, if you please, and do not allow it to catch the walls when turning corners."

They walked for five minutes through corridors of green and gold, staring into rooms lined with agate and porphyry. They looked at each other in wonder when they proceeded through a faded gray silk salon full of precious objects in lapis lazuli, rock crystal, bronze, and ivory. Treasures that had been sent to the Russian court from the four corners of the world had been arranged carelessly here and there—a jade chair from China, a miniature carriage carved out of red onyx, a bowl of the finest kiri wood inlaid with gold, and, in one room, a child's toy made entirely of oddly shaped pearls.

The room into which they were finally led came as a surprise, because it was small and had a false ceiling that gave an impression of intimacy, a rare commodity in Russian palaces. A fire was blazing in the hearth and on two red silk sofas four ladies were sipping tea.

The czarina rose and led Laurel and her father to meet her other guests.

"This is Laurel Holman, about whom I have just

154

been talking, and her father, Mr. James Holman, who has come to Russia to paint our portraits. Mr. Holman, meet my sister, the Grand Duchess Elizabeth, the Countess Bettina Pavlovna, the Countess Cherchenko, and my friend Anna Semyonovna. Now, do show us the portrait you have brought. We are all *most* impatient to see your work."

The servants were dismissed and Holman cut the string around the portrait and stripped off the paper wrapping. Then, with a smile at the impatience of the ladies, he unwrapped Laurel's portrait.

There was a gasp of shock and admiration at the originality of the conception. In Russia, portraits were portraits, formal, regal, and each one similar to the other. This one showed Laurel with stars on her dress and a look of such intense eagerness in her eyes, the czarina understood at once that the girl was in love. As she was not in love with the grand duke, perhaps she was in love with the man at whom she had been gazing in the portrait. Alexandra looked at her sister and smiled conspiratorially. Then she turned to Holman.

"I should be pleased to sit for you, Mr. Holman. Shall we start on Monday after lunch? You will come to the Winter Palace, of course, and choose the room you would like to use for the background. We have so many to choose from, I do hope you will find something original."

Holman rose and kissed the czarina's hand, bowing respectfully as he knew was the custom on receiving an imperial commission.

"I thank you, ma'am. This will be a high point in my career and I look forward to it."

"My sister also wants a portrait, do you not, Elizabeth?"

"Indeed I do, Mr. Holman. I should like to be portrayed with my children in the snow, if that is possible."

"Everything is possible, ma'am, and you'll have exactly what you want."

When Holman had drunk his tea, he took his leave and went in search of a location for the portrait. He was accompanied by a servant, so he would not get lost in the corridors full of priceless treasure. The rooms of the Winter Palace were magnificent, each one more so than the last, but Holman could not settle on any of them. His image of Alexandra was one of an ethereal, almost ghostly creature, a fey, fairylike, elusive being full of tears and mystery, secret joy, and unimagined strength. She was a wood nymph in a crown that she despised, an enchantress with ferns in her hair, too subtle ever to mix with the bizarre and uncaring society of St. Petersburg.

Holman was getting weary of the gilded atmosphere, when, looking out of the window, he saw a garden full of beautiful white doves sitting in tall cedar trees. The trees were shaded from gray blue to darkest green, and one dark, brooding cedar of Lebanon dominated the scene. There was a lake nearby, and a ghostly statue of Aphrodite, the goddess of beauty, to the right of the composition. He knew at once that he had found his location for Alexandra's portrait.

Laurel was eating a sugar cake and drinking her third cup of tea when the Grand Duchess Elizabeth leaned forward and said curiously, "You've told us so much about America and all the ladies who do just as they please, but you haven't told us who commissioned the portrait of you. Did the grand duke want the portrait the moment he saw it?"

"He did, ma'am. He offered Poppa one thousand guineas for it, and then two thousand, then finally ten thousand."

"Mr. Holman must have been delighted."

"Oh, no, he was annoyed. The grand duke couldn't understand that the portrait's a commission that's already been bought. It belongs to someone in England and can't be sold twice. He even asked my father to do a copy, and that really riled him. He never does copies and he was so annoyed he had to go to bed to get out of the grand duke's way."

"Andrei will get one of his servants to take the portrait while your father's out, and you'll never see it again."

Laurel's eyes widened and she blushed angrily at the thought of such presumption.

"Surely he'd not stoop to theft?"

The czarina interrupted with unusual sharpness. "That man would stoop to anything to have his way. You had best leave the portrait here in my personal gallery, where it will be safe. Now, tell us some more about the portrait of Mrs. Gould which your father painted in New York."

"Mrs. Gould wanted to be painted on her husband's yacht in a seaman's hat and reefer jacket."

The Russian ladies laughed outrageously at this and the czarina had to wipe the tears from her eyes.

"Did Mr. Holman agree?"

"He protested, ma'am, and suggested white linen with a sailor collar to give a nautical look, but she was adamant, so Poppa did the portrait and Mrs. Gould was delighted with it and hung it in her salon. It makes everyone laugh when they see it, and perhaps that was what she intended."

"And the Duchess of Marlborough, what kind of portrait did she want?"

"She had hers done with the parterre as a background and she just wrote Poppa again to ask for another one on his return to England. That's to be done in her boudoir."

A babble of shocked, delighted chatter broke out on hearing this. The Countess Cherchenko looked sternly at Laurel to see if she was telling the truth.

"Are you quite sure she wants it painted in her *boudoir?*"

"Yes, ma'am. The duchess will be shown with her two sons in a beautiful ball gown, as if the children are admiring her as she leaves for a reception."

"What does she call the children, pray?"

Laurel smiled at Consuelo's witty comment on her sons.

"She calls them the 'heir' and the 'spare,' Countess. Poppa and I thought her quite the wittiest lady in England."

Gales of laughter greeted this and the ladies chatted animatedly for some time. At five, the cups were placed upside down to signify that they had finished tea. Servants came and cleared the table, disappearing obediently from sight at a signal from the czarina. Then, one by one, the guests took their leave, until only Laurel and the empress were left in the room.

"I shall send a servant to find your father. Until then, do stay and keep me company, my dear."

"I'll be glad to, ma'am."

"May I ask you a question, a very personal question, Laurel?"

"Of course you can."

"Who commissioned that wonderful portrait of you and what is the place used as the background?"

Laurel stared into Alexandra's blue eyes, confusion entering her mind. She could think of no reply but the truth.

"Lord Allandale commissioned it, ma'am. He lives at Wentworth Saye, not far from Blenheim Palace, and the background of the portrait's his conservatory, which is what he especially wanted."

"Is he in love with you?"

Laurel shrugged, her face scarlet. Talk of Penn made her realize how much she missed him, and she wanted to rush back to England on the very next train. She chose her words carefully when she replied: "Lord Allandale paid a lot of attention to me when I was in England and I enjoyed his company very much, but I've not heard a single word from him since I got here."

"Our post is lamentably bad, Laurel. You must not take the lack of letters seriously. The truth is, the postal authorities here are archaic in their attitudes and the distances very great. Some news comes to us many months after it has happened in Europe, some not at all. Only travelers arriving from Paris or London bring with them newspapers and the immediate news of what is really happening in the world."

"Maybe that's the reason."

"And you, what do you feel for this man?"

"I like him very much, ma'am. I do hope I'm not in love with him, though. I don't really know much about men, to tell the truth."

"Why do you hope you aren't in love?"

"Because Penn Allandale's the most handsome and splendid man in Oxfordshire and every woman in the county craves him."

The czarina smiled a secret smile. Then, inclining her head, she looked questioningly at Laurel.

"Did you say Penn Allandale? That stands for Pennington, does it not?"

"It does, ma'am. He's a second cousin to the Prince of Wales and indirectly related to your family. He mentioned it to me when I told him I was coming to St. Petersburg."

"I shall say nothing of all this to any of my friends, so your love for Penn can remain *our* secret, which is the wisest thing for it to be."

Laurel lapsed into silence, then spoke sadly. "I'm not in love with Penn, at least I don't think I am. I just think of him all the time and wish he'd answer my letters, and at night I lie in bed and imagine him riding his chestnut horse through the corn fields near his home. Wentworth Saye was the loveliest place I'd ever seen in my life, ma'am, all surrounded by poppy fields and daisy meadows and honeysuckle hedges. I felt as if I was in paradise."

Suddenly tears fell and Laurel looked in alarm at the czarina.

"I'm so sorry. It's just that now we've talked of Penn I realize how much I long to see him."

"You are in love, however much you do not wish to be, and I very much think that he is in love with you. That is why he wanted your portrait to be set against that beautiful conservatory of his home. Someday the portrait will hang on the wall of the family gallery for everyone to see, and they will point to the rare orchids and to your beautiful face and say how very lovely you were. That is what Penn intended. He was already preparing to show you to the future generations of his family in the most affectionate light."

Alexandra stared into the fire, her romantic soul touched by Laurel's dilemma. Then, when Holman returned, she rose and led him and his daughter to the anteroom, where a servant was waiting to take them back to their carriage.

"I have enjoyed our meeting, Laurel, and I thank you, Mr. Holman, for bringing the portrait for me to see. Be assured that it will be safe in my care. I shall so look forward to our sittings."

"Thank you for your kindness, ma'am. I plan on doing the finest portrait I've ever done. I'll have no excuses not to, because I've certainly got the most beautiful sitter."

The Holmans were driving through the city, when a messenger from the British embassy in a hat cockaded in red, white, and blue galloped alongside the carriage and called for the driver to halt. Then, saluting Laurel, he handed her a letter on cream vellum, a dark red seal at the rear.

"This is for you, Miss Holman. It was sent in the diplomatic bag from London, and I was on my way to deliver it at the Vladimir Palace when I saw you."

"You're most kind."

Tearing open the envelope, Laurel found a letter from Penn. Her face alight with pleasure, she read the contents of the note in sheer delight: *Dearest Laurel, I've had two letters from you since you left for Russia and have sent four in return. As you answer none of my questions, I am unsure if you have received any of them and am therefore sending this one in the diplomatic bag. We are all well at Wentworth Saye, though I am missing you dreadfully. Clarissa sends her love and Hugo his respects. I've had to throw myself into work since your departure in order not to go insane. New stables are being constructed, the east wing has just been decorated, and an avenue of laurel trees planted from the house to the entrance gates. I hope you understand the significance of that! I've missed you so grievously that I'm now known as a surly and unsociable fellow and my womanizing has ceased. It's a fearsome thing to have one's brain and heart occupied by a beautiful young woman whose image will not go away, no matter how hard a man tries. Seriously, do write and tell me you are well and safe and happy, as I am half-dead from worrying about you. And give the czar my respects, if you should meet him. We were introduced once when we were very young on his visit to England. I hope Mr. Holman will have been allowed to paint the czarina. Her face is a dream, with a quality rarely found in modern times. Take care of yourself, won't you, and have the satisfaction of knowing that you have enslaved me completely. I send you my affection, my admiration, my devotion— and my respects to your father. Penn Allandale.*

When Laurel entered the Vladimir Palace her face was transformed with pleasure. She ran at once to her room and hid the letter in a niche in the wall of her dressing room. Then she waltzed around the room, finally throwing herself down on the bed and closing her eyes blissfully as she imagined Penn busying himself improving the house so he would not have time to think of her all the while.

When the clocks chimed six, Laurel rose and walked into the dressing room. Tonight she was going to the theater. She must look her best and make her father proud. Her mind turned again to thoughts of Wentworth Saye and she took out Penn's letter and read it again and again. When Polinka appeared to take instructions on which dress to put out, Laurel was staring dreamily into space.

"Are you all right, ma'am?"

"I'm fine, I was just thinking of . . . happy times."

"You look like a woman in love."

The blush that suffused Laurel's face surprised her maid, who thought gleefully that that was just what the American was, only she was not in love with the Grand Duke Andrei. Polinka began to sing loudly in her enthusiastic peasant voice. Whoever he was, he was making life far more interesting than it had been before the lady's arrival. Who could tell what might happen next? Perhaps there might be a duel at dawn, or a suicide by the grand duke to the accompaniment of the Gypsy guitars of which he was so fond. Polinka's overactive imagination dwelt on endless possibilities. She could hardly wait to know what would come to pass.

5

The sea frozen, the railway lines unusable, St. Petersburg had become a winter wonderland isolated from the rest of the world. The scene outside Laurel's window at the Vladimir Palace was like a Christmas card. On the road, coachmen in New Year uniforms of scarlet-caped coats were driving troikas to and fro, tiny silver bells on the reins tinkling merrily. By the palace railings a man was singing to the tune of a barrel organ. On the frozen streets, men and women were picking their way warily along, their heads bowed against the icy wind from the river. Stark leafless trees silhouetted against the pink winter sky were hung with lanterns, and the arch with the clock at the end of the Morskaya was decorated with crosses made from evergreens and conifers sprinkled with flakes of newly fallen snow.

Some officers of the Royal Guard rode by, their faces stern. They did this at ten each morning and were considered by many to be one of the finest sights in the city. Their breastplates shimmered in the winter light. Their backs were ramrod straight, their bodies seemingly carved out of stone. All the proud heritage of Russia was obvious in these men, whose job it was to guard the Divine Ruler and his family. It was a sacred duty and all of them were hand-chosen for their looks, their military ability, and their background.

Laurel moved away from the window and sat gazing at the fire. She had come to St. Petersburg with her father so he could earn enough money to give him security for his future, and he was certainly doing that. She glanced at the czarina's portrait in the corner of the room and knew that it was one of the finest things he had ever done. An air of ghostly calm and tranquillity pervaded the portrait, and its understated background and the statue of the goddess Aphrodite. This czarina compelled the onlooker's attention in a way she found impossible to do in real life. Her blue eyes were intense in their expression and her filmy, iridescent silk dress and the matching opals around her neck ambivalent, much like the lady who had sat so patiently for the portrait.

By contrast, the Grand Duchess Elizabeth's picture was a symphony in white, painted against the snowy background of St. Petersburg's gilded spires and faded campaniles. Her beautiful features and the merry faces of her children in their scarlet velvet hoods stood out vividly against the simple setting. On seeing the portrait, she was delighted. Her sister's reaction to her own portrait had been less dramatic. The czarina had simply sent for her husband and together they had stood, holding hands, for a full fifteen minutes as they weighed every facet of the painting. Then she had praised Holman lavishly and asked him to do another portrait of her young daughters.

Since that day, commissions had come in as fast as the painter could handle them. He had already accepted a request to paint the Countess Korolenko on her bed of imperial sable, the Countess Shuvalova in her new gold troika, the Princess Imeretinskaya in her palatial malachite salon, and the young princesses skating on the lake of the czar's residence at Tsarskoye Selo.

When Holman entered the salon, he found his daughter pensive, as she had so often been of late. He hurried to her side and sat facing her, concern filling his heart.

"Are you all right, honey? You've seemed so down this past week."

"I've been hoping to have a Christmas card from Penn, and none has come. I just keep thinking about him, Poppa, and wishing he was here, but he's thousands of miles away and he doesn't even write. One letter in four months isn't enough. Why doesn't he make contact with me?"

"Penn told you he *had* written, and I believe him. He isn't the sort of fellow who'd lie about such a thing. Trouble is, the post here's so god-awful you might never get his letters and he might not be getting yours."

Laurel had not thought of this and looked increasingly troubled by the possibility.

"Do you really think he might not have had mine?"

"Sure do."

"Oh, Poppa, what shall I do?"

"Just leave everything to Penn. Once he realizes how things are, he'll fix something so you can communicate. You just see if he doesn't."

Laurel knew her father was right. Penn would do what had to be done and find a way to make contact with her. She turned to Holman and talked of his new commission: "Did you make a good start on the portrait?"

"I certainly did. The Countess Korolenko's pretty and she knows how to sit still, so I'll get on faster than I hoped. I hear Andrei's planning to take you to the ballet tonight."

"Yes, he is. I'm going to meet his mother for the first time and I'm not looking forward to it."

"She's of no importance to you. Just relax and be yourself. If she's rude, ignore her. Old dames like that hate being ignored."

The grand duke rushed into the palace on his return from the Princess Sophia's house and asked a servant to bring Laurel to his office immediately. Then he walked back and forth, his face paler than usual, his hands clenching and unclenching. For weeks, since her return from Italy, his mother had avoided mentioning or meeting the Americans. Now she could avoid the meeting no longer, but had refused adamantly to sit with Laurel in the family box, an action that, in Russian social terms, amounted to a monstrous insult. Andrei wondered how to break the news to his guest, when she appeared at the door.

"Stephan said you wanted to see me."

"Come in please, Laurel, I must speak with you."

"Has something bad happened? You look upset."

Andrei rang for coffee with some of the almond biscuits he knew were Laurel's favorites. Then he turned to her and spoke his mind for the first time since her arrival.

"I fell a little in love with you when I met you in England at the Duke of Marlborough's house. That was why I invited your father to visit St. Petersburg. I hoped and still hope that in time you will see the value of my love and treat me as more than a friend."

Laurel greeted this statement with some confusion, unused to the grand duke's being so direct.

Andrei continued when she remained silent: "When you and Mr. Holman arrived in Russia, my mother was in Italy visiting relatives in Rome. She was away, in all, for over half a year. Now, as you know, she has returned. She is displeased that I invited you here at all, as she detests foreigners and in addition loathes any woman in whom I am interested. On the one hand, she tells me she wishes me to marry. On the other, she always makes such difficulties for the women that I think of marrying that they take flight and will have nothing further to do with me. I do not refer to lovers, only to women I have in the past considered marrying."

"Why are you saying all this, Andrei?"

"You must know my feelings. Since you came here I have longed for you with all my heart, but you have shown in every action that you care little for me. I *want* you, Laurel. I desire you and dream of you every night."

"Please don't say any more. I know your feelings, but they aren't matched by my own and I can't change how I am."

Andrei moved nearer and looked into her eyes, a faint smile playing on his lips.

Almost afraid, Laurel retreated toward the door, her heart pounding because she knew he had been tempted to make a move toward her that both would have regretted.

"Has something else happened, Andrei, that has made you tell me all this?"

"It has. Tonight, at the ballet, my mother will be forced to meet you, as you are going there by imperial invitation. However, she has refused to share our family box with you. It is an insult and I beg your forgiveness most humbly. I do not know how to save you from embarrassment before all of society."

The coffee arrived and was poured, the tiny sugar biscuits handed out. Laurel was unperturbed by the news. If Andrei's mother chose to act like a jealous lover, why should she worry? She told him she would take care of the problem, amused by his chagrin.

"But what can you do? How will you conceal the truth?"

"I'll write a note to the czarina explaining that I can't attend the ballet."

"But she commanded you to go."

"No, Andrei, she *invited* me to join her party after the performance, but if I can't share your box and I can't sit in the stalls with the locals, because all the seats are bought months in advance, I just can't go. It's not important. Poppa and I can go together another time."

Andrei shook his head at her easy acceptance of the insult his mother had instigated.

"I do not understand your American ways. One does not write to the czarina without permission."

"I don't see why not."

"And what of the other things I told you?"

Laurel looked into the burning, feverish face, conscious of the tension in the grand duke and the desire that was increasing with each new day until it was tangible.

"I'll be honest with you, Andrei, more honest than any other woman you'll ever meet. I came to Russia for one reason, and one reason only—to give my father a chance to earn some security for the future. I had to come with him because his health hasn't been so good lately. I'd much rather have stayed on in England. Since I arrived in St. Petersburg, you've been very kind to me and I owe you the truth. I don't love you, though I like you well enough and I've enjoyed our outings together. I'd never marry you, because I couldn't marry a man I didn't love madly. I know it's romantic and silly by modern-day standards, but that's how I was raised to think."

"You could learn to love me—that is what happens to women in marriage."

"I don't believe that you *learn* to love someone, Andrei. You either love them or you don't. In any case, I'm not sure I could learn to love Russia. I'm an American, and our two countries are worlds apart."

"I would change everything you disliked. Love makes all things possible, and for a Romanov, nothing can be denied. You would only have to command me."

Laurel shook her head wistfully at his eagerness.

"What you say is very romantic and I never realized the extent to which you were willing to go to make me love you. But it wouldn't work, our two worlds are poles apart, and they could never meet. Now, I'd best go and arrange things for this evening."

When she had gone, the grand duke sat alone, enjoying the scent of camellias she always left behind. He had never met a woman so honest, so baffling, so impossible. What, he wondered, must he do to find the way to her heart, to be the man of her choice? Nothing was impossible for a Romanov. That was what he had always been taught from childhood, and he believed it. He must simply try harder to please her.

Andrei went to his desk and wrote an order to the jeweler to make a necklace for Laurel in the form of a choker of camellias, the flowers to be made of pearls, the leaves of emeralds, and the stamens of tiny topaz stones. Then he went to the garden and picked a single red rose from the hothouse and sent it to her room. She disliked ostentatious displays from the florists of St. Petersburg and was prone to tearing off the wrappings angrily because the flowers had been suffocated. Andrei had learned to take note of all her desires. Soon, he told himself, she would realize that he loved her above everything else in the world.

Laurel wrote a brief note to the czarina, saying that she could not join the imperial party after the ballet, because it had been found there was not enough room in the grand duke's family box for her to be present that evening. She also mentioned that the new portrait and that of the czarina's sister were ready for collection.

An hour later a messenger arrived with a cossack escort to collect the two paintings. He handed a note into Laurel's hand, bowed low, and left the palace.

Reading the brief message, Laurel was amused by the czarina's perception and determination: *Dear Laurel, You will be escorted to the imperial box on arrival at the Maryinsky Theater. Please inform the Grand Duke Andrei and his mother that this is an imperial order.*

The Maryinsky Theater was famous as the most romantic and impressive in the city, with the finest dancers, the best orchestra, and a scintillating prima ballerina, Mathilde Kschessinskaya, who had been the czar's mistress before his marriage. The interior was decorated in ice blue and gold. The audience reserved what tickets were on sale months in advance, though most of the seats were passed down from generation to generation. Uniforms were obligatory for men, full evening dress and jewels for the ladies. The first row of the parterre was reserved for nobles of the highest rank and officials of the court. The imperial box occupied an exalted central position toward the rear of the hall.

The audience watched as the Grand Duke Andrei took his place in the family box, followed by his mother, aunt, and Cousin Amalia. There was much speculation about the fact that his American guests were absent, and a few knowing members of society told their friends how the Princess Sophia had been proclaiming her detestation of foreigners all over the city since the day of her return from Italy. Obviously she had refused to share the box with the American, who had therefore been obliged to stay at home.

The czar entered the imperial box in a scarlet dress uniform. The audience rose to its feet, as was the custom, many nudging each other when it was seen that the imperial party comprised the Grand Duke Serge and his wife, the czarina's sister Elizabeth, Miss Laurel Holman and her partner for the evening, the Count Cherchenko's youngest and most handsome son, Sandro, plus the ever-present Anna Semyonovna, a friend of the royal family. Some of the audience looked to the spot where Andrei's mother was gazing at the American, dressed in pure white crinoline, with something close to loathing.

The Countess Oblimova whispered to her husband,

"Sophia Feodorovna has turned quite gray with annoyance!"

"Good! Let us hope she next turns into a pillar of salt. I cannot stand that awful woman!"

The czarina stood tall, her regal face and slim but impressive figure silencing all comment. Then, as the imperial party took its seats, the overture commenced and the haunting strains of Tchaikowsky's *Swan Lake* filled the auditorium. On the entrance of the prima ballerina there was thunderous applause. Then the audience sat in complete silence, watching as the story unfolded in all its enchantment.

Laurel was entranced by the size of the stage and the beauty of the costumes and feathery white tutus. She could barely keep from applauding every move when the prima ballerina pirouetted faultlessly, held arabesques interminably, and moved like a tiny doll within the proscenium arch. The story was sad and tears filled Laurel's eyes as she thought of Penn Allandale and their enforced separation. The orchestra was powerful and moving, the corps de ballet perfection, the atmosphere electric. Laurel held her breath as solo followed solo, each one more perfect and more astonishing than the last. All thought of her sadness disappeared as the magic of the ballet wrought its spell on her. When the curtains fell for the first intermission, Laurel remained still, gazing at the spot where Mathilde Kschessinskaya had been taking her bow.

The czarina leaned forward and addressed her, a smile on her lips. "Come, Laurel, it is time to order some refreshments. Would you like champagne, wine, coffee, or almond milk?"

"Almond milk, please, ma'am."

The czar turned to his American guest.

"Does our ballet please you, Miss Holman?"

"It's truly wonderful, sir. I felt as if it were all real and happening right there before my eyes. I never saw anything as impressive before, not even at the Royal Ballet in London."

Flattered by her comment, the czar turned to his wife.

"It would please me if Miss Holman and her father were to attend the fancy-dress ball next week. Could you find yourself a costume in time for Thursday, young lady?"

"I could, sir, and I'm sure Poppa will love thinking about what he wants to wear. We've never been to a fancy-dress ball before."

"Come as something original, I beg you. That will not be difficult for you and Mr. Holman, because you are naturally different from other people. Most of our friends, however, will appear as Marie Antoinette, Peter the Great, or Louis XIV. It will make a splendid sight, but a rather monotonous one, I'm afraid."

Laurel turned to her young escort, the twenty-year-old son of Count Cherchenko.

"Tell me, Sandro, what are you going to do in life when you finish your education?"

"I'm the youngest son, ma'am, so I shall manage Papa's estates."

"Call me Laurel—no one ever calls me 'ma'am.'"

"Very well, ma'am . . . Laurel." Sandro blushed to the roots of his blond hair.

Laurel continued, pretending not to notice his shyness, "Where will you live when you manage your father's estates?"

"Papa has properties in Yalta, which is in the south of our country, in Kiev, and outside St. Petersburg at Tsarskoye Selo. That is probably where I shall have my base, though I have only just left school and nothing has yet been decided. I love the country much more than the city, however, and am happy with my future prospects."

"I love the country too, but I haven't been there yet. I suppose the roads are impassable because of the snow."

"No, they are not impassable, at least not to Tsarskoye Selo, because that is the road to the royal country residence, which is cleared each day. I go every Sunday to roast chestnuts on the fire with my sister Katinka. She lives in the house and will act as my housekeeper until I marry. Perhaps you would like to dine with us next Sunday, Laurel? I would personally collect you from the Vladimir Palace and bring you home safely. You have nothing to fear, I always carry a rifle in winter in case we encounter wolves."

"I'd love to see your house, Sandro."

His face lit with pleasure and he shook her hand.

"I am the luckiest man in St. Petersburg! Katinka and I have never entertained an American before.

My sister will be thrilled to have the opportunity to meet you."

The czarina, who had been listening to the exchange, turned to Laurel.

"Count Cherchenko's house is a wonder. See that Sandro remembers to show you the summer pavilions while you are there. They are a wonderful sight, second only to our own Rose Pavilion at Peterhof. You really must stay in Russia until the spring, so you can see them when they are covered in blossom and not in snow."

When the grand duke heard that Sandro had invited Laurel to the country, he was enraged and called her to his office to be reprimanded.

"You will not go to the country with that boy!"

Furious at his tone and the rage he was displaying at her acceptance of the invitation, Laurel spoke sharply. "Don't tell me what I can and cannot do. I'm your guest, not your mistress."

"You will not go, I say. It would humiliate me before all my friends in St. Petersburg."

"Why are you acting like this, Andrei? You must know by now that I won't be dictated to. I just *won't* be ordered about as if I were your possession. In any case, it's time you accepted that your reason for inviting me to Russia hasn't worked out for you. I'm here to help Poppa complete his commissions, not to be your woman, and you *must* understand that."

Realizing that she could not be turned about by force, Andrei appealed to her better nature.

"I invite you instead to one of my own country

houses. Or, if you like, I will take you to visit Moscow. You would find that a most fascinating place, I promise."

"I'd rather stay here in St. Petersburg. My father's busy right now and needs my help."

"Laurel, please say at least that you will come with me to the fancy-dress ball at the Winter Palace and also to the christening of the czarina's daughter on the eighth of March."

"I already agreed to come to that. Now, let's stop arguing about nothing at all."

Andrei sat by the fire, determined not to lose his temper or to panic at her attitude, which was so alien and unbelievable to him. He remembered then that he had something for Laurel and looked down at her with an affectionate smile.

"I bought you a special present. It is not jewels or furs or clothes, because you said Russians had no originality and always bought those things for their friends. Can you imagine what it is?"

Laurel looked around the room, curious to know what new toy Andrei had found for her. Usually his taste ran to expensive trinkets from the court jeweler. Surely he had not bought a gift himself instead of sending Stepan for it.

Andrei returned with a cardboard box and handed it to her. Inside, Laurel found a tiny white kitten with a big pink satin bow around its neck. She picked it up, kissed it, and waltzed with it around the room.

"This is a lovely present! Thank you, Andrei. I do so love kittens."

He was so happy to see that he had pleased her, and he almost threw his arms around her, but already he had learned caution and chose instead to talk of the fancy-dress ball.

"You are keeping your costume a secret, as is your father. I could find out nothing at all from him."

"You'll see why when we appear at the ball. Poppa designed our costumes himself, and Lotty's making them up for us. She told me she never saw anything like them before in St. Petersburg. I just hope they don't cause a scandal and that the czar has a sense of humor!"

The following Sunday, Laurel went to the country with Sandro Alexandrovich to see the Cherchenkos' fabulous country house. She was shown the summer pavilions the czarina had mentioned. They were immense cedarwood structures with quaintly carved interiors, not unlike peasant houses, except that these were constructed of the finest woods and filled with the most expensive furniture. Unlike many of the royal residences, the buildings were the essence of hominess, and Laurel knew at once what had appealed to the czarina. She turned and smiled at Sandro.

"It's a wonderful sight. The pavilions are truly places for lovers and passion on bearskin rugs in front of the fire, like we read about in novels. Have you a girlfriend, Sandro?"

Nonplussed by her directness, the young man looked at his hands. Then he gave a helpless shrug.

"I am in love, but my father does not approve of my choice."

"Why not?"

"Mitzi is half Russian and half Chinese. My father disapproves greatly of what he calls the undesirable classes."

"Is she very beautiful?"

"The most beautiful woman I ever met, even more so than the czarina and you."

"Tell me all about her, Sandro."

He held out his hand affectionately to Laurel.

"Thank you for being my friend and letting me talk of Mitzi. I shall try to be of service to you someday in return. The truth is that love has made only unhappiness for me. I love my father and hate to deceive him, but nothing in the world will ever stop me loving Mitzi."

"You should marry her and *then* tell your father."

"He would disown me."

"It's unlikely, but if he did, you'd just have to earn a living like ordinary people do and your father would have to find himself a new estate manager. I don't think he'd want a total stranger in charge of all his affairs, would he?"

"I do not know. If he did dismiss me, I suppose I could find work. I know everything about farming and forestry and estate management. Come, let's go back to the house and I shall show you my portrait of Mitzi. I keep it hidden in my room in a chest."

"Does your sister know of your feelings?"

"Of course, but Katinka cannot help. Papa is a

very stubborn man and determined to be the head of his family. He wishes everyone to obey him, and he will settle for nothing less than total obedience."

"We'll talk of it again over dinner and I'll give you the best advice I can."

"I shall be in your debt forever, Laurel, if you find a solution to my problems. Perhaps you would not be offended if I also gave *you* a word of advice?"

"Please do."

"Take care in your dealings with the grand duke. Since he was a small child Andrei has had his own way in all things, and he has come to expect it. With you, he has not, and for the moment he is showing patience and restraint. That is because he still hopes you will change your mind about him."

"And if I don't?"

"He can be a very dangerous adversary. I would not put *anything* past him. Some of his actions have been shrouded in rumor and mystery."

Laurel stared into Sandro's innocent blue eyes.

"Do you mean Andrei might try to take advantage of me against my will?"

"Perhaps. He might do anything, even hide you away in a far-off place until your will is broken. I only mention this, Laurel, because it is obvious to me that you are unaware of the grand duke's true depths. Once Andrei hardens his heart against someone, that person had best get out of St. Petersburg with great haste."

* * *

The night of the fancy-dress ball was icy cold, with a skin-stripping wind coming from the sea. Snow was falling steadily and there was a rumor that the coach-man of a leading aristocrat had been found frozen to death after having been ordered by his master to wait outside a house on the Dzerzhinskaya.

Laurel and her father entered the grand salon of the Winter Palace together and were announced by the stout-faced majordomo.

"Mr. James Holman and his daughter, Miss Laurel Diane Holman."

The aristocratic men and women of St. Petersburg, in their gilded lace and bejeweled costumes, turned and gasped at the astonishing outfits of the painter and his daughter. Holman was dressed as a lion with a huge ruff of sand-colored "mane" around his impressive head. The costume was made of thick pile velvet with a bejeweled tail that swung from side to side as he strutted by.

Laurel was dressed like a tiger. She wore a daring outfit of brown and gold sequinned material; on her face she wore a mask and over her hair a hat in the form of a tiger's head. Though she was covered from top to toe in the tight-fitting striped material and had a skirt to cover her legs and a swirling tiger-skin cloak overall, she caused a sensation. Everyone crowded around her to see this daring ensemble, one that could only have been worn by a foreigner.

The czar moved forward and greeted the pair.

"I complained that all our guests would come as Marie Antoinette and Peter the Great and I was almost right. But I see that you are different. How very refreshing to encounter such originality."

Laurel looked at the enormous crowd in the room and then back to the czar.

"How many people are here tonight, sir?"

"Two thousand were invited, but many more have come. It is often so, but there is room for three times as many in this room, so we need not be perturbed."

Laurel was dancing with Sandro Alexandrovich when she saw Andrei's mother gazing at her in horror. She ignored the lady, tired of the Princess Sophia's obvious dislike and the way she insisted on showing it so openly. When Sandro returned her to her father's side, however, Laurel was horrified to see the princess coming toward their table.

The matriarch of the family looked down at her in disdain.

"We have not met before, Miss Holman."

"No, ma'am, we haven't."

"I came here only to tell you that your costume is obscene. For a woman to expose part of her body in public is a disgrace which has never been perpetrated in this city before, and I am surprised that Andrei allowed you to leave his home in that condition."

"The czar has complimented Poppa and me on the originality of our costumes."

"He, like all the men in our family, is a fool."

"You're indiscreet to say it, ma'am."

"I shall not wish to meet you again, Miss Holman. Women who pursue my son are rarely those who are good for his future, and you are the most dangerous thus far, because Andrei cares for you."

"Dangerous for you or for Andrei?"

"How dare you!"

Laurel took a deep breath and spoke evenly, despite the tension of the moment. "For your information, I came to this country at your son's invitation so my father could paint some of the leading members of society. I've no interest in Andrei, nor ever shall have, and time will prove that I've spoken the truth. Andrei's charming and kind, but he's a spoiled womanizer who loses interest in his women once he's possessed them. I want a man who'll love me forever and I don't intend to settle for anything less than that. Now, if you'll excuse me, I have to return to my friends."

With that, Laurel walked back to the spot where Sandro and his sister were standing with the wife of the governor-general of St. Petersburg. Holman joined her in seconds, a proud smile on his face.

"You did well with that old woman. She nearly had a fit when you walked away from her. Imagine her saying that you were pursuing her son. He's never done anything but pant after you since we arrived!"

"I shouldn't have been so rude to her."

"Nonsense! It'll do her good. Now, you just forget her. We came to Russia to make money and you came to see a bit of life before you go back to England and marry Penn."

"You make it sound as if it's all been arranged."

"It will be, mark my words. Come on, now, let's

dance. I like these fast, twirling waltzes they're so partial to out here."

The prizewinner in the ladies' fancy dress was the Grand Duchess Elizabeth in a silver wig and panniered dress as the Empress Catherine the Great. The male winner was James Holman as the lion. His prize was a solid gold fob watch that he knew would look well on the waistcoats Lotty was making for him. Delighted by his win, he looked in concern at Laurel as she stood on the edge of the circle of guests, her expression far away. Pushing though the crowd, he put his arms around her.

"Is something wrong, honey?"

"Nothing, Poppa."

"Come on, now, what's wrong?"

"I wish I was home or in England, Poppa. St. Petersburg's a shallow place for all its parties and fun. It has no real heart and I'm fed up with living in a place where no one thinks of anything but gossip and adultery."

"I'll be ready to leave by the end of April."

Laurel beamed. "Will you *really*? You're not just saying that to make me happy?"

"I intend to paint like a demon so you can be reunited with Penn before you know it. They tell me England's great in April."

Laurel threw her arms around her father's neck and kissed him delightedly.

"I love you dearly, Poppa."

"That's more like my girl."

*   *   *

In early March Laurel went with Andrei to the christening of the czarina's baby at the Cathedral of St. Peter and St. Paul. All society was present and the scent of lavender, musk, and bergamot mixed with that of damp sables and the incense sprayed by bearded priests in white and gold. The atmosphere was heady and typically Russian.

The baby cried throughout the ceremony, a portent that was said to bring luck. The czarina remained serenely beautiful, her eyes on her child and on the gilded altar with its symbolic figure of Christ. She was praying that the next time she became pregnant she would bear a male heir to the Russian throne. It was her desire, her obsession, her anxiously awaited duty. Of course, she loved her little daughters, but in Russia only a son was important.

The ceremony was nearing its close, when the cathedral was filled with the sound of frenzied shouting, cheering, and screaming from the square beyond the doors. Some of the congregation began to fidget. Many of the children present nudged each other and one little boy ran to the door and then called to his mother, "Mama, come and look! A pink-and-yellow cloud has just fallen out of the sky."

Count Orlov rose from his seat at the rear of the cathedral and told the boy sternly to return to his own seat. Then, looking out into the vast square, he stared in astonishment at the sight before him and beckoned his friend to come to his side. The two men appeared so taken by what they saw that another joined them and then another, until there was a small crowd looking out.

When the priests had intoned the final blessing, the czarina and her husband walked with the imperial party from the cathedral. As soon as they had gone, most of the congregation rose, and after hearing another burst of uproarious cheering from the crowds in the square, rushed outside.

Laurel moved up the aisle with Andrei, curious to know what it was that had driven half the occupants of the city to run to see what was happening in such a frenzy. She followed her fellow guests to the chilly square and in the white light of a winter's afternoon saw a magnificent pink-and-yellow balloon eighty feet wide descending slowly onto the cobblestones. It was too far away for her to see any detail of what was happening, but she noticed a number of soldiers from the Volynsky Regiment running to rope in the craft. Then, to the ecstatic cheers of the crowd, two intrepid travelers stepped out. Drawing nearer, Laurel realized to her joy and utter astonishment that it was Penn Allandale and his brother, Hugo.

She rushed forward to see Penn, but he was already lost in the crowd, hoisted on the shoulders of the military men who had helped him land. An announcement was made to the effect that the two men had just broken the world long-distance record by flying all the way from Paris to St. Petersburg. This was greeted by yet more delighted cheering and calls for the gentlemen to make a speech.

Laurel was jostled by the crowd, her face alight

with joy. At last her eyes met Penn's and he called out to her: "Couldn't get here by sea, because the harbor's frozen, and couldn't get here by train, because the rails were frozen, too. Had to think of *some* way to see you again. How are you, my darling?"

Laurel held out her hand to grasp his, but Penn was swept along by two dozen hefty hussars overjoyed to be part of his triumph. She began to feel giddy from relief and joy and dozens of conflicting emotions. Imagine it! Penn had flown all the way from Paris by balloon, because that was the only way he could be with her. Poppa had been right. Penn *had* found a way to do what he wanted to do!

Andrei stood alone on the porch of the cathedral, watching as Penn was feted by the crowd. Laurel's face was a picture, alight with joy, sensuousness, delight, tears, and laughter, all the emotions of a woman in love. He sighed wearily. So this was his rival. Probably it was the same Englishman who had commissioned the portrait of Laurel and which had been kept by the czarina so that he could not appropriate it. The action still rankled Andrei's unforgiving nature. He recalled the day he had first met Lord Allandale at Blenheim Palace, as he was leaving with the Prince of Wales. They had disliked each other on sight even then. Perhaps Laurel had been the reason for their feelings of animosity. Perhaps the Englishman was her lover or her suitor. The dark side of Andrei's nature came to the fore and he decided to watch and wait and do everything in his power to keep the two apart. With one last glance in Penn's direction, he turned and walked away from the crowd toward his home.

That evening at dinner Laurel was unusually animated. Penn had sent her a secret message of only three words, but they were the words she had longed to hear him say from the moment she had realized her own feelings. The note said simply "I LOVE YOU." Laurel kissed it fervently, knowing that she would keep it forever and read it every night. Someday, when she was old, she would frame it and put it on the wall of Wentworth Saye. She shook her head at her own daydreams. Penn might love her, but would he marry her? There was a long way to go yet before they could be together for life.

Penn had chosen to stay at the Hotel Europa, overlooking the River Neva, in a suite with tightly sealed windows that were not at all to his liking. When he asked for them to be opened, he was told loftily by the manager that this was impossible. He wrote a note to a friend at court, who informed the czar of their English visitor's discomfort. Within an hour a section of one of the glass panes had been cut out with a diamond from the imperial collection.

Able to relax at last, Penn began to leaf through some of the twelve hundred invitations he had received since arriving in the city. He was finding it difficult to concentrate, however, because he was troubled that Laurel had not made contact with him. He had been in the city for one and a half days, had attended a celebration dinner at the Winter Palace, two court felicitations, and a reception, all without seeing the woman he loved and had traveled so far in near-arctic conditions to be with. Bemused by this and troubled about the rumors of the grand duke's infatuation for Laurel, Penn decided to go at once to the Vladimir Palace to find out if she was unwell or simply disinclined to see him. Now that he was in Russia, there was no excuse for letters not to be received, no reason why they could not keep in touch.

Penn was about to leave, when a footman appeared and announced Miss Laurel Holman. He rang the bell, ordered coffee, and then went to the anteroom to greet the woman he loved.

"My dearest Laurel, what are you trying to do to me, reduce me to a mass of nervous rubble?"

She ran to greet him, hugging him to her heart and clinging to him, tears rolling down her cheeks.

"I am so delighted to see you, Penn, but why haven't you replied to my letters? Poppa's just dying to see you and show you the portrait he did of me in the conservatory at Wentworth Saye. We were expecting you for dinner last night."

"You sent me an invitation?"

"Of course we did. I sent Stepan with it to the hotel."

"I've written to you four times since I arrived and sent the notes with the porter to deliver to the Vladimir Palace."

"To hell with servants and their inefficiency! We're together and everything's golden."

"You're here and I'm here and I shall ignore everything except the most important reason for being in Russia, which is to see you. Dearest one, now that we're together, I can't remember all the things I wanted to say to you. How are you? How is your father? Have you missed me as I've missed you? Come, let's sit together by the fire and talk as if we were never apart."

Laurel looked down, suddenly uncertain whether to reveal her true feelings. She knew that she must, but she felt shy after the long separation.

"I've missed you dreadfully, Penn. Russia's no place for the likes of Poppa and me. We're just not used to a life of balls and parties and people who like nothing better than matchmaking, gossiping, and gambling. I'll be so relieved when we can return to England."

"Thank God the atmosphere of the place didn't please you."

Servants appeared with coffee and lemon cakes served on violet-sprigged Sèvres porcelain. Penn gazed at Laurel, examining anew every feature on her face, every movement of her hands, her wrists, her fingers. She was even lovelier than he remembered, and as fresh and wholesome as she had been before. Even her clothes were perfect; he liked her tilted pillbox hat covered in tiny blue flowers, the velvet jacket with a tiny waist, and her double-draped skirt. She had thrown her sable cloak on the chair, as though she were well used to its priceless feel. There was a new assurance about her that pleased him, and something else, a sense of knowing what she wanted from life. Penn closed his eyes, trying desperately not to blurt out to her all the things he knew required the proper moment.

They talked for a while of mutual friends, the journey Penn had made in the balloon, Hugo and Clarissa and Wentworth Saye. Then, with an impish smile, Laurel offered to take him on a tour of the city.

"I want to show you some of the many contrasts of this city. I tell you, Penn, there are people so rich they keep trunks of emeralds in their cellars because there's no room for them in the house, and others so poor they have to beg bread from the bakeries every morning. You've never been anyplace like it before."

"I look forward to being educated in the oddities of life à la Russe."

"What else have you been looking forward to?"

"To this."

He took her in his arms and kissed her on the lips, gripping her body with an urgency that forcibly communicated itself. Laurel's hat fell to the ground, but she made no attempt to pick it up. She only closed her eyes and let him hold her against the door as he kissed her cheeks, her throat, and her lips until she moaned from unfulfilled desire. She was touched when he gazed down at her.

"Do you still want me, Laurel?"

"I want you more than ever, and for always."

"I love you and have loved you since that first day when I found you in your gig, gazing at the lake of

Blenheim as if you were in fairyland. I want to marry you when we return to England."

"Is that a proposal, Penn?"

"I can't think what else it is. I should kneel or make a speech, I suppose, but between us there's no need for speeches. I love you more than anything in the world and I know now I always will. What better reason could we have to marry?"

Laurel threw herself into his arms and kissed him again and again with increasing eagerness and delight. All her dreams had come true and at this moment in time she was the happiest woman in the world.

"Oh, Penn, I'd marry you right here and now if it wouldn't disappoint your family, but I'll marry you the minute we get to England, maybe right there on the docks!"

Delighted to be in each other's company again, they went out and visited the market, walking around the stalls like tourists, examining inlaid wooden objects from the Ukraine, silver work from Georgia, embroidered caps and caftans from Uzbekistan, and exotic amber jewelry from Lithuania. Everywhere they went there was the smell of Russia, a mixture of boiled cabbage, damp leather, sweat, and the expensive odors of amber and chypre. The people's voices were shrill, the accents many and varied against the background sounds of St. Petersburg—the rumble of carriage wheels grinding on granite-inlaid roads and the contrasting sweet chimes of bells in a nearby church.

From the market they went to the arcade where

Lotty's establishment was situated. The dressmaker was charmed by Penn's looks and his elegant gray tweed jacket. How strong he was, how stern and iron-willed. With a sweeping gesture of welcome, she invited the couple upstairs to her private rooms and told her assistant to take charge of the store. Once there, Lotty was only too pleased to show Penn her designs, especially the book of wedding dresses that had so enchanted Laurel on the day of their first meeting. While he looked at them, she questioned him gently.

"How long do you plan to stay in our city, Lord Allandale?"

"I hope to remain here until April or May."

"And why did you not stay at the Winter Palace or in the British embassy, as important visitors usually do?"

Penn gave her a flashing smile and spoke the truth. "I prefer to have some privacy, Madame Lototsky. I only came to Russia to see Miss Holman, and it's easier for us to meet and talk outside the formality of the palace or the embassy."

"Call me Lotty, all my friends do."

Penn looked into the twinkling blue eyes and Lotty blushed with pleasure at his small confidence. Then she turned to Laurel.

"You are looking radiant, my dear, and I am sure I know the reason. I shall be making one of my wedding dresses for you before long, I think. Which one are you going to choose?"

"I like the one with the skirt covered in camellias.

I think it's a dream dress and I want one just like it for my wedding."

"Yes, that is a wonderful gown. But tell me, do you want all this to be kept a secret?"

"No, you can tell everyone in the city as far as I'm concerned, Lotty. I'm proud of Penn and proud that people should know I love him."

Madame sighed, her face suddenly still. Evidently Laurel did not understand the grand duke's nature. Lotty did her best to be diplomatic, waiting until Penn had gone down to the shop to choose a gift for Laurel before gently reminding the young lady of her position.

"In order not to upset the grand duke, who most certainly believes himself in love with you, I think it would be safer to keep your attachment to Lord Allandale a secret. Here, this is the key to my dacha on the island of Kammeni Ostrov. Use the house whenever you wish. You and your fiancé can be alone there, because no one goes to the islands during the winter."

Penn heard this as he rejoined the two women.

"You're most kind, Lotty, and we appreciate it."

"Enjoy yourself, my dear sir, skate, ride in my troika, and make big fires with logs from the store. You need to be alone, and in Russia that is not easy. Always there are people watching and servants who listen to your every word."

Lotty's face became dreamy and Penn was touched by her memories.

"I was in love once, you know, only foolishly I

chose a Russian suitor. He fought a duel over nothing at all and died an hour later. We had known each other for only six months, yet I thought my life had ended with his. Love is a disaster for many people. You must take care and guard your own most jealously, so it can be preserved forever and ever."

On her return to the Vladimir Palace, Laurel found herself confronted by Andrei, who was ashen with rage. Controlling himself, he eyed her radiant face and the beautiful clothes he had bought for her pleasure and his own.

"We had an appointment to eat lunch together, but you forgot! It is unlike you to be so thoughtless."

"I sent a message telling you I shouldn't be home for lunch, Andrei. I'm sorry if you didn't get it. It seems to me your servants do not deliver things reliably. I didn't get four separate messages from Lord Allandale, and he didn't get mine. Where's Poppa, anyway?"

"He is in his studio, as always."

"What's wrong?"

"Where have you been? Or am I not allowed to ask?"

"I took Penn Allandale around St. Petersburg and showed him everything, the market, the arcade where Lotty has her shop, the cathedral and all the lovely buildings along the Moika. We didn't see all the canals, of course, but Penn felt as if he'd seen five hundred of them. He said his feet felt two sizes bigger than they had yesterday."

"I am not concerned with Lord Allandale's feet. I

am concerned that you accompany him openly around the city. Everyone will think you are his mistress."

Laurel's eyes blazed and she looked at Andrei as if he were a beetle to be trodden underfoot.

"That's insulting. Take it back at once!"

"Forgive me. I have been mad with jealousy."

"You never did get one thing straight, Andrei. Since I came to Russia I've made a few friends, like Sandro and Katinka and Mitzi and Lotty. I have friends in other places too, and I'm very loyal to them. Penn's one of my English friends. He was very kind to Poppa and me when we were in Oxfordshire. You surely wouldn't expect me to ignore him when he arrives in Russia. In any case, I don't *want* to ignore him. I like Penn and I like him a lot."

Andrei sat in the high-backed leather chair, lighting a cigar to calm his nerves. His heart was pounding from fear of losing Laurel to the Englishman. What did one do to capture such a woman? How did one curb her willfulness? He hated it and yet it was part of her charm. Confusion and violence filled his mind and he had no idea what to try next.

Laurel took off her hat and looked down at him with a sympathetic smile.

"Penn's going to the ball tonight. I'll introduce you, and I'm sure you'll get on."

"I already met Lord Allandale when I was in England and have no desire to meet him again. In any case, half the aristocrats of St. Petersburg will be in line to shake his hand, and I refuse absolutely to join in the adulation. Imagine the insanity of flying half-way across the world in a balloon in the middle of winter. How could any man have contemplated such a thing?"

Laurel became angry again at this.

"I'm getting very tired of your jealousy and your bitterness."

"It is your fault, all of it."

"Don't waste your time being jealous on my account, Andrei. I'm not the woman for you, I've told you that many times. Accept it, because if you don't, you're going to be very unhappy. I don't love you and I'll never love you. I just want you to be my friend."

At eight, when she was about to leave for the ball, Laurel went to the door of her room and found it locked. She walked through to her father's bedroom and found that locked too, and every other exit from their suite. Holman was dining with Lotty that evening, unable to resist either her veal cutlets or her wondrous store of scandalous stories. Nonplussed, Laurel began to shout for Polinka, but she had been given the night off. She was about to ring for a servant, when she heard someone calling to her from the hallway outside.

"What is wrong, Miss Holman? Are you ill?"

Laurel realized that this was the voice of Yelena Ivanovna. She ran to the door and called through to the young woman outside. "I'm locked in and can't get out. Bring the grand duke, will you, please."

"Andrei just left for the ball at the Winter Palace."

"He *left*! Why didn't he wait for me?"

"He said you were ill and would not be going. What can I do to help you, Laurel?"

Furious that Andrei had played such a trick on her, Laurel sat on the bed trying to still the pounding of her heart. She knew quite well that he had locked her in her room to prevent her from appearing before his friends in society on the arm of Penn Allandale. He could not stand the thought of her dancing with the Englishman and as usual was determined to have his way at all costs, like the spoiled child he still was. She rose and went back to the door.

"Yelena! I want you to do something very important for me."

"Of course I will. I was on my way to visit you, as you had suggested, when Andrei said you were unwell. What do you need?"

"Go to the Europa Hotel and ask for Lord Allandale. Tell him I need him urgently, and bring him here at once."

Time passed slowly. Laurel lit the candles in her room and sat on the bed, still furious at what had happened. She was about to take off her ball gown, when she heard Penn's voice on the other side of the door.

"What's going on, Laurel? Miss Ivanovna said—"

"I've been locked in my room. I suppose Andrei didn't relish the idea of my dancing every waltz with you."

"Did he not, begad! Well, we'll show him the error of his ways. Wait a moment and I'll be back."

Laurel was sitting on the bed, when the door crashed open. With it came six of the grand duke's largest servants, who fell to the ground at her feet. Behind them she saw Penn standing in the hall, dressed in white tie and tails. She ran to him as he held out his arms to her, and kissed him passionately on the mouth.

Yelena gazed at the couple, her face transformed by the realization that Laurel was madly in love with the handsome Englishman. The American had told the truth when she said she had no interest in the grand duke. As the servants disappeared, carrying the broken door with them, Yelena withdrew discreetly to the parlormaid's pantry nearby, looking in one last time as Laurel and Penn continued to kiss and caress each other, oblivious of their surroundings.

"Thank you for coming to rescue me when I needed you."

"I shall always be near when you need me, Laurel. That is my main aim in life, that and making you the happiest woman in the world."

Within minutes Yelena was in her carriage and heading for her mother's home in the country. She had decided at last to follow Laurel's instructions to the letter and to try to win back Andrei's affection by transforming herself once again into the distant, beautiful creature she had been on leaving the Smolny Convent. For the first time in months, Yelena smiled happily. She was reliving the moment when Laurel had thrown herself into Penn's arms, a look of sheer ecstasy on her face. Yelena knew then that she would have a good friend in her endeavors, and she was content.

Penn looked down at Laurel, his face alight with desire.

"I have an idea. If the grand duke doesn't want to see us dancing together at the ball, let's oblige him. Let's go away for a few days. I know the perfect place, and had arranged to take you on a visit there this weekend."

"What about my father?"

"Write him a note and explain what happened. Then go and change your clothes. We'll leave the palace immediately."

They rode out of the city in a gilded troika to a country house on the Gulf of Finland. Its facade was painted daffodil yellow and it had shutters of faded gray, like houses in the Mediterranean region. In front of the house were a frozen lake and a wood of magnificent conifers. Far to the rear of the property was a hunting lodge that had been built by Catherine the Great as a love nest. The main house had steps carved out of solid rock that led to a tiny pebble beach and the frozen sea, and there were toboggan slopes to the rear, framed by hedges full of scarlet berries.

Enchanted by all she saw, Laurel was thrilled to be alone with Penn in this secret, isolated place, with a charm all its own. She felt a surge of excitement as she was led inside the house. This was the moment she had been waiting for with great eagerness, the first time she and Penn had been together and alone since his declaration of love. The next few days would, she knew, change everything in their relationship. They would achieve a new intimacy and become true partners in life. Shivering in anticipation, Laurel allowed Penn to lead her upstairs to the bedroom that had been chosen for her. The magic days of love were about to begin.

Within an hour of their arrival, servants were preparing a delicious punch of orange liqueur and fruit, and the cook was making dinner. The fire was warm, the atmosphere homey, the rooms brightly colored and styled in the manner of ages long past. Then wood and stone, rock and crystal had been used in preference to the copied French styles of gilded panels and Louis XIV chaises longues so adored by the present generation.

Laurel sat at the table watching as the meal was served. It consisted of a soup of potatoes, cream, and nutmeg, a delicious casserole of venison with walnuts, sorbet with anise and violets, and a liqueur of glowing amber made from plums ripened in the late-summer sun of a past year. She raised her glass to Penn.

"I'm so glad Andrei locked me in my room. To us, my darling."

"To the future and to love."

"I didn't tell you how proud I am of you for breaking the record with the balloon flight. I was so thrilled to see you again, I forgot all about your achievement. I had no idea you were such an expert in aviation."

"It was nothing."

"It was something very special, and you know it, but the most special thing is being together again. Now, tell me about the house. Who owns it and how long can we stay?"

"It belongs to a friend of Hugo's, who's given us permission to use it whenever we want. Before we return to the city we'll visit the hunting lodge and picnic by the sea. I'm told the lodge has to be seen to be believed, like all the love nests created by the Empress Catherine the Great. Dearest Laurel, all I really want is to make every minute we have together unforgettable."

"I love you, Penn. I love you so very much."

He reached across the table and kissed her hand. Then, together, they went and lay in front of the fire on a big sofa covered in Persian velvet. Hours passed like minutes as they renewed old acquaintance, whispering confidences and moving inexorably nearer the moment of passion, ever closer to the point where they would commit themselves totally to each other for life.

Penn kissed her until her cheeks burned like fire. Then he untied the buttons of her dress and kissed her breasts and tasted the skin of her neck and shoulders. The more he loved her, the more he wanted to do all there was to do to a woman. He held back, though, conscious that they had been apart for such a long time and that Laurel might need time to make her decision.

Laurel closed her eyes, her head swimming from excitement and passion. At last they were together, and within a few days Penn would make love to her as she wanted him to. She felt his mouth on hers, his tongue exploring her, and cried out from the violence of her desire. She was thrilled when he picked her up and carried her upstairs to her room.

"I shall sleep in my own room tonight, but soon I'll come to yours. I want to make love to you, Laurel, and I cannot wait much longer for us to be one."

The grand duke arrived home in an expansive mood. Not only had Laurel been prevented from dancing with Lord Allandale, but the Englishman had disappointed everyone by not appearing at all. Perhaps he had been waiting for Laurel at his hotel.

When Andrei had had a brandy and discussed a staff problem with Stepan, he went upstairs, taking the key to the Holmans' rooms from his pocket. It was then that he saw the broken door. Wild with rage, he ran to the hall and summoned his manservant.

"Who broke down the door and on whose orders?"

Stepan moved forward, showing none of the ironic amusement he was feeling at the fact that for once someone had defied the master in his own home.

"Lord Allandale was summoned from his hotel, sir, when Miss Holman found herself locked in her suite. Her father was out, you see, and the young lady was very upset. It was Lord Allandale who ordered the muzhiks to break the door. I believe he feared she might become hysterical."

Andrei walked from the palace, took his horse, and rode immediately to the Europa Hotel. He was informed that Lord Allandale had not yet returned from the country. Mad with jealousy, Andrei wrote a card for Penn and handed it to the head receptionist, with instructions that he was to give it into the Englishman's hand. The card said simply: *I do not tolerate foreigners entering my house and breaking down my doors. I demand satisfaction and will send my seconds to call on you.*

Pistols at dawn were to be the order of the day.

6

Penn and Laurel had been in the yellow house for twenty-four hours, hours that had passed in a golden haze of kissing and talking of romantic things. They had skated together on the frozen sea, howled with laughter as they sped down the hill on toboggans. They had eaten delicious food and had drunk some of their host's champagne. Now they were riding together to the hunting lodge with a winter picnic prepared by the cook that included an insulated container of hot soup, delicious pelmeni, and Easter cakes or kulichi, with hot coffee and Armenian brandy to wash it all down.

The hunting lodge was situated within sight of the main house, but as they neared the sea, a thick fog descended from the bay. Suddenly, in the swirling white mist, they had to feel their way to the entrance, almost missing their direction as they moved the short distance from the horses to the door. Then, miraculously, it was there in all its glory and beauty, lit by dozens of yellow and pink candles, just as Penn had asked.

Laurel walked inside, her face glowing with pleasure. Catherine the Great had built this lodge as a love nest, and what a love nest it was. In the light of the roaring log fire, the walls shimmered and gleamed. On closer inspection, Laurel saw that topazes had been embedded in the gilded plaster, thousands of them, all sparkling and giving off glowing amber lights. The ceiling was of Karelian birchwood paneling, the snuffboxes, ashtrays, and goblets of etched gold in the form of mythical animals and unicorns. Before the fire there was a daybed eight feet long and eight feet across, covered in lynx skins piled one on top of the other in glorious profusion. The blond furs, the gleaming walls, and the orange light of the burning wood created a scene that was at once barbaric, splendid, and, to Laurel, unforgettable.

Penn turned to her, his face very still.

"This is like something out of a dream. It's truly a place meant for love and lovers."

He moved toward Laurel, kissing her gently on the lips, then with more urgency, provoking her to passion. He spoke gently, with infinite tenderness.

"Take off your clothes. Now is the time for us to

make love, as we've been wanting to make love ever since we first met."

Laurel opened her mouth to protest, but she knew that she had no desire whatever to prevent what was going to happen. Her fingers began to tremble as she fumbled with the fastenings of her jacket, and she was relieved when Penn took over and untied them himself.

"Remember above all else that I love you, my darling, and I've waited a long time to show you how much I care."

"I'm scared, Penn."

"Don't be. Love's a great adventure, and we are destined for each other."

Laurel felt his hands becoming more fevered in their movements as he lowered the petticoats, revealing her legs. Then he knelt before her and kissed her thighs and her stomach and the tips of her breasts as they pushed over the camisole top. She let him push her back on the couch, watching in silent fascination as Penn untied the last satin bows of her drawers. Dizzy from desire, she urged him to hurry, not caring that he might think her wanton, and unable to resist the longing to feel his body naked at her side.

Throwing the drawers aside, Penn looked down at the woman he loved. He had never seen a softer, more curvaceous body, and it took his breath away. While Laurel lay, holding out her arms to him and urging him to join her, he lifted off the heavy sweater he was wearing and stripped off his shirt, cravat, and riding trousers. He saw her eyes widen as he took off the last of his clothes and stood for a moment towering above her, a splendid male animal all blond and bronzed and eager for love. Moving to her side, he fingered the silken skin of her face with gentle attention, kissing her cheeks and her forehead and her ears as he whispered words that inflamed her beyond imagination.

"Come and kiss me like you first kissed me in Paris. Make me love you even more, if that's possible. Laurel, you're trembling so, what's wrong?"

"I want you, but I'm afraid I'll be hurt."

"If it hurts at all, it will only be for a moment. Hold my hand, dearest one. I'm going to make love to you as no one else ever has and no one else will again."

For a while she was so inflamed by the feel of his nakedness against her own, she could do nothing but allow him to touch her and explore her body as he chose. Penn's hands wandered at will over her arms and her neck, his fingers caressing her breasts, her nipples, and the flatness of her stomach before moving to provoke her within her very core. And all the while he kissed her, his lips warm on hers, his body becoming more eager by the second as he whispered words of love.

"You are so beautiful and exciting."

"I love you, Penn."

"Raise your knees . . . that's right. Now, kiss me again. When we kiss, my heart and yours are one, just as our bodies will be in a moment."

Laurel shuddered from sheer delight as his mouth

touched hers, his tongue moving inside her so she forgot everything but the fact that all the strength and resistance had gone from her. Love was at last entering her life, and she wanted it more than anything in the world.

Finally, in a brief moment of lucidity, Laurel opened her eyes and saw Penn parting her thighs. One moment he was poised above her like an eagle soaring in the sky. Then she felt a sharp stab of pain, followed by a gradual moving crescendo of elation. She cried out, wild from passion and desire, "I do so love you, Penn. I adore what you're making me feel."

"Hold me, my darling, and we'll soar to the heights together."

His body moved like a rapier, faster and faster, until in a moment of vibrant abandon he cried out as he felt Laurel contract in the final moment of passion. His body joined hers in the last exhausting seconds of their embrace. Then he moved to her side and cradled her in his arms, panting from spent desire and the excitement of the moment.

For Penn, love had been a revelation, and he wondered if he would ever achieve such happiness again. He kissed Laurel's cheeks and her fingers and whispered in her ear, "I feel like a king. You were truly wonderful."

"Love's not at all like I imagined. I think I might get to like it far too much."

"Thank heaven for that. I'm rather fond of it myself, so we shall please each other endlessly."

For a long time they lay in each other's arms,

Helene Thornton

staring at the fire and idly stroking each other's bodies.
Penn looked down at the beads of sweat on Laurel's
forehead, the glow in her cheeks, the secret smile
around her lips. She was happy and he was content.
Kissing her cheek, he asked her what she wanted to
drink. "We have champagne or some of that delicious fruit nectar the cook made."

"I'm thirsty, so I'll have the fruit cup."

"I love you dearly, Laurel. You're the only woman
in the world for me."

"And I'm going to love you always and always,
Penn. I may even get to be horribly jealous like
Andrei."

"We should return to the house, I suppose, but it's
too nice by the fire on such a cold day."

"Let's sleep here tonight and tomorrow. Then we'll
go back to St. Petersburg and I'll have a talk with
Poppa. What am I going to tell him? Will he see the
difference in me? I'm so happy, I'm certain there's a
light shining like a beacon out of the top of my
head!"

"Tell him the grand duke locked you in your room
to prevent your being with me. Tell him we're going
to get married as soon as we return to England. Tell
him you love me and I love you. That's all he'll need
to know."

"Kiss me, Penn."

Their lips met and their naked bodies touched.
Penn stroked her hair and bowed his head to kiss her
breasts. Desire surged again as he ran his fingers
lightly over her body, enjoying Laurel's shivers of

anticipation, her cries of pleasure and passion. When he entered her, he was overjoyed by her response, her newfound confidence in loving, and the way she was willing, without shame, to guide him to those places that most excited her. He felt like a knight in shining armor as he loved her with all his heart in their secret pavilion of passion.

In the still of the night, Laurel lay in bed listening to the sound of Penn as he slept at her side. His breathing was deep but gentle, his right hand on her thigh. She looked at the glowing fire and was amazed by her own longing for him. How wonderful love had felt when Penn had shown her the way, how satisfying and full of unexpected delights. She thought then of the grand duke and was apprehensive about his reaction on her return after this unannounced absence. Sandro and Lotty had both warned her that Andrei could be vengeful. Surely Andrei would not try to do anything to Penn?

Oh, Penn, my love. Soon to be her husband. Penn would speak to her father on their return. Laurel's mind turned to considering her father. Of late he had spent most of his evenings at Lotty's apartment, entranced by her food and her style and her sense of humor. In her heart, Laurel knew that romance had entered Holman's life in the autumn of his days, just as it had entered her own. She leaned forward and kissed Penn's cheek as he slept. Then she kissed his neck and his shoulders and the fingers that had so recently provoked her to ecstasy.

The night was icy and the fire a mere glow. Laurel

stepped out of bed and turned over the ashes, throwing on some twigs, and then, as they blazed, more wood to increase the warmth. She was about to return to bed, when Penn held out his hand to her.

"Come here and pay the penalty for walking around naked in the middle of the night."

She smiled roguishly at the taunt.

"I like the penalties you impose far too much. Don't make me a slave to them."

"I adore you, even though you're a trifle shameless. Oh, my dear, you're cold. Come closer, closer, really close, *that's* the way to get warm again. Dear God, there isn't a man in the world as happy as I am at this moment. I wish morning would never come."

"Morning might be even more beautiful and the sun might forget it's the middle of winter and shine."

"The daffodils were in bloom when I left Wentworth Saye."

"Are you homesick, Penn?"

"A little, but only to be there with you. That old house was never the same, once you went away. It looked the same and we knew it was the same, but somehow the heart and spirit seemed to have gone from the place and from me."

"Penn, teach me how to love you. I want to spoil you as if you were an Eastern potentate and bone idle in the ways of passion."

"Don't say such inflaming things. I'm a simple Englishman and unused to the ministrations of Eastern temptresses."

Laurel moved toward him and within minutes they

were in their own private world, two beings in love with love and with each other. She kissed Penn's thighs and his stomach, moving up slowly until their lips met in a passionate embrace. As always, the kiss melted something within her and she began to writhe with longing.

"Make love to me, Penn. I want to be loved until I'm too tired to speak."

"Your word is my command."

Laurel smiled at the twinkle in his eye as he threw back the bedclothes and ran his hands lightly over her naked body. As the fire sprang to life, she raised her legs so they were wrapped around his shoulders and closed her eyes as Penn made her his own. She was surprised to find that love was becoming even more intoxicating as time passed and she grew used to it. Then the movements of passion quickened and she abandoned herself to them, allowing Penn to provoke them to a peak of ecstasy that left both gasping in each other's arms. When passion was spent, Laurel snuggled in his arms and kissed his cheek.

"You're the most wonderful lover in the world."

"You're not qualified to judge me, but I'm happy you think so."

"For me that's what you are."

"Dearest one, I *am* qualified to judge, and I can tell you that you are the perfect lover."

Outside in the distant countryside a cockerel crowed to welcome the dawn. Laurel and Penn closed their eyes and slept, their bodies entwined, their faces content, their passion momentarily spent.

On his return to the Europa Hotel three and a half days after he had left it, Penn found the grand duke's message waiting for him. He read it, turned it back and forth, half-puzzled, half-amused that any man should challenge him to a duel for releasing a lady from a locked room. Ignoring the message, he went to his room and was unpacking when Andrei arrived with his seconds and asked if he preferred pistols or sabers. Raising an eyebrow in mild rebuke, Penn looked hard at the Russian, who seemed to be in the grip of a profound and feverish emotion. He knew at once that the reason for the duel had nothing to do with the broken door, but was instigated by Andrei's jealousy and hurt pride over Laurel.

Penn spoke equably, despite his misgivings about the wisdom of the duel. "I choose pistols, sir. The usual rules, I assume?"

"Of course. Will tomorrow at eight suit you, Lord Allandale?"

"It will, though I cannot understand why you should challenge me over such a trivial matter. Someone locked Miss Holman in her suite at the Vladimir Palace. Any servant would have done what I did in your absence from the house."

"If a servant had done it, I should not be perturbed, but you are not welcome in my home, sir. The reason for that must be obvious to you. I am in love with Laurel Holman and have been since the day I first met her. You are a potential suitor and therefore my rival."

"Surely you're man enough to allow Miss Holman

to choose her own partner in life? She is more than capable of deciding with whom she wishes to spend the rest of her days."

Andrei looked incredulously at the Englishman, with his blond hair and arrogant blue eyes.

"Why should any woman choose her man? Women do not know their own minds. Miss Holman will choose me if she is led to do so and is allowed to remain in Russia for long enough to appreciate my character and worth. That is how it is in life, and nothing you say will change it."

Penn sighed as the grand duke moved to the door. Russians had no idea that these were modern times and were inclined to treat women as chattels, as their ancestors had always done. He decided it was time to put an end to the fiasco.

"I must tell you, sir, that Miss Holman and I are engaged to be married. We intend to marry as soon as she and her father return to England. I'll thank you, therefore, to keep your foolish and childish imaginings to yourself. You may indeed be in love with Laurel, though from what I hear in society you have the reputation for falling in love rather often, and then only until your passion is sated. Miss Holman is not in love with you, though. She never has been and never will be and has told you this clearly on a number of occasions."

"She has discussed me with you?"

"I asked Laurel if she were aware of the rumors circulating in this city that she is your mistress. She told me the truth of her feelings and realizes now that her reputation has been compromised by remaining so long in your home and by being seen with you in St. Petersburg on many occasions."

His face pale with rage, his fists clenched, Andrei strode to the door.

"I have nothing more to say on the subject. I shall await you in the appointed place at eight A.M."

With that he walked from the room, slamming the door behind him. Penn had been the cause of all his troubles with Laurel, and he knew that now. He did not pause to reflect on his own nature and its effect on Laurel's opinion of him. He sought only to find a scapegoat for the fact that he had been persistently unsuccessful with the woman he desired. Now he had one and he began to hate Penn with a virulence that was insidious, dangerous, and disproportionate to his circumstances.

At dawn it rained and the birch forest to the north of the city smelled of damp leaves, humid earth, and the first spring flowers. The morning sea mist was beginning to clear and everywhere birds were singing. It was a beautiful site for a lovers' meeting, though it was known to the local people as the field of sorrow, because so many young officers had lost their lives in duels fought in these deceptively peaceful green glades.

Andrei strode through the ferny undergrowth, followed by his second. His face was intent, his mind focused on the only thing that mattered to him at this moment, to rid himself of Penn Allandale and leave the way free to the courtship of the woman he adored.

He was glad the Englishman had chosen pistols, because he was a fine shot and confident of his abilities, even in the hazy morning light. He wiped his forehead of water that kept dripping from the overhanging trees. He must arrive at the appointed spot looking well groomed and confident. Otherwise the Englishman might think him apprehensive, and that would be intolerable to his pride.

Penn rode in a carriage as far as the outskirts of the wood. Then, accompanied by his brother, he moved toward the clearing where the duel would take place. He was angry with Andrei for forcing the issue, and longing to be home again in England, far away from the madness that was Russia. He began to think of Wentworth Saye and the night he and Laurel had danced together under the moon.

Then Hugo spoke to him and brought him back with a jolt to the unpleasantness of the present. "There they are, Penn. The grand duke's all in black, like a damned crow. He's looking rather impatient, if you ask me."

"He's a fool."

"Certainly is, and absolutely crazy to allow you to choose pistols."

They moved forward into a clearing surrounded by thick-trunked trees, ferns, and golden broom. The grand duke's second drew near and proffered the weapons.

"You know the rules, Lord Allandale?"

"I do, sir."

"You will walk twenty paces. Then, on the order

from the dueling master, you will turn. On his second order, you will fire. Monsieur le Brunet will officiate, if you are in agreement."

"I have no objection to Monsieur le Brunet."

Penn took off his gray flannel jacket and stood checking the pistol meticulously and ignoring Andrei completely.

The grand duke weighed him from head to toe, frowning at the crisp white shirt, the riding breeches, and the flannel waistcoat. An Englishman always looked like nothing else in the world but an Englishman. Andrei wondered why it was that when a Russian bought his clothes from the finest tailors of Saville Row he still looked like a Russian. He moved forward and spoke with Penn.

"I am ready when you are, Lord Allandale."

"At your service, sir."

"Let the maître take his place."

The two men stood back to back as the dueling master called out the rules. Then they began to pace slowly across the clearing. On the order to turn, they moved to face each other.

The dueling master called the final order: "When I give the word, gentlemen . . . FIRE!"

Two shots rang out in the silence of the early morning, startling the birds from the trees, so they rose in the air like an undulating black cloud. Andrei's shot grazed Penn's head, singeing a few of the blond hairs by his ear. Penn's caught the grand duke in the upper part of the shoulder, whirling him around so he crashed to the ground.

Andrei's second ran to his master's side.

"Come, Excellency, you are not seriously hurt. It is but a flesh wound. I shall take you back to the palace within the hour."

The servant motioned for the carriage to be brought as Andrei began to curse his adversary. "Damn the Englishman! Damn him to hell and purgatory!"

"Indeed, sir. Now, let me help you. Stepan is waiting in the carriage with the doctor, and we shall have you back home in St. Petersburg in a moment."

Hugo ran to his brother's side and threw his arms around Penn.

"Another inch and that fellow wouldn't have been able to bother you again."

"I didn't want to kill him. I aimed only for his shoulder."

"I know you did. He'll be out of your way for a few days at least."

"Not a word of this to Laurel, at least not until I have a chance to explain."

"Of course not. She'd be dreadfully upset and might go and beat the very dickens out of the grand duke for challenging you at all."

"Let's get back to the city. We'll be in time for a late breakfast at the Europa. Then I have to go to the Winter Palace. The czar asked me to call on him at two-thirty to explain the principles of ballooning."

"He's violently opposed to dueling, Penn."

"So I hear. Let's hope he knows nothing of this morning's escapade."

Penn passed the Maryinsky Theater on his way to

the Winter Palace. He saw that the staff were preparing for a children's performance later in the day. Already huge samovars had been placed outside the stage door and young girls in pink-and-white fichus were arriving alongside boys from the local academy, naval cadets, and court pages. As they entered the theater, each one received a box of candy and a portrait of the czar. Penn paused to watch the throng of eager young people. Then he moved away, his face pensive. He was thinking that the British ambassador had been right when he said in private that the Russian aristocracy trained their sons to wield the whip and their daughters to cultivate the passivity appropriate to court debauchery. Even at this tender age there was something arrogant in the eyes of the young men and a docility in the girls that appalled him.

As he walked on, Penn thought of Laurel, who was anything but docile. For a moment he savored the thought of her naked body in bed in the firelight glow. How lovely she had been, how giving and full of sensuality. As each day passed, he loved her more and could not bear to think that he might ever lose her. He had made a vow never to hurt her and always to do everything in his power to make her happy. It was a vow he took seriously, and whatever he did, wherever he went, he looked for things to share with Laurel, small presents to buy that would amuse her.

Penn was entering the Winter Palace when the czarina's personal servant beckoned to him.

"Lord Allandale, the czarina wishes to see you at once, if you please."

"I have an appointment with the czar at two-thirty."

"It has been canceled. The czar has a chill and has been put to bed."

"I'm sorry to hear it."

"It is nothing, sir. His Excellency will soon be well again. He is very strong and capable of overcoming all illnesses within a few days."

Penn was led to the same private suite where Laurel had had tea with the czarina. He found the lady alone and dozing before a roaring fire. He closed the door softly and approached her, bowing a greeting when she opened her eyes.

"Lord Allandale at your service, ma'am."

"My dear sir, how very kind of you to visit me. My husband is unwell and so I wished to steal you for an hour."

"I'm delighted to be stolen, ma'am."

The czarina rang for tea to be brought. Then, with an elusive smile, she sat opposite Penn on a stiff-backed chair covered in royal-blue silk.

"I wish you to tell me all about your duel with the Grand Duke Andrei."

Taken aback by her knowledge, Penn gazed into the enigmatic blue eyes.

"May I ask how you knew of it, ma'am?"

"I know everything that goes on in this city, Lord Allandale, at least almost everything. This is a place where the walls really *do* have ears."

Penn's eyes twinkled and he smiled at the mysterious woman before him.

"On the night of Count Orlov's ball, which I was invited to attend with Miss Holman, someone locked her in her suite at the Vladimir Palace. She assumes it was the grand duke, because no one else would dare do such a thing. Mr. Holman was out and in desperation Laurel sent for me. I hurried to the palace from my hotel and ordered servants to force one of the doors. Laurel was released, to her relief and mine."

"Then what happened?"

"The grand duke took exception to my action and challenged me to a duel."

The czarina thought about this and spoke resignedly. "Of course it was not the true reason for the challenge, as I am sure you are aware."

"I'm in love with Miss Holman and have asked her to marry me on her return to England. The grand duke thinks himself in love with Laurel and he refuses to take note of her wishes in the matter. That is the core of the problem, ma'am."

"Andrei Vladimirovich has always been like that and he will not change. Now his pride has been hurt, he will be worse, and I fear his jealousy greatly."

"It's unfortunate for me and for Laurel. We're in love, ma'am and we'd like to be together without the constant threat posed by the grand duke."

Tea arrived with tiny diamond-shaped smoked-salmon sandwiches, pastries full of cream and raspberry purée, and a dish of iced biscuits decorated with cherries. The czarina watched as servants handed Penn his tea. She was weighing his face, his hands, and his English manners, which fascinated her.

"You are unusually honest, Lord Allandale."

"It's one of my faults, ma'am. My father always hoped I'd enter the diplomatic service, but he despaired of my discretion by the time I was ten."

Amused by the statement, the czarina spoke disdainfully of the Corps Diplomatique. "Diplomats are boring. They are trained to talk about nothing at all and never to pass a real opinion. I get so very tired of listening to their platitudes. May I ask how long you will be staying in St. Petersburg, Lord Allandale?"

"I must return home to England in May."

"And Miss Holman?"

"Her father hopes to have all his commissions finished by then so we can go back together on the train. The czar asked me to leave the balloon here so it can be shown at the British Exhibition in October. I'm to give your husband some lessons in flying it before I go, and no doubt he'll put the knowledge to good use during the summer months."

"The czar will be like a child with a new toy, and so will his friends. Tell me, Lord Allandale, would it help you and Miss Holman if I were to ask the grand duke to undertake a mission for me? Perhaps we could make an imperial invitation for him to accompany us on the Easter holiday to the Crimea."

"It would help enormously, ma'am, though I doubt he would accept any invitation that took him out of St. Petersburg."

The czarina rose and rang for a servant, looking sternly down as she did so at Penn.

"He will have no choice but to accept. An imperial invitation is a command."

Andrei was lying in bed, feverish and furious at the humiliating outcome of the duel. Stepan had just changed the dressing on his shoulder, and Andrei was gazing resignedly across the vaulted room, with its dark red Gothic hangings, to the garden, where he could see Laurel looking for spring flowers under the trees. She was wearing one of the simple sprigged cotton dresses she had brought with her from England and looked more radiant than he could ever remember. He looked closely at her face and knew in his heart that Lord Allandale had made love to her. He was shocked that Laurel had finally allowed herself the luxury of passion. Perhaps she had been longing for the Englishman all winter. Perhaps he had simply been blind to the fact that she was a woman in love, madly in love with the handsome aristocrat from Wentworth Saye.

Andrei sighed wearily as spasms of pain rippled from shoulder to arm. He had still not recovered from the shock of realizing that despite Penn's seeming lack of interest in the duel, he had turned out to be one of the finest marksmen he had ever encountered. Andrei knew instinctively that his rival's shot had been placed precisely where it would damage only his pride and not his body on a lasting basis. The Englishman could have shot him clean through the heart, but he had increased the humiliation by allowing his adversary to go free. For Andrei, this was a fate worse than death.

Stepan was about to administer a sedative to his master when one of the ground-floor footmen appeared with a message from the czar.

"This came for you by imperial messenger, sir."

"Dear God, what now!"

Andrei scanned the contents of the note and threw it down on the floor, speechless with rage and chagrin at the invitation that amounted to a most unwelcome royal command. The czar had written in his usual enigmatic tone: *I am worried about you, Andrei Vladimirovich, and am instructing our physician to call on you at eleven. If he advises it, you must accompany the family to Livadia for the holiday. Alexandra joins me in sending our best wishes for your speedy recovery. Nicholas R.*

Andrei looked beseechingly at Stepan.

"When the physician comes to see me, tell him I am too ill to be examined."

"Very well, Excellency, but I doubt he will heed what I say."

"And bring Miss Holman to me at once, if you please."

"I will go and look for her, sir."

"She's in the garden under the trees. Hurry, Stepan, don't stand about staring into space."

Laurel entered the room, wrinkling her nose at the scent of ether and antiseptic. Looking down at Andrei, she was not surprised to find him still agitated, his eyes regarding her like a wounded animal. She remembered, however, that only a few hours previously it had been his intention to kill Penn, and this made it easy for her to harden her heart against him.

"You wanted to see me, Andrei?"

"Say you forgive me for fighting the duel. I am very ill and need your forgiveness."

Laurel sighed at the man's cunning.

"You're not seriously ill. I checked with Dr. Zonanov after his visit and he said you have a shoulder wound and a very slight fever, which is from your overwrought emotions and not your injury."

"Damn you! Don't you ever believe what I say?"

"You don't ever tell me the truth, so I can't believe what you say. Now, why did you ask to see me?"

"I have decided that I would like to convalesce in the south, where the weather is so much milder than here in St. Petersburg. Will you and Mr. Holman come with me? We could travel with the imperial party to Livadia, the czar's summer palace in Yalta, which is in the Crimean region. The gardens there are the most beautiful in all of Russia, with tropical plants and vegetation just like that which is found in the Mediterranean."

Laurel looked thoughtfully at the sick man. Obviously Andrei had been given an imperial invitation to accompany the czar and members of the court to the Crimea for the Easter holiday. It was equally obvious that he had no desire to leave her in St. Petersburg with Penn Allandale. She tried to pacify him until she could verify if her suspicions were correct.

"I'll think about it, Andrei."

"Tell me by tonight, promise it."

"I'll do no such thing. I'll think about it and when I've decided I'll tell you my answer. I have to ask Poppa first how he's getting on with his work."

The imperial physician was just arriving as Laurel left the palace. He made an ornate bow to her and then swept inside, followed by his four assistants. Outside the palace gates, the beggars were gathering for their daily bread at the door of the bakery. Two peasant women were standing on the pavement, staring up at the great house. They had obviously arrived for the Statute Fair, which would be held in two weeks' time, and would spend the interim period working as extra staff in one of the palaces of the city during the holiday period, when family and friends from far and wide were apt to appear unexpectedly for reunions.

Laurel looked again at the awed faces of the two peasant women and remembered her own reactions to the palaces of St. Petersburg on first arrival in the city. Now she had grown accustomed to the size of the houses and the legions of servants. She had even grown used to the extremes of the Russian temperament, though she would never learn to like them. She stepped down from the carriage outside the Europa Hotel and asked the doorman to dismiss the driver. Then she went at once to Penn's suite.

They embraced and held each other close, kissing

again and again. Then they sat facing each other across a breakfast table loaded with boiled eggs, salami, mild cheese, black bread, white rolls, butter, marmalade, and a samovar of tea. As she filled her plate, Laurel told Penn what Andrei had said.

"I think he's been issued with an imperial invitation, and you know what that means. He won't be able to refuse it."

"I've been issued with one, too. The czarina invited me to take you to stay at the Royal Palace of Peterhof on the Gulf of Finland and to visit one of her favorite summer pavilions in the grounds. I am so happy I could burst."

Laurel's face glowed with inner excitement at the prospect of the trip in store. Then, remembering she had not seen Hugo since his arrival in the city, she inquired about him. "Where's Hugo? I expected to see him yesterday at dinner."

"Hugo went to Moscow to visit our good friends the Benettis. They're Italian and living in the city at the house of Prince Youssoupoff. Carlo's an artist, like your father, though with a very different style, and he's doing the prince's portrait. Tell me, have you any idea when Andrei will be leaving the city?"

"He didn't actually say he was leaving, but I think he'll have to go with the rest of the imperial party on Sunday. There's not much wrong with him except hurt pride, jealousy, and a stiff shoulder. The bullet went clean through him and the flesh is healing fast. I checked with his doctor to make sure Andrei didn't lie about his condition."

"If you're right, we'll leave soon after for the Rose Pavilion."

"What a lovely name. What kind of place is it?"

"It's a summerhouse in the garden of the royal palace. According to the czarina, it's the most beautiful little house in the entire world. She believes we shall be staying there chaperoned by Lotty, and I shall have to arrange that the staff are well tipped so they report it that way!"

"Oh, Penn, I just remembered, Tuesday of the following week is my birthday. Poppa'll be expecting us to have dinner with him."

"We'll come back after a few days and take your father and Lotty out to celebrate. Then, if you like, we'll go back to the Rose Pavilion until we're tired of each other."

Laurel's face clouded at the thought.

"Don't ever say that, Penn, not even as a joke. I'll never tire of you and I can't bear to hear you mention it even in fun."

"I was teasing, my darling. Remember one thing: I'm the fellow who almost had his ears frozen off flying thousands of miles to see you. I love you, Laurel. I love you more than anything in the world, and I'll love you for as long as there's breath in my body."

Laurel ran to him and let him take her in his arms, her face close to his, her mouth searching for his. Feelings so strong they were overwhelming swept through her and she felt mad with a beautiful passion, an overwhelming feeling that nothing in the world mattered but herself and the man she loved. Penn's hands were gripping her, making her shiver with anticipation, and she closed her eyes as he kissed her, filling her with such weakness and anticipation she could think of nothing else. Content to be where she knew she belonged, she relaxed and forgot all about Andrei and the outside world. For the moment, pleasure was the important thing, and pleasure was synonymous with being close to Penn.

Spring came suddenly that year, as was often the way in Russia. Unaccustomed to this swift transition from white winter landscape to rain-filled streets and bridges over ever-rising waters, Laurel woke to the sound of birdsong and the sight of buds on the cherry trees outside her window, pale green in the golden sunlight. How different everything looked now that the sun was here, how joyous and alive. She leapt out of bed and ran to the window, smiling because the gardeners were all working at the tasks that came with the new season. Some were cutting dead wood off the trees, some wheeling barrows of fertilizer to the kitchen garden. On the periphery of the lawn stood Andrei's mother, talking with Stepan. Laurel wondered why Andrei had not taken Stepan with him to Livadia. Then she shrugged. He had probably left the young man to spy on her, but Stepan would never find her where she and Penn were going. He would not even be able to hazard a guess as to their destination.

Laurel went to her dressing room and looked at the clothes Polinka had packed for her visit to the country. She and Penn would return for her birthday party, which Lotty had insisted on giving at her own apartment. After that, they might cruise on the royal yacht or accept Lotty's invitation to go to the beachhouse on Kammeni Island, to be alone and safe in that secret place. Laurel sat on the edge of the bed, thinking how lucky she was. Her father had so many commissions he was in his studio working from dawn to dusk. His friendship with Lotty had made him happy, and for the first time in many years he was totally relaxed and at ease with life. Thanks to the czarina, Andrei was far away in the Crimea, leaving the way free for Penn to be at her side. Laurel was profoundly grateful for this, and so excited she could remember nothing but the fact that at four that day the man she loved was calling to collect her. They were going away to a beautiful house together, to enter even deeper into their world of romance. She shivered excitedly, longing more with each passing moment for the time when they would be together for always.

They drove out of the city as cannon fired from the Kronstadt, proclaiming the rising of the waters. Laurel wondered if there were going to be really grave floods, as there had been many years previously. Answering volleys came from the city, and colored lights on the roof of the Admiralty Building twinkled their messages on the state of the waters, these anxiously watched by the rich of the city, who feared damage to their homes.

On the outskirts of the city, they saw crowds of

women emerging from the steamy interior of a laundry, their feet bound in cloth tied with straps, their black clothes and red kerchiefs standing out in the mist of late afternoon. Farther on, the troikas of two noblemen were racing on an empty piece of road, the screams of the cossack drivers like the raving of madmen in the nearby asylum. When the race was over, the two men leapt out and exchanged gold coins. It had all been for a wager, even the life-risking antics of the coachmen.

Laurel shook her head resignedly. Russia was the only place she had ever been where a man would risk his life on the turn of a coin, and sometimes for no reason at all, except that he was bored. The temperament was alien to everything she had been taught to value, and it was unnerving to see its effects all around her each day. More and more she thought of the peace of rural England, the jovial shepherds of Wentworth Saye, and the staff of the house, whose homey faces were so very different from the nervous ones of Russian servants. She recognized her condition for what it was and was content to experience the nesting instinct that comes to many women about to be married.

Twelve versts from the city, along the coast road overlooking the Gulf of Finland, there was a concealed turning that led to a pillared entrance guarded by two blue-clad cossacks. Penn leaned forward and handed an imperial order to the guard, who ran to open the gate. Then he drove through, looking back in satisfaction when the cossacks locked the doors behind them. Turning to Laurel, he kissed her cheeks.

"We're marooned here—isn't it a wonderful prospect?"

"I'm going to love being marooned with you."

"Let's hope the czarina remembered to inform the staff that we're arriving, or we'll be the hungriest guests that ever visited the place."

"Look, Penn, over there, isn't that something special?"

Rounding a bend, they saw the Rose Pavilion, a charming old house with tall chimneys, pointed dormers, and pergolas of deep pink roses. The pink-painted walls had been muralized with flowers, the painter depicting large cabbage roses around the windows and doors. A team of gardeners who looked after the property had improved on this and had planted real climbing pink roses in a circle around the perimeter of the property and then over the pergola that led to an ornamental lake covered in bright yellow water lilies. Bees buzzed in pink and peach azalea bushes in the front garden and a white cat looked curiously out over the water at the lovers, who were sitting together in the carriage, entranced by the scene.

At that moment, a servant began to brush the forecourt with a long-handled broom. Upstairs, a maid in frilly white opened the windows and shook her duster. And somewhere in the rear of the house they could hear a woman singing.

Laurel took Penn's hand in her own.

"This is paradise, isn't it?"

"It's quite beautiful. No wonder the czarina insisted I bring you here. She may seem distant to many people, but I believe she's a romantic at heart. She told me this was her husband's favorite property in the early days of their marriage."

"Let's go look inside."

Maids rushed to welcome them, and a butler in black and white led them to their rooms and then left them alone. Minutes later, a young man in livery appeared and asked what they wanted to eat that evening.

"We have fine fish from the river, with lemon rice, also wild goose or ptarmigan. The cook is most pleased to have guests in the house. To follow, he begs to suggest a violet soufflé, which is one of his specialties."

When they were finally alone, Penn and Laurel sat gazing about her bedroom. A fire glowed in the grate. The four-poster was hung with cobwebby white lace, the walls painted with cabbage roses in pink and cream like those on the exterior of the house. The carpets, hand-knotted of cyclamen and amber silk, had been designed in a circular pattern depicting a flower garden surrounded by tree ferns and vines.

Penn walked through to a bathroom handsomely fitted with bronze and then to his own bedroom, where the walls were painted with camellias. The courtship had begun in a Tudor mansion in rural England and was continuing in a fairy-tale pavilion in the middle of Russia. Smiling, happy, and relaxed, he prayed silently that the romance would never go out of their lives, that for himself and Laurel there would always be magic and enchanting places where memories would be made that they would cherish forever.

In the early morning, they went rowing on the lake, accompanied by the white cat. Spring sunshine filtered through the overhanging willow trees, dappling Laurel's face and the white silk of her dress. In the distance they could hear field hands singing an Eastern hymn and through a break in the trees could see young peasant girls with cornflower circlets in their hair taking food out to the workers. After the passionate lovemaking of the previous night, the atmosphere was serene, peaceful, and idyllic.

Penn rowed from the lake down a channel that led to the jetty by the sea.

"If I keep on rowing, we'll end up in England. Then I'll marry you and keep you there forever."

"I couldn't go without Poppa. If I left him behind, he might get ill and I'd have a bad conscience about it for the rest of my days. In any case, Andrei might get it into his head to take Poppa hostage against my return."

"Andrei's a thousand miles away, or might as well be."

"I'm so happy we're alone at last. I'm just greedy for every second of your time."

"You have them all. You always will."

"Let's walk a little way on the beach. Poppa and I

used to love walking on the beach back home in America."

They walked from the jetty, where the boat was moored, to a headland half a mile away. There, windswept but refreshed, they stood looking out to sea at the distant coast of Finland. In the opposite direction there was a seemingly endless vista of the Russian countryside, with its neatly plowed fields planted with wheat, rye, and millet. Below them, the palace looked a magnificent structure like Versailles. Only the Rose Pavilion remained invisible from their vantage point, a secret paradise that existed only for those with a reason to visit it. Few in St. Petersburg even knew of its existence, and for this reason it seemed all the more precious to the lovers. Like Wentworth Saye, it was part of their story, their courtship, and the golden days of their first lovemaking. It was also a place of refuge from the scandals of a superficial court.

One evening at the Rose Pavilion, Penn went riding in the dusk. On his return, he found Laurel waiting for him by the lake, a glass of white wine in her hand. She was dressed in the lavender-blue satin gown she had worn on the night of the dinner party at Wentworth Saye, which Consuelo had given her. He rode to her side and looked down at her with such naked desire it took her breath away.

"Why did you choose that dress tonight?"

"It's the eve of my birthday and I was hoping you might dance with me in the moonlight when the chimes of midnight strike."

She looked at him as he sat the white stallion, the most perfect man she had ever seen. His face was suntanned, his blue eyes soft on hers, and as he dismounted and secured the horse, Laurel felt a shiver running through her body, a bewitching, haunting feeling that she enjoyed and feared for its addictive effect on her.

Penn hugged her to his heart.

"May I have this waltz, young lady?"

Laurel kissed his cheek and drifted into his arms as a solitary violinist began to play. She was touched when she realized that the man was picking out the melody of the waltz from *Bal Rosé*, the same haunting tune the musicians in England had played that night at Wentworth Saye. The violinist was joined, seconds later, by other musicians, until, as dusk turned to dark and servants hurried from the pavilion to light the big rose-scented candles on the terrace, a full orchestra was to be heard in the silence of the night.

Some of the staff stayed to watch as Penn and Laurel danced by, she in her lavender-blue dress that shimmered like the moon, he in his white silk shirt and English tweeds, not caring about his clothes, only how he felt as he held the woman of his dreams in his arms and danced with her to paradise.

For dinner they ate tiny shellfish served with a sauce that smelled of the sea, then sturgeon wrapped in fennel leaves, and chicken stuffed with truffles. They relished a soufflé decorated with gilded rose petals and drank a liqueur made of cuckoo flowers and honey. Then, when the servants had gone, they lay together in front of the fire on a daybed of crushed silk velvet. Outside, a nightingale trilled its song to the moon. Inside, the lovers were preparing to make this night more enchanting and more memorable than any had been before.

Penn poured the last of the wine and bent down to pick Laurel up into his arms.

"I have one other surprise for your birthday."

She kissed him and snuggled happily in his arms as he carried her upstairs to bed. On entering the room, she smelled the roses before she saw them. Then, as Penn lit the lamps, she gazed about her at an incredible sight. The whole room had been lined from floor to ceiling with large pink roses of intense fragrance and great beauty. Whereas, until a few hours ago, the only flowers had been those of the artist's imagination, these were real in all their freshness.

Penn placed her on the bed and kissed her gently.

"I want you to have this for your birthday. I do hope it fits. Lotty helped me about the size. The flowers on the walls are French Jacqueminot roses, specially chosen for their fragrance. But the rose on that ring is a real rose of England."

Laurel gazed down at a box of black velvet inside which nestled, on a bed of shimmering white satin, a ring of chased gold with a half-open rosebud fashioned from rubies, pearls, and diamonds. She put it on her finger and held it there, afraid lest she drop it.

"It's just the most beautiful ring I ever saw. The

rose is like the ones in your garden at Wentworth Saye."

"You remembered them—I wondered if you would."

"I remember everything about the house, every blade of grass in the garden, every red poppy in the fields, and every orchid in the hothouse. I loved all of it so very much."

"This is your engagement ring, Laurel. The next one I buy you will be a wedding band."

Her eyes filled with desire, and recognizing the urgency of her longing and the eagerness of his own, Penn kissed her on the lips, lifting her onto the bed and taking off the loose silk robe she had chosen for the latter part of the evening. Her body was rounded and soft, yet strong and braced for love. The breasts were heavy, the nipples pointed and hard. It was a body to make any man weak from longing, one made for love in all its glory. He kissed Laurel again, savoring the honey taste of her. He was thinking how he adored the way she wound her arms around his neck and pressed her body against his own. He spoke his innermost thoughts to her.

"I love you more than I ever thought it possible to love any woman."

"Make love to me, Penn. Make love like you did before. I'm longing to float on a pink cloud all the way to heaven."

He kissed her neck and her shoulder, the tips of her fingers, and the tips of her toes. Then, hastening to remove his clothes, he slipped into bed at her side. Within seconds he was rapturously exploring the secret places of her body with gentle hands and an inquiring mouth. Their embraces grew more fervent, until Laurel lay panting at his side. When the moment came for him to enter her, he was excited by her cry of desire. He could feel the warmth of her breath on his neck and the pounding of her heart next to his own. At the moment of passion, they clung together, looking into each other's eyes as sunbursts of emotion exploded within their minds and bodies.

After love, they lay curled like kittens around each other, exhausted by emotion spent. This was the moment they both adored, when Penn stroked Laurel's hands and cushioned her head against his chest, all the while reflecting that nothing in the world was as perfect as having made love with the woman he worshiped.

"Each time, love improves when I am with you. You've made me the happiest and luckiest man in the world."

"I adore you a little more each day, Penn."

"Don't ever stop loving me. I should die if I ever lost you."

He kissed her on the mouth, his lips eager on hers. Then he returned to stroking her face and saying those things she longed to hear, the little endearments that are typical of men and women in love.

They were still lying together when they heard a loud hammering at the front door of the Rose Pavilion. Laurel sat up, hear heart beating wildly.

"Who on earth could that be?"

"God knows, but he's in a fearsome hurry."

Looking at the clock, Laurel saw that it was one in the morning. She got up and ran to the window. Below, servants were lighting the lamps, and in the eerie green glow of the gaslights, she realized that the caller was their good friend Sandro Alexandrovich. Laurel called out to him from the balcony outside her room. "Is something wrong, Sandro? Is Mitzi ill?"

"No, I came to warn you that the grand duke returned unexpectedly to the city this morning. He's raving mad about the fact that you are missing and has been making threats against Lord Allandale's life. Your father told me to come and find you. I did so through the czar's estate keeper, and if I can find you, so can Andrei. It seemed best to come here at once to warn you."

"You're the very best of friends."

"I married Mitzi three days ago and told my father afterward, like you said, Laurel. He just told me he hoped I should not live to regret it. You were right. Getting married to my dearest one was so much easier than we had thought."

"I'll come down right away."

"Don't hurry. I have ordered some tea and will be quite content."

At eleven the following morning, while Sandro and his new wife were breakfasting on the terrace and Laurel and Penn were picking flowers on the lower terrace, the carriage of the grand duke appeared in the drive. Sandro looked hard at the servant and gave him his final instructions.

"Remember what I told you to say if the grand duke asks you any questions. What I have told you is an imperial command."

"I shall not fail you, sir."

Andrei was nonplussed to see Sandro and his doll-like wife sitting on the terrace eating breakfast together.

"I did not expect to find you here, Sandro."

"Nor I you. I thought you were in Yalta with the imperial party."

"I was, but I made an excuse to leave. My wound has been somewhat infected and I wished to see my own physician in St. Petersburg."

"How was Yalta?"

"Beautiful as ever, and boring as ever."

At that moment Laurel's laughter echoed from the lower garden. Andrei leapt to his feet, his face paling with anger.

"Laurel is here?"

Sandro replied imperturbably, all the while continuing his breakfast, "We invited her and her fiancé, Lord Allandale, to come to see the Rose Pavilion. Mitzi and I believe it to be one of the very prettiest houses in the area."

"Lord Allandale is not her fiancé."

Sandro spoke firmly but with infinite gentleness. "Yesterday, on Laurel's birthday, Lord Allandale gave her a ring. I am quite sure they are engaged to be married, Andrei."

The grand duke sat quite still, his face as pale as tallow. He had returned to the city in a long and harrowing journey to prevent the couple being together, but despite everything, Allandale had triumphed. Hatred of Penn overcame his reason and he wanted only to wipe the Englishman from the face of the earth. Instead, he rose and took his leave.

"Tell Laurel I called, if you please. I wished her to know that Mr. Holman appears unwell, and I have taken the liberty of calling my own physician to attend him. When she is ready, perhaps she will return to St. Petersburg to see her father."

"Of course she will, but won't you see her and tell her yourself?"

"No, I have much to do and must leave at once. I am at your service, my dear Sandro, Madame Cherchenko."

With that Andrei rose and went to his carriage. During the journey back to the city he began to make new plans. He had been too gentle with Laurel and he realized it. Now he felt it was necessary to break her as one broke a wild horse in order to make it amenable to one's desires. Allandale had let it be known that he must return to England shortly. Laurel and her father had planned to return with him. In the light of the painter's illness, however, they would probably have to delay their departure. If only he could separate Laurel from the man she loved, Andrei knew Russia would do the rest. With her vast, empty spaces, her poor communications, and her fearsome weather, she had eventually defeated every conqueror from Genghis Khan to Napoleon. She would do the same with the Englishman. Once Allandale was gone, Laurel would know only what *he* told her of what was happening in the outside world. Andrei began to feel calm again. If he had luck, patience, and was prepared to be totally ruthless, there was still a chance to win the day.

7

St. Petersburg, May–June 1899

On Whit Monday they held the Statute Fair, an old
custom not unlike a marriage market. In the park,
the young girls lined up under the lime trees, their
parents standing shyly behind them. Some were maids
in palaces overlooking the park, some shop assistants.
Many were so poor they wore darned dresses, even
for this auspicious occasion. Opposite the girls stood
a line of young men, their parents loitering nearby,
wondering what was going to happen, what manner
of marriage could be arranged on this sunny spring
day.

Polinka stood her ground as a handsome young
farm worker from the wooded hills north of the city
walked by, then turned and walked past again. Under the trees, she could see Laurel and Penn watch-

ing this quaint pantomime and could not help noticing how radiant her mistress was. Becoming engaged had changed the American, making her more beautiful, more animated, and less given to periods of sadness at being in Russia, far away from the man she loved. Polinka primped her hair and fixed the farmer with a dreamy look, the kind of look she had seen Laurel give Penn on many occasions. To her delight, the young man returned and stood eagerly before her.

"I'm Gavrilo Kazimirovich Stegunov."

"Polinka Appollonovna at your service, sir."

"Can I talk to your father?"

"Dad! Come here, will you."

Polinka watched anxiously as the two men stood together discussing her marriage portion, the quantity of her linen and clothes, her household accomplishments. Then, when everything had been arranged, Gavrilo turned to her and shyly took her hand in his big hamlike fist.

"Let's go and walk around the riding enclosure. I like to see the fine folk on their horses. Someday I want to own a horse of my own."

"We'll own one, maybe two. Before we go to the riding ring, can we go and meet Milady first? There she is, standing under the trees. She came with me today to give me courage. She's the best mistress I've ever had."

"She's very grand and very beautiful."

"She's American and the gentleman with her's English. He fought a duel with the Grand Duke

Andrei Vladimirovich and near blew his head off for love of the lady. It was ever so exciting!"

Polinka led her fiancé toward the spot where Laurel and Penn were waiting. When they were face to face, she introduced Gavrilo with obvious pride. "This is my fiancé, ma'am. His name's Gavrilo Kazimirovich and he's one of the estate workers at the Count Kutsov's property. He's never been to St. Petersburg before. We're going to get wed in the autumn, when they've brought in the last of the wheat. After that I'll be living in the country again, just like I used to. You were right when you said that someday the earth would call me. I've been fed up for weeks with the city. I keep dreaming of working in the fields and wearing flowers in my hair."

Laurel stepped forward and shook the young man's hand, pleased by his firm grip and honest blue eyes. She was amused to see Polinka gazing enthusiastically at her fiancé's rocklike shoulders and big, bearlike body. Laurel wished them both the very greatest happiness in the future. "Congratulations, Gavrilo. I hope you and Polinka will prosper and that your children will grow to be healthy and content with life."

Not understanding a word of English, he turned questioningly to Polinka, who explained what had been said. Then, with a bow, he led his new fiancée away to walk by the lake and throw stale bread to the ducks. He was thinking that he had found himself a most intelligent and ambitious young woman, one who would show him how to realize his longing to own a little plot of land and a cottage he would build himself for his family. The Statute Fair had worked its spell and Gavrilo was well pleased that the tedious journey to St. Petersburg had been worth all the trouble.

Penn and Laurel left the park by the enclosure where the aristocrats were riding horses that were for sale on this day of celebration. The men were stiff-backed and proud, the horses magnificent, the women sitting sidesaddle in dressage outfits, many of them performing to the music of an out-of-tune local band. Now and then an officer of the guard galloped by, startling everyone, and as Penn and Laurel left the park, a troop of cossacks in blue came in through the side gate, their wild-eyed faces almost hidden under the bearskin hats that were their pride and joy. Later they would perform daring feats of equestrian skill for the assembled guests. Then they would drink too much and sleep it off in the far reaches of the park.

Penn and Laurel rode in a carriage to Lotty's apartment. She had insisted that Holman be moved there so she could give him her undivided attention. His ailment had been diagnosed as kidney stones and there had been much pain to bear. His condition was still too poor to consider traveling home from Russia, and so he was marooned in Lotty's house, cared for, adored, attended constantly, but pining to be able to return to England, so his daughter could marry the man she loved.

On entering the sick man's bedroom, Laurel saw

that her father was feverish again. She sat at the bedside, looking down at him sadly.

"Is the pain very bad?"

"Not so good, honey. I guess there's another stone to pass. It'll come tonight and then maybe I'll feel easier. How're you, Penn? I hear you have to leave by the end of this month."

"I'm afraid so, sir. Some legal problems concerning probate of my father's estate have come up that require my urgent attention. I should have gone in May, but I couldn't resist staying on here to wait for you and Laurel."

"I'll do my best to get better so's we can travel together, but right now I don't feel sure of anything."

"Don't worry, Mr. Holman, Laurel and I are in love and a few weeks' delay isn't going to cause a disaster. Wentworth Saye and I shall be waiting eagerly for your arrival, whenever it is."

"Did Hugo get away yesterday?"

"He left on the midnight train for Paris. I shall look forward to having his account of the trip. My brother detests trains, but the journey by ship is just too long."

"And what of the grand duke?"

"He's curiously quiet at the moment. He's been away in Kiev and last night announced that he was going to visit his property in Moscow till the end of this month. It's a mercy that he's managed to accept the fact that Laurel and I are in love."

Laurel sighed, uncertain in her own mind that Andrei had done anything of the kind, but she said nothing of her apprehension to Penn. It certainly looked as if Andrei had accepted her situation. He had, of late, been seeing Yelena again, frequently in the company of his mother. The Princess Sophia, lacking any other woman who could interest her son, had decided to work hard on encouraging Yelena to complete the transformation she had begun and to behave in a manner befitting a future leading society woman of St. Petersburg. Surprisingly, the young woman had reacted with wisdom and graciousness, taking criticism from the princess and doing her best to mold herself in the right image for the future. She no longer entertained Andrei at her house and saw him only when accompanied by a chaperon. The city gossips were nonplussed by her behavior and by Andrei's. Had the grand duke lost interest in the beautiful American? Or was he playing a waiting game? Those who knew him well pointed out that Penn Allandale was due to leave for England on the thirtieth. After that, who could tell what might happen?

In the middle of June, the czarina opened the Royal Palace of Peterhof for a fete to celebrate the advent of summer. She invited Penn and Laurel to stay with the imperial party, together with her sister and husband, the Cherchenkos, and a few chosen members of the inner circle of friends.

In the country, life was very different from the routine of St. Petersburg. Formality was banished completely and the ladies wore white voile dresses, the men light cottons and straw boaters. The days were spent rowing on the lake, fishing from the jetty, picking and pressing wildflowers, and gossiping furiously. In the evenings, which were hot and still, all the windows of the palace were left open, and often dinner was served on the terrace under an awning of yellow roses and laburnum.

The czarina became a different person when she was with her family, and everyone remarked on the change in her. Gone were the black moods and depressions that affected her in the city, together with her frequent angry withdrawals from rooms full of people she neither knew nor liked. In the country she felt like a real person, able to spend all her time with her husband and children, just as if she had never become the empress of all Russia.

One evening, on the birthday of the czar's cousin, a masked entertainment was held in the summer ballroom of the palace. Laurel dressed in a gown of diaphanous emerald chiffon, a string of pearls wound around her slim neck, a garland of daisies and ivy leaves in her hair. Her mask was in the form of an owl's face and she could not resist rushing to Penn's room to show him her changed appearance.

"How do I suit being an owl?"

"You look beautiful, even in that curious get-up."

"What's your mask like? The czarina chose them herself, you know. I can't wait to see what she ordered for you."

"She obviously has a sense of humor. She gave me

this and told me she thought it suited my personality very well."

Penn drew from his pocket the black, shiny velvet mask he had been given, depicting a panther, the legendary wild animal of the jungle.

Laurel looked at his evening dress, at the blond hair that shone so distinctively in the glow of the candles above them.

"You'll make a very good panther—an English panther, anyway."

"They don't have many panthers in Oxfordshire. I do hope my behavior won't disappoint the czarina."

After dinner, the mazurkas began and the company grew jolly. The czar, always so remote and tense, unwound enough to ask four of the ladies to dance with him. Then he approached Laurel, smiling that elusive smile she had come to know very well.

"I recall you once putting me at my ease by telling me that you were not the best of dancers, Miss Holman, but I think it was not true."

"It's true enough, sir, though I've improved since I met Lord Allandale. I do so want to impress Penn, and I'm scared to death of treading on his toes."

"He's a very lucky man and I hope he knows it."

"I'm in love, so I'm the lucky one."

"May I ask when you plan to marry?"

"As soon as Poppa and I return to England. My father's not well right now, but when he's better, we're going to Penn's house in England so I can be married from there. I dream about it all the time and can't think of much else. I'm getting to be a very dull young woman."

"That you could never be, Miss Holman. Now, shall we try to steer a safe course around this very small ballroom?"

When the czar returned her to her place, Laurel saw that Penn was waltzing with the czarina. The lady usually refused invitations to dance, because she was known to be nervous and inclined to break out in a sweat when touched by a stranger. Laurel was relieved to see Alexandra's face relaxed and smiling as Penn guided her with his usual skill, so there were no moments of hesitation on the royal lady's part. Under a canopy of lilac and jasmine, the two waltzed in perfect harmony. Laurel looked across the room to where the czar was watching his wife's unusually relaxed performance with gentle pride. She was touched by his obvious love for his wife and the czarina's overwhelming need for her husband. That was how it should be in life, but rarely was.

Laurel wandered outside and stood under the moon, gazing out at the sea. How beautiful the countryside was, how peaceful the night. The whole area was scented with lilac, the sounds of music mixing with the lapping of the sea on the rocks below. Laurel thought how her life had changed since the day she had left America and how strange it was that it was such a short time ago. On the voyage to England she had still been a young and immature girl, inclined to stare at the grand passengers with whom she and her father were traveling and with a habit of practical joking that many found unamusing. Remembering her own gaucheness, Laurel passed down an avenue of lime trees in the direction of the Rose Pavilion. At Blenheim she had learned a great deal by watching Consuelo, the Duchess of Marlborough. She had soon mastered the art of walking tall, of dancing gracefully, of speaking in a well-modulated voice, and not laughing too loudly at jokes. Then she had met Penn and the final transition from schoolgirl to woman had taken place. For him she had longed to be a true lady worthy of Wentworth Saye and the Allandale family background. Almost overnight she had felt herself maturing and falling in love and she had prayed so hard that Penn would love her too. Russia had been a new experience, opening Laurel's eyes to good and evil, superficiality and depth, wealth in all its forms and poverty at its most tragic. Here she had learned to deny Andrei his spoiled whims, to handle Yelena's moods and Andrei's mother's dislike. She had made friends with the most powerful family in the land and had become a real woman in Penn's arms. Now all she wanted for the rest of her life was to be with the man she loved. All her hopes and her plans were fixed on Penn. All her ambitions were ambitions to be realized with him and with their family in the future. He was the perfect man for her, the only man, and Laurel knew it as surely as she knew that dawn would come or night would fall.

She was approaching the door of the Rose Pavilion when she heard a footfall behind her. Turning, she saw Penn coming after her with a wrap. She ran and hugged him delightedly, kissing his cheeks and his hands.

"I hope you're following me, Lord Allandale."

"Indeed I am. I fear I'm developing some of brother Hugo's bloodhound tendencies. The truth is, I don't like you being out of my sight for more than a few minutes. Here, I brought your wrap in case you felt cold."

Penn stood, holding her in his arms in the moonlight, with nothing but the sound of crickets chirruping in the grass to disturb the peace of the starlit stillness.

"Kiss me, Laurel."

She stood on tiptoe, her lips searching for his, and they kissed and kissed again, their bodies close, their breath coming fast through their lungs. Laurel gazed into Penn's eyes as his mouth brushed her cheeks, her nose, her forehead, her shoulder.

"This is a magic night, like all the nights we've spent together. Dearest Penn, I do so want you. If we were home at Wentworth Saye, I should lock you in my bedroom and refuse to let you go."

"Let's go upstairs without further delay."

"Don't tempt me! The czarina might send someone to look for me, and just imagine what would happen if we were found together."

"The czarina retired to bed ten minutes ago. I fear my dancing exhausted her, or perhaps I said something that shocked. I told her I loved you so much I couldn't bear to be without you for a moment. She blushed to the roots of her hair."

Laurel ran inside and upstairs to her room. Penn

followed, taking the steps two at a time and ignoring the startled glance of a servant sitting in the porter's chair in the hall. To please the czar's desire for decorum, he had been allocated a room in the main building of the palace and Laurel one in the pavilion. Now they were going to be together in the room where they had made love so many times before.

Locking the door firmly behind them, Penn sat in the moonlight watching Laurel as she undressed. First she took off the chiffon skirt and hung it in the dressing room. Then she untied the shimmering bodice and stood before him in her lace camisole and frilly drawers. This was the way Penn loved best to see her, unpinning her hair and dropping the flowers from it on the ground. While she was so occupied, he began to kiss her neck and her shoulders. Then he took the brush and began to run it through the red-gold curls, smiling when Laurel closed her eyes in pleasure at his touch.

"You look like a kitten. If only you could purr I should believe you a member of the feline breed."

"I purr whenever you touch me, Penn. It's just that you don't hear it."

She untied the camisole and let it fall on the fur rug. Her breasts were already longing for his touch and her heart fluttering with anticipation. Pulling the long white satin ribbons of the drawers, she let them fall to the ground. Then she turned to Penn and wound her arms around his shoulders.

"Take off your clothes, and hurry. I do so want you."

"I must go to the pantry and find some champagne. I have a devil of a thirst tonight."

Penn wandered to the pantry adjacent to their room and returned with two glasses of champagne from the cold cupboard. Then he slipped off the dinner jacket, the shirt with its diamond studs, the trousers, shoes, and all the paraphernalia of formality, revealing the slim, hard-muscled body Laurel adored.

Within seconds they were together, lovers burning with desire. Penn kissed her neck and her chest and the breasts thrust so eagerly to him for his adoration.

"Oh, my darling Laurel, it's so good to be here with you again. This pavilion is *our* place and I shall always remember it as something very special."

"You don't have to return to the party, do you?"

"I do, but not for a long time yet."

They kissed and tasted and stroked each other's bodies, shivering from desire and the prospect of love.

Laurel lay on her back and then rolled onto her stomach, so Penn could kiss her back and the nape of her neck. Then, as she cried out from desire, he lifted her so she was astride him, enveloping his hardness with the softness of her own body. She threw her head back in reckless abandon and led him swiftly to the climax of passion.

At the moment of giving, a storm exploded outside and the room reverberated with the sound of rumbling, crashing thunder. Chandeliers tinkled, shutters rattled, and the house was filled with noise. Purple lightning filled the sky and blinding white flashes made the atmosphere electric. The summer storms of St. Petersburg were legendary, but this one was more intense than any Penn and Laurel had seen before, and they sat up in bed together, delighted.

"My dear Laurel, I shall not have to go back to the ball now the storm has broken. Everyone will think we took a walk together and got caught in the downpour. They'll imagine we're sheltering until it is over and then retiring to our beds."

"Our separate beds."

"That's what I hope they think."

Another clap of thunder pierced the air and somewhere in the distant peasant houses dogs began to bark and children to cry. Laurel snuggled happily in her lover's arms, truly content. When Penn was near, nothing in the world frightened her. When he was at her side, holding her in his strong arms, kissing her and making love to her, nothing could change the joy she felt in the nearness of his body. She closed her eyes, fulfilled and happy to be in her favorite place, listening to the storm raging outside the windows. She was with the man she loved above all else in the world. The elements could do as they pleased. All that mattered was that she and Penn were safe in the Rose Pavilion and in each other's arms.

On the last day of the czarina's country house party, a messenger rode out to Peterhof with a note from Andrei. It was brief and to the point:

My dear Laurel,
Your father is gravely ill. Please return at once to the
city. Lotty is with him constantly, but the doctors
may have to operate, and for that they will need
your permission. Andrei Vladimirovich.

Penn helped Laurel into the carriage. Both were
pale-faced and tense at the news about Holman. The
czar had insisted on dispatching the imperial physician immediately to the palace, with instructions to
await Laurel's arrival and report on her father's
condition. Penn sat very still, determined to do everything in his power to help, but uncertain if
Holman's condition had already passed the point of
no return. He held Laurel's hand and did his best to
sound reassuring.

"I cannot say anything to comfort you, except that
I am here and I shall do everything I can to help you
in the trying days ahead. I shall stay at your side,
even if it means moving you from the palace to the
Europa Hotel. We must stand no jealous nonsense
from the grand duke."

Laurel's eyes filled with tears as she sat looking out
at the brown fields of Russia, her vision blurring so
the workers in the cotton smocks and little children
by the roadside became out-of-focus figures in the
shimmering heat of midday. She was thinking how
hard her father had worked all his life and how
success had come very late to him. She recalled his
thrill at making money at last from his painting. Of
late he had even talked of building an extension to

the house in Vermont, so she and Penn could bring their children for summer holidays. Laurel thought wistfully of the beach parties and the sailing that were popular on the coast of New England and how her children would someday love running wild in the woods of Vermont and adventuring in their grandfather's studio, with its trunks of costumes, faded sepia photographs, and old paintings. Now her father might die far away from home. She gripped Penn's hand for comfort and sat in silence all the way back to the city.

A troop of Chevaliers Gardes on magnificent chestnut horses rode by as the carriage paused to make the turn into the forecourt of the Vladimir Palace. Penn saw that Andrei was waiting for them at the door, his face stern, his body full of tension. For a moment he wondered if the grand duke would refuse him entry to the property. He decided to take it for granted that under the circumstances even Andrei would play the gentleman.

Stepping from the carriage, Laurel looked up into Andrei's stern face, her eyes full of questions. "How's my father? Is he any worse than earlier in the day?"

"He is gravely ill and cannot be moved. May I have a word with you, Lord Allandale?"

"Of course, sir. Laurel, forgive us for a few moments. Perhaps you should go and see your father."

"Lotty is with him. She has been here for four days and will not return to her shop. Every woman in St. Petersburg is begging for delivery of new clothes, but Lotty has a mind to cure Mr. Holman by willpower alone."

Penn thought wistfully of Lotty, with her steely determination and endearing admiration for the painter. Then he turned to the grand duke and inquired what it was he wanted. He was surprised by Andrei's reply.

"We have had our differences, Lord Allandale, because we are both in love with Laurel. For the moment, however, these must be put aside. I need your help most urgently."

"I am at your service, sir."

"Mr. Holman is going to die if this stone does not pass, and the doctors have informed me he is too weak to undergo an operation. To be truthful, they can do no more. I have heard, however, of a woman who lives far south of the city, who makes medicines reputed to melt such stones. I would ask if you would take me there to buy some of the medicine. We should have to travel in your balloon. To go such a distance by road would take too long and we would risk getting stuck in the mud after the storms of the past few days. There is no railway line in that direction, hence my suggestion."

"I'll arrange for us to take off by noon."

"Thank you. At least we shall be able to do *something*. I cannot stand another night in this house, waiting for Mr. Holman to die."

Laurel sat at Lotty's side until six in the evening, changing the cold compresses on her father's head and giving him medicine prescribed by the doctors.

He was barely conscious and in such intense pain he could only speak in a whisper. He was determined, however, to give her a message.

"Go home with Penn if I get too sick to travel."

"Try hard to get some sleep, Poppa. Penn's here with me and he's not leaving for ages yet."

"Dear God, what a time for me to get sick."

"Now, you just quit worrying, Poppa. We'll all get by and we'll go right back to England once you're cured. Penn's not going to vanish because we're delayed."

Lotty looked her age as she sat in the same dress she had worn for four days, all the makeup washed from her face. She had been in love only twice in her life. The first time, at twenty-one, she had been passionately involved with a Russian, who had died in a duel, the cause of which she had long since forgotten. The second time, love had come on first sight of James Holman, with his pixie face, diminutive stature, and overwhelming talent. Having seen his paintings, she had admired him even more, though she had said nothing of her feelings for him. Then, one evening, as she was serving dinner to him in her apartment, Holman had confessed to having fallen in love with her. He had proposed marriage and invited her to return with him to Vermont, to the white clapboard house he so adored. Lotty had been speechless with delight. There had been many men in her life since the days of her youth, but this was the only one who had wanted to make her his wife. Holman had drawn the white house for her, together with small portraits of some of his friends. Lotty kept these drawings by her bed and each night repeated the names of Holman's friends, so she would be able to greet them in a familiar way when she arrived in America. Now, as she sat looking at the painter's ashen face and the sweat running in rivulets down his cheeks, she knew that he was weakening. He would not survive much longer if the stone did not pass. She spoke softly to Laurel, her face haunted but not yet resigned to the inevitable. "We must pray for a miracle, my dear. Come, let us kneel together and ask for God's help."

They knelt at the bedside, their hands clasped, their eyes closed, while Lotty said the prayer: "Merciful Lord, help James Holman to get better. He is such a *good* man and so very kind. How can you resist helping him to be whole again? Please, if you are there watching him suffer, hear our prayer and help him to get well."

At eight-thirty, Andrei and Penn returned with a bottle of foul-smelling green liquid. Ignoring the protests of the doctors, the two men insisted on dosing the sick man with the mixture. Then they adjourned to the dining room for the evening meal.

Lotty refused to leave Holman, but Laurel went down and sat with the two men. It was obvious that the grand duke was in an expansive mood and eager to explain what they had done.

"We went in search of this miracle woman, whose medicines cure fevers, stones, and the gout. She is an old and most frightening creature, but I believe she is wise. Lord Allandale also felt that she knew much more about the body than most Russian doctors."

Penn poured himself more wine and turned to Laurel.

"The woman is part Russian and part Chinese. Perhaps that explains her knowledge of medicines, herbs, and bodily functions."

"I hope the medicine works. We don't have much hope left if it doesn't. Poppa's weakening all the time."

"We shall know by morning. Andrei and I intend to give your father another dose at eleven tonight, one at four in the morning, and then again at eight."

"I'll stay up with him and give Lotty a break. She keeps falling asleep in the middle of a sentence. You've got to get her to sleep, Penn."

"I'll try, but she's a very obstinate woman."

Andrei rang for his manservant.

"Please take Madame Lototsky's keys and go to her shop, Stepan. Bring back some clean clothing for her, tell the maid where she is and that she will be staying here until Mr. Holman recovers."

"I will leave at once, sir."

"When you return, ask Lotty to come to my study."

"Very well, sir, though I doubt she will leave Mr. Holman."

Andrei turned to Laurel with a reassuring smile.

"Do not worry, I shall arrange for Lotty to sleep in the room adjacent to your father's. In that way she will perhaps consent to rest. I shall tell her that Mr. Holman needs her to be strong and that she must eat and sleep so she can support him during his convalescence. She is in love with him, of course, and dreams of marrying him. She simply cannot stand the thought that he may not recover."

"My father proposed marriage to Lotty a few weeks ago. I was so happy when he told me, I could have shouted hurray from the rooftops."

"I did not know that they were to be married. Now I understand Lotty's desire to stay at your father's side."

Laurel returned to Holman's room, leaving the two men to discuss their flight. Despite his intention to ignore Penn as much as possible, Andrei had been mightily impressed by the Englishman's cool head, courage, and ruthless determination to get to his destination and back before nightfall. In the midst of the seemingly deserted Russian countryside, Penn had summoned men to assist with the balloon, as if by magic. His lack of the Russian language had meant nothing, because he had such a commanding presence the peasants seemed to understand what was required without endless orders. Andrei looked at the tweed jacket Penn was wearing, with its unusual chamois patches at the elbows, cuffs, and collar. He decided to have one made just like it, and a pair of boots in the English style, too. While Penn told him about his research into aviation, Andrei became so engrossed he was shocked when his companion rose, looked at his watch, and moved to the door.

"Time for Mr. Holman's next dose of medicine. Do come and help me administer it."

"Of course, Lord Allandale. With a man as sick as Laurel's father, two pairs of hands are better than one. You will stay here as my guest until all this is over, of course."

"How very kind of you. I shall be delighted to accept your hospitality."

At nine the following morning, Holman opened his eyes and smiled at Lotty.

"I'm hungry. Could you find me something to eat?"

Lotty burst into tears and wailed for all the tension of the past week. It was some time before she could reply. "I'll go at once and tell them what you want."

"Stop your crying, too. The fever's gone and I feel the need to pass a whole lake of water. I reckon this stone's about to lose its fight with my insides."

"Oh, my dear, this is a miracle."

"Sure is. For a while there I thought we were in trouble."

For days the medicine was administered and Holman continued to improve. He was still weak, emaciated, and given to falling asleep all the time from sheer exhaustion, but the stone had passed and the danger was over.

Lotty returned to her atelier and went into a phase of feverish activity. Dresses were completed and dispatched, new orders taken, but none for after the summer's end. At that time, Lotty knew she would be leaving Russia forever. Looking down at the ring on her finger, she smiled sentimentally. Even the ring Holman had chosen for her was original, an eye of sapphire blue stones, just like her own, surrounded by diamonds, pearls, and emeralds, so its effect was almost hypnotic. He had told her the eye was guarding her on his behalf whenever they were apart and would report to him if she misbehaved. Enchanted by the idea, the man, and the fact that she was about to marry at last, Lotty sang in her bedroom and in her bath, living for the evenings, when she would return to the Vladimir Palace to spend the night caring for the man she loved.

Laurel arrived at the Europa Hotel in a dress of cornflower-blue lace. She was wearing the sapphire earrings Andrei had bought her to match the outfit and was so happy, her radiant face had even caused comment in the streets of St. Petersburg. There, hardened soldiers, cynical society women, and men with an eye for a beautiful lady had greeted her and congratulated her on her father's miraculous recovery. This had made Laurel realize for the first time how very long she had been away from home and how many people she knew in Russia. Andrei had been right in a way, when he said that Russia was her second home.

On seeing Penn, Laurel ran into his arms and kissed him joyfully.

"Poppa got up today and walked a few steps with me and Lotty to support him."

"He'll be fighting fit again in a month or two."

Laurel's face clouded when she thought of the weeks she and Penn would be apart.

"I do *so* want to come back to England with you."

"I know you do, and I dream of nothing else. This is a cruel blow of fate to us, Laurel. I had not expected that we should ever be separated again. However, Mr. Holman cannot just be abandoned, not even to Lotty's tender care."

"I know. If anything happened to him in a strange land when I was far away, I'd never forgive myself."

"Dearest Laurel, I love you with all my heart. You know I don't want to leave you to return to England, but I have no option. I cannot leave the legal problems there any longer."

"Have you booked your tickets?"

"I leave the day after tomorrow at eleven in the morning."

Tears began to fall down her cheeks and Laurel looked so distressed he went to her side and held her to his heart.

"Tonight I'm taking you to the island of Kammeni Ostrov to see the Gypsies. We'll have a memorable evening and dance til dawn. Then we'll go to Lotty's dacha and sleep till noon together."

"I keep wondering how I'll be able to get through a single day without you, Penn. We've hardly been apart since you arrived in Russia."

"Just remember all the while that I'm thinking of you, loving you, and waiting for you to come to England for our wedding. I'm yours now and forever. Don't ever allow doubt to enter your mind."

The White Nights of St. Petersburg had arrived, when it was light from dawn till midnight. Then a luminous blue light appeared that lasted until sunrise. These legendary evenings were scented with the heady perfume of rose, pansy, and heliotrope that lulled the senses into sheer delight. Until foreigners had experienced the White Nights, they had no idea how powerful was the spell cast by this romantic, climatic phenomenon, no sense of how their lives could change when night became day for a few short weeks. In the magic days of summer, all inhibitions were lost, new lovers were taken and old ones discarded. Men went in search of excitement and adventure, and wives, normally staid and self-satisfied, felt the urge to visit the country, to listen to the rousing Gypsy music that inflamed them as nothing else could.

On the island of Kammeni Ostrov, the rich were in residence for the summer, in weekend houses painted sugar pink and buttercup yellow, pistachio and palest lilac. Parties were held most evenings, and on fine nights, from ten P.M. the Gypsies entertained in a clearing by the sea. These were the Gypsies who had always had a hold over the emotions of the noblemen and women of the Russian court. Their tantalizing bodies, haunting music, astonishing dancing, and melancholy songs contained all the contrasts of the Russian character, and as they performed in the cedar-bordered clearing, every man and woman watching them felt a tug at the soul, a climaxing of emotion that nothing could equal.

Laurel saw a fire twenty feet high and burning brightly, turning the blue dusk, with its solitary star, into the setting for a painting. The Gypsies were dressed in red and gold, orange and silver, the women in backless dresses that revealed almost all their lean, hard torsos and luscious breasts. The men were wearing thick sashes over loose satin trousers and wide-sleeved blouses. The performances seemed spontaneous, though Laurel had no idea if they really were.

First, there was a rousing chorus from the entire Gypsy assembly, then individual acts by a group of children, their scarlet costumes decorated with tiny silver bells. A male singer with a lyric-tenor voice followed, then two dancers, whose lithe brown legs and full, switching skirts excited every man in the audience.

The pièce de résistance was Mounija, the principal performer, who danced a fiery solo representing the marriage ritual of a Tatar princess of Gypsy legend. The performance was so erotic, so deliberately designed to entice, that not a sound came from the audience as they sat on the ground by the fire, hypnotized by the power of the Gypsy's personality, the forbidding command of her almond-eyed face. Mounija's body bent like the branches of a stripling. Her legs were exposed to the thigh by the split in her skirt. As the climax of the dance came, she threw herself on the ground, her legs spread-eagled, a violent throbbing of passion running through her body, as if she were transfixed by a phantom lover. The music died, the dancer relaxed and was still, and the clearing echoed to loud applause, cheers, and cries for an encore. Some of the men forgot themselves and kissed their wives or lovers with passionate abandon. One couple hurried away into the woods, unable to contain their desire a moment longer.

Penn put his arm around Laurel and spoke spontaneously in admiration of the spectacle. "Gad, what a sight, what an atmosphere! If this continues, we shall have to adjourn to Lotty's place long before we planned."

"Mounija was beautiful. I wish I looked just like her."

"Don't be ridiculous! You look beautiful even in the sunlight of midday. That lady is certainly alluring, but she is long past the age when she can face the daylight."

"I never realized I could be jealous of you, Penn. I think I love you far too much."

He looked into the amber eyes and kissed the tip of Laurel's nose, enchanted by her innocent envy of the Gypsy.

"Always love me too much and always be a little jealous. I want you to love me so single-mindedly you'll never have room to love anyone else."

Large chunks of roast suckling pigs were served from the tips of silver sabers, along with baked potatoes full of sour cream and goblets of heady red wine. Then second helpings of everything were brought, with more wine and brandy for the men. The company grew merry and some of the stiff society ladies got up and danced with the Gypsies to the tune of a battery of guitars. Laughter greeted their efforts and those of the men to imitate the movements of the exquisite Mounija.

When the meal was over and the aristocrats exhausted from their efforts in the dance, a new band appeared and played a recital of guitar and balalaika music. Songs as old as time were sung and the performance ended with a medley of all the most popular Gypsy melodies, with choruses for the audience to sing. For some this was a touching moment and tears fell as they remembered the happy days of their youth. For others it was a moment of joy and emotion and they sang with abandon the lilting melodies they had known since the beginning of time.

Laurel was touched to hear the sound of Russian voices raised in a fervent outburst of sentiment, happiness, and spiritual abandon. Nowhere else in the world had she heard folk sing as they sang in this land of contrasts. Nowhere else in the world were total strangers willing to display their souls as they did here on the island near St. Petersburg. She and Penn rose and took their leave with regret, pausing when a Gypsy child ran after them and proffered a silver charm for luck. Laurel handed the child a coin and then gave the charm to Penn.

"I hope this brings us luck and the happiest possible future together."

"It will remind us of a wonderful evening in Russia."

"I just want it to bring us together again so quickly we can forget we've ever been apart."

They walked together along a pebble beach in the pale light of dawn. Here and there, Penn bent to pick up an interesting stone and Laurel held them for him, a tiny pure white pebble shot with silver, a pale pink stone worn smooth by the waves, a shell that reflected the colors of an opal in the sunlight of morning, a heart-shaped stone that he handed over to her with a wistful shake of his head.

"I wish my heart were as hard as that stone, but it isn't, and I'm already wondering how I shall manage to live without you till your return to England."

"I'll be there by the fall, maybe sooner if Poppa recovers his strength fast."

"That's three months away. Dear God, I shall have built another set of outbuildings and extended the garden and created a new paddock by then. My only comfort when you're far away is in building something splendid for your return."

Laurel paused and kissed him tenderly on the mouth. Then they walked on together, hand in hand.

"That's Lotty's villa on the headland, Penn. She told me it was right on the point. Isn't it pretty?"

"Charming, though pale blue walls and dark green shutters are Mediterranean, not Russian in style."

"She built it for her old age, but now she's in the process of selling it to Count Korolenko, who's been looking for something on this island for many months."

"Come, let's go and see what kind of house Lotty chooses for her leisure."

The house was simply furnished in the finest taste, with solid mahogany furniture in the old Russian style. There were comfortable sofas in restful colors of beige, stone, rose, and ivory. Outside the windows, the woods were full of cooing pigeons, and a narrow path led to the vegetable garden tended by a venerable retainer.

Laurel and Penn went to a bedroom in the turret of the property and found the morning sun streaming through the rose silk curtains. So tired were they, that they undressed, embraced, and fell into bed, holding each other close for a few moments until sleep claimed them.

Outside in the bay, a foghorn hooted as the mist came down and visibility shrank to a few yards. In the garden, a maid was picking flowers for the lunch table and the cook was chopping, pounding, and whipping the ingredients for a special meal and winking knowingly at her husband as they gossiped about the new arrivals.

"If I know anything, they'll appear for dinner, not lunch. They've been up all night with the Gypsies."

"They're a good-looking couple and very young."

"I'll make something fortifying for dinner so they have plenty of strength for a night of love."

"You're a fool, Anna, a romantic fool."

"So's Madame Lototsky. She told me to make everything perfect for these two, as they're going to be separated before long and they're fearfully upset about it. They're in love, that's certain. He never took his eyes off her for a moment. I always thought Englishmen were cold, but I know now I was wrong."

Laurel woke at three on a lazy summer's afternoon. The mist had cleared from the bay and the view from the window was sensational, all the way to the distant coast of Finland. In the sunlight, the sea shimmered like a million sapphires and the sky was cloudless azure blue. There were dozens of small white yachts racing in the bay, and below, on the beach, a group of children were watching the proceedings and calling to their favorite captains. In the garden, the old servant was asleep under the plum tree and the house was silent, because the staff were taking a nap. The only sounds were those of distant fishermen singing traditional songs of the sea and the cry of a curlew circling overhead.

Laurel went from the window to the bed and sat looking at Penn as he slept. How handsome he was, how very calm, peaceful, and in control of his life. The fair hair and suntanned skin lit by the rose light of the curtains made him resemble a Greek god sleeping in the sunlight of Mount Olympus. Laurel kissed his toes, then his calves, his knees, his stomach, his chest, smiling when he stirred and reached out for her.

"I love you, Penn. Why don't you wake and say good morning."

"Good morning. Come to bed."

She lay at his side, continuing to kiss his cheeks and his ears and his neck, savoring the scent of his body with its indefinable masculine smell that reminded her of haymaking days in the countryside. Seeing that he was still half-asleep, she began to whisper mischievously to him.

"In my imagination you look just like a Greek god sleeping on Mount Olympus. I want you so much and I'll want you every hour of every day when you're gone. I'll think of nothing but the lovely times we've had together these past few months and of being with you again at Wentworth Saye. You're my life, Penn, and don't you ever forget it."

The blue eyes opened and he sat up and looked into her face, sensing the melancholy and apprehension that were edging into her mind as the moment of parting approached.

"Greek god indeed! It's a fascinating thought, but I'm an Englishman and I dream only of you. If it helps you accept your own distress, I shall be plagued by this separation more than you'll ever know, because I had not expected it. I had vowed I should never be separated from you again, and I shan't, once we're wed. But today we're together and we mustn't allow the thought of parting to spoil everything."

"Kiss me, Penn, make me forget what I want to forget and think only of you."

They kissed lightly, playfully, slipping easily toward that state of desire from which there was no return. When Laurel tried to break away from him to catch her breath, Penn pursued her around the bed, ever the masterful lover.

"Don't try to escape me. This is no time for titillation."

"Your kisses make me lose my breath!"

"You're supposed to lose your breath. Your heart's supposed to pound. Listen to mine, it's beating only for you."

Inflamed by his words, she cried out as Penn proceeded to kiss her, lingering over her nipples and the mound of soft amber hair that covered the center of desire. When he had kissed her from head to toe, she felt herself lifted and lowered gently onto the hardness of his body. Suddenly, white-hot passion flared and they were both lost in the undulating, languorous movements of love, each one's mind invaded by longing so forceful it wiped out everything but the sensuousness of the moment. Laurel felt sweat running down her back as Penn continued to provoke her, his hands on her breasts, his body inside hers forcing her to that explosion of passion, when a thousand stars would fill her mind.

When the moment came, her very core seemed to contract with the exquisite pain and pleasure of the orgasm that left her weak and silent at his side, her eyes closed, a faint smile on her lips.

After love, they lay together idly debating what to do with their day. Penn had worked it all out to the letter, though he cheerfully admitted that plans often had to be changed or abandoned when two people were in love.

"In a moment I'll ring for breakfast. I'm as hungry as a hunter and I'm sure you are too. Then I'll take you fishing at that little lake we saw a mile inland from here. If we're lucky, we might catch some trout to eat for dinner. Then we'll return to the house, have a leisurely meal, and go walking by the pier. You can plan the evening. We can either stay in the house or go and have champagne in one of those picturesque bars by the quayside, where they play the balalaika. I've taken a fancy to those instruments. I think I'll buy one and get Hugo to learn to play it. He's marvelously musical, unlike me."

"Let's decide what to do later."

"That's what I like to hear. It means we'll come to bed early and make love till dawn."

The lake was picturesque, remote, and overhung with weeping-willow branches, their long, light green fronds providing a cool cover of shade. As Penn and Laurel sat in the rented craft, drinking ice-cold white wine and eating the picnic made for them by Lotty's cook, they were impressed by the peace and quiet, the privacy of this tiny paradise. Now and then a dragonfly descended, its blue-green wings shining in the sunlight. There were trout, carp, and perch to be fished and pink-tipped water lilies growing around the periphery of the water. No houses had been built in the immediate vicinity, so it was the most secret and private of places in which to be together, and both were so content in their intimacy, they felt able to sit together in silence, enjoying the moment.

After an hour, they secured the fishing lines and went below to a tiny cabin painted in the peasant fashion with flowers of the field and hedgerow. The owner's wife had put meadowsweet and old-fashioned pink roses in earthenware pots to scent the cabin with the fragrance of the wild. The bunk was narrow and covered in a counterpane of hand-embroidered white linen. The floorboards were stenciled with flowers and vine leaves, making the room a miracle of color and ingenuity.

Laurel gazed about her, touched by the simplicity of this white-painted craft. After the palaces and mansions of the city, the bejeweled rooms and gilded boiseries of the grand duke's lavish home, this simple boat with its painted interior reminded her of the real world beyond the gilded domes of St. Petersburg. She realized with something of a shock, as she sat drinking wine with Penn, just how homesick she was, not only for the little house in Vermont and the beautiful country mansion in Oxfordshire, but also for the reassurance of reality. Someday, she knew, the months spent in Russia would seem like a dream, a mirage of the mind, to be assimilated and then forgotten, because they had nothing to do with the real life she wanted to lead in the future.

Penn finished the last of the wine and stood looking down at her.

"Let's go for a swim."

"I'd love that. It's so hot I feel at least a hundred years old."

"Let me help you with those buttons. You know, you're the most exciting woman to undress. I swear you only wear so many buttons, ties, and ribbons to send a man wild."

Laurel kissed him eagerly, her face full of happiness.

"I only want to send *you* wild with desire. If I can do that, I'll be happy."

Penn dropped the gray-and-pink skirt to the ground and threw the white blouse after it. Then he untied the ribbons of her camisole and put it on the chair with the drawers and Laurel's shoes. Unable to resist her nakedness, he traced a finger from her neck to her waist, circling the breasts and smiling as the nipples hardened under his touch. Taking off his own shirt and the riding trousers he had worn for the walk from Lotty's dacha, he held out his hand to Laurel and they ran upstairs to the sunlit deck.

"I'll race you to the jetty and back."

They dived overboard and swam side by side through the cool, clear water. Green fernlike plants tickled their bodies and fish passed under them, circling curiously as they trod water, laughing delightedly on reaching the landing stage. Forgetting that they had agreed to have a race, they swam back the long way around the periphery of the lake, keeping to the shade of the trees. The water was limpid, the atmosphere sybaritic, and as they neared the boat, Penn caught up with Laurel and kissed her passionately on the lips.

"Come here, nymph of the lake, I have a fancy to make love to you in twenty feet of water."

"I never drowned from passion before. Take care you don't get us trapped in the weeds."

Closing her eyes, Laurel shivered from excitement as their bodies touched and their lips met. The moment was one she would long remember, with the sun dappling through the trees, showing their naked bodies in darkness and then in light. As Penn pulled her to his side and wound his legs around her, they sank a little, and Laurel fought him, suddenly afraid of sinking below the surface. Then she felt the moment when their lips and their bodies became one and she relaxed, content to allow the water to move them where it pleased. Their cries rang out, with no one but the birds to hear. Their bodies began to thresh in a violent, throbbing duel of passion, until the violence of their longing for each other was dissipated and Penn began to kiss her ardently, telling her again and again how much he adored her.

"You're the most exciting woman in the world for me. When I'm loving you I feel at least ten feet tall."

"Kiss me again, Penn."

He held her and kissed her on the lips, tasting the familiar sweetness of her, mingled with the water of the lake.

"All my plans have gone awry, thank God. I do so hate keeping to a timetable. Do tell me what *you* want to do, Laurel."

"I just want to be with you. We'd best take the boat back, I suppose. Then we'll go back to Lotty's for a late lunch or a very early dinner. Afterward we'll wander the quayside and see the end of the race. You can take me to one of those balalaika places and we'll get tearful at the thought of parting."

"We'll do nothing of the sort. We'll dance and sing, even though we don't know the words. Then we'll go back to the dacha and watch the White Nights turning to blue. I shall love you till I'm so weak I can't contemplate returning to England. If I don't control my reluctance to go, I shall succumb to the temptation and stay here with you. Then Wentworth Saye will end in the ownership of the government instead of my family."

"That would never do. I plan to raise my children there."

"How many children?"

"I don't know, maybe two or three or four."

The blue eyes looked with great intensity into Laurel's own, making her forget the prospect of Penn's departure and think only of the moment. They had been together for one last day of loving and it had been an unforgettable one. She swam at his side back to the boat, scrambling aboard with his help and shaking her head of water, all the while complaining that her hair had become frizzy, just as it had been when she was a child.

From his place among the trees at the side of the lake, Andrei withdrew and walked slowly back to the distant dacha of his friend Gustave, which was situated on the other side of the far hill. He had had no idea that Laurel and her lover were using Lotty's house for their last few days together and had had in mind a morning's fishing, when he had come upon a scene of such intense and passionate abandon it had taken his breath away. Despite his better judgment, Andrei had stayed until the couple returned to the boat, naked but unashamed, laughing like naughty children at what they had done.

As he walked on, he was going over in his mind the memory of Laurel's naked body, the tiny waist, the long, slim legs, the full breasts with their pointed rose-pink nipples. He had never seen such a sensuous creature, nor ever would again. He had never imagined that Laurel would be so uninhibited, so vibrantly, violently sensuous that she would make love to the Englishman in broad daylight, not caring who might see their coupling. Desire beat at his temples and Andrei knew then that he must have her, whatever the consequences. He would do whatever it was necessary to do from now on in order to possess Laurel's body. He would lie and cheat, scheme and plot. He no longer cared if she loved him, and had accepted that she never would. He knew only that he must have her or go mad from the obsessive desire that he had been controlling for so long.

Unlike his entrance into St. Petersburg, Penn's departure from the Finland Station was accomplished in comparative privacy.

Laurel accompanied her lover to the train and went aboard with him to help him settle in the elegant blue-upholstered interior. Then she sat silently at his side, struggling to control the panic that was gradually filling her heart.

"I can't believe the moment's come, Penn."

Outside, the guard blew his whistle for visitors to leave.

"You know how I hate to say good-bye, my darling. Let's just say au revoir."

Tears fell when she heard this, and Laurel could only nod her reply. Penn took her in his arms and kissed her gently on the cheeks.

"I love you and will kiss you a dozen times a day in my imagination. Perhaps because we are so very close, you'll feel it on your cheek and your mouth and your neck."

"Don't say that! Parting's bad enough without your giving me reasons to think of you every hour of every day. Promise me you'll take care of yourself. Don't take any risks once the shooting season begins, and don't ride that mad horse Hugo told me about. I wish to God you weren't taking the balloon with you."

"I was going to leave it here, but I saw how rough the czar's friends were with it and I didn't want it ruined before I returned for the exhibition. Misha and I shall fly it back from the Polish border to London."

"Does that Russian know about balloons? Has he the same skill as Hugo had?"

"He's an expert, Laurel. He knows what he's doing better than I. Now, please don't worry. I shall arrive safely in England, just as I arrived safely in Russia."

A whistle was blown, the second and final summons for all visitors to leave the train. Laurel rose, went outside, and stood on the platform, looking up at Penn, who held her hand through the open window. She was touched to see his stern face and to hear his voice breaking with emotion as he wished her a last good-bye.

"Till we meet again at Wentworth Saye, my darling."

"I love you, Penn. I love you with all my heart. Godspeed and God bless you."

The train pulled out of the station, slowly at first and then with increasing speed. Laurel stood waving a silk kerchief until Penn's golden head was a mere speck on the horizon. Then, when all sign of him was gone, she sat on a bench on the platform and sobbed distractedly, not caring who was watching or what they thought of her grief. Penn had left her and gone back to England. Weeks of separation lay ahead. For the hundredth time she cursed the fact that she had ever come to Russia. Then, remembering his face at the moment of their farewell, she cried again for all the anguish the parting had caused.

Penn had given her a gift before leaving the Vladimir Palace, and Laurel struggled, after a while, to unwrap it. She found inside the tissue-wrapped package a locket, obviously a very old locket, which had on one side a photograph of Penn and on the other a miniature of Wentworth Saye. With the gift he had written a note: *My dearest Laurel, This is the locket my grandfather gave to the woman he loved above all else in the world. I give it to you in the hope that it will remind you of me and that you'll wear it for our wedding day. Pray that the time will pass quickly and we'll find it easy to forget this horrible separation. I adore and love you with all my heart. I always have and shall always. I kiss you and will dream of being with you again very soon. Penn.*

Laurel rose unsteadily and put on the locket, her eyes going over and over the contents of the note. Somehow, wearing the locket that had belonged to Penn's beautiful and much-loved grandmother made her happy and she did her best to conceal her grief. Slowly, still stunned from the agony of their parting, she moved back along the platform to the spot where she knew the coachman was waiting to take her back to the Vladimir Palace. It was then she saw Andrei standing in the center of the station concourse. When he saw her tearstained face, he hurried to her side.

"I hope you are not angry that I came to collect you, Laurel. I thought you might be upset and did not wish you to be alone."

"I'm glad you're here. I'm just so tired and upset I don't feel sure of anything, not even getting back to the palace."

Andrei's eyes gleamed as he lifted her into the carriage.

"Come, I shall cover you with a blanket. Your hands are cold and you are looking unwell. Dearest Laurel, you must rest for a few days and allow me to take your mind off your sadness. I know you do not love me and that your mind is full of Lord Allandale, but at least you can permit yourself the luxury of using my affection for you to keep you from becoming morbid about the parting."

"You're very generous and I truly appreciate it, Andrei."

"I am yours to command, as I told you a long time ago."

They rode through the city, each thinking his own thoughts. Laurel was reliving the moment of Penn's departure and going over all the happy days they had spent together in St. Petersburg and the surrounding countryside. Andrei was intent on following the plan he had made. He must take care and exercise the greatest self-control. If he was clever and lucky, Laurel would be his before long. He looked up at the sun as it shone down on the majestic buildings of his city. He was feeling happier than he had felt since the day of Penn's arrival. At last Lord Allandale was far, far away. It was *his* turn now to gamble for the lady.

8

Laurel had been working all afternoon on the background of one of her father's portraits and was cleaning her hands with spirit to remove the paint. Of late, to keep her mind off thoughts of Penn, she had worked very long hours. Holman was painting again, but could no longer work the number of hours each day he had before his illness, and both had agreed that he should take on no further commissions. He was also working more slowly than previously and had to rest frequently, so estimated that the work outstanding would take until the end of August to complete. The return to England had been tentatively arranged between father and daughter for September, and each morning Laurel marked another day off the calendar in her dressing room. Like a sleepwalker, she was living life on a superficial level, her eyes on the distant and perfect prospect of being with her lover again.

Andrei was in his carriage approaching the Shuvalov Palace when he saw a friend he had not seen for months alighting from a droshky nearby. He called out a greeting. "My dear Josef, how are you. It is so long since you were in St. Petersburg."

"Andrei! Come and join me for a drink."

Ordering his coachman to stop, Andrei joined his friend in the lounge of the nearby National Hotel, with its faded tapestries and frescoes of Russian history from the days of Genghis Khan. They ordered coffee, brandy, and pirozkhi and Andrei listened as Josef talked of the trip from which he was returning.

"I went first to Finland to see Mama. Then I traveled to England in the vilest ship anyone ever had the misfortune to encounter. I went all over the country, from Scotland to Land's End, and enjoyed it immensely, despite the weather. Then I visited Paris and spent two months suffering at the hands of a most beautiful creature. I tell you, Andrei, her thighs were like vises and it was all I could do to concentrate on anything when she was near. I escaped from her eventually on the train to Berlin and then came here on the express direct to St. Petersburg. I arrived half an hour ago."

Andrei saw some newspapers sticking out of his friend's valise.

"Have you finished with the newspapers, Josef? I would enjoy having some real news."

"You can take them. I read them from cover to cover during the journey and have no further use for them. There is a photograph of my French lady friend, Mademoiselle Lalage, on page four of *Le Matin*. You will be green with envy when you see her."

"Indeed I shall not. I am in love and living like a monk."

"Who is it this time?"

"Her name is Laurel Holman and she is American. Her father is a famous portrait painter and they came to St. Petersburg at my invitation so he could accept commissions from my family."

"And why are you living like a monk?"

"It's a long story and I won't bore you with it. Let us say simply that Miss Holman is not the kind of woman who wears red for any man."

"Poor fellow, to be in love with a virgin must be hell. They are so dreadfully dull, or had you not noticed?"

"Laurel is as bright as a diamond and as hot as burning coals. I dream of her every night and can do nothing but desire her, even to the detriment of my health."

"My dear Andrei, this doesn't sound like you. You're obviously in need of an evening out with the Gypsies of Yelagin. Don't waste your time on foreigners. Most of them are schemers and the rest are frigid due to a very strict upbringing."

"Laurel is neither of those things. She is the perfect woman. Unfortunately, she is in love with another man."

"Really! Have you quarreled over her?"

"We fought a duel months ago and I lost. Lord Allandale is one of the finest shots in England, a fact of which I was unfortunately unaware at the time of challenging him. I believe he could have killed me, had he wished it. I am therefore in his debt, damn him!"

"An Englishman, eh? They're hell as rivals because one can never tell what they are thinking. They seem so cold, though according to Mademoiselle Lalage they burn pretty bright once they take off their blazers."

They drank more coffee and toasted each other's future in love, when Josef looked up at Andrei.

"What did you say that English rival of yours was called?"

"Lord Allandale. I believe his first name is Pennington, though they call him Penn. He comes from the county of Oxfordshire and is a friend of the Duke of Marlborough and indirectly related to the Romanovs."

"Hand me that paper, will you? I've been reading those newspapers for days on end and seem to find the name familiar."

Josef leafed through the papers, turning them back and forth to where the foreign news was printed. In *Le Matin* he found what he was looking for and handed it with a flourish to Andrei.

"Is that the fellow? If it is, your worries are over."

Andrei stared at a large, clear photograph of Penn and Hugo Allandale on the day they had left Paris for St. Petersburg in their balloon. The caption over the picture was clear and to the point: the Englishman, on his return to England, was still missing after his balloon had drifted off course over the sea, somewhere in the northern wasteland. Underneath the headline and the photograph, there was a more detailed account describing the circumstances of the disappearance. The two fliers had failed to keep one of the preset rendezvous arranged by Penn between Poland and London. Search parties had been sent out to no avail and the two fliers had been posted missing, presumed dead.

Andrei looked again at the photograph, remembering the day when he and Penn had gone out together in the balloon. How efficient Allandale had been, how commanding and sure of himself. Now he had come down somewhere over the vast emptiness of northern Europe and perhaps been killed. This was the chance Andrei had been waiting for, the moment when he was sure he would be able to wrench Laurel from her love for the Englishman and into the real world, his world, where she belonged. He remained for another half-hour sharing stories with his friend. Then he returned to his carriage and told the coachman to drive him immediately to the Vladimir Palace.

Laurel was in her room daydreaming about Wentworth Saye when she received a summons from Andrei to come at once to the library. She went to her dressing room, changed into a clean blouse, and made her way down to the dark, book-lined room, where she found him sitting behind the ebony desk looking fixedly at a newspaper before him. As she entered, Stepan handed her a brandy. Laurel shook her head.

"You know I never drink brandy."

"I thought you might wish one today, Miss Holman."

"I'm better without it, thanks."

Stepan turned to his master, who waved him away. He left the room at once, sick with apprehension on Laurel's behalf. The American was madly in love with the Englishman, whatever the grand duke's feelings on the subject. Now, with Lord Allandale dead, what would she do? In his heart Stepan knew that Laurel could never love Andrei, that her whole world might crumble in this calamity. He wondered if he dared inform her father and Madame Lototsky of what had happened, so they could come at once to support her. Then he shook his head. The grand duke had given orders that for the moment *he* would do all that must be done, and his word was Stepan's command. Resignedly the young man went below to the servants' quarters and sat with a melancholy face, waiting to be summoned.

Andrei looked up at Laurel and then broke the news in a quiet, firm voice. "I am afraid I have some very bad tidings for you. They concern your fiancé, Lord Allandale."

She sat facing him across the desk, her knuckles white on the arms of the chair.

"Say it quickly, whatever it is."

Andrei pushed the newspaper toward her, watching as the color drained from her face. To his surprise, Laurel did not cry out, but sat stiff-backed and rigidly controlled, her eyes on his as if hypnotized.

"Is Penn dead? For God's sake, tell me the truth, Andrei?"

"I have just met a dear friend of mine on his return from Paris. The news is that both men were found dead a few days after this article was published. Josef knew all the latest tidings, because he left Paris on the express train for St. Petersburg only two days ago."

Laurel stared at the paper, trying to grasp the hideous significance of the words. She could only think how handsome, healthy, full of love and life Penn had looked at the moment when he had stepped on the train. He could not be dead, yet Andrei had said that he was, and the newspaper report virtually corroborated that hope was gone. Like a woman in the middle of a nightmare, Laurel rose and left the room. Hastening back to her suite, she threw herself on the bed, her eyes fixed on the ceiling. Feelings of intense panic rose in waves from her stomach to her throat. Her head ached, her heart beat like a gong, and she had neither the strength nor the inclination to ring for a servant to call her father. Again and again Andrei's words rang through her mind. Penn was gone from her life! There would be no future happiness together at Wentworth Saye, no children to carry on the Allandale tradition. She turned to face the wall, and lay there unable to think or speak, nausea rising within her and despair filling her heart.

Polinka entered the room and found her mistress lying quite still on her back, her eyes fixed on the ceiling. It was almost time for dinner, yet it was obvious that Laurel had made no effort to dress. Puzzled, Polinka approached the bed and looked into the empty face. Panic filled her when she realized that her mistress was quite unaware of her presence. She shook the distracted woman's shoulder and called to rouse her. "Tell me what's wrong, ma'am. Has something bad happened? Speak to me, will you! Dear God, what's to be done? I'd best go and fetch Stepan."

Instinctively realizing that some terrible shock had sent Laurel speechless, Polinka ran down the corridor to the servants' quarters and called for Stepan to come at once. Then, seeing Holman returning to his suite from the studio, she ran to his side.

"Your daughter's ill, sir. I think she must have had a shock and now she can't speak for dread of thinking of it."

Holman went at once to Laurel's bedroom and sat at her side, taking her ice-cold hand in his own.

"Tell me what's wrong, honey. I know something awful's happened, but what is it? You just have to say something to guide me so I can help you."

Laurel lay, her face seemingly composed, hearing only the indecipherable sound of voices that seemed to be coming from a distant place. She was imagining herself in Lotty's house on Kammeni, kissing Penn's body as he lay sleeping. Then she began to relive the moment when they had first seen the Rose Pavilion and the pergolas of scented pink blossom, the lake covered with yellow water lilies and bright green frogs. Those had been the days of paradise and perfect love. Both had known in their hearts that the early meetings at Wentworth Saye and the lovemaking of the Rose Pavilion were enchanted days never to be bettered. A solitary tear fell to Laurel's cheek and was wiped away by her father.

Holman rang for a servant and instructed him to bring the grand duke at once. Then he asked Stepan to go and find the physician and insist he come to the palace without delay. Afraid and uncertain what had caused this strange malady in his daughter, Holman remained at Laurel's side, stroking her hands and trying to encourage her to come back from the place to which she had chosen to withdraw.

When Andrei appeared in the room, he looked in puzzlement at Laurel's impassive face.

"What is wrong with your daughter, Mr. Holman?"

"I'll ask you that, sir! Has Laurel had a shock of some kind? I demand to know what the hell is going on here. An hour ago she was working happily in my studio. Now she seems to be in a trance."

Andrei hesitated. He had not expected this reaction from Laurel and knew that her father would be angry with him for provoking it.

"I am afraid I am responsible for giving your daughter the shock, sir. I received this today, and with it the news that Lord Allandale has been killed, together with his Russian copilot in the balloon."

Holman leafed through the newspaper cutting, his face paling as he reached the final sentence.

"It says nothing here of Penn's being dead. Till I read that, I'll not believe it, and neither will Laurel."

"My friend Josef Valentinov informed me that it happened about two days after this report. He has just returned to St. Petersburg from Paris."

"You should have gotten me to tell my daughter the news. Penn's the most important thing in Laurel's life, always has been, always will be."

Shocked to hear this, Andrei spoke with more than his usual vehemence. "Laurel cannot love Lord Allandale forever. To do that would be to waste her life on a mere memory."

"It's her life and she'll do what she wants with it. You'd best leave us now, sir. There's no place for you in Laurel's life right now, nor will there be."

"You are mistaken, Mr. Holman. I am in love with your daughter. At least I can *try* to help her over the anguish of Lord Allandale's death."

"We'll see about that. Right now we need to rouse her if we can. Laurel can't lie here like a sleeping beauty forever."

For days the doctors came and went, giving tonics and potions to wake the patient and other concoctions to make her sleep. None, however, was able to rouse her from her stupor, and on the fourth day Holman went to Lotty's apartment and asked her to come and sit with the sick girl.

"I think Laurel's so shocked she just *can't* come back to us. She's kind of stuck in her grief and going over and over every goddamned hour she and Penn ever spent together. It's obvious that those thoughts are much happier than the ones she's faced with right now."

"She needs to cry, but perhaps she cannot or dare not let out her grief."

"Help her, Lotty. I've sat there for hours trying to call her back, but I can't do a goddamned thing. I never felt so helpless in my life."

"I'll pack a bag and come immediately after lunch. The Grand Duchess Elizabeth will have had her last fittings by that time and I can close the shop without any problem. Now, you are *not* to upset yourself, James. Lotty will take care of everything."

The czarina sat alone in her room, thinking of all her sister had told her about Penn Allandale's tragic death. Shocked and profoundly disturbed, she wrote a personal message of sympathy and sent it to Laurel's father, with another to the British ambassador that was simple but touching: *We are distressed to hear the news about Lord Allandale. Please convey our sympathy to his family in this most trying time.* When she had considered Laurel's situation further, Alexandra called the imperial physician and sent him to the Vladimir Palace to report on the young lady's condition. Then she hurried to the study, where her husband was going through his dispatch boxes, and told him all that had happened.

"Lord Allandale has been killed on his journey back to England and the shock of the news has affected Miss Holman's mind. She is bedridden at the Vladimir Palace, unable to respond to anything and unable even to recognize her own father."

"How do you know this?"

"My sister told me and she heard of it from Madame Lototsky. Lotty is going to sit with Laurel to try to help her back to reality, but they say she is most gravely ill."

"I mean, how do you know about Lord Allandale's death? There has been nothing about it in our press."

"It was reported in the Paris newspaper *Le Monde* apparently. No doubt *we* shall receive the news in six months, if ever!"

"How very dreadful. Miss Holman is so very much in love with the man. What can we do to help?"

"No one seems to be able to do anything. She seems to want to die and will eat nothing at all."

"She must be brought with us to the Crimea for the summer. At Livadia there will be nothing to remind Miss Holman of her fiancé and the weather there is so very agreeable to the recovery of invalids."

"If you agree, I shall issue a royal invitation to the Holmans. My dearest one, I am so glad you agree with me that she would be best out of St. Petersburg."

"We must do what we can for that young lady. She is a most charming and amusing person and this is her first taste of tragedy. Unlike the Romanovs, she is not inured to it and will have to learn how to adjust her life to its harsh demands."

Andrei became frantic when Laurel continued in her withdrawn condition, refusing to eat or speak and sleeping only infrequently. The cook was informed of her condition and ordered to tempt her with the finest delicacies money could buy. Smoked salmon was piled in the thinnest slices, with lemons sent from the czar's own glasshouses. Tiny blinis full of red caviar were placed before her with chickens cooked in champagne and nightingales rolled in foie gras. Laurel appeared not to see the food. If she succeeded in swallowing a mouthful of anything, she immediately vomited it, so great was the shock to her system, so intense her pain. Andrei decided it was imperative she be removed from the palace at once. In her room Laurel would surely be remembering the night when Lord Allandale had broken down the door to rescue her or the evenings they had all spent together during Holman's illness. Desperate to retrieve the beautiful creature before she died of grief or starvation, he took the unprecedented step of visiting his cousin, the czar, to ask for permission to accompany Laurel to Livadia for the summer holiday.

Nicholas looked with a certain detached curiosity at his cousin. Andrei was as pale as snow and in his usual state of agitation. No doubt he was in love with the American, inasmuch as he could ever love anyone, but the czar's mind was troubled by the wildness of the grand duke's manner and his determination to hurry the young lady away from the city, far from all familiar sights and the friends she had made since her arrival. Andrei's feverish desire for Laurel was obvious, and whenever he spoke of her, it increased. What did it mean? Why was he persisting in wooing the young woman, whose heart so obviously belonged to another man? When he saw the grand duke's hands trembling violently, the czar softened and took pity on his condition.

"You may come with us, Andrei, but you will have to stay in your house in Yalta, while Miss Holman and her father stay at Livadia with us. My wife and I do not approve of the fact that this young lady's reputation has been compromised by her association with you."

"I agree, of course, and I shall make sure Laurel is ready to leave for Yalta on the first. Let us pray a change of scene will wake her from her reverie. Anything else would be impossible to contemplate."

Laurel woke from her state of shock two days before she was due to leave for the south. Lotty was at her bedside, reading a book about America. It was after midnight on a fine summer night, the only sounds in the room a servant singing in the distant cellar and the ever-present rumble of carriage wheels on the Nevski Prospekt outside. In a whisper Laurel spoke to the woman at her bedside. "Where am I?"

"You are at the Vladimir Palace. You have been ill and unable to wake because you had a shock."

"Who are you?"

Lotty gazed into the beautiful amber eyes that seemed curiously empty of expression. Did Laurel not recognize her, or had the shock robbed her of her memory? She rose and gave the feverish girl a glass of spring water, kissing her cheek gently and stroking her hands.

"Do you not know me, my dear? I am Lotty, your very good friend."

Laurel looked from the heart-shaped face with its big blue eyes to the jet necklace and tasteful white silk blouse that was so beautifully made. Somewhere in the recesses of her mind, she knew that she had met this woman before, but a foglike barrier descended when she tried to think about it. Raising her hand to her forehead, she looked uncertainly at her companion.

"I'm sorry, I don't seem to recall you. I feel so strange and weak, and when I try to think hard, I can't. What's wrong with me?"

Laurel tried to get out of bed, but sat down with a start on the chair.

"I'm dizzy. Have I been suffering from a fever?"

"You have not eaten for almost two weeks and you would drink only water."

Holman entered the room and stood in the shadows, watching the daughter he loved as she sat on the edge of the bed. Laurel's face was ashen, with dark blue shadows under the eyes. She had lost an enormous amount of weight and was barely able to stand. As he listened to the two women talking, Holman realized that she had also lost her memory and was now in that curious limbo where sadness and happiness mean nothing, because reality has slipped away. He moved toward her and held her in his arms.

"You're awake, honey. I'm so pleased you're improving at last."

She recoiled, her eyes wide with fear. Holman hastened to reassure her. "I'm your father and I'm here with Lotty to look after you. Tomorrow we're all going to the south for a holiday, so you can get well again. We'll be staying at the czar's house in Yalta and they tell me it's just great there. The sun will shine and there'll be beautiful houses and yachts and beaches and lots of friends to care for you. You'll be yourself again in no time at all, you just see if you're not."

Lotty motioned for the servant to put a tray on Laurel's bed. Then she fed the patient with consommé and chicken breasts hastily ordered from the kitchen. Within minutes of eating, Laurel fell into a deep sleep. Lotty put the tray on the table and turned to Holman as he sat staring down at his daughter, tears of anguish falling down his cheeks.

"Try not to upset yourself too much, James. She will return to her normal self someday, when her body and her mind are ready to accept the shock of Penn's death. At least she has eaten something, and at Livadia I am sure she will grow strong again. We will have to do everything we can to reassure her, though. Laurel is going to need all the confidence we can give."

That night Andrei ran upstairs and entered the darkened room where Laurel was sleeping. He had been told after midnight that she had awakened during his absence from the house and that she had eaten some food. He also knew that at this moment Laurel remembered nothing of the past. He looked down at her, holding the candelabrum over her as she slept. In losing her memory, she would remember nothing of his rival, Lord Allandale. This was such a golden piece of luck that Andrei was intoxicated by joy. He began to make plans for their stay in Yalta. He would overwhelm Laurel with gifts and affection, and on the clean slate of her mind imprint his own image. If she recovered her memory at some time in the future, it would be too late. She would be his by then and he would never let her go. He leaned over the bed and kissed her forehead. Then, like a phantom of the night, he swept from the room, his sable dressing gown rustling behind him on the ground.

The area around Livadia was more Mediterranean than Russian in its vegetation, the dark good looks of the people, and their extravert way of speaking. Palm trees lined the streets, their widespread branches outlined against a deep blue sky. Roses, lilac, and oleander bloomed wild in the hedgerows, and everywhere there were tiny cottages painted pink, white, and yellow, contrasting piquantly with the legendary palaces of Yalta.

The Southern Palaces were the fantasy homes of rich aristocrats from St. Petersburg, Kiev, and Moscow. Most, like Livadia, were white, square, and pillared in the neoclassical style. Others were so astounding they defied description. Count Orlov's house was a copy of the summer residence of the Mongol ruler Genghis Khan, with a shimmering green-tiled roof, Chinese curved ends to the terrace, and a staff of Orientals said to perform sword dances after dinner. There were houses in the Chinese, Turkish, and Japanese styles, and one with walls of Persian stained glass that looked like a kaleidoscope when lit by thousands of candles for evening fetes. In that house the guests were required to wear Oriental dress, to indulge their host's desire to be sultan of all he surveyed. It was rumored that the man kept a harem of blond Circassian beauties to complete the fantasy during his summer visits to the area.

Into this exotic atmosphere the royal party arrived with their two hundred trunks of luggage. These were carried from the train with countless pantechnicons of bedding, paintings, and personal items beloved by the czarina. Porters and palace retainers ran to arrange the transfer of this mammoth mound of baggage. Then the imperial party walked regally along the platform and into a line of carnation-bedecked horse-drawn carriages for the journey to Livadia.

The streets of Yalta with their picturesque houses were as unlike those of St. Petersburg as a parrot was to a lark. On the coast road ahead was the magnificent white-painted palace of the czar, its walls gleaming in the sunlight of midday. The air was heavy with the scent of roses and jasmine, and local people stood waving a greeting at the roadside. The czar's daughters chattered excitedly, because this was their favorite home, far away from the gray streets around the

Winter Palace, where the little girls knew their mama was bitterly unhappy.

Laurel went to the carriage set aside for her, Andrei, and her father. The beauty of the surrounding countryside had impressed her and she was feeling more relaxed than she had felt since coming out of her state of shock. Andrei kept pointing out things of interest, obviously pleased when she reacted favorably to his superior knowledge.

"That is the old royal yacht, which is moored here for most of the year. The one next to it belongs to the Grand Duke Serge, and over there, behind the wall of rhododendron, in his home. Adjacent to it is the mansion belonging to my friend Prince Mdvani. It is painted claret red and covered from roof to terrace with blue flowering plumbago. Some consider it the very prettiest house in Yalta."

"I should like to see it someday."

"You shall, my dear Laurel. We will have lunch with the family within the week, I promise. And now we are almost at Livadia. You and your father will stay here as the czar's personal guests. I shall be at my house overlooking the harbor. I invite you there for lunch whenever it would please you."

Laurel looked into Andrei's eyes, obviously troubled that he would not be staying in the same place as she and her father. She did not notice the gleam of satisfaction her dependence gave him, the flush of triumph her need brought to his cheeks. She was too busy gazing at the white mansion, with its terrace full of oak tubs of flowering orange trees, where two hundred staff were lined up to greet the royal family. On the lawn, an orchestra was playing favorite tunes of the day. When she heard the musicians, something tugged at Laurel's heart and a solitary tear fell down her cheek. Suddenly the happiness of the moment vanished and the gray phantoms of her mind returned to frighten her. She shivered, conscious of the feeling that she was about to remember something that had been banished like a leper from her consciousness. She closed her eyes, praying for the strength to overcome whatever it was that had so disturbed her sanity.

The following morning, Laurel woke to the sound of birdsong. Over the windowsill of her room, tendrils of Indian convulvulus were creeping, their purple bells and shiny green leaves a picture of beauty that would last only for one day. Then they would die, spiraled and tightly shut like the emotions she was hiding, even from herself. She rose, walked to the window, and looked down at the lawns and the surrounding land.

On the terrace, Alexandra and her children were eating breakfast and laughing delightedly at a family joke. In the garden, Nicholas was inspecting a patch of new woodland planted since his last visit. Laurel's attention was caught by the sight of a flower-bedecked carriage that appeared at the far end of the drive, its leather upholstery almost obscured by a lavish trimming of tiny pink daisies. The driver was Andrei, and as he passed her window, he called up to her, "Get dressed and come and have breakfast with me at my house."

Laurel wandered absentmindedly to the dressing room and put on the first outfit that came to hand. She did not brush her hair and look at her reflection in the mirror. Since arriving in the south of Russia, she had been conscious of a curious compulsion to return to St. Petersburg that preoccupied her and was inexplicable, because she liked Yalta and was impressed by the kindness of the staff and the other guests. Still, something within her told her that she should be in the city, and she paused for a moment before leaving her room, to wonder why it was that when she had been in St. Petersburg she had wanted to run away. Now that she was far away, she wanted to return. Was she going mad? People kept appearing, who expected her to recognize them, but she recognized no one at all. The only thing that kept haunting her mind was a tune that she could not even hum from start to finish. Something told her the tune was important, because it kept entering her mind in tantalizing phrases. Laurel knew it was connected with some happy event or events that must be recalled, but she could do nothing to hasten the return of memory.

Impatient with herself for her condition, Laurel ran down to the terrace to join Andrei. It was a beautiful, sunny day and her father had said she must enjoy this holiday and not try to force memory to come back. Afraid lest she stay forever in ignorance of the past, Laurel decided to obey him and to avoid the thoughts that disturbed, the brief flashes of an elusive face that haunted her very soul. In that way, perhaps, her mind would heal itself and she would return to the real world she had lost.

On reaching the driveway, she greeted Andrei with a smile. Perhaps if she put on a brave face she would suddenly become normal again. Ever hopeful that her condition would change, Laurel stepped into the carriage and was driven away.

"Have we far to go to your house, Andrei?"

"About three versts from Livadia along the most beautiful and scenic road. You will see the property long before we reach it, because it is perched on the edge of a cliff."

"Don't you get scared it might fall in the water? I'm scared of everything right now."

"We Russians believe in fate. If the house is meant to fall in the water, it surely will, and I with it. If not, I have nothing about which to worry."

The house was unusual and Laurel felt at ease there at once. It had been built by a female ancestor who longed for the wooden farmhouse where she had spent her youth. The exterior was boarded in silver birch, the garden full of scented flowers in shades of lilac and white. There were only five rooms and a terrace that clung to the precipitous cliff overlooking the bay. Outside the dining room there was a paved area overhung with honeysuckle and occupied for the most part by the cook's three cats. Laurel walked to and fro, taking in every detail of the scene.

"The views from up here are magnificent, Andrei.

I compliment you on your taste in choosing such a dramatic site."

The grand duke glowed with pride. Already Laurel's attitude to him had changed and he was ecstatic to think that she would soon be his.

"It was not I who chose it. I have only improved the property after it was left to me."

He watched as Laurel returned to sip her breakfast coffee and to eat some of the fresh white bread he had ordered for her enjoyment. She was looking better, but remained very thin and drawn. Her habit of keeping a certain distance between them was also unchanged, though she was pleasant and keen to hear his stories of the past. Now, though, her moods altered without warning, and often Andrei knew something had struck a chord in her troubled mind. He ignored these moments, diverting her attention as best he could, ever fearful that she might remember that which he wanted her to forget.

"Look over there, toward the horizon. Did you ever see such a sight, Laurel? That is the czar's new yacht sailing toward the harbor, with an escort from the Russian Navy. It is one of the very finest ships in the world, and so large even I shall get lost below-decks."

Laurel gazed at the white ship as it steamed slowly into port with its accompanying destroyers, their flags flying to honor the arrival of the sovereign. She was about to turn to Andrei, when she saw a tall blond Russian walking along the quayside toward the harbormaster's office. Her eyes settled on him and she turned very pale.

"Do I know that man, Andrei?"

He looked over the parapet, frowning, because from the back the young man was the image of Penn Allandale. With a confidence he did not feel, Andrei shook his head.

"He is a sailor who works for one of my friends. You have never met him."

"I was scared, because he seemed familiar. Sometimes I think folk are familiar that I never met before, and yet I don't recognize my own father. I do so hope I'm going to be better soon."

"Of course you are. I shall personally see that you are cured."

Laurel watched as a servant hurried to pour more coffee at Andrei's command. Her heart was beating very fast and she knew that something had stirred in her mind. Her deliberations were interrupted, however, when Andrei rose and held out his hand to her.

"I will show you the interior of my home. Then we shall go to see the countryside around Yalta, which is most beautiful. I wish to take you today to the house you wanted to visit, the red one with the blue flowers growing all over the facade. We have been invited to lunch there and will be eating some turkeys from my friend Ivan Nitichenko's farm. He plans to change the eating habits of our entire country, though I fear Russians will always prefer ducks and geese to his elegant white birds."

"Isn't the czar expecting me for lunch today? He

said something about my joining his friends for the meal."

"I have excused you for this one day. Everything has been arranged, Laurel. Relax and let us enjoy each other's company."

For many days Laurel led the quiet life, visiting the town with her father, buying pretty souvenirs in the market, and adventuring around the grounds of Livadia. Once, she purchased a fourteenth-century cross of gilded satinwood, its painted images long faded by time. When asked what she intended to do with such a large and ancient relic, she replied that it was to go in the hallway of her home. On being questioned more closely, she became tearful and could not remember where her home was or what it looked like.

Realizing that she was still very tense, Andrei took Laurel out one morning and bought her a magnificent shawl from a Bukhara merchant. It was made of heavy woven silk in many shades of cream. Thrilled by the gift, she sat on the terrace outside her bedroom, looking closely at the interwoven designs in their subtle, barely contrasting colors. One of the figures was a knight in shining armor, his back very straight as he sat his horse, ready to charge into battle. An image flashed into her mind, of a man on a white horse, his back very straight as he sat looking down at her. But where had she met him? And why could she still not remember his face?

Andrei had been playing tennis with the czar, who had been called away to receive an imperial messenger. Left alone on the court, Andrei put down his racket and sat on a wooden bench, looking up at the terrace where Laurel was sitting on her white iron chair, gazing into space. They had been in Yalta for almost three weeks and she was becoming more preoccupied and withdrawn. Restless, bored by the warm weather, the domestic atmosphere, and the endless evenings of charades, chess, and music, Andrei had decided to take Laurel to dine at the Villa Miliza, a notorious but highly luxurious meeting place for men of the aristocracy visiting Yalta. Perhaps the excitement of the establishment would convey itself to her troubled mind. Certainly there was no danger of anything there reminding Laurel of Penn Allandale. Andrei thought with longing of the young ladies of the villa, of the nights he had spent in the establishment in the past, wining and dining and making love till dawn. At the Villa Miliza everything was possible for the man who could afford to buy happiness.

There was an aquarium set into rock walls at the entrance to the villa. In it, blue and silver fishes swam between fernlike fronds of waterweed and white coral. Some of the fish were small and sleek, others with frilly pink gills. One was black, aggressive, and ugly. In this cavernous grotto, surrounded by creatures of the deep, a transition took place between the real world outside and the world of fantasy within. Men who were normally shy became bold when pampered by the legendary Miliza, and those who were too forward or impolite to the staff were given a lesson in good manners before being thrown out into the street by one of Madame's cossack doormen. It was not for nothing that the establishment was the talk of Yalta.

Laurel entered from the grotto into a room lit by violet-colored candles. The walls were darkest blue, the ceiling painted with stars. Food smells mixed with the scent of cigar smoke and the heady perfumes of sandalwood, patchouli, and tiger lily worn by the women. Some of the guests were dancing, some dining, and one solitary couple sitting on the terrace with a bottle of champagne, just looking into each other's eyes.

Andrei led her to a luxuriously furnished private room high above the main concourse and ballroom, where they could see everything but not be seen by the other guests. Delighted to be in her company, he took off her cloak and helped her to her seat, delighted that she had dressed for the occasion in one of his favorite outfits, a shimmering amber ball gown, the skirt scattered with topaz stones. She was undoubtedly the most beautiful woman in the establishment and Andrei was proud of her. In an expansive mood, he looked across the table at Laurel and explained his plans for the evening.

"We shall dine here. Then we will dance. Afterward we are invited to drink liqueurs at Prince Mdvani's house, you remember, the place you liked so much the other day when we called there."

"Of course, I thought it was a wonderful house and he was a truly charming man."

"What do you wish to eat, my dear Laurel? They have nothing but the best at the Villa Miliza."

"I'm not really hungry."

Andrei looked perplexed. Then he spoke determinedly. "I must insist that you eat. You have to try to regain your strength or your father will worry himself into another illness, and we would not wish that, now, would we? Have a soufflé of salmon to begin, or a dish of Miliza's red soup. I *love* the red soup they serve here."

"All right, I'll try it, and then I'll have chicken in cream and tarragon sauce."

"And I will order beef flamed on the sword. I adore the drama of its presentation. Now, tell me about your day. What does the czarina talk about when you and she are alone together? Tell me everything."

"She tells me about her children, about the changes she and the czar want to make in the house. Today she told me about a lady who lives in England called Consuelo. She's a duchess and a very amusing person. I laughed so much I had to wipe the tears from my eyes. It was a tonic, I can tell you."

Andrei's face darkened and he wondered what the czarina was trying to do. If Laurel could be made to recall Consuelo, Duchess of Marlborough, did it follow that she might also remember Lord Allandale and his house near the Palace of Blenheim? He questioned Laurel again about her conversation of the afternoon. "Where does the duchess live?"

"She and her husband have a magnificent house in

England. He's one of the leading aristocrats of the country, though she's American by birth. Apparently it's the way of his family to marry wealthy Americans."

"And who are their friends?"

"I don't know. I suppose the Duchess of Marlborough is known to everyone in England."

Satisfied that Penn had not been mentioned, Andrei relaxed and enjoyed his dinner. Even Laurel seemed impressed by the lavish service, the presentation, and the wonderful dishes brought to tempt her appetite. The waitresses were peasant girls in beribboned headdresses and hand-embroidered blouses. Musicians attended them as they ate, and the most beautiful and melodic Gypsy songs were sung to please them. Andrei was delighted to see that Laurel was eating hungrily. A little color had come to her cheeks and he ventured to hope that she might be returning at last to normality.

At the end of the meal, he held out his arms to her and led her to the dance floor.

"Come, they are playing a waltz and I want to dance."

Under a canopy of scented yellow jasmine, a dozen couples were drifting by. The women were wearing fabulous outfits of lace, chiffon, and heavy satin, the men in uniforms of every shade and style. At the edge of the floor, two small Negro pages were swinging scent sprays full of attar of roses, and the air was balmy with the gentleness typical of the southern provinces, that were renowned for soothing the senses and relaxing the most troubled mind.

They waltzed around and around the ballroom, barely speaking. Then Laurel felt Andrei guiding her outside to the marble-floored terrace. There, under the light of the full moon, he kissed her on the lips. She closed her eyes, knowing that this should excite her, but his lips were cold and there was a savagery about him that frightened her. She pulled back and looked reprovingly into his eyes.

"You hardly know me! You shouldn't be so familiar."

"My dear Laurel, you and I have known each other for a year. You just don't remember the past and all we have done together. Kiss me again and don't be so cold. Coldness only excites me, and I swear I cannot be held responsible for my actions if you continue to treat me in this fashion."

Gripping her in his arms, Andrei kissed her again, mad with desire when he realized that the dress had slipped from her shoulders, revealing the fullness of her breasts. He was about to overwhelm her protests and carry her upstairs to one of the bedrooms above the ballroom, when she stiffened and gazed in utter joy at a man who had appeared out of the nearby woods on a pure white stallion.

Suddenly Laurel broke free of his grasp and ran like a gazelle toward the rider, calling joyfully, "Penn! Oh, my dearest one, I thought you were dead and now you're back and I'm so . . ."

Laurel halted, her face draining of all color as she neared the rider and realized that he was a total stranger. Memory returned with a sickening lurch and she knew that it was not Penn Allandale, because *he* was dead and would never again come riding through the woods to greet her. With a muttered apology to the rider, she turned back and stumbled into Andrei's arms.

"I thought it was Penn. God, but I remember everything now. He's dead and nothing will *ever* be golden again!"

"Don't be such a fool! You are young and will fall in love again. I promise you will be happy someday, Laurel. Try to believe it."

She looked at Andrei in sudden anger and exasperation.

"For you, falling in love's very easy. You can fall in love every week or every month if you feel inclined. My feelings aren't at all like yours. For me there'll only ever be one man, and that's Penn Allandale."

"Damn him! I am sick of hearing his name!"

"Go away! I can't bear to hear you saying that you damn the man I love."

Realizing that he had made an error, Andrei put his arm around her and spoke gently, placatingly. "I'm sorry, Laurel, but I am so in love with you. I keep hoping that you will learn to love me now the man of your first choice is dead."

"I want to go back to my father now, Andrei. Please take me home. I need time to think and to get over the shock of coming back to life. How long has it been since I forgot everything?"

"It has been many weeks. I brought you here to Yalta in the hope that this new place would help you feel better. It is so very restful in the south, and the climate is agreeable. I was sure you would think it the very finest place for a new start in life."

"I don't feel alive at all."

"You will. We can none of us look back, Laurel. We have to be brave and to go on with our lives. That is what you will have to do, whatever you think at this time."

"I don't think anything at all. I can't imagine the future without Penn. I panic every time his image enters my mind. All I ever wanted was to be with him. All I ever knew was Penn. He's the only man I ever loved and who ever really loved me."

"There will be others. You are a most beautiful woman."

"Men might want me, but I won't want them. I'm a woman who can love only once."

"You are too young to know any such thing, believe me. Life is not always black and white. There are shades of feeling that you will learn to appreciate in time."

That night, when Andrei had gone home and her father had retired to bed, Laurel lay in her room thinking of the man she loved. She wanted to kiss Penn, to hold his hand and hear him whispering the sweet, loving words that had so delighted her, words of loyalty, eternal devotion, and passion. When she tried to think of a future without him, she found it impossible. Every plan she had ever made had been connected with him, and she had made so many. She had planned the places they would visit, the changes they would make to Wentworth Saye once they started their family, the routine of living that would please him best. Now, in one savage moment, everything had gone. There was no future, at least none she could look forward to with eagerness. Again and again feelings of panic came into her mind, and she paced the room from midnight till dawn, unable to allow herself to sleep until daylight came, and even then only when a maid agreed to stay at her side. Suddenly the thought of being alone was terrifying, and Laurel's last thought before going to sleep was to wonder how long this anguish would last. Would she ever again be happy? Would she ever laugh and make jokes? Where would she live? How would she fill her days? Could a woman who had tasted the heady wines of passion to the exclusion of all else ever settle for the bread-and-water existence of loneliness and uncertainty that lay ahead?

As the clocks struck six, Laurel fell into an uncertain slumber, tossing and turning on her bed as she tried to assimilate the unacceptable fact of Penn's demise. Still it was impossible to believe that the golden man of her dreams was no more, and in the stillness of early morning she imagined his body next to hers, his lips on hers, his hand entwined in hers, his voice telling her his plans for the future, their future, the future that could never be.

9

Yalta–St. Petersburg, September 1899

The czar and his family had returned to the city, but
new guests had arrived at Livadia for a holiday.
These included Sandro Alexandrovich and his wife,
Mitzi. Though the Holmans were also due to leave
for St. Petersburg, they decided to stay on for a few
days so they could spend some time with their friends.
Then, Holman had informed the grand duke, he
would be finishing his final commission and taking
Laurel back to America. Only there did he feel she
had any chance of recovering from the anguish of
Penn's death.

Andrei had taken the news with seeming calm. He
had already made meticulous plans on what to do if
Holman tried to remove his daughter from the country,
and he would not hesitate to put the plans into
operation, whatever czarist disapproval they might
provoke. Not only were feelings of love involved, but

also the Romanov pride. Every man in St. Petersburg would think him a fool if he let the woman he desired slip through his fingers. Every woman would know herself to be second best to his passion for Laurel and would lose interest in him. Only Yelena and his mother would continue to support and pamper him. For a moment Andrei's face softened as he thought of the young woman who had transformed her life for love of him. Yelena would always be there, waiting, hoping he would marry her. Laurel would not. She must be imprisoned in an ivory tower and forced into acceptance of Russia and his passion. Instead of thinking of her as a woman, Andrei had already begun to think of Laurel as a wild creature to be broken before being tamed.

In the countryside around Livadia, the haymaking was in full swing. The mowers' shirts were scarlet and white and the men sang lusty choruses as they marched back to their villages each evening. This was the season when local matchmakers sipped tea at nightly gatherings and negotiated marriages between the peasant families. Often wedding processions could be seen from the upper windows of Livadia, the young couples dressed in their best, a priest walking behind with children holding lighted candles and crowns of painted wood that would be placed symbolically over the bridal couples' heads. The end of summer was the season for lovers and newly married couples to prepare for the long winter ahead. It was the time when young men thought of passion and young girls prepared quilts and embroided blankets for their dower chests.

In the gardens of Livadia there were pink and violet asters and sweet peas growing in scented profusion all around the terraces. The leaves on the trees were turning crimson and gold, the air still warm and heady. Only in the early morning could one tell that winter was not so very far away. Then, in the hours of dawn, the air was chill, the smells of smoke and newly turned brown earth typical of the season and reassuring in their pungency and richness. It was the perfect place to find peace, to recuperate from sadness, but gradually Laurel had found its silence and inactivity exhausting. She longed for a pace of life that was familiar and the sights and scenes of her American home.

On the day before they were due to leave for St. Petersburg, Laurel and Andrei went for a picnic with Sandro and his wife. A dozen servants accompanied them to carry baskets of food, blankets, wine coolers, and water. The place chosen for this al-fresco feast was a riverbank overlooking one of the vineyards of the region.

The grapes were being gathered by migrant workers, locals, and children, and the air was loud with the sound of singing. Larks trilled in the trees above, and the young women picking the grapes were tanned deep cinnamon brown by the sun. The atmosphere was balmy, the landscape golden, and as the menservants lit fires and unpacked the baskets, Sandro turned to Laurel with an enthusiastic smile.

"I'm so glad you and Mr. Holman stayed on for a few days. This is my very favorite time of the year and I defy anyone to have visited a place as beautiful as Yalta. When I was small, this was the time I looked forward to with all my heart, because the weather is so wonderful and I love the harvest scenes. Also, one knows that winter is not far away, and I much prefer the snow to the enervating days of midsummer."

"What are your plans when the holiday ends?"

"Mitzi and I will return to my father's estate near St. Petersburg, so our child can be born there in December. After that, God willing, we will remain at the farm until the spring, when we hope to return to Yalta. Papa has promised that if I do well with the estate he will give me a house here, so we shall be able to spend two holidays in the south each year. But tell me of your plans, Laurel."

"Poppa and I are going back to St. Petersburg tomorrow, so he can finish his last portrait. Then, at the end of September, we'll be returning to America. We've been away a long time and we're anxious to get home. The memories that will come back to me in the city won't help me get over Penn's death."

"Of course not. You will recover more quickly in your own country, where you and he were never together."

Andrei turned away so Laurel would not see the look of anger on his face. Inscrutable as ever, he watched the workers in the fields, unaware that Mitzi was gazing at him with that curious, childlike, but knowing expression of hers. He turned to face her when she addressed him. "Will you accompany your guests out of Russia, Andrei?"

"I dislike farewells and will leave Laurel and Mr. Holman at the Finland Station, with their permission."

"And you, Laurel, will you not miss all your friends in Russia? We have come to love you so very much."

"I'll miss you, but I know it's time to go home. I have to replan my whole life, and I can't do that here. When I'm in St. Petersburg, everything will remind me of Penn. Once I'm in Vermont I'll be able to think straight again. At least that's what Poppa and I are hoping."

Andrei felt impatience rising in his gullet, and he strode over to where the servants were unpacking food and setting up the fire.

"Come, Laurel, we have heard enough of your sadness. You are with friends and we have some wonderful things to eat. We must be happy and forget about Lord Allandale."

As the meal was served, everyone began to tell stories and to laugh, as if they had not a care in the world. There were smoked salmon, red caviar, black caviar, and mountain-deer cutlets from the Caucasus. Afterward, pork sausages and potatoes were roasted on the fire, a task these privileged aristocrats were unaccustomed to and therefore found all the more amusing.

Sandro took a fork and served some of the sausages and potatoes on green-and-gold Dresden plates. Servants stood by, filling the potatoes with sour cream, while he turned to Laurel.

"How many sausages and potatoes for you?"

"One of each, please."

"Your appetite will improve when you return to St. Petersburg. It's obvious that the air of Yalta is too balmy for you. People who are born in the northern climates often find it so."

"I'm just not hungry of late, Sandro. Poppa keeps complaining that I'll get too thin."

"You're still beautiful, don't worry. You always will be beautiful, even if you get as thin as a raindrop or as fat as a Christmas goose."

Andrei frowned at the compliment and turned to reprimand his young friend. "You will make your wife jealous, Sandro. A married man should not make such lavish compliments to another woman."

Sandro smiled conspiratorially at his enchanting wife.

"Mitzi is never jealous. She knows I love her more than anything else in the world, and that is enough. She knows too that Laurel *is* beautiful. That is a fact, and my wife understands my admiration. *You* should not be jealous, Andrei. Jealousy is an emotion that causes nothing but sadness."

"Unfortunately it is one to which I am frequently a victim."

A light breeze ruffled the trees around the clearing, making the fire burn more brightly. The servants brought white wine for the ladies and a heady red for the men. Then, as the dove-gray clouds of evening edged into the sky, the women from the nearby vineyard finished their work, formed a line, and walked in pairs from the field. They were singing one of the harvest hymns traditional to the area, their clear treble voices touching in the simplicity of their emotion.

Laurel smiled across the picnic spread at Andrei.

"I remember you once showed me a painting of harvest scenes in the Crimean region, and I thought it the loveliest in your country collection."

"You are a romantic. You love always the things which bring emotion, and you care nothing for the value."

"It's true. Poppa raised me to appreciate beauty and not money, though we both know that money's one of the important things in life."

"In St. Petersburg I shall take you to see the paintings of my friend Pavel Frantsevich. Like you, he prefers things that are touching to those that are grand. You will like him and his home on the Fontanka. I shall also show you a house which you can use for the remainder of your stay in Russia. It is in the country, forty versts from St. Petersburg, and no doubt you will be happier there."

"You've been so kind to me and my father, Andrei. I just don't know what we'd have done without you these past weeks."

"You do not have to be without me. I am here and I remain your devoted servant."

St. Petersburg was icy cold and Andrei hurried to wrap Laurel in furs when they arrived on the Imperial Train. As they moved along the platform toward the carriage that was waiting to take them to the Vladimir Palace, they looked across the gray waters of the gulf at the oak, ash, and birch trees that had already lost all their leaves. As they did, an icy wind blew across the Neva, making their faces tingle and their eyes water. Andrei called for the coachman to hurry. Then he turned to Laurel and her father, conscious that both were shivering and uncomfortable with this sudden drop in temperature.

"I warned you it would be very different here from in the south. Many of our citizens catch their death of cold when returning to the city from Yalta."

Holman pulled his fur coat up over his ears.

"I'm half-frozen already, so I can believe you, Andrei. Are you all right, honey? You're as pale as tallow. I hope you're not getting a chill."

"I'm fine, Poppa, but it's a shock to realize the change in the weather. I'd forgotten just how cold this city can be."

Andrei piled another lynx rug over Laurel's knees and a long wrap of arctic fox over her shoulders.

"In truth, this city was built in the worst possible place, but one cannot change it now. It is too late, and in any case, no one would really like to interfere with the work of the Emperor Peter the Great. We Russians are very proud of all his achievements."

At the Vladimir Palace the Holmans were helped to descend into the forecourt by a host of eager servants. Fires had been lit in their suites and in all the main rooms of the property, and the atmosphere was warm and welcoming. Fine food smells drifted up from the kitchen, and in Laurel's bedroom she found a gift on the bed and next to it a pile of invitations. She rang the bell for Polinka, who came bounding into the room, her face alight with pleasure.

"Welcome back, ma'am. Are you feeling better after your holiday?"

"I'm getting better, thanks. I've been hoping you'd still be here when I returned. When do you leave to get married?"

"I decided to stay on till you go at the end of the month, milady."

"That was very kind, and I'm grateful. I'd have missed you if you'd gone."

"You've got dozens of invitations, and one very important one to the fete of Peterhof. They hold it every year before they close the place down for the winter. Sometimes they have it in the French style, sometimes in the English style, and once they got everyone dressed up as Turks for the occasion. I believe it's quite a sight."

"What's the gift?"

"I don't know, milady. It's from the grand duke. Probably he's been to the court jeweler's again."

Laurel tore the silver tissue wrappings from the gift, revealing a carved cedarwood box about twelve inches by eight by six. Attached to the box by a solid gold chain was a key. This she inserted into the lock. On opening it, she stood motionless, gazing at a shimmering collection of diamonds in every shade imaginable. There were yellow, rose, and blue stones, and ones that scintillated like stars. Laurel looked from the stones to Polinka and then back to the diamonds. She ran her fingers through them, astounded by their number and their obvious price- lessness.

"I never saw so many diamonds in my life. What does this mean? Why has the grand duke given me such a gift?"

"It's your parting present, I suppose, ma'am. He used to collect diamonds when he was young, as I recall. He kept them in cabinets in his bedroom, and they were terrible to dust. Oh, aren't you lucky. You'll be rich for the rest of your life now you have those. Mr. Holman won't have to paint a single por- trait ever again unless he really wants to."

Laurel left the box on her bed and ran downstairs to find Andrei. He was sitting by the fire in the salon, his eyes thoughtful, his hands placed together at his chin, as if in prayer. She went to his side and sat on the velvet stool near his feet.

"I came to ask you about the gift you sent me."

"Did it please you, Laurel?"

"I never saw anything so astonishing in my life. Polinka told me it's part of your diamond collection."

"That is true. I used to collect the stones, but I gave up a few years ago when I reached the age of twenty-five. I had so many they began to take up too much room in my suite and in trunks in the cellars. Also, acquisition began to bore me, as I recall."

"Are you quite sure you want to give me all those stones, Andrei?"

"Don't be so serious, my dear. It is a gift to amuse you. Play with them, design yourself some jewels to be made with the best of the stones, or do whatever you please with them. They are only diamonds, and not to be taken seriously. I gave them to you to make you happy and to show my affection for you."

Laurel moved to sit in a massive Chinese chair of carved kiriwood and ebony. As she gazed into the fire, she was trying to fathom Andrei. Why, when he knew she was leaving St. Petersburg, had he given her such a gift? She shook her head, unable to understand the way his mind worked. Perhaps he had decided to assure her financial future, because money meant little to him but everything to her. Perhaps he felt, in his devious way, that for as long as his diamonds were in her possession she would never forget him.

Servants brought a trolley loaded with pastries, bread, preserves, and the barely ripe cranberries beloved by all Russians. Another trolley held a solid silver samovar of tea. The majordomo approached Andrei and informed him that his mother had sent a message asking him to dine with her that evening.

Andrei looked annoyed as he wrote a reply and sent it to his mother. Then he turned to Laurel.

"I arrived only a few minutes ago, and already my mother knows of it! I swear she is more efficient in her network of spies than the czar's secret police."

"Will you go and eat with her tonight?"

"I have made my excuses, because I do not wish to leave you alone on our first evening back in the city.

335

Also, in the morning I am invited to a bear hunt. It will take place near the country house I intend to offer you for the rest of your stay. You must accompany me there when I go."

"I wouldn't enjoy a bear hunt, Andrei."

"Of course you would. It is most exciting. However, if you think it might upset you, I shall leave you at the house and return after the hunt to show you my trophies. It is decided, Laurel, say no more. Let us enjoy these wonderful cream cakes Monsieur Gaston has made for us. It was a fine idea of yours to take on a French patisseur."

For a while they ate and drank, and Laurel thought about the country house Andrei was offering her and wondered why he was doing this. During the months of her stay in Russia, he had adamantly resisted the idea of her living in the country. Now, on the point of her departure, he was urging her to get out of St. Petersburg. More puzzled by his behavior by the minute, she decided to tell him about her plans. "I've had lots of invitations from your friends and my own, but I don't feel like socializing right now. Shall I turn everything down?"

"It will be best if you go at once to the country, I think. I will visit you there, and perhaps I shall come to stay, if you do not object. There is much to see and do in that area, and you have already visited everything of interest in St. Petersburg."

"I think I should accept the czarina's invitation to the autumn fete at Peterhof. She'd think it odd if I didn't. After all, she invited me to Livadia and looked after me as if I were part of her own family."

Andrei looked increasingly apprehensive at this, and Laurel wondered again why he now wanted her out of the city. Had he some new liaison he was trying to conceal from her? Was he afraid of her discussing her imminent departure with his friends, because this would cause him to lose face? Was he afraid of someone telling her something he did not want her to know? In the days before Penn's death, Andrei had craved the usual social life of the city, which included attending every ball and party of note, and he had wanted to attend them all with her. Now he wished to keep her from mixing with the people she knew. Laurel sighed, too distracted still by the thought of her lover's death to be able to work out the quirks in Andrei's nature. No doubt he had his good reasons for wanting her far away, but it was obvious he was not about to divulge them.

Men gathered in the birch wood outside the dacha Andrei had put at Laurel's disposal. There were twenty of them in all, each one from the privileged class of St. Petersburg. In addition there were cossacks, muzhiks, and grooms to watch the horses once the party moved into the forest on foot. The air was loud with the sounds of hounds baying, horses whinnying, and servants calling. The colorful scene became unreal as a fine drizzle came down through the ever-present mist of morning, making the house seem ghostly and unreal.

Laurel watched from her window as the men prepared for the hunt. Most of Andrei's friends were fair and handsome in that angular, high-cheekboned Russian way. One was swigging brandy out of a solid gold flask. Another was cuffing his groom on the ear for some indiscretion. Andrei was deep in conversation with a friend, his face unnaturally pale. Laurel wondered what bad news he had just received, what wager he had lost, what enemy had survived a duel.

She retired from the window as a horn was blown to signal the departure of the hunters. The thought of the bear in his solitary splendor, traditional master of these woodland areas, being hunted by a crowd of bored aristocrats from St. Petersburg was upsetting, and to keep her mind off it Laurel took a book from her luggage and sat in the boudoir reading. She was about to ring for coffee, when a slip of paper fell from the pages of the novel. On it Penn had written: "This is just to remind you that I love you more than anything in the world. I've written lots of these notes and hidden them for you to find, in case you ever get tempted to forget me."

Laurel burst into tears and sobbed as if her heart would break. All the anguish of her loss returned and she was terrified of being alone, terrified of the future and the interminable years when she would have to live with nothing but memories to sustain her. Nausea rose in her gullet, and her head began to ache. As always at times like these, she could think of only one thing: getting out of Russia and back to the little house in Vermont. There, if anywhere in the world, she would get well again. But she would surely never recover the joy of living that had once been hers. From this moment on, Laurel knew, she would have to fight for every happy moment, every second of hope. She sobbed then, heartbroken by the note, yet thrilled to have it in her hand. It was a real and precious souvenir of the man she loved, and she would keep it for the rest of her days.

At five in the afternoon, as dusk was falling, Andrei returned triumphant from the hunt. Behind him, two dozen grooms were dragging in the carcasses of the black bears that had been killed. In time these would be skinned and the skins cured for use around the dacha. His friends were drinking a potent punch of vodka and Armenian brandy. As they drank, they kicked the carcasses with due disdain and told stories of their own bravery to each other. Leaving them in the courtyard, Andrei went in search of Laurel. He was eager to show her the rewards of his expedition and anxious for her praise.

On entering the bedroom, Andrei saw that Laurel's face had taken on the haunted look that had become so familiar since her lover's death. His mood changed and he felt annoyance instead of jubilation. His voice was terse when he spoke. "I killed a bear and my friend Grisha another. Altogether, five were slaughtered, which is something of a record. Soon I shall have the skins cured and put in your bedroom. You always like the bearskins on the floor of the west wing of the palace, and I shot every one of those myself."

When she did not answer, but simply stared in mute horror at the carcasses of the bears in the courtyard, Andrei spoke impatiently. "What is wrong, Laurel? Why are you looking so sad? You always become depressed when you are left alone for a few hours."

"I found a note from Penn in my book and it made me remember him and all the lovely things we did together when he was alive."

"You *must* stop tormenting yourself with thoughts of the past. You will ruin your life because of Lord Allandale, and no man is worth that."

"I loved him, Andrei, and I just can't stop loving him. It's only a few weeks since you told me he was dead, and I haven't had time to get over it."

"Tomorrow I shall be taking you to the fete of Peterhof. That is a spectacle that will take your mind off everything and one you will never forget. We shall enjoy ourselves immensely, and you will not even think of Lord Allandale for a moment, I promise. In fact, I forbid you to mention his name again in my presence. He has haunted you for long enough and he is ruining my life. I do not wish to be ruled any longer by a dead man."

Laurel realized that Andrei knew nothing of love. Yelena had been right when she said he loved only the hunt and pursuit of women. His heart had obviously never been deeply affected by anyone, nor ever would be. Perhaps he had no heart. Perhaps he could not love anyone or anything with a selfless passion. Laurel lapsed into silence, conscious of

Andrei's annoyance, but caring nothing for it. Her mind was already set on leaving Russia and being free of his all-too-possessive desire. She was angry too that he presumed to tell her not to mention Penn, that he longed to oust the Englishman from her mind and her memory. This she resented and fought. Penn was the most precious thing in her heart, and she would treasure every memory of him for the rest of her days. In time, she realized that she would cease grieving, but until then she wanted nothing to do with Andrei's jealous instructions to forget the man she loved. She looked defiantly over to where he was standing, relieved when he left the room without further comment.

The fete of Peterhof was a night of momentous happenings. The czar and czarina were determined to show that despite their reclusive natures they understood power and the need to manifest it. To this end, they had decided on this occasion to rival the glories of Versailles, by copying one of Louis XIV's lavish entertainments held there in past centuries. The fete would last for days, during which commoners, aristocrats, and local peasants were all invited and allowed to intermingle. Eighteen hundred servants were needed to light the quarter of a million colored lanterns in the grounds. Some of these were shaped like flowers, some like suns, moons, or vases, and all glowed with a coral-and-gold light, so the palace seemed suspended in the midst of a fascinating fairyland.

Under the trees, six thousand carriages belonging

to guests who had already arrived were drawn up and guarded by muzhiks. In the garden and on the terrace, thirty thousand pedestrians were strolling by and gazing at the splendidly lit interior of the palace. Some of the aristocrats from St. Petersburg were due to arrive by ship, others in splendid white yachts, their flags flying to celebrate the occasion. By contrast, peasants from a nearby village kept arriving in carts. They were dressed in their Sunday best, their faces flushed in anticipation of seeing the czar, who was not only royal but also, in their eyes, divine.

The ball commenced at seven. Courtiers, members of foreign ambassadorial staffs, diplomats, and distinguished visitors to the city appeared to be presented, each one in the national dress of his country. Outside the window, people were still arriving and the sound of carriages, carts, and troikas mingled with the lilting cadences of the orchestra in the ballroom. Around the walls sat the chaperons of young society girls. To distinguish them from the guests of high order, they were dressed in purple, black, or gray with pearls around their necks and thin fur stoles around their shoulders. On this auspicious occasion, the Chevaliers were on duty in ceremonial white-and-gold uniforms, a head taller than most of the people in the room. These handsome, aristocratic soldiers were gazed on in awe and admiration by many a peasant girl in white dimity with daisies instead of diamonds in her hair.

The czar and czarina sat together on a raised platform, watching the parade of dignitaries and visitors making ritual obeisance to them. When the last had backed away from their presence, the mazurkas began and the rooms became noisy with the sound of rejoicing. Peasants danced with each other, aristocrats with members of their own class. Nothing was stolen from the palace, because the possessions of the Divine Ruler of all Russia were sacred, like his person, to be revered and admired but never touched.

Laurel entered the room on Andrei's arm. She was wearing the most beautiful dress she owned and knew that this would be her last appearance in Russian society. She had done her best to make herself as beautiful as possible, so she would be remembered as an attractive woman and not one with tear-stained red eyes. Her dress was sugar pink, with a skirt so vast men and women stood back to give her room when she passed by. The bodice was décolleté and edged with white osprey feathers, as was the undulating hem of the outfit. In her hair Laurel wore a tiny dove made entirely of diamonds, its outspread wings fashioned from the same feathers as on the dress. She wore no other jewels and her slim figure and pale, serious face gave her the air of a vision as she walked from room to room, looking in avid curiosity at the astonishing sight of the rich and the poor, the mighty and the serf, the beautiful and the ugly, all mixing together on one of the two occasions each year when everyone, regardless of his rank in life, was allowed to pay tribute to the czar.

As Laurel moved on, cooling her cheeks by gently wafting herself with the osprey fan, many a man sighed with longing for her. But it was accepted that the American had loved and lost the great passion of her life, and the aristocrats of St. Petersburg, ever lovers of tragedy, let her be and treated her with respect.

The czar danced the first cotillion with Laurel as his partner, his hand firmly on hers, his voice reassuring. "I am so happy you came to the ball, Miss Holman. I was sad to think we might not see you again before your departure from Russia."

"I shan't be in St. Petersburg very much from now on, because the grand duke is anxious that I move to the country."

The czar looked puzzled at this statement.

"How very odd. Usually Andrei hates the country and everything to do with it."

"I know. I've been trying to work out why he wants to hide me away all of a sudden."

"I think it would be best if you and Mr. Holman came to stay at the Winter Palace for the final days of your sojourn in our country. It will give you the chance to say good-bye to your friends in St. Petersburg and there will be no difficulty in getting to the station. Journeys from the country can be so very difficult at this time of year, and we cannot have you missing the train."

"Thank you, sir. I'll enjoy being at the palace, and so will Poppa."

At one A.M., when Andrei had plied her with pink champagne and she had danced with all her friends and waltzed the last waltz with the czar, Laurel wandered alone through the park of Peterhof, along the avenue of lime trees, and past the ornate fountains to the lake. From the last stone step that led to the water, she stood looking across at the Rose Pavilion. Tears began to fall down her cheeks as she remembered the nights of love she and Penn had experienced there, the long, sultry days of early summer when they had ridden in the countryside nearby and adventured in the woods. Without being fully aware of what she was doing, Laurel began to walk around the lake in the direction of the pavilion, picking a flower here and there and sniffing the mellow scent of autumn that was everywhere. Just to see the Rose Pavilion made her happy. To go inside it once again would be paradise.

Andrei followed at a distance, well aware of where Laurel was going. He had drunk too much vodka and was in no mood to indulge her in her grief. When she entered the pavilion, which was deserted of staff and guests, he followed, closing the door behind him and startling Laurel from her reverie.

She turned to look at him, troubled by his attitude and the suddenness of his appearance.

"What are you doing here, Andrei?"

"I followed you, though you try constantly to elude me. Perhaps I have finally reached the point where I am tired of being eluded."

"I wanted to be alone with my memories."

"I know. You wanted to remember Lord Allandale, as you remember him every hour of every day. Well, I am sick of Lord Allandale and I am sick of your grief and your constant longing for your lover. He is dead and it is time you accepted it."

"Don't shout, Andrei."

"I am utterly tired of being patient with you, Laurel. I am bored by your dwelling on the past. Tonight you are with *me* and I find it insupportable that you spend every hour we are together thinking of another man, a man who is dead."

Laurel made for the door, determined not to listen to the tirade, but Andrei barred her way.

"No, my dear, tonight you will elude me no longer. Tonight you will be mine, not the woman of Lord Allandale."

"Let me go at once! You're drunk and don't know how offensive you're being."

"Because now I have the courage to demand?"

Laurel flew at him and beat his chest with her fists, all her anger and pent-up hurt being expelled on him. Then, hitching up the wide skirt, she tried to leave by the rear entrance of the pavilion.

Andrei ran after her, snatching at the skirt to stop her and tearing it from floor to waist. When he saw the curve of her thighs, he rushed forward and tore off the bodice, so Laurel was half-naked before him. He was surprised to see no fear in her, only naked fury and loathing. This excited him, and he mocked her vulnerability.

"If you go back to the palace in that condition, you will cause quite a stir."

"Damn you, Andrei. Is this all you really care about? Yelena Ivanovna told me once you wanted to treat all women like concubines. Is that what you want of me?"

Andrei roared his answer back at her with true defiance. "It was all I *ever* wanted of you. Now, be silent. Tonight you will be mine and there is nothing you can do about it. If you scream, no one will hear you. There are one hundred thousand people in the palace and the grounds, all of them making noise. In any case, the Rose Pavilion is too far away."

"Let me go at once! I won't be threatened by you any longer."

As Andrei came at her, Laurel picked up a walking stick from the hall stand and brought it down on his head. He deflected the blow, taking a riding crop from the wall and hitting her hard across the back while she screamed out. Then he picked her up in his arms and carried her upstairs, ignoring her cries and her frantic struggles to escape. Once there, he locked the door and threw her down on the bed. When Laurel tried again to run to the window and jump, Andrei slapped her so hard she fell, momentarily stunned, to the ground.

Stripping off his clothes, so he was naked before her, Andrei approached the bed and snatched off the camisole and drawers that were her only covering. His eyes were alight with excitement and he was muttering under his breath. "I have wanted you for so long and have never waited with such patience for any woman. I want to explore your body, to dominate you and make you *beg* me for my love. I want to be your master, Laurel, and I shall, because

I am a Romanov and stronger than any ordinary mortal."

Laurel clawed his chest and kicked and shouted, her mind reeling with horror. But the weeks of eating little and sleeping only for a few hours of daylight had taken their toll and before long she felt her strength ebbing. Then tears came and she began to plead with him. "Let me go, Andrei! For God's sake, think what you're doing."

"Never! You are mine now and I want you to do with me all the things you ever did with that Englishman. You desired him, I know, and you do not desire me, but you will please me or it will give me pleasure to beat you until your spirit is broken."

"You could never break my spirit, Andrei. You can beat me and you can steal my body, but you'll *never* make me want you. I'll just curse you to the end of your days."

"I am already cursed, and my whole family too. The soothsayers foretold it a long time ago. In any case, your body is worth any punishment that might come my way in the future, and nothing you say will stop me."

Andrei's body was slim, hard, and stronger than Laurel had ever imagined. He did not kiss her or show even the smallest sign of affection. He simply grasped her breasts and opened her most secret places, as if taking possession of them. Forcing her thighs apart, his fingers sank deep into the moist membranes that no man but Penn had ever touched. Then, unable to contain himself any longer, he entered her and in a crescendo of feverish abandon made her his own. His cries of desire satiated echoed in the night, like the wild sounds of the troika drivers in St. Petersburg. At this moment in time, he was having his way, and that, above all else, was Andrei's pleasure. He did not even look at Laurel to see what effect he was having on her. He cared only that he was dominating her for the first time since their meeting in England. She was his. Her body was entirely at his disposal, to do with as he pleased. He was triumphant at last.

In the early hours of the morning, Laurel lay on the edge of the bed, staring at the wall. It was almost dawn and she was trying to work out how to leave when she had no clothes to wear. Afraid to make any noise in case Andrei woke, she tried to sit up, feeling the bruises on her body and her arms and thinking herself a dozen years older than the previous night. Anger clouded her mind, but she was conscious that if she told her father what had happened he might feel obliged to avenge her. Then, like Lotty's first love, he would be killed, because Andrei was one of the keenest duelists in the city. If she did not tell her father, she would have to stay at the Vladimir Palace with the man who had ravished her, pretending nothing had happened and risking a repetition of the events of the night. Laurel decided to tell Lotty and to ask for her help. The departure date would have to be brought forward and she would move into Lotty's apartment, on the pretext of having new clothes made at very short notice. The decision made, Laurel was about to rise and take Andrei's shirt and trousers, so she could sneak out of the woods under the cover of darkness, when his hand began to touch her breasts and he pulled her toward him.

"Come, I want you again. This time, try to pretend that you want me. Be my whore and pleasure me."

"Don't touch me. I detest you and I always will."

Andrei threw back his head and laughed wildly.

"But you are mine now, my dear Laurel, and you will never escape me again. I have possessed every part of your body and you will be unable to wipe me from your memory."

He kissed her, despite her struggles, his lips cold on hers, his fingers tightening on her nipples until Laurel cried out in pain. Then he forced her to lie on her back with her head over the edge of the bed, her legs held down by his iron grip. He was about to enter her, when Laurel kicked him out of the way and ran from the room.

She ran downstairs to the front door of the pavilion and was struggling with the bolts when she felt the horsewhip on her back and saw Andrei, his face wild with excitement, beating her as she had never been beaten before. She screamed desperately, hoping someone would hear. Then she felt him lifting her and carrying her to the fur rug in the hall. Half-conscious and sobbing bitterly, Laurel was thrown down and held under Andrei's heel.

Playfully Andrei turned her this way and that, all the while piercing her body with his manhood in a relentless, seemingly endless pursuit of pleasure. Finally, when he was mad with longing for her, he cried out and fell spent and exhausted on the ground at her side. Unlike Penn, who had been so affectionate after love, he seemed to detest her and pushed her aside roughly once his desire was satisfied. Then he lay, watchful and suspicious, guarding her, taunting her, and finally pleading with her. "You are the only woman in the world for me. Say you forgive me for what I have done. I waited so long to love you, and you provoked me beyond human endurance."

"Damn you and damn your ideas of love. You're a madman and I hate you as I never hated any man in my life."

"I adore even your loathing."

Laurel lay silent, choking with frustration because she dared say none of the hateful things she wanted to say. She had been used like all Andrei's women were used and knew she must get away or be exploited again and again until all his pent-up lust was dissipated.

Andrei frowned at her continuing silence.

"Tell me you forgive me. I *beg* your forgiveness."

"I have nothing to say to you. I'm going to get up in a moment and go back to the city. When I arrive I'll be moving out of the palace and into Lotty's apartment. Then I'll leave Russia for good. If you try to stop me, I'll tell the czarina what you did and show her the marks on my body. She'll believe me before she'll believe you, and you know it."

"Will you go naked to St. Petersburg?"

"I will if I have to. The dress you tore can stay right here as evidence of what you did last night."

"You are threatening me, Laurel?"

"I'm telling you what I'm going to do, Andrei, that's all."

He rose and began to pace the hall, his face angry and spoiled.

"You are the most difficult woman I was ever unfortunate enough to meet. I have wished many times that I never met you that day at Blenheim. My mother was right: foreigners are nothing but a disaster. It is impossible to understand their ways."

"I'm an American and I know what I want in life, and what I want isn't you and it isn't Russia. Now I'm leaving here, Andrei. Just don't try to stop me."

He looked resignedly down into the golden eyes.

"I will drive you back to the city and find you some clothes."

"I won't go with you. I shall *never* go anywhere with you again and I don't even want to see you once I leave here. Do you understand me, Andrei, or are you so stupid you can't see what you've done!"

"At least take the clothes from the next room. I put them there last night for you."

Laurel stared aghast at this statement, her face paling with fury.

"You *knew* I'd come here to the Rose Pavilion, didn't you? You planned every last second of this, long before we arrived at Peterhof. You're an animal, Andrei. You don't even deserve my loathing."

Looking into her eyes, Andrei saw hatred, anger,

and something he could not identify that was pity. Rising, he followed her to the bedroom and watched as she dressed in the clothes he had brought. He felt helpless as she left the house without another word and marched past the sleeping peasants at the far side of the lake. There he saw her taking one of the equipages for the ride back to the city.

Andrei returned to the bedroom, still thinking of the exciting happenings of the night. He was tired from his exertions and excited by Laurel's disdain. As he stretched indolently on the bed, he could think of nothing but trying to persuade her to let him use her body again. Normally, when he had possessed a woman, he lost all interest in her, but Laurel's coldness had ignited burning flames within him that nothing would ever quench. She was and would remain forever the unattainable woman, the creature whose body could be stolen, but whose passion and desire were hers and hers alone.

When he had slept for an hour, Andrei woke refreshed. He rose, dressed, and rode at speed to St. Petersburg. It was time to arrange the final act in the drama, and he was eager at the thought of putting his plan for Laurel's capture into operation. It did not occur to him that she might tell anyone what he had done the previous night. He was the Grand Duke Andrei Vladimirovich Romanov, and no one had ever denied him his way.

Holman was not particularly surprised when Laurel left the palace and took up residence in Lotty's apartment. He was astonished, however, when she insisted that they leave Russia within a few days.

"What's wrong, honey? Has something happened to upset you? Tell me what's going on."

"I can't tell you about it right now, Poppa, and I can't stay on in St. Petersburg one moment longer than I must. I want to go home to America right now."

Holman looked hard at his daughter, but decided not to ask any further questions. Obviously Andrei had begun to press his attentions on her with more than his usual persistence, and Laurel, rightly, wanted nothing to do with him. That very day Holman decided he would go to the station and book tickets on the train for Paris. First, though, he would make sure that no opposition could be put in their way by the grand duke. To ensure this, he would call on the czar and czarina at the Winter Palace and then purchase the tickets with a warrant of royal approval. On his return to the Vladimir Palace, he would varnish his last portrait and then tell Andrei with confidence that their stay in Russia was over. Holman hurried upstairs to his room and took his wallet, passport, and travel pass from the desk. Within minutes he was ready to leave. His face was thoughtful as he ran downstairs to the waiting carriage and made his way toward the Winter Palace. He did not notice that Stepan was following him.

Andrei arrived at three in the afternoon and called for Stepan to make his daily report on the activities of the Holmans.

"Miss Holman moved to the apartment of Madame Lototsky, so her clothes can be finished in time for her departure. Mr. Holman went first to the Winter Palace to take his leave of the czar and then to the station to buy the tickets to Paris. He did this with a royal warrant, sir."

"Damn him! He has learned too many of our Russian ways."

"Indeed he has, sir. He is now upstairs in the studio varnishing the last portrait. His servants are packing the trunks and Mr. Holman has given instructions to move his luggage to the Winter Palace. Apparently the czar invited the Holmans to stay there, if they wished, for these last few days in our country."

"Send for Golitsin and the police chief I mentioned to you earlier in the week."

"I took the liberty of doing it already, Excellency."

"Well done, Stepan. You are my right hand. I don't know what I would do without you."

Andrei sat for a long time meticulously planning his moves in the entrapment of Laurel Holman. He had already made his wishes known to the head of the Okhrana, the czarist secret police, and now intended to inform the chief of the St. Petersburg civil police, who would in turn send a messenger to the German border post, where the final act of the piece would be played out. Andrei smiled at the thought of the tigerish fury Laurel would show once she realized that she was trapped forever in Russia. He wondered if she would cry and plead for mercy. Or would she dissolve into tears of grief and be unable to rally her courage? Whatever her reaction, one thing was certain, she would be his forever and unable to leave Russia again. Until she settled to her fate, Andrei planned to keep her captive far away from St. Petersburg in a family-owned fortress near Samarkand. There he would have her for his own, far, far away from czarist supervision.

Andrei had reckoned without Laurel's own willingness to be as devious as any Russian. On Lotty's advice, she was at that moment having tea with the Princess Sophia, her implacable enemy since the days of her first arrival in the city. Aware that Andrei had the power to prevent her from leaving Russia, Laurel had decided that the only person who would help her unconditionally to her freedom was the woman who had longed for her departure from the moment of first meeting.

Princess Sophia gazed at her visitor with a calm, ordered face that hid the inner turmoil she was experiencing. She had had to admit that the American had courage to come to the house of an enemy and ask admittance as if she were a friend. Curious, unable to do anything but accept the young woman's presence, the princess settled with her tea and her sugar biscuits on the gold brocade sofa and listened attentively to what Laurel had to say.

"Please tell me everything, Miss Holman. You would not have come here at all unless you had something of great importance to tell me. As I am old, I have all the time in the world to give you, so please take what you need."

"I'm leaving St. Petersburg on the twenty-third, ma'am. My father will be with me, and Madame Lototsky too, because she and Poppa are due to marry when we get to the States. We'll be traveling by train from the Finland Station."

"I am delighted to hear that you are going to return home to America."

"I knew you would be, and that's why I came here. I'm afraid your son might try to stop me leaving Russia, and I'm anxious to prevent his doing it. You're the only one who can really influence Andrei and help me get away."

The princess sat very still, complimented by Laurel's faith in her power over her son, but offended that the American should imagine Andrei might try to prevent her departure. She answered with caution, "What grounds have you for your suspicions, Miss Holman?"

Laurel sighed. She had hoped it would not be necessary to discuss what had happened the previous night with Andrei's mother, but now it seemed the only way. She spoke calmly, without emotion, her hurt and anguish at the events of the previous night held in the tightest self-control. "When I arrived in Russia I was already in love with a truly wonderful man. His name was Penn Allandale and he came from Oxfordshire in England. In those first months in St. Petersburg, I missed Penn so badly I thought I'd have to return to England to be with him. Then he arrived in Russia in his balloon and I was so happy I wanted to shout my happiness from the rooftops.

Penn and I were very upset by Andrei's jealousy around that time. Your son invited me here because he thought he'd fallen in love with me. Right from the beginning he detested Lord Allandale and was determined to do everything he could to interrupt our courtship."

"My son has always been a very jealous man. I am afraid it runs in our family."

"When Penn returned to England in June, I expected to join him there eight weeks later, in early September, to marry him from his home in Oxford-shire. Then Andrei found out that Lord Allandale and his Russian copilot had been killed on their way through Central Europe. I . . ."

Tears began to fall down Laurel's cheeks like early-morning dew on the petals of a rose. She continued her story, however, staring out of the window at the garden like a woman in a trance.

"In a way, my whole life ended the moment I heard of Penn's death. I got ill and lost my memory. Andrei was so very kind to me. He took me to the south with the czar's own party of guests so I could recover my wits at Livadia. As time passed, though, he became exasperated at my grief and eager for me to let *him* replace Penn in my affections."

The princess sighed, knowing that the young lady was speaking the truth and fearing what might be coming next. Laurel's voice caught with emotion as she rose, took off her jacket, and unbuttoned her gilet, revealing pale, flawless skin fearsomely bruised and marked by two sharp whip lashes.

"Last night, at the fete of Peterhof, Andrei made love to me against my will. I'd gone on my own to visit the Rose Pavilion, where Penn and I had had so many wonderful times. Andrei followed me there, locked me in the house, and used me until his desire was satisfied. I came back to the city this morning. I've moved out of the palace, and Poppa's booked our train tickets for the journey out of Russia. My father's moved into the Winter Palace at the czar's invitation, and I'll be going there too for the last few days. I've not told my father what happened, though I have told Lotty. Then I came here to tell you, because you're the only person who can control Andrei and make him see sense. I don't love your son, ma'am. I never loved him and never encouraged him to think I ever could. I don't want to see him again *ever*. I just want to go home. Do you understand?"

The princess sat quite still, her face twitching with distress. She was very pale and able to control her grief at Laurel's words only with the greatest difficulty.

"I am grateful to you for coming to me, Miss Holman, and am most desperately sorry for what has happened. I know you must be telling the truth and I cannot say anything in mitigation of my son's behavior. Andrei is a man who has always liked to have his way, and he will never change. On the subject of your departure, however, I can surely be of help. I will see that my son is summoned here urgently from the station, so he cannot harm you or follow in his private train. I will also talk with him and make sure he does not attempt to molest you further prior to your departure. Is it your intention to tell the czarina what Andrei did to you?"

"No, ma'am. I've no desire to ruin Andrei, just to get out of Russia safely and hurry back home to America."

The princess rang for fruit liqueurs to be brought, and Laurel sat with her former enemy, savoring the subtle taste of mirabelle, prunelle, fraise, and noisette. Then, with a shy smile, she rose and extended her hand to the older woman.

"Thank you for seeing me, ma'am. I'm grateful you're going to help me and my father, whatever your reason for doing it."

"I misjudged you, Miss Holman. I am getting old and cantankerous and I fear my son inherited his jealousy from me!"

"I misjudged you too, but I'm glad I came to my senses before it was too late. I must go now. Poppa and Lotty are taking me to lunch on the island of Yelagin. Lotty says I have to keep occupied so I won't think of what happened last night. We're going to eat bluefish fresh from the sea, just like we do back home."

"You long for your home, don't you, Miss Holman?"

"I long for Penn, but he's gone, so I just want to get back to America, where I know I'll be safe. I'll live the quiet life there and work so hard I'll get over my nightmares. I just hope I can be normal again someday."

"I wish you good fortune, Miss Holman. Have no fear that I shall help you in every way I can. My power is not inconsiderable, and I have the advantage of knowing the way my son's mind works. You will leave St. Petersburg at the appointed time, that I promise."

Relieved by what she had done, Laurel drove in her carriage past the market, where peasants were arriving in carts full of fresh country produce. She had reached the Bolshaya Millionaya, where the British embassy was situated, when she saw Hugo Allandale entering the building. Overjoyed to see a familiar face, she told the coachman to halt and then dismissed him, waiting till he was out of sight before rushing inside the stately building, calling out to her friend. "Hugo! Wait for me, it's Laurel Holman. Oh, I am *so* pleased to see you. What are you doing here? I truly never expected us to meet again in St. Petersburg."

Hugo turned with a joyful smile and held her in his arms.

"My dear, whatever happened to you? You're so thin, and we've not had a single letter from you. Have you been ill?"

"I wrote four," Laurel replied, then sighed. "But I gave them to Stepan to post, like I always do."

"Come in. I'm busy unpacking and can't find a thing. We finally managed to get the balloon back and now we're here to put it on display with the British Exhibition next month. It's a new one, of course, and in the very latest style. I swear it could be flown all the way to the Pole and back again in complete safety. Now, tell me all your news."

Laurel shrugged wearily as they walked into the ambassador's salon and sat down on an English chintz sofa.

"When I heard about Penn's death, I got ill and lost my memory from the shock. My father and Andrei took me to Yalta with the imperial party to convalesce, but I haven't been the same since. The joy's gone out of my life, Hugo, and I just can't imagine the future without Penn. All my hopes and plans were connected with him, and I *still* can't really believe he's gone. How are you and Clarissa recovering from the tragedy?"

Hugo stared at her, speechless from shock at Laurel's words. Then his eyes moved toward the door, where his brother was standing listening to what had been said. Taking Penn's signal for caution, Hugo held Laurel's hands and spoke gently. "My dear Laurel, you have been wrongly informed about all this. It's true that Penn was in a frightful accident and was lost for over two months when his balloon was blown off course and came down over Lapland. It was a veritable wilderness, you see, and he had a dickens of a time getting back to civilization. His Russian copilot died of exposure when they were only twenty miles from safety."

Laurel listened uncomprehendingly, her face turning very pale.

"What are you telling me?"

Noticing Hugo's constant glances at the spot behind her near the door, Laurel turned and looked straight into the anxious blue eyes of Penn Allandale.

With a cry of utter joy, she ran to him, sobbing hysterically from shock. "Oh, dear God be praised, you're alive, Penn! They told me you were dead. I can't believe you're here! I can't believe we're together again!"

Penn held her to his heart, kissing the trembling hands and trying to calm her distress. His voice was gentle, despite the anger he was feeling. "Who told you I was dead, Laurel?"

"Andrei found out about it. He had a French newspaper with a report of the accident. One of his friends had brought it back from Paris, or so he said. Then a few days later Andrei was told you were dead."

Penn looked hard at Laurel, noting the lines of suffering on her face, the gauntness of her body.

"Damn Andrei for what he's done to you. I ought to kill him for this."

"No, no, it's just that in Russia they never get the newspapers until months after they come out in London or Paris. I suppose he got an incorrect report."

"There never was a report of my death. He made it all up to trick you. Oh, my dearest, how you must have suffered and how *I* have suffered from not hearing from you. I imagine Andrei made his servants give him any letters you sent to the post."

Laurel tasted the bitter tears that were falling down her cheeks and thought furiously of all the sadness she had suffered in the past few months. Hatred of Andrei filled her heart, and fear too, for now she knew that he was both ruthless and evil. She looked eagerly at Penn.

"Poppa and I are due to leave Russia on the train in a few days' time. I'm so scared Andrei will try to stop us. If he finds out you're alive, he'll certainly *never* let me go!"

Penn held her close, frowning because she was trembling violently from head to toe and so thin he could feel her ribs sticking out of her bodice. Feelings of intense love and pity filled his heart and he knew he must take her home to England at once and away from the Russian who had wanted her so obsessively for so long. He knew also that Andrei had lied cruelly to give himself a chance with Laurel, a chance she would never have granted. He whispered to her as she snuggled in his arms. "Come, we'll eat lunch together in my private room. Then you and I must talk. I'll take you home to England, Laurel, so you have nothing further to fear. Andrei has played his last trick on you. From this time on we shall simply forget that he exists."

"But the exhibition. You just arrived for it."

"To hell with the exhibition. I came here to see you and hurry back with you to England, and that's just what I'll do."

"Penn, there's something terrible I have to tell you. Perhaps—"

"Perhaps nothing. We're together, and that's all that matters. We'll marry within the month, and from that moment on, life will start anew for both of us."

Laurel began to sob desolately, and Penn motioned for his brother to leave them. Then, having watched her closely for a while, he asked what was wrong, what had happened to disturb her so dreadfully.

Laurel knew she must tell the truth of what Andrei had done to her, even if it meant the end of the love affair. No marriage could be founded on a lie, and she was conscious that it might take many weeks for her to recover from the shocking experience, weeks that would cause Penn distress unless he knew the reason for her condition. Tearfully she recounted the happenings of the past few days and then the incident of the previous night at Peterhof.

Penn moved away from her and stood with his back to the place where she was sitting. He was so enraged he could barely keep from rushing out and going to the palace to challenge the grand duke to one final duel.

"You realize, Laurel, that honor dictates that I challenge Andrei over this. I shall kill him, I swear I shall kill the bastard!"

"Please do nothing. If you killed him they'd put you in prison and I'd never see you again, which is just what he wants more than anything. I want to leave here and go to Wentworth Saye with you. I want to settle down with you, Penn. Don't let pride dictate your actions. We don't *need* revenge. We need each other. Please, I've already thought you dead on one occasion. I don't want to find out that it's true and that Andrei has killed you just when we've been reunited."

Realizing at last how she had suffered, how her

mind needed the panacea and reassurance of his love, Penn knelt before her.

"You're the woman I adore and respect, Laurel. You're the person I dream of at night when I'm asleep, and think of in the early hours of each morning. I don't care that Andrei used your body, only that it hurt and damaged you. For my part, from this moment on we're one person. We'll be spending our whole life together, and no one is going to spoil our love for each other."

"I adore you, Penn. You'll never know how much."

"I know you've been hurt, and I can't get out of my mind what Andrei has done, but for the moment we must forget him. You and I are what matters, and getting you back to England safely is the priority."

"What if he tries to stop me leaving?"

"I don't think he can, though he's mad enough to try. Don't worry, dearest one. Hugo and I will ask Sandro's advice and help in making a plan. You have nothing to fear. We Allandales are nothing if not inventive, and no Russian is going to get the better of us, I assure you."

"When Andrei realizes you're here, he'll know you'll try to find me and take me back."

"That's true. It might be best if you get out of his way completely. If he can't locate you, he can't question you to find out if you know of my presence in St. Petersburg."

Over lunch they brought each other up-to-date on the happenings of the intervening weeks. With many loving glances, affectionate kisses, and promises of devotion, Penn reassured Laurel that what had happened the previous night made no difference at all to his feelings for her or to their future together. Inwardly he continued to seethe with rage that Andrei had gotten away with ruining Laurel's happiness, paining her mind with thoughts of death and her body with the imposition of his lust. He decided to think more of this when Laurel had gone. He must find a way of letting Andrei know that nothing had changed in his feelings for her and nothing ever would. He would marry her whatever the grand duke tried to do. He would also make sure the Russian knew that his despicable behavior would become known in England and he would no longer be welcome among the ranks of the nobility who had once considered him a respected friend.

Laurel's shock at discovering Penn was alive was so great, it was decided to send for Lotty to come and collect her. She was kissing Penn passionately and listening to his plans for the future when the dressmaker appeared at the door on the arm of Hugo Allandale.

On seeing Penn, Lotty let out a whoop of delight and rushed to kiss him resoundingly on both cheeks. Finally she settled in a chair, cooling her burning cheeks with a fan.

"I cannot believe it! Lord Allandale is alive. Dear God be praised for his great mercy."

Laurel ran to kiss Lotty, laughing when the older woman began to wipe the tears of sheer happiness from her eyes.

"Don't cry, Lotty. Everything's all right again and my life just started anew."

"My dear Laurel, my dear Penn, what can I say? This is surely the happiest day of my life. Now, tell me what I can do to help. You must not let Andrei know you have met again. He will be as dangerous as a trapped animal when he realizes that you are here in St. Petersburg."

Penn stepped forward and knelt at Lotty's feet, his face earnest, his voice eager to impress on her the need for secrecy.

"I don't want you to tell anyone but Mr. Holman of my return, Lotty, not one single soul. We're afraid Andrei may attempt to prevent Laurel from leaving Russia. If he knows I'm back, he'll certainly attempt to do so, whatever the czar might try to do to control him. I'm going to arrange something with my friends to keep Laurel out of the grand duke's way, but until I have, we must be cautious."

"It will be best if you go at once to the Winter Palace, Laurel. I will fetch your father, and there you will both be safe. I will also go to Andrei's dacha to collect what few things you took there and tell his staff you have left for an even more distant property on the gulf, where you will be spending your last days in the city. If Andrei questions the staff, that is what they will tell him, and perhaps he will feel reassured that you know nothing of Penn's arrival. I had best close my shop down and come with you to the palace, if the czar will permit it. Otherwise Andrei will never believe that I have not heard of Penn's being alive and told you the news."

Penn kissed Lotty's cheeks and shook her hand.

"I'm so grateful to you for all your help in this. I hope someday to be able to repay you for your loyalty to Laurel and me."

"There is nothing to repay, Penn. We are a *family* and I have waited so long to be part of one. There is not a thing in the world I would not do to help you both to the happiness you so richly deserve."

When Lotty had gone to collect Laurel's father, Penn called for a British-embassy guide and had him accompany her to the Winter Palace. They kissed good-bye with a long, lingering embrace that ignited both as it always had. Laurel caught her breath, thinking how she had so recently thought that for her emotion was a thing of the past and passion a faded memory. Then, with a backward glance at Penn, she left the embassy by the ambassador's private entrance and hastened away to the Winter Palace. Within an hour her father would join her and they would begin the tense wait for the moment when they would make their attempt to escape from Russia forever.

10

St. Petersburg, September 1899

Outside the window there was a chestnut tree, its leaves turning flame red and orange and drifting to the ground in the autumn breeze. In the room there were fur rugs, a glowing fire, and a canopied bed carved with doves of peace. The house, which Penn and Laurel had never visited before, belonged to a friend of the British ambassador. Andrei knew neither the owner nor the location. The lovers had come here because they were longing to be together and considered it safe to meet only in a place where they were unknown. It was the first time they had been alone together since their meeting at the embassy. They were about to make love and their feelings of joy and happiness knew no bounds.

Entering the bedroom of the deserted dacha, Penn looked around at painted walls and ancient carved furniture. Laurel, he saw, was trembling from joy and anticipation, fear of pursuit, and what he recognized as a certain apprehension. She was afraid lest her experience with Andrei had robbed her of her precious ability to enjoy their lovemaking. He was confident, however, that nothing in the world would ever rob her of her sensuality and desire for happiness. It would be necessary though to prove to her that her body was still perfect in his eyes, her passionate nature unaffected by the happenings of the past few weeks. Experiencing the same thrill he had always felt when she was near, Penn watched as Laurel began to undress.

"How wonderful it is to be alone with you at last, my dearest one."

"I've been dreaming of making love with you, but I never thought it would happen again. I used to try to imagine you as you'd been and pretend you were with me. I used to love you with my mind, knowing I couldn't love you with my body."

"Don't think of those unhappy days anymore. Oh, my darling, I know you've suffered grievously and I have suffered hell. My whole family did their best to cheer me during our separation, but I was something of a tribulation to them in my anger and my hurt."

"I adore you, Penn. My life's taken on a whole new meaning since we've been together again."

"Kiss me and don't be afraid of anything. You and I are meant for each other and we always shall be. Nothing Andrei's done could ever change that."

Laurel kissed him on the mouth, emotion bursting like a meteor from her after all the tension of the past few months. When their lips met, she savored the feelings the kiss brought. Then, for a moment, she looked into the eager eyes of her lover and saw again the magnetic quality that had so drawn her to him in the first place. She kissed him again, crying out when he began to touch her body.

"Hurry and make love to me, Penn. I want to know if I can still feel the thrill I used to feel before Andrei hurt me so badly."

As the sun fell in the sky and the light in the room turned to coral in the autumn evening glow, they hurried to bed. Naked, delighted to be together, and excited beyond all measure at the prospect of love, they hugged each other between the linen sheets in the big bed, where generations of Russians had made love, given birth, and breathed their last.

Penn lay on his elbow, gazing at Laurel's body and watching the pleasure in her face as he ran his hands over the petal smoothness of her skin. A shiver ran through her and she arched her back, desire overwhelming her and communicating itself to him with a violence that was tangible. So forceful was her longing, he grasped her to his heart and kissed her on the lips, lingering over the wetness of her mouth and enjoying the breathless panting of her chest. As she moaned with pleasure, he moved down and caressed her throat, her breasts, her stomach, and the shapely thighs that always excited him.

"You smell of camellias, even when there are none around. I've been dreaming of the scent of your body for so long."

Laurel wound her legs around him, her face a picture of contentment.

"I love you, Penn. I was so worried I might not be able to show you just how much, but you were right: nothing will ever spoil what we have for each other."

He kissed her breasts and her nipples, taking them in his mouth and gently biting them.

Laurel writhed under his touch, low cries escaping from her as her body began to melt with desire. Her eyes were closed in sheer delight and already she had forgotten all the bad times of the past few months. Penn was loving her as she had longed for him to love her during the black days when she had thought him dead. Passion filled her heart and she pushed him gently back on the bed and began to kiss his body, tasting his skin and gently exploring his hardness with her fingers. His cries of pleasure were intoxicating and when he took control and laid her back on the soft down pillows, Laurel raised her legs and wrapped them around his waist, her eyes still closed, all her instincts crying out for the moment of penetration, when they would be one. When it came and he entered her body, slowly, inexorably moving inside her, she went wild and struggled to evade the piercing thrusts of his masculinity, because the ecstasy was too much to bear, the happiness almost too great after the months of despair and uncertainty. She gasped as his body undulated before her.

"This is what I've been dreaming about for so long. This is what I wanted to feel, just you and me together, Penn. I love you so dearly, my darling."

Penn felt her contract and then the sudden and liberating spending of passion from his own body. He was so happy, tears came to his eyes, and to hide them from her he took Laurel in his arms and held her tightly, kissing her head and her hands and the tips of her fingers. Then he smiled, suddenly drowsy and content.

"I feel as if I flew all the way to Russia without the aid of my balloon."

"You made me feel as if I were floating on a cloud."

"By the time we've all spoiled you to death at Wentworth Saye, you'll soon recover from your ordeal, I promise. After that, I shall spend my life making you happy and devoting my time to you and the children we'll have someday."

"Are we really going home, Penn?"

"Of course we are. I came to Russia especially to bring you back to England."

"I'm afraid of Andrei and what he might do. I think he's a little mad. He has power, you know, and connections with men in the secret police and all manner of characters in the militia. God knows if the czar's aware of some of the things he does. Perhaps he'll even stop the train and have me smuggled back to St. Petersburg without anyone knowing. Andrei could hide me for months in one of his houses in Moscow or Kiev and no one would ever know."

"Hugo and I have worked out a plan and I assure you the last thing Andrei will be able to do is take you off the train. What time do you leave, by the way?"

"We're on the noonday train tomorrow."

"We've not had much time, but everything has been taken care of. Sandro did most of it, in case I was being followed by Andrei's men."

"Will Hugo travel with us?"

"Hugo will play a big part in your escape from Russia. He'll travel part of the way with you, but then he'll return to St. Petersburg as if nothing had happened. Now, you are not to worry, Laurel. We've arranged a few surprises for the grand duke and we've planned for every contingency, with Sandro's help."

"I'm tired, Penn."

"Sleep awhile. Then we'll eat dinner and return to the city. You'll have to help me cook it, I'm afraid. I was worried that the servants might gossip and had them dismissed until morning. We don't need any interruptions from Andrei at this crucial time. If he came here in search of you, I should be obliged to shoot the fellow."

They ate potatoes roasted on the fire, with a joint of cold beef Penn had brought with him from the British embassy. The meal was enjoyed in the bedroom, before the fire, both of them dressed in night clothes, both eager to kiss and hold hands like conspirators thrilled to be part of a great adventure. Penn explained his plan to Laurel and then they talked of Wentworth Saye, of Consuelo, Duchess of Marlborough, who had sent Laurel a good-luck charm. Penn spoke wryly of his neighbor. "Perhaps Consuelo knew we'd need the good-luck charm. She certainly has a rather low opinion of the grand duke these days."

"She's a very clever person. I wouldn't be in the least surprised if she knew everything that had happened."

"She's waiting for your arrival with great eagerness. I swear she plans to help make our wedding the talk of Oxfordshire for generations to come."

Laurel looked at Penn in his blue silk dressing gown that matched the color of his eyes. If anything, he was even more handsome than she remembered. She smiled across the table at him, bending forward so he could kiss her again and laughing when her nightdress caught in the hot butter from the baked potatoes.

"How did my portrait look when you hung it in the gallery at Wentworth Saye?"

"It was perfect. Everyone agrees it's the most sensational painting in the house. Your father is certainly full of new ideas. My sister says the portrait blows a breath of fresh air into all those dusty old pictures of ours."

"Right now Poppa's quaking in his boots in case he can't leave Russia and spend some of the money he's earned here. He's absolutely convinced Andrei will do something to stop us."

Penn watched with pleasure as Laurel changed the butter-stained nightdress for a voile negligee. Then, taking her on his knee, he questioned her gently. "Have you anything in particular that *you* want to take with you?"

"I have the clothes Andrei ordered for me, but I intend to leave those behind, because they'd only remind me of him. I have the furs and jewels he gave me, which will also be left behind. I have a box of diamonds of every color and size that he gave me just before the ball at Peterhof."

"Those must definitely be left behind!"

"Apart from that, I have very little, a few clothes I bought myself, an icon Lotty gave me, and a new hat or two."

Penn smiled at her independence, wondering what Andrei would do when he realized that the young lady had left everything he had bought or given her in the suite he had reserved for her use. His pride would be hurt and he would surely find it hard to accept such a complete rejection. All thoughts of the grand duke disappeared from Penn's mind when he saw Laurel's legs through the muslin of the negligee. With a playful lunge in her direction, he was tantalized to see her running away from him. He began to pursue her, excited by her cries.

"Don't chase me, Penn. You know how it makes me scream. Don't do that! Now you've untied my wrap. . . . Oh, I like that, do it again, do it again, don't ever stop."

On the floor of the bedroom, amid the opulent karakul and lynx fur rugs, Penn kissed her and fondled her breasts till Laurel closed her eyes and begged him to love her. "I want you, Penn. I want you to make me dream dreams no one else can."

"Don't trap me like that with your thighs. That

kind of behavior is enough to send a man wild as a savage."

"Be my savage, I like it when you pretend."

He loved her masterfully, commanding her passion, so it surged like the sea with majestic power. Their hands met, their lips searched feverishly for each other, and their bodies mixed with all the sweetness of honey. The climax came like a summer storm and then they lay entwined, kissing and whispering words of love so precious to both. Everything in the world was perfect now they were together again.

In St. Petersburg, Andrei was driving with his mother along the Moika Canal, when he encountered an old friend en route to a wedding in a gardenia-bedecked carriage.

The man, Count Valerian, leaned forward and called out a greeting. "I saw your English friend Lord Allandale yesterday, Andrei Vladimirovich. Obviously the reports of his untimely death were unfounded."

Princess Sophia started violently. Andrei turned pale. However, he raised his hand in a greeting to the count and then continued imperturbably on his way.

His mother chose to be diplomatic. "I suppose Lord Allandale has come to show off his balloon at the English Exhibition. I had heard that aviation was to be the theme."

"Perhaps that is why he is here."

"Did you *know* he was alive, Andrei?"

"I had been told that he was dead, but one can never tell about such things."

The princess knew at once that her son had lied to Laurel in order to have his way with the girl. Despite her devotion to Andrei, she felt a certain revulsion at this and fell silent as they passed down the silent tree-lined avenue with its interlacing canals.

Andrei was appalled to hear of Penn's arrival at the city. It could not have come at a worse moment, and would, he felt sure, complicate everything. Obviously Allandale would ask Laurel's whereabouts, and someone was sure to tell him that she was staying in the country. He decided to send a message to ask her to come to see him at the Vladimir Palace, promising to bring his mother as chaperon if Laurel agreed. If she refused to come, he would ride out to the dacha and persuade her to leave at once for a more remote property belonging to a friend. Restive, afraid of anything ruining the all-important culmination of his plans for the Holmans' journey, Andrei forgot about his mother and the people who kept greeting him as he sat at the princess's side. He was concentrating all his energies on making sure he could capture the object of his lust and keep her forever.

On arrival at his home, Andrei went to the library, wrote a note, and called for Stepan to deliver it to Laurel. He was working on the details of his plan for getting Laurel to Samarkand, when the servant returned unexpectedly early and handed the note back to him. Andrei looked up questioningly at Stepan.

"What happened? Why did you return so quickly?"

"Miss Holman was not at the dacha, Excellency. I thought it best to hurry back and inform you at once."

"Where has she gone?"

"The staff said only that she and her father moved out two days ago, having accepted an invitation from one of their friends to visit a remote country house on the gulf. I believe it is far from St. Petersburg, sir, but I was unable to ascertain the name of the property or the owner, because the servants knew nothing."

Somewhat mollified that the house was an even greater distance from the city, Andrei was nevertheless perturbed. There was so little time before Laurel's departure from the station of St. Petersburg. Would she come and visit the city before leaving? He thought not, conscious that she would want to keep as much distance between herself and him as she could. He wondered if any of her friends would visit her and tell her of Lord Allandale's arrival. He decided to send Stepan to keep watch on the Englishman and to take action if he moved out of St. Petersburg. If he did not, then there was no reason to suspect that Allandale knew of Laurel's whereabouts, and by the time he found out, she would be well out of his reach.

On the twenty-third of September, on a bright, sunny autumn morning, Laurel, her father, and Lotty arrived at the Finland Station for their journey to Paris. It was a blustery day, already cold with the approach of winter, and all three were thinking their own thoughts at this auspicious moment of departure.

For Lotty it was the end of an era and the start of a

new life. Her youth had been spent in her native Hungary, the years of her early womanhood in Russia, where she had encountered tragedy and sadness as well as success. She was a wealthy woman, a woman in love, and despite the tension of the moment, radiant.

For Holman, leaving Russia was a profound relief. He had never liked the mechanical glitter of the place, the sophisticated ways copied from Parisians, the wild temperament of the inhabitants, who swung from euphoria to melancholy in the space of a few hours. He had worried about Laurel's love for Penn and their enforced separations. Above all, he had been appalled by the way Andrei had tracked her constantly, as if she were a rare and beautiful animal. Now, at last, they would be free of the Russian's ever-watchful presence, and that was the best news of all. Holman squeezed Laurel's hand to encourage her.

"Only five minutes to go before we leave. Perhaps Andrei won't show at all."

"I hope he doesn't, Poppa. I surely don't want to see him ever again."

"How're you feeling, Lotty? Any sadness at leaving home?"

"Russia was never really my home, James, only a place where I settled for a while. I feel no distress at going away."

Laurel heard a commotion at the end of the platform and saw Andrei with a retinue of palace staff hurrying toward her. The servants were carrying gifts wrapped in colored paper, bottles of champagne, and solid silver ice buckets of caviar. She motioned for her father and Lotty to get into the train, fearful lest Andrei try to delay their departure. She was pleasantly surprised when he urged her to follow.

"The train is about to leave and we cannot allow you to miss it. My servants will put the champagne in the suite your party will occupy, and the food will be served for your lunch. I could not resist coming to say good-bye."

Laurel replied formally, already a stranger to the man before her. "It was kind of you to think of us, Andrei."

"Where did you vanish to during the past few days? I thought you were to stay at the Winter Palace for the last part of your visit to Russia."

Laurel smiled ingenuously, avoiding telling him that that was exactly where she had been with her father and Lotty, though Andrei's servants had been led to believe otherwise. She answered lightheartedly, "One of Lotty's friends invited us to visit her house on the gulf. It was horribly cold, but my stay there gave me a chance to think and settle my mind a little. I do that best when I'm far away from cities."

"And what did you decide, may I ask?"

"I decided I was right to go home to America. Home's the only place for me right now, and it will be till I'm over Penn's death."

Pleased that she obviously had no idea that Allandale was alive, Andrei stood in his sable cloak on the windswept platform, waving as the whistle blew and the train moved slowly out. Drops of rain began to fall, but he ignored them. He was intent on watching the train till it was a mere speck in the distance, and all the while, he smiled the cunning smile of triumph his servants knew so well. It would take time to do all that he would have to do to win Laurel to his way of thinking, but he was still confident that victory over her could be his. With an autocratic nod to the stationmaster, who bowed low, Andrei strode back along the platform to his carriage. He had received an urgent message to visit his mother, and as always, was anxious to obey her. He gave the order to the coachman and then sat back, considering his next move.

Three days after the journey began, on reaching the border in the early hours of the morning, passengers on the train from St. Petersburg to Paris were wakened by stewards and asked to produce their passports. Border police inspected these, and most of the people were allowed to return to sleep little worse for the unwelcome intrusion.

On arriving at James Holman's berth, the police chief saluted and called for an interpreter. Then he asked Laurel's father for his tickets and passports, and for all the members of his party to be brought to the berth.

Lotty appeared minutes later, smiling sleepily at the officer, who saluted and asked her where the third member of the party was. She replied easily, displaying no tension or sign of apprehension: "Mr.

Holman's daughter is the third member of our party. Here is her ticket."

"But where *is* she, milady?"

"Laurel had to return to St. Petersburg. As there were only two stops between the city and the border, she stepped off the train at the first. I am *sure* the guard will confirm all this for you, as he was called and asked to check her ticket, which was of the nonexchangeable type."

The policemen looked from Holman to Lotty in fear and uncertainty. Their chief had been ordered to take Laurel Holman off the train and to send her by imperial express back to St. Petersburg, where the Grand Duke Andrei Vladimirovich was waiting for her. Terrified of what would happen to them if they failed to comply, the policemen followed their chief from the train. The guard was called to confirm Lotty's story. Then the police chief returned to Holman's compartment.

"May I ask, sir, *why* the young lady returned to St. Petersburg. I shall need all the facts for my report, you understand."

"Of course you do. My daughter left something valuable behind in the city and insisted on going back to fetch it."

Lotty translated Holman's words, all the while fixing the officer with a look of sympathy and understanding.

"Were you instructed to question Miss Holman, officer?"

"No, milady, my orders were to put her on the

imperial express back to Petersburg. If she is not here, however, I cannot fulfill my orders and there will be trouble, terrible trouble, you'll see."

"You must tell the truth, sir, and the truth is that she discovered she had left something of value behind in the city. She refused to leave Russia without this object, which is of *immense* meaning to her, and so returned to collect it. Women are like that, as you know. So often we leave behind things that we love. Then we simply cannot continue our journey without them."

The police withdrew and went into a conference. Within minutes they had decided to search the train, and this they did with the greatest diligence, from one end to the other. Then, in the pale gray light of dawn, they stood by as the train crossed the border and left Russia. Their faces were pale and anxious and they were all wondering what punishment would be meted out to them by the grand duke when he learned what had happened.

Holman stood at the window with Lotty, his arms around her shoulders. Outside, there was nothing but a vast emptiness of flat brown fields tinged with gold in the morning sun. Tense from the rigors of the search, Holman gazed at the fields and spoke softly to the woman he loved. "They were thorough. I'll give them that."

"They always are, James."

"Praise be we didn't follow my plan and try to hide Laurel on the train. If we had, they'd have found her and sent her back to Andrei in St. Petersburg."

"Lord Allandale's plan was perfect for the situation. He is a clever man, my dear. Normally, foreigners have great difficulty in understanding the Russian mentality, but he does not. Sometimes we forget that Russians also have difficulty in understanding the ways of visitors to their country. Of all the foreigners I have met, the English are the most awkward to fathom, and Penn is harder than most to understand."

"He's as straight as a die!"

"He is honest, it's true, but as an Englishman he is also capable of doing *anything* to have his own way. The grand duke will soon discover that it is very hard for a Russian to think like an Englishman!"

"I wonder where Penn and Laurel are now, and what they're thinking."

"They will be together, and to them that is all that matters. Now, you are not to start worrying, James. Come, we will drink some of the grand duke's champagne and eat some of his caviar. Then we will make a toast to the future of those we love. We are *free* from Russia and everything to do with it. We must not allow fear to enter our minds."

After stepping down from the train forty miles from St. Petersburg, Laurel entered a covered coach and was driven at speed by Hugo Allandale to the estate of Sandro Alexandrovich's father. Sandro had agreed to complete the second stage of the journey with her. For his part, Hugo would return to the British embassy in St. Petersburg as if nothing untoward had happened. He was quite unafraid in this

387

difficult situation. As an Englishman, Hugo considered himself to be the equal of ten Russians in courage and guile, though he knew well that if the grand duke ever realized that he had played an important part in getting Laurel out of the country, he would rot forever in one of the notorious jails of the city, perhaps the infamous one where all the dungeons were below sea level and regularly flooded. With a shrug, Hugo prepared to ride back to St. Petersburg. Within twenty-four hours, Andrei would know that Laurel had eluded him. Perhaps he would know sooner, depending on what his own plans had been. Hugo asked himself for the tenth time that day just what the Russian's reaction would be. How far would he defy his cousin the czar? How ruthless would he be?

Sandro drove Laurel at a fast gallop to the estate of one of his friends, almost a hundred and fifty versts from the city. There he left her with Penn, who was already waiting for her arrival. The two men shook hands, embraced, and bade each other farewell, their faces radiant as they clasped hands.

Penn's gratitude was obvious when he spoke to his young friend. "I'm so grateful to you for all you've done for Laurel and me. No man ever had a better friend."

"I am sorry to lose you, Penn, but someday we shall meet again, perhaps in England."

Laurel went to Sandro's side and kissed his cheeks. "My dearest friend, I do so *hate* good-byes. I feel as if I've known you all my life, and now that we're parting, it hurts."

"I would like to thank you for the advice you gave me when we first met, Laurel. To you it was very simple advice, because you are an American and able to think in the Western way. But that advice changed my life. Now I am married to Mitzi, and our son's birth has reunited us with my family. We have our little house in Yalta and our home on the estate near St. Petersburg. Most important of all, we have each other and are truly the happiest couple in the world. It is more than I ever dared hope to achieve, and you alone are responsible."

"No, you are. I gave the advice, but *you* acted on it."

Sandro kissed her hand and then stood back as Laurel and Penn entered a three-horse troika for the last stage of their escape from Russia. It would be a twenty-mile dash to the far northern coast, the part of the journey that was by far the most risky, because of the flat terrain and the endless open spaces patrolled by cossack guards. Sandro waved as they drove off, their faces merry, their bodies swathed in furs against the biting Arctic winds. When they had disappeared into the blue dusk of evening, he felt empty. Would he ever learn if they had arrived safely in England? Or would Russia, with her enormous distances, make future contact impossible? He walked inside the old farmhouse and sat for an hour thinking of all the happy times they had spent together. He remembered the night when he had been Laurel's partner at the ballet and had fallen under the spell of her beauty and her forthright opinions. Despite his desire to see the couple safely home to England, he could not help feeling that he had lost greatly by their departure.

When Andrei heard that Laurel had disappeared from the train, he smashed everything in the dining room of the palace in a wild, raging tirade of fury. Crystal glasses and decanters littered the ground, next to fragments of valuable porcelain and vases of great value hurled from the sideboard in blind, destructive anger. All his pent-up frustration and hurt pride came out at last and the self-control he had manifested in the early days disappeared as he roared for the servants to come and carry out his orders.

"Stepan! Go at once and bring the head of the Imperial Cossack Guard to me. Tell him I wish twenty volunteers to be summoned at once for special duty."

"Yes, sir, I shall hurry to bring the officer to the palace."

"Malenkov, go with a message to the head of the Okhrana. Tell him I wish to see him at eleven P.M. in my study."

"He goes to bed each night at nine, Excellency. Everyone in the city knows it."

"Damn you, go and give him the message and see you bring him back with you. He can sleep when I have found Miss Holman."

For hours after the departure of the servants, Andrei paced the room. The head of the Cossack Guard had been and gone, running with his orders like a man in a nightmare. Of the head of the Okhrana there was no sign. The head of the St. Petersburg civil police was also conspicuous by his absence. Andrei held his aching head in frustration, sure that some malevolent spirit was working against him, that his luck had finally run out. He had no idea that his mother had engineered the absence from their homes of most of the men he was likely to call on in his frantic search for Laurel.

Finally, unable to stand the waiting any longer, Andrei called for a groom and told him to prepare the fastest troika team. He had decided to follow the cossacks to the railway station, where Laurel had stepped off the train. She would surely have been a most conspicuous figure in such a primitive region, and someone must know in which direction she had gone. He ran down to the courtyard of the palace, got into the troika, and drove off into the night. He would not sleep again until he had Laurel safely under lock and key in St. Petersburg. If necessary, after the drama of her escape from the train, he would make sure that she was never again allowed to go free. He had decided that she must be broken before she could be trusted to do what he wished her to do, to live as he wished her to live.

Penn and Laurel were watching an arctic fox hiding from an eagle. The fox reminded them of their own situation, because they knew only too well that they would already be the subject of a manhunt. The resources of the Russian state police were exceptional, and both were subdued, if happy, as dusk came and Penn lit a campfire so he could roast the game birds he had shot earlier in the day. As he worked, he told Laurel of the plans he had made for their departure.

"You must sleep when you've eaten, because at dawn we'll cross the causeway over there. I chose that small island as our point of departure."

"But it's deserted. How will you find the men to help you take off?"

"Sandro's arranged everything. He says there'll be good men there who'll know how to do what's required."

"I hope he's right."

"He's always been reliable."

They ate wild ptarmigan and bread toasted on the embers of the fire. With this meal of smoky flavors they drank rich red wine and some flowery subrovna. They were drinking black, acrid Russian coffee when Laurel grimaced.

"After these months in Russia I shall be forever content with English food."

"You'll have us all eating clam chowder within a week, and you know it!"

"I may, but I'll learn to cook roast beef to please you, too."

"Mrs. Anderson does the cooking for us at Wentworth Saye. All you have to do is be yourself and be happy. We need you, Laurel, and we all love you very much."

She lay down by the fire, her eyes growing heavy with tiredness.

"I'll believe I'm really out of Russia when we're a thousand miles away from here. I wonder whether Andrei's already called in the soldiers to search for us?"

"I imagine he will have. He's not a man to leave any stone unturned."

Laurel shivered, afraid and tired of the suspense. Her only thoughts were of getting out of Russia, and these went around and around in her head all the time like a carousel. Finally she held out her hand to Penn.

"Hold me for a little while. I'm scared and tired and longing to be home with you."

"Try to sleep. I shall have to keep watch throughout the night, and at first light we'll leave for the island. Just remember all the time that I love you and that we're almost out of this accursed country."

Penn kissed her cheek and her ears and her mouth, enjoying the way she responded with eagerness and affection. When he had wrapped Laurel in a blanket, he went to the edge of the clearing and sat guarding her for the rest of the night. There were no noises to disturb the peace of the countryside, no visitors, animal or human, to cause disruption. The time passed slowly and Penn occupied himself with making plans for their future together. Then, wet from a heavy dew and tired to the very core of his body, he rose, stretched, and went to throw more kindling on the fire. Dawn was breaking in a thin line of gold on the horizon. He took his binoculars and looked around in every direction. It was then he saw another line, this time of blue-clad Imperial Cossacks, riding from the far distance toward the spot where he and Laurel were camped. It would take them half an hour or more to arrive, perhaps longer, as the ground was sodden. Penn hurried to rouse Laurel and made ready to break camp, proud when she asked no questions but simply hastened to the small boat at the water's edge.

As they were rowing toward the island, Penn explained what he had seen.

"Some cossacks of the Royal Guard are riding over the far hill. I imagine Andrei will be with them. He'd be unable to resist the possibility of my being arrested!"

"Don't joke about him, he's dangerous."

"To hell with Andrei. We're going to show him a clean pair of heels very shortly."

Laurel thought of Andrei. He was a Romanov, and therefore, in his own eyes, divine. No man could say no to him. No woman would dare disobey him. Was it possible, she wondered, that he really imagined he could take her by force and imprison her in one of his palaces? Suddenly she knew that that was exactly what he planned to do. Shivers ran through her body and she kept looking behind her and watching as the cossacks became more clearly visible, a thin blue line intersecting the dun-colored distant plain. The line moved forward at what seemed like a considerable pace. They were coming nearer and would reach the shoreline before long.

At that moment, Laurel noticed a man on the beach of the island toward which they were heading. He was watching them intently through a spyglass.

"Look, Penn, there's a man on the shore and he doesn't look like a peasant from these parts."

"Maybe he's one of Sandro's friends. I have to agree he doesn't look like a local."

Penn took the binoculars and gazed at the figure on the shore, who was waving an enthusiastic greeting to them.

"Gad, Laurel, that's Sandro's brother, Pavel! I recall meeting him at the Winter Palace when he came to have lessons in ballooning with the czar's party. No wonder Sandro was able to guarantee that the men would be here in time if they're all his personal friends and family. It wouldn't surprise me if he's invited the entire St. Petersburg Balloon Squadron to see us off."

They were hauled onto the shingle beach and then led to a field on the far side of the island, where the wind was less blustery. There they found two dozen men in tweed jackets and caps, hurrying to complete the inflation of the balloon. The atmosphere was merry. Coffee was being served with a breakfast of wild rabbit and bread toasted on the fire. One of the younger men was playing an accordion and singing in a light tenor voice.

Laurel turned to Penn, her face troubled by the relaxed manners of the men. It was obvious that these charming aristocrats had no idea of the urgency of their situation.

"We must make them hurry, Penn."

"We'll be gone in fifteen minutes, I promise. Don't worry, Laurel. Sandro and his brother have taken care of every eventuality."

"In fifteen minutes the cossacks could be here."

"They'd have to swim across, and though it's not far, cossacks are notoriously unhappy about entering water. That was why I chose the island."

At that moment Andrei was setting an example to the Cossack Guards, by entering the water with his horse, raising his rifle above his head, and attempting to get across to the island. Some of the soldiers hesitated before plunging after him into the current. One was swept away and many cried out in terror as they struggled to retain their balance in the icy depths. Only Andrei continued grimly on, his eyes on the island. He cared nothing for the cold or the risks or his hunger and exhaustion. He cared only to take back what he considered to be his and to punish the Englishman for his presumption in trying to steal Laurel. This was Russia, and in Russia the Romanovs were omnipotent. It was a fact Andrei was longing to make clear to his rival in the only way possible.

The balloon was inflated, the two passengers settled in the basket with hampers of food and water. With much waving and well-wishing, Sandro's friends and family began to cast off, unaware that on the hill behind them the pursuing cossacks were mustering.

Penn looked lovingly into Laurel's eyes.

"This is the moment we've been waiting for. I can hardly believe it's here."

"Say nothing till we're safely out of Russia."

"In a few seconds we shall be."

The cossacks rode down, their sabers drawn. Members of the St. Petersburg Balloon Squadron fell back, though one had the presence of mind to slash the balloon's last guide rope before hiding behind a boulder on the shore.

While the cossacks rode up to Pavel and began to question him, the pink balloon rose majestically in the cloud-gray sky. Penn held Laurel to his heart, overjoyed to be free, to be alone with her and on his way back to England and the home he loved. Nuzzling her to his heart, he saw that the cossacks had ceased all activity and were sitting in the saddle, staring up at the billowing craft that had eluded them. Pavel was waving good-bye, having produced his trump card for the captain of the Cossack Guard, an imperial command to the members of the Balloon Squadron to assist in the departure of Lord Allandale and Miss Laurel Holman in every way possible. The command was signed by the czar himself, and on seeing it, the cossacks had been ordered to fall back.

Only one man stood apart from the rest, and when Penn saw what he was doing he made ready to gain height, to take the craft above the clouds, where it would be safe.

Andrei loaded his rifle and tried the sight. He had to make an adjustment before attempting the difficult shot. Impatiently he mounted his horse and galloped forward, the better to see his target. Then, taking careful aim, he was about to squeeze the trigger, when some heavy sacks of ballast were thrown down from above, stunning him with a savage blow to the head. Dropping the rifle, Andrei fell to the grassy knoll, furious at the ribald comments of some of the cossack escort. Tears began to fall down his cheeks, and without a word, when he was able, he stumbled to his feet, mounted his horse, and rode back to the beach to make the crossing back to the mainland. He had lost Laurel. Having tried everything he knew, he had still lost her to the Englishman. He wanted to cry out, to rage and scream at fate, but he was too tired and too dispirited to do anything. Humiliated, hurt, exhausted to the point where tears continuously fell down his cheeks, he struggled back to the shore and then galloped forward alone in the direction from which he had come. He was wondering if he would be the laughingstock of St. Petersburg for what he had done.

In the Vladimir Palace, Princess Sophia was waiting for her son's arrival. When Andrei appeared, his face bruised and tearstained, his clothes filthy, she greeted him with a kiss and linked her arm in his as they went upstairs to his private suite.

"My dearest Andrei, I can see from your face that Miss Holman is gone. Try not to take it so hard."

"She went with that accursed Englishman after all I have done for her, all I have lavished on her in love and money."

"She left everything behind. Stepan found all the clothes you had bought her, and the furs and even the diamonds, in her room."

On hearing this, Andrei ran past his mother and up the stairs to the rooms Laurel and her father had occupied until recently. There, amid the priceless furniture and Oriental wall hangings, were the clothes and the jewels and the furs and the boots and everything he had bought her. He bent and took the note she had put at the bedside. It said only the briefest of good-byes: *Dear Andrei,*

I've asked Polinka to put out in my room all the things you bought me. I can't take them home with me for reasons you'll understand better than most. On my father's behalf I thank you for inviting us to St. Petersburg. For my own part, I wish I had never come here and I don't ever want to return or to see you again. I'm sorry it has to end this way, but you only wanted me for a lover and I only wanted you for a friend. Laurel Holman.

Andrei walked around the room, opening the wardrobes and gazing at the sensational clothes inside, the bejeweled boxes of rings and necklaces all made to Laurel's own designs. The furs seemed to hold her perfume, and he held them to his cheek and closed his eyes, allowing the memories of the past year to filter slowly through his mind. Finally he came to the box of diamonds Laurel had left behind and looked at it in uncomprehending silence. He had never met a woman who could treat diamonds with disdain. How was it that Laurel could reject even that most beautiful symbol of his regard for her? He sat in the armchair, staring at the bed in which she had slept until so recently. His mind was in a turmoil and he could think of nothing but his loss. For as long as he could remember, he and all his family had been taught that to be a Romanov was to be all powerful. Andrei sighed despairingly. If the American had taught him anything, it was that being a Romanov, or anyone else for that matter, meant nothing at all when love was the dealer of the hand.

In the pink balloon, high above the blue waters of the Gulf of Finland, Laurel and Penn were kissing. A long and dangerous journey lay ahead, but they were together and deeply content. If God willed it, they would be married within the month. If ill luck came and the balloon went down, they would die together. Penn voiced their thoughts as they drifted at last over the Finnish coast. "Look, my dear, that is the Russian coast we have just left. Below us is Finland. Whatever happens now, we'll not land in czarist territory."

Tears of relief and happiness fell down Laurel's cheeks.

"Thank you for bringing me out of that country, Penn. I'm *longing* to be home with you."

"You'll never have seen a welcome like the one we'll get when we reach Wentworth Saye. Even Flannegan will allow himself a smile, and that doesn't happen often. You know what a devil he is for keeping his dignity."

"I just want to *be* there and to hide away forever."

"With me, I hope?"

"With you, for always."

"Hold my hand, Laurel. The wind's rising and we're going to need to keep our wits about us."

"Nothing can stop us now. We're going home where we belong."

11

Wentworth Saye, Autumn 1899

On a chill morning in late October, carriages began to rumble from the ancient town of Woodstock into the courtyard of Wentworth Saye. Some of the guests had come from London, some from nearby Blenheim. The Prince of Wales arrived in a revolutionary new automobile that broke down at the gate and had to be towed into the grounds by the estate manager's horse. Ever the extravert, the prince stepped forward to be greeted by Penn.

"My dear friend, how are you? I hear you had a few adventures in Russia. Do tell me what happened. I had a note from my cousin Andrei the other day. He was more than a little put out by your sudden departure."

"The grand duke committed an unpardonable breach of gentlemanly behavior against my fiancée, sir, about which my lips are sealed. I eventually managed to get her out of Russia with the greatest difficulty and considerable subterfuge. Hugo only arrived back a week ago, after being questioned for days by the security police. I honestly thought he was going to be arrested."

The Prince of Wales looked hard into Penn's angry face and understood what had happened. Displeased, he entered the house, angry that he had been responsible for introducing the grand duke to Laurel in the first place.

"From this day on, Andrei will not be welcome in England. I have always found his desire to have his own way rather tiresome, but your story is a shocking one and I am displeased."

"I knew you would feel that way, sir."

"How is the bride . . . and where is she?"

"She'll be arriving shortly from Blenheim. The duchess insisted on sending Laurel with full honors, and the runners have been called."

"They normally send for the runners only to collect a new Duchess of Marlborough!"

"Apparently Consuelo insisted."

Penn led the royal guest into the hallway, which had been decorated from floor to ceiling with pink and purple asters. Solid silver punch bowls were being carried in by the servants and Clarissa was supervising the final decoration of the table, her face flushed with excitement. Seeing the Prince of Wales, she curtsied gracefully.

"Welcome to Wentworth Saye, sir. It's a great day

for a wedding, isn't it, a real English autumn morning, just the kind Laurel loves."

"She'll be more English than any of us before long!"

"With respect, she won't, sir. Laurel's American to her bones and we love her just how she is. We need someone like her to shake the cobwebs out of us all at Wentworth Saye."

"Show me the chapel, Clarissa. I hear you and Penn have had it restored at last."

"We have, sir. This is a very special occasion and Penn was determined to marry in the same place as his grandfather, so we had to have the renovations completed."

Laurel was standing in front of the mirror in her wedding dress. It was a dream outfit, just as Lotty had promised, the skirt made of two hundred and fifty yards of the finest silk chiffon appliquéd with Tudor roses and fleurs-de-lis. The décolleté neckline was revealing but elegant, the waist a tiny circlet of jeweled flowers. As a headdress she had chosen an arrangement of veiling with camellias and miniature orchids from Penn's hothouse. At her throat she was wearing the Allandale pearl-and-diamond choker, just as Penn's beautiful American grandmother had done.

She turned as Consuelo entered the room and greeted her.

"Dearest Laurel, the carriage is ready and the runners are waiting on the forecourt. Your entrance is going to cause quite a sensation."

"I'm so excited I could burst. My cheeks aren't red, are they?"

"They're a lovely pink. Now, stop your fussing and let me take you downstairs."

They walked together through the gilded corridors of Blenheim to the forecourt, where, long ago, the warrior Duke of Marlborough had assembled his soldiers. There Consuelo stretched out her arms and embraced Laurel.

"Good luck, my dear, and a wonderful, happy life."

"Thank you for all you've done for me, Consuelo."

"Think nothing of it. I did it because I like you and because I need a very special friend as my neighbor at Wentworth Saye."

Laurel stepped into the carriage that had been decorated with cream and pink roses. Instead of horses, ropes had been attached to the sides so it could be pulled by the legendary Blenheim Runners—the coachmen, gardeners, grooms, and odd-job men employed by the family, who, on special occasions, were allowed to indulge their desire for excitement by dressing up in bright blue uniforms and pulling the tiny carriage at speed to its destination.

At a signal from the head groom, they moved off. Laurel waved good-bye to the assembled guests on the forecourt. Then she looked ahead at the grounds of the palace, remembering the day when she had first driven her gig through the pastures and met the handsome Englishman who had captured her heart. Life had changed totally since that sunny spring morning. Many good and bad things had come her way, but nothing had altered her feelings for Penn, and she knew nothing ever would. As she rode through the iron gates of Blenheim and out into the street, where crowds were waiting to cheer her on, Laurel was ecstatically happy. She was about to marry the man she loved, and the world was golden again.

At the gates of Wentworth Saye, the postman called a greeting. Two shepherds in calico smocks threw wildflowers into the carriage, and a little girl, sitting in a governess cart with her mother, cried out that the bride looked just like a fairy princess.

Penn was standing with his brother and sister on the forecourt when he heard the sound of cheering. Straining to look down the drive, he caught sight of Laurel's carriage being pulled by the Blenheim Runners. As it drew near, he saw her in all her beauty, so vulnerable and excited by the moment that her face took his breath away. He hurried down the stairs to meet her and help her from the carriage.

"Dearest Laurel, you are the most beautiful bride I ever saw."

"I'm yours, and that's what I've wanted to be ever since the night we first danced in the conservatory. I didn't realize it then, of course, but I knew it the moment I left you on the station in Paris."

"This is our day, and one we've waited for for such a long time."

"I love you, my darling, and I'll love you forever, even when I'm old and bent and bad-tempered."

Penn threw back his head and laughed delightedly at the phrase.

"For me you'll always be beautiful. One of the great advantages of a passion such as mine is that it is blind to the faults of my intended."

They were separated then as Penn hastened with his brother to the chapel and Laurel made her way to the porch, where her bridesmaids were waiting to hand her her bouquet and arrange the billowing skirt. She saw that the bouquet had been made exactly as she had asked, of white camellias, miniature orchids from the hothouse, wild blue violets, and maidenhair fern. It was an old-fashioned posy and a copy of the one Penn's grandmother had carried. The head bridesmaid kissed her cheek and wished her luck.

"It's going to be the very prettiest wedding this house ever saw, Laurel."

"I want every minute of it to be memorable."

Flannegan went into the salon, where Clarissa, Lotty, and Holman were drinking champagne.

"May I have a word with you, Miss Clarissa?"

"We're about to leave for the chapel. Will it not wait?"

"I think not, ma'am. Two gifts have just arrived that necessitate some advice. This is from the Czar of Russia, as you can see."

Clarissa opened the gift and found inside the heavy parcel a veritable treasure trove. There was a Louis XV mirror, a solid gold vase studded with rubies, a diamond-and-platinum chain, and a set of gold-and-sapphire cufflinks designed by the court jeweler.

Flannegan moved forward with another, smaller gift.

"And this is from the Grand Duke Andrei. He sent a note with it, as you will see."

Clarissa looked from Flannegan's impassive face to the box on the table. When she opened it, she gasped at the sight of the shimmering green stones within. Surely these were emeralds, and worth a king's ransom. She looked to Holman, helpless and confused. "My brother will order me to send these back, I am sure of it."

"I don't think they should be returned. They should be held in trust for Penn's children and for future generations of your family, in case hard times ever come."

"Dear me, what am I to do?"

Flannegan spoke with his usual confidence. "Read the note, Miss Clarissa."

She looked down at the note, which displeased her immensely. If a note of such familiarity, talking of diamonds previously given as a gift, were displayed with the other wedding presents to the public, Laurel's reputation would be ruined forever. Clarissa read the note again: *You did not like the diamonds I gave you, so I send these beautiful emeralds as a final tribute to our friendship. I remain, always, your servant, Andrei Vladimirovich Romanov.* Before she realized it, Clarissa had crumpled the note in her hand and given it to Flannegan to throw away. She had been told nothing of what had happened in Russia, but knew from her brother's fury whenever Andrei's name was mentioned that the grand duke had committed some unforgivable breach of good manners where Laurel was concerned. She was relieved when Flannegan spoke again. "May I make a suggestion, Miss Clarissa?"

"I should be obliged if you would, Flannegan."

"The grand duke and the czar are both from the same family, are they not?"

"They are Romanovs."

"They have quite different reputations. The czar is a family man and respected in the world. The grand duke is something of a black sheep, with a fearsome reputation, if you'll pardon my presumption, ma'am. I think it might be best not to embarrass the master and his new wife by displaying any gift from that gentleman. Perhaps we should simply put the box of emeralds with the czar's gifts. In that way it would cause no comment at all. Everyone knows the imperial family are lavish in their presents to close friends. Also the emeralds would look well placed in that charming gold vase. Do you approve of the suggestion, Miss Clarissa?"

She looked uncertainly at Holman and Lotty for some sign of their agreement. When they nodded, she turned to Flannegan.

"Do what has to be done and say nothing of all this to *anyone*."

"My lips are sealed, miss."

Flannegan walked imperturbably out of the room

to arrange things as he had been arranging them at Wentworth Saye for twenty-five years.

In the flower-filled chapel, the organist struck up the notes of the wedding march. Laurel moved forward on her father's arm, a radiant bride about to embark on the greatest adventure of her life. As Penn looked around, she impulsively held out her hand to him. Then, together, they stood at the altar, listening as the priest said the words they had waited so long to hear.

About the Author

Helene Thornton is the author of THE MIS-
TRESS FROM MARTINIQUE, CATHAY, and
PASSIONATE EXILE. She was an actress in
England before turning full time to writing and
now resides in France. Her next book for Signet
will be FABLES.

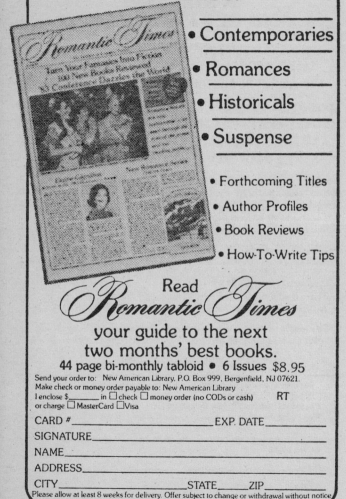

Romantic Fiction from SIGNET

Sensational Reading from SIGNET